SURFACE CHEMISTRY

By

Dr. A. Goel

DISCOVERY PUBLISHING HOUSE
NEW DELHI-110002

Published by:

DISCOVERY PUBLISHING HOUSE
4383/4B, Ansari Road, Darya Ganj
New Delhi-110 002 (India)
Phone : +91-11-23279245; 23253475; 43596065
E-mail : discoverybooksindia@gmail.com
discoverypublishinghouse@gmail.com
namitwasan9@gmail.com
web : www.discoverypublishinggroup.com

First Published: **2006**

Reprinted: **2023**

ISBN: 978-81-8356-150-1

Surface Chemistry

Printed at:
Infinity Imaging Systems
Delhi

Preface

This book has been written for the students of under-graduate and post-graduate level of the various universities in India. A special feature of the book is that the text has been illustrated with a large number of line diagrams and the data presented in the form of numerous tables for reference and comparison. In the preparation of text standard works and review by renowned author have been freely consulted and the reference given chapter wise. At the end of the book will be found useful by those who wish to make a more detailed study of the topics discussed.

We are extremely grateful to our respected Managing Director Shri Tilak Wasan, Discovery Publishing House, for valuable and active cooperation. We humble request our students and chemistry teachers to send us their constructive criticism and suggestions which we shall be using in the publication of the next edition.

Author

Contents

Pages

Preface

1. **Surface Chemistry** 1

Introduction, Characteristics of Adsorption, Sorption and Occlusion, Adsorption of Gases on Solids, Physical Adsorption, Measurement of Adsorption Isotherms or Experimental Methods of Determining Gas Adsorption, Various Adsorption Isotherms, Determination of Surface Area, Heat of Adsorption, Adsorption Isobars, Chemisorption, Adsorption From Solution, Alternate Definition of Surface Excess, Adsorption by Porous Solids, Surface tension and Surface Free Energy, Capillary Condensation, Wetting Phenomena, Applications of Adsorption.

2. **Equations and Transport Phenomena in Gases** 100

Collision Diameter, Barrometic Formula, Mean Free Path, Equation of State, Effect of Height on Distribution, Barometric Formula by Taking Into Account the Variation of Acceleration due to Gravity with Altitude Above the Earth's Surface, Derivation of the Barrometric Formula Taking Into Account the Variation of Temperature with Altitude, Molecular Chaos, Collision Number and Collision Frequency, Limitations of Van Der Waals Equation, Calculation of the Boyle's Temperature from Van Der Waal's Equation, Modified from of the Van Der Waal's Equation, The Derthelot Equation, The Equation of Kammerling Ones, The Beattie-Bridgeman Equation of State, The Clausius Equation, Maxwell's Law of Distribution of Velocities, Transport Phenomena in Gases, Degrees of Freedom, Law of Equipartition of Energy,

Average Values, Maxwell's Distribution for Kinetic Energy, Experimental Verification of Maxwell's Distribution Law.

3. **Solutions and Their Theories** **165**

Meaning of Solution, Type of Solutions, Vapour Pressure of a Liquid, Lowering of Vapour Pressure, Ideal Solutions, Non Ideal Solutions, Raoult's Law Applicable to Binary Solutions of two Liquids, Relative Lowering of Vapour Pressure, Measurement of Lowering of Vapour Pressure, Osmosis, Relation Between Lowering of Vapour Pressure and Osmotic Pressure, Theories of Osmotic Pressure and Supermeability, Osmotic Pressure, Van't Hoff's Theory of Dilute Solutions, Measurement of Osmotic Pressure, Measurement of Boiling Point Elevation, Abnormal Colligative Properties of Solutions, Colligative Properties, Colligative Property Measured $\propto$ Mole Fraction of the Solute, Abnormal Osmotic Pressure.

4. **Physical and Constitutive Properties** **227**

Chemical Constitution and Optical Activity, Optical Rotatory Dispersion, Molar Refraction or Refractivity as an Additive and Constitutive Property, Optical Exhalation, Refrachor, Viscosity and Chemical Constitution, Molecular Refraction, Molar Volume of Liquids, Mecleod's Relationship—The Parachor, Refractive Index, Optical Activity.

5. **Catalysis and Kinetics of Heterogeneous Reactions** **259**

Catalysis, Types of Catalysis, Theory of Homogeneous Catalysis, Function of a Catalyst in Terms of Gibb's Free Energy of Activation, Theory of Heterogeneous Catalysis, Quantitative Treatment of Adsorption (Theory of Heterogeneous Catalysis), Absolute Rate Theory in Heterogeneous Gas Reactions, Classification of Catalysis, Acid-Base Catalysis.

1

SURFACE CHEMISTRY

INTRODUCTION

It has been known that the surface of a liquid is in a state of strain or unsaturation due to the unbalanced or residual forces which act along the surface of a liquid. Similar to it, the surface of a solid may also have residual forces or valencies. Thus, *the surface of a solid has a tendency to attract and to retain molecules of other species (gas or liquids) with which such surfaces come in contact. This phenomenon of surfaces is termed* as adsorption.

As the molecules remain only at the surface, and do not go deeper into the bulk of the solid, the concentration of adsorbed gas or liquid is more at the surface than in the bulk. Hence this discussion may follow up by the definition of adsorption.

"Adsorption is a technical term coined to denote the taking up (Latin, surbere, to suck up) of gas, vapour, liquid by a surface or interface".

Differences between Adsorption, Absorption and Sorption : Adsorption is a surface phenomenon whereas absorption is a bulk phenomenon in which the substance assimilated is uniformly distributed throughout the body of a solid or liquid to form a solution or a compound.

The phenomenon of adsorption and absorption are illustrated in Fig. 1.1.

Adsorption should be distinguished carefully from absorption.

(i) In absorption, the substance is distributed throughout the body of a solid or a liquid to form solution or a compound. On the other hand, adsorption only takes place on the surface and not in the-body of adsorbent. Thus, adsorption is a surface phenomenon, and absorption is a bulk phenomenon.

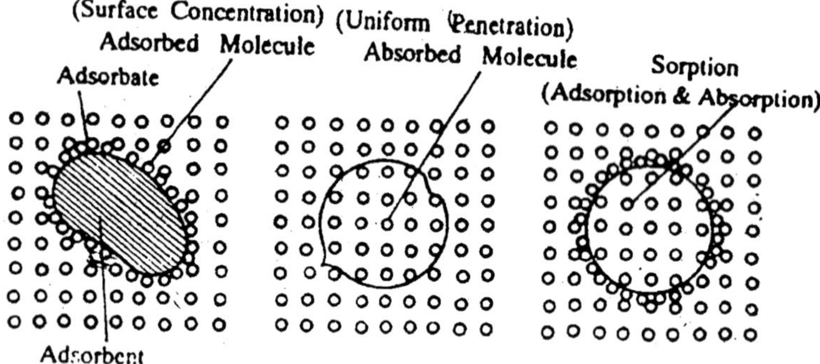

Fig. 1.1 : Illustration of adsorption, absorption and sorption.

(ii) In absorption, the concentration of the adsorbed molecules is always found to be greater in the immediate vicinity of the surface (Adsorbent) than in the free phase (Adsorbate). On the contrary, absorption involves bulk penetration of the molecules into the structure of the solid or liquid by some process of diffusion.

(iii) In case of adsorption, the equilibrium is easily attained in a very short time whereas in absorption the equilibrium takes place slowly.

(iv) Typical isotherms for adsorption and absortion are shown in Fig. 1.2.

If x/m is plotted against p or c the graph should be a straight line in adsorption [Fig. 1.2 (a)] and a typical curve for absorption as shown in the Fig. 1.2(b).

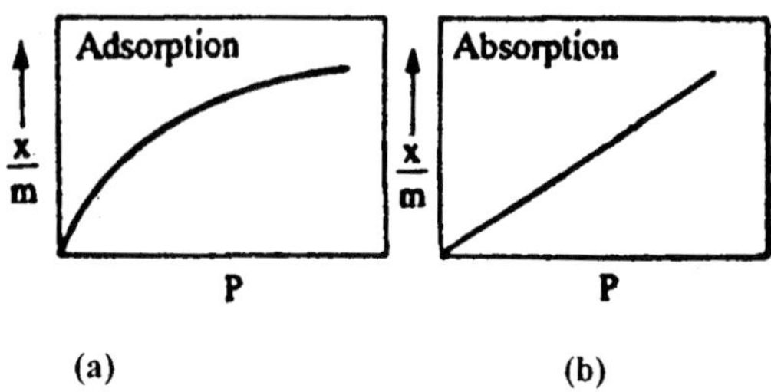

Fig. 1.2 : Typical isotherms for (a) adsorption, and (b) absorption respectively.

Examples for Adsorption and Absorption

(i) Water vapour is absorbed by anhydrous calcium chloride while it is adsorbed by silica gel.

(ii) Ammonia is adsorbed by charcoal while it is absorbed by water to form ammonium hydroxide.

$$NH_3 + H_2O \rightarrow NH_4OH$$

(iii) Decolourisation of sugar solution by activated charcoal is another example of adsorption. In this example, charcoal adsorbs rhe colouring meterial and thus decolourises the solution.

(iv) The colour of the lake test for aluminium ions is due to adsorption of dye (litmus) on the freshly precipitated aluminium hydroxide.

(v) When a hot crucible is allowed to cool in air, a film of moisture is formed at the surface. This is the case of adsorption of water vapour on the surface of a crucible.

(vi) When sponge is put into water, it takes up water. It is an example of absorption.

Nomenclature Used in Adsorption : The meterial on the surface of which adsorption takes place is called the *adsorbent* and the substance adsorbed is called the adsorbate. The common surface separating two phases, where the adsorbed molecule concentrates is referred to as the *interface*. The larger the surface area of the adsorbent, the more the adsorption. Due to this reason colloids are good adsorbents due to their high surface area per unit mass although they have very small dimensions.

Adsorption stands for different concentrations of a substance at an interface. If the concentration is more at an interface, the adsorption is said to be *positive*; if the concentration is less at an interface, the adsorption is said to be *negative*. The reverse process of removal of an adsorbed substance from the surface of a solid is known as *desorption*.

Examples of Adsorbents

(a) *Silica gel :* It acts as a good adsorbent and is prepared by mixing sodium silicate with 10% hydrochloric acid at 50°C.

(b) *Metals :* Metals act as good adsorbents and are being used for contact catalysis.

These are prepared by the reduction of their oxides or of the salts under suitable experimental conditions. Examples are Ni, Cu, Ag, Pt and Pd.

(c) *Colloids* : As colloids possess high surface per unit mass due to their small size, they act as good adsorbents.

Examples of Adsorbates : There are various gases (He, Ne, O_2, N_2, SO_2, NH_3 etc.) and substances in solution (NaCl, KCl) which can be adsorbed by suitable adsorbents.

CHARACTERISTICS OF ADSORPTION

The various characteristics of adsorption are as follows:

1. Adsorption is a spontaneous process and takes place in no time.
2. The phenomenon of adsorption can occur at all surfaces and five types of interfaces can exist: gas-solid, liquid-sold, liquid-liquid, solid-solid, and gas-solid. The gas-solid interface has probably received the most attention in the literature and is the best understood. The liquid-solid interface is now receiving much attention because of its importance in many electrochemical and biological systems.
3. It is accompanied by a decrease in the free energy of the system, *i.e.*, A G. The adsorption will continue to such an extent that A G continues to be negative. Eventually, magnitude of AG decreases to zero. When AG for further adsorption reaches a value for zero, adsorption equilibrium is said to be established.
4. As the process of adsorption involves loss of degree of freedom of the gas in passing from the free gas to the adsorbed film there is a decrease in the entropy of the system.

It follows from the Gibbs-Helmholtz equation

$$\Delta G = \Delta H - T\Delta S \qquad ...(1)$$

or

$$\Delta H = \Delta G + T\Delta S \qquad ...(2)$$

where ΔG is the change in free energy, ΔH is the change in heat content, ΔS is the change in entropy, and T is the temperature of the system.

As the entropy and free energy decrease in adsorption, the value of ΔH decreases. This decrease in heat content (ΔH) appears as heat. Hence the adsorption process must always be exothermic.

SORPTION AND OCCLUSION

In many examples, the initial rapid adsorption is followed by a slow process of absorption of the substance into the interior of the solid. In these cases, the effects of absorption cannot be distinguished from those of adsorption. Therefore, the two new terms were introduced:

1. *Sorption : The process in which both adsorption and absorption take place simultaneously is generally termed absorption.* This term was suggested by Mcbain (1909). Examples are
   (a) The uptake of gases by zeolites is a striking example of sorption.
   (b) When hydrogen is taken up by charcoal, it first condenses on its surface. This is adsorption. After some time, the hydrogen diffuses slowly into the interior of the charcoal forming a true solid solution and, hence, this is absorption. So the charcoal has adsorbed as well as absorbed hydrogen gas. Therefore, it is an example of sorption.
   (c) The direct dye-stuffs taken up by cotton fibres are also in the adsorbed as well as in the absorbed state.
2. *Occlusion :* In 1886 *T. Graham* proposed the term occlusion which possesses a similar significance to sorption. But this term occlusion is restricted to the sorption of gases by metals only.

ADSORPTION OF GASES ON SOLIDS

I. Introductory

The study of the gas-solid adsorption process has excited the interest of both academic and industrial scientists for many years, and the reactions are not hard to find. Industrially, it is known that this phenomenon'8 plays an essential role in the catalytic process. The ability of surface tu selectively accelerate the rates of many chemical reactions is the basis of much of the heavy-chemical production in the world.

It is generally believed that all gases or vapours are adsorbed on the surface of all solids with which they are in contact. The phenomenon was first described in 1773 by Schcele. who discovered the uptake of gases by charcoal.

II. Factors on which Adsorption Depends

The phenomenon of adsorption of gases by solids depends upon the following factors:

(i) *Nature of the adsorbent and, adsorbate :* The amount of the gas adsorbed depends upon the nature of the adsorbent and thsgas (adsorbate) which is to be adsorbed.

Gases like SO_2, NH_3, HCl and CO_2 which liquefy more easily are adsorbed more readily than the permanent gases like H_2, N_2 and O_2 which do not liquefy' easily; This is because the easily liquefiable gases have greater van der Waal's or the mntccular forces of attraction or cohesive forces.

As the critical temperatures of the easily liquefiable gases are more than the permanent gases, it follows that higher the critical temperature of the gas (adsorbate), the greater the extent of adsorption.

(ii) *Surface area of the adsorbent* : The extent of adsorption of gases by solids depends upon the exposed surface area of the adsorbent. It is well known that larger the surface area of the adsorbent, the large will be the extent of adsorption under given conditions of temperature and pressure. It is for this reason that silica gel and charcoal obtained from different animal and vegetable sources become activated because they possess a porous structure and thereby render a larger surface.

(iii) *The partial pressure of the gas in the phase* : For a given gas and a given adsorbent, the extent of adsorption depends on the pressure of the gas. Adsorption of a gas is followed by a decrease of pressure. Therefore, in accordance with Le Chatelier's principle, the magnitude of adsorption decreases with the decrese in pressure and vice-versa. The variation ofadosrption with presure at constant temperature is expressed graphic'ally by a curve known as adsorption isotherm.

(iv) *Effect of temperature* : For a given adsorbate and a adsorbent, the extent of adsorption depends upon the temperature of the experiment. As discussed earlier, adsorptiop usually takes place with the evolution of heat. Therefore, according to the *Le Chatelier's principle*, the decrease in temperature will increase the adsorption and vice-versa. An example is that if the temperature of the coconut charcoal is lowered from –29° to –78°C, the amount of nitrogen gas adsorbed increases from 20 to 45 ml under the same pressure.

III. Types of Adsorption of the Gases on Solids

Based off the nature-of .forces, between the gas and the solid surface, there are two types of adsorption :

1. *Physisorption or Physical Adsorption* : If the physical forces of attraction hold the gas molecules to the solid, the adsorption is known as physical adsorption or physisorption. The forces of attraction bringing about physical adsorption are :
   (i) Permanent dipole moment in the adsorbed molecule,
   (ii) Polarisation,
   (iii) Dispersion effects,
   (iv) Short range repulsive effect.

In case of physisorption, the forces of attfaction which hold the gas moleoules to the solid are very weak. Therefore it is characterised by a low heat of adsorption, usually of the order of 40 kJ per mole. This value is of the same order of magnitude as the heat of vaporisation of the adsorbate and lends credence to the concept of a weak 'physical' bonding. Physical adsorption is usually observed at low temperatures or on relatively 'inert' surfaces. Examples of physisorption are as follows :

(i) Adsorption of various gases on charcoah

(ii) Adsorption of nitrogen on mica.

2. *Chemisorption or Chemical adsorption* : If the chemical forces hold the gas molecules to the surface of the adsorbednt, the adsorption is known as chemisorption. In this case the adsorbate undergoes a strong chemical interaction with the unsaturated surface and gives rise to a high heat of adsorption, usually of the order of 400 kJ per mole. Chemisorption is often characterised by taking place at elevated temperatures and is often an activated process. It may be dissociative, non-dissociative or reactive in nature. Some examples of chemisorption are:
   (a) Ethyl alcohol vapours condensed on the divided nickel.
   (b) Adsorption of oxygen on tungsten.
   (c) Adsorption of hydrogen on nickel.
3. *Distinction between Physisorption and Chemisorption* : Exact differentiation between chemical and physical adsorption is often difficult and usually unprofitable. To the practising chemist a physically adsorbed species is usually considered to be an adsorbed material that can be completely removed faom the surface, without decomposition, by prolonged evacuation at room temperature or by heating to 120°C. This experimental

choice of conditions is completely arbitrary, and the final decision is always left with the experimenter. However, the advent of infrared spectroscopy had led to a better means of distinguishing between the two processes.

We know that the infrared spectrum of a molecule arises as a result of the vibrations of the atoms within the molecules. If the molecule is physically adsorbed, the infrared spectrum is altered only slightly and small frequency shifts, usully less than 1 percent, are pbeservcd. During the chemisorption process, the symmetry of the adsorbed molecule is completely different from that of the gaseous molecule. In this case a completely new infrared spectrum is observed and band shifts and intensities are far removed from those of the gaseous absorbate.

Let us illustrate this method by considering the IR spectra of acetylene in solution and adsorbed on silica and on palladium coated silica. These spectra are shown in Fig. 3 in which (a) represents the infrared spectrum of acetylene in liquid solution, (b) represents of acetylene on porous silica glass, and (c) of acetylene on porous silica glass coated with palladium. The IR spectrum on silica [Fig. 1.3(b)] is like that in solution [Fig. 3(a)] except for a small shift to lower frequencies, but the IR spectrum on palladium [Fig. 1.3(c)] is completely different and contains extra new bands. These spectra can be explained by saying that the latter case is a chemisorption with formation of new bonds (Fig. 3(c)] whereas the former case [Fig. 1.3(b)] is a typical physical adsorption.

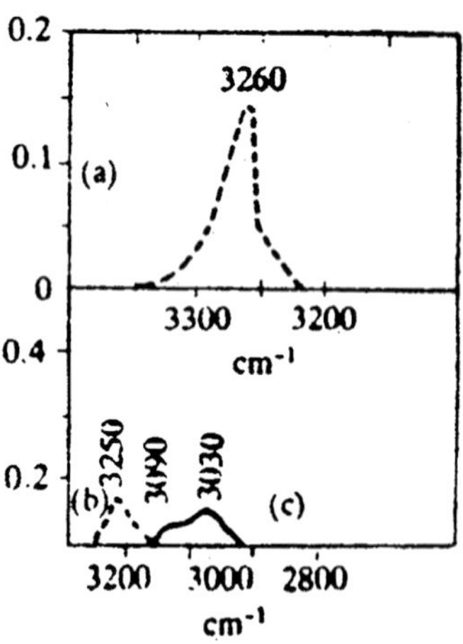

Fig. 1.3 : Infrared spectra of (a) acetylene in liquid solution (b) acetyl DC on porous silica glass (c) acetylene on porous silica glass coated with palladium.

4. *Differences between Physisorption and Chemisorption* : The various differences are as follows:

(a) *Specificity* : Physisorptions are non-specific. Thus, every gas is adsorbed to a lesser or a greater extent on all solid surfaces. On the other hand, chemisorptions are more specific in nature. A gas will be chemisorbed on such solids only with which it can combine chemically.

(b) *Speed* : Physisorptions are instantaneous. Chemisorptions may sometimes be quite slow depending upon the nature of chemical reaction involved. A rough estimate is that adsorbable impurities of air are adsorbed by gas masks in a contact of less than 0.01 second.

(c) *Reversibility* : Physisorption equilibrium is reversible and is rapidly established. Chemisorption is irreversible. Physically adsorbed layer can be removed very easily by changing pressure or concentration. On the other hand the removal of a chemisorbed layer, however, requires much more rugged conditions such as high temperatures, etc.

(d) *Heat of adsorption* : Physical adsorption is generally characterised by low heats of adsorption which is about 40 kJ/mole or less. Chemisorption is characterised by high heats of adsorption, viz. 40 to 400 kJ per mole which indicates that forces are similar to those involved in chemical reactions. Therefore, it is highly probable that gas molecules form a chemical compound with the surface of the adsorbent.

(e) *Nature of the adsorbate and adsorbent* : Physical adsorption like condensation can occur with any gas-solid system provided only that the conditions of temperature and pressure are suitable. The Chemisorption will take place only if the gas is capable of forming a chemical bond with the surface atoms.

(f) *Effect of pressure* : As the pressure of the adsorbate increases, the rate of physical adsorption increases. The rate of Chemisorption decreases with the increase of pressure of adsorbate.

(g) *Effect of temperature* : Physical adsorption occurs to an appreciable extent at temperatures close to those required for liquefaction of adsorbed gases. Generally, Chemisorption occurs at high temperatures. But certain examples are known in which it occurs at low temperatures. Chemisorption increases at first and then falls off with rising temperature.

A graph drawn between amount adsorbed (x/m) and temperature (T) at a constant equilibrium pressure of adsorbate gas is called an adsorption isobar. Adsorption isobars of physisorption and Chemisorption show one important difference (Fig. 1.3) and this difference is used for experimentally distinguishing Chemisorption from physisorption. While the physical adsorption isobar shows a decrease in xjm along the rise in temperuture the Chemisorption isobar shows an initial increase with temperature and then the expected decrease. The initial increase shows that, like the chemical reactions, Chemisorption also needs activation energy. However, the latter decrease indicates that at higher temperatures desorption does occur in Chemisorption process. Frequently durfng the high temperature desorptions the evolved gas carries with it some atoms of the adsorbent as well in a chemically bound form.

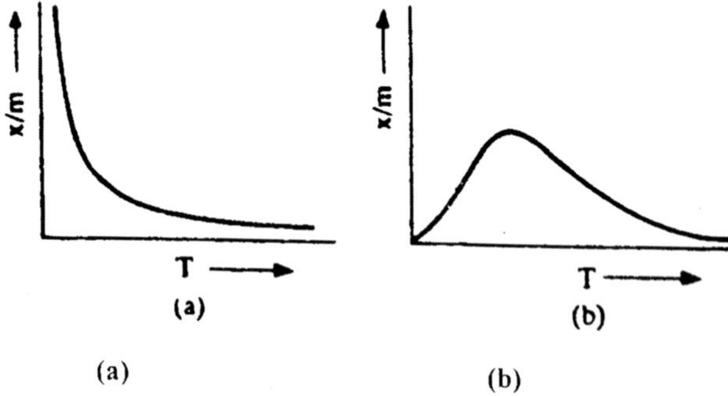

(a) (b)

Fig. 1.4 : Adsorption isobars : (a) Physical adsorption, (b) Chemisorption.

The various differences between physisorption and chemisorption are summarised in Table 1.1.

Table 1.1

Physical adsorption	*Chemisorption*
(i) It involves physical forces.	(i) It involves transfer of electrons gas and solid between.
(ii) Heat of adsorption is generally less than 40 kj/mole.	(ii) Heat of adsorption is 40–400 kJ/mole.
(iii) It is reversible.	(iii) It is not reversible.
(iv) It is a general phenomenon which will occur with any gas-solid system provided only that the conditions of temp and pressure are suitable.	(iv) It will only take place if the gas is capable of forming chemical bond with the surface atoms.

(v) Multilayers are possible in physical adsorption.	(v) Only monolayer is formed.
(vi) It is appreciable at low temperatures and high pressures with the increase	(vi) It can occur at high temoeratures. The rate of chemisorption decreases of pressure.
(vii) No appreciable activation energy is involved.	(vii) Chemisorption is an activated phenomenon and involves appreciable activation energy.
(viii) It is an instantaneous process.	(viii) It may be rapid or slow.
(ix) Physical adsorption is a function of coverage of surface.	(ix) It is adsorbed at fixed sites on the surface. These sites are known as active centres.
(x) Not very specific.	(x) Often very specific.

PHYSICAL ADSORPTION

Types of adsorption carves. As discussed earlier, the magnitude of adsorption depends on the pressure of the gas and the temperature of the experiment for a given gas and a given adsorbent. Hence, the amount of the gas adsorbed is a function of temp and pressure only. Mathematically, it can be expressed as

$$a = f(P,T.) \qquad ...(1)$$

where a is the amount of gas adsorbed, P is the pressure, and T is the temperature. When equation (1) is represented graphically, three different curves are obtained.

(i) *Adsorption Isotherm* : If the temperature is kept constant and pressure is changed, the curve between a and p is known as adsorption isotherm.

$$a = f(p) \text{ if T is constant.}$$

(ii) *Adsorption Isobar* : If pressure is kept constant and temperature is varied, the curve between a and T is called the adsorption isobar.

$$a = f(T) \text{ ifp is constant.}$$

(iii) *Adsorption Isostere* : If the amount adsorbed is kept constant, the curve between p and T is known as adsorption isostcrc.

$$p = f(T) \text{ if a is constant.}$$

Types of Adsorption Isotherms (Physical) : Seven types of physical adsorption isotherms have been reported. These are give below lin the Fig. 1.5.

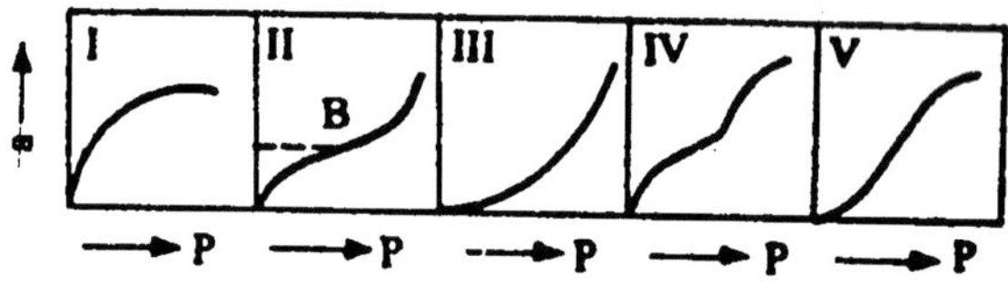

Fig. 1.5

Type I. This type of curve is obtained in such cases where mono-molecular layer is formed on the surface of the adsorbent.

This curve shows that a saturation state is reached. It means that there is no change in the value of 'a' (the amount adsorbed) with the increase in pressure onwards. This type of the curve is rare. Example is the adsorption of nitrogen on charcoal at –195°C.

Type II. This type of isotherm has a transition point 'B' which represents the pressure at which the formation of monomolecular layer is complete and that of the multi-molecular layer is being started. For many years it was the practice to take point B at the knee of the curve as the point of completion of a monolayer, and the surface areas obtained by the method are fairly consistent with those found using adsorbates that give type I isotherms.

Example is the adsorption of nitrogen on silica gel at –195°C.

Type III. In this type of isotherm there is no transition point. In this the multi-molecular layer formation starts even before the formation of monomolecular layer is complete.

Example is the adsorption of bromine or iodine vapours on silica gel at 79°C.

Type III is relatively rare and a recent example of this is that of the adsorption of nitro-gen on ice. This type seems to be characterised by a heat of adsorption equal to or less than the heat of liquefaction of the adsorbate.

Type IV. In this case there is a tendency for a saturation state to be reached in the mutiinolecular region as well. In fact this can be regarded as a duplication of the lind type. Example is the adsorption of benzene vapours on ferric oxide gel at 50°C.

Type V. This isotherm indicates multi-molecular layer formation in the beginning. At higher pressure, there is a tendency for 'a' (amount absorbed) to remain constant. It means that the saturation state has been reached. Example is the adsorption of water vapour on charcoal at 100°C.

Type VI and **Type VII.** There is a need to recognise at least the two additional isotherms shown in Fig. 1.6 These are expected for non-wetting adsorbate-adsorbent systems.

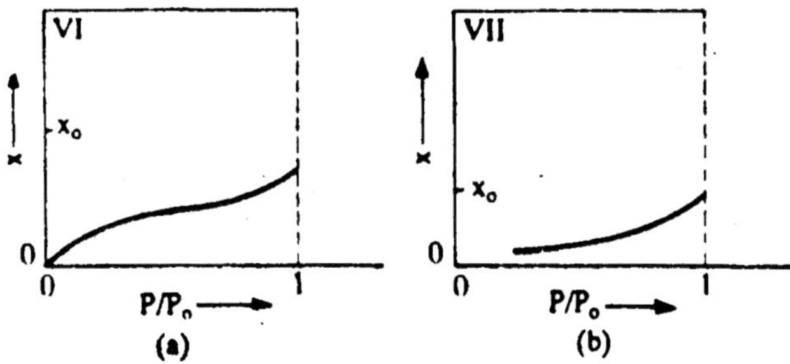

Fig. 1.6 : Two additional types of adsorption isotherms expected for non-wetting adsorbate-adsorbent systems.

MEASUREMENT OF ADSORPTION ISOTHERMS OR EXPERIMENTAL METHODS OF DETERMINING GAS ADSORPTION

The two principal methods of measuring adsorption equilibrium are classified as volumetric and gravimetric, depending upon *whether the amount ofadsorped gas is determined by means of experimentally measured pressure and the gas-law relationship of the gas phase or by direct measurement of the weight gained by the adsorbent; both methods require a certain amount of vacuum technique.*

Let us discuss these methods one by one.

1. *Volumetric or Manometric Method :* This is the most widely used technique which makes use of pressure-volume measurements to determine the amount of adsorbate gas before and after exposure to the adsorbent. The apparatus suitable for this is shown in Fig. 1.7.

In Fig. 1.7. A is a sample bulb, B and C are gas burettes and manometer, D is vapour-pressure thermometer and a is a three-way stop-cock. The adsorbent, usually a powdered solid, is kept in bulb A, which is maintained at the desired temperature of adsorption T_1.

When measurement is made with the apparatus as shown in Fig. 7 one first deter-mines the "dead space" or the gas volume in bulb A. upto three-way stop-cock a, and this is done by evacuating the line and then admitting some non-adsorbed gas such as helium to some pressure and volume reading on the manometer and burette. Stop-cock a is then turned so as to connect A and C, and the change in pressure and volume readings is noted. The helium is then removed and the adsorbate gas is admitted while stop-cock a is closed. The amount of gas is determined from the manometer and burette readings. The stop-cock is then turned so as to connect A and C and from the new readings taken after a suitable equilibration time, the amount of adsorbed gas can be calculated. D is the vapour pressure thermometer, in the same bath as the sample bulb.

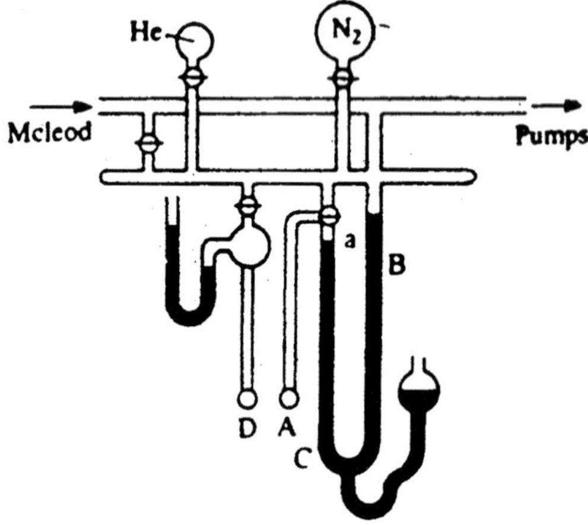

Fig. 1.7

The specific amount adsorbed, expressed as cm^3 at STP per gram of adsorbent is calculacdby

$$V = [(\Sigma\Delta\ V_{dose}) - V_{unads}]/W$$

where $\Sigma\Delta V_{dose}$ = Total amount adsorbate (gas) In the system.

V_{unads} = Total amount of unadsorbed gas.

W = Mass of the adsorbent.

Successive points on the isotherm are determined by admitting another ΔV_{dose} and so reaching another equilibrium pressure. The adsorption isotherm, thus, determined is reported graphically by plotting V vs p.

2. *The Gravimetric Method of Measuring Adsorption* : By the gravimetric method of determining the adsorption isotherm, the amount of gas adsorbed is weighed using a vaccum microbalance. Vacuum microbalances, that are suitable for adsorption measurements, have been classified by Rhodin as follows :

   (a) Cantilever type

   (b) Knife-edge type

   (c) Torsion type and

   (d) Spring type.

Fig. 1.8 shows a diagram of apparatus for measurement of the amount of adsorption by the additional weight of the adsorbent with the aid of a quartz-spring balance designed by J. Mcbain and A. Bakr.

In quartz spring, 3 is a cup with adsorbent, 4 is the ampule with liquid adsorbate (or cylinder with gaseous absorbate), 5 is a manometer, 6, 7 are thermostats and, 8, 9 and 10 are stop-cocks.

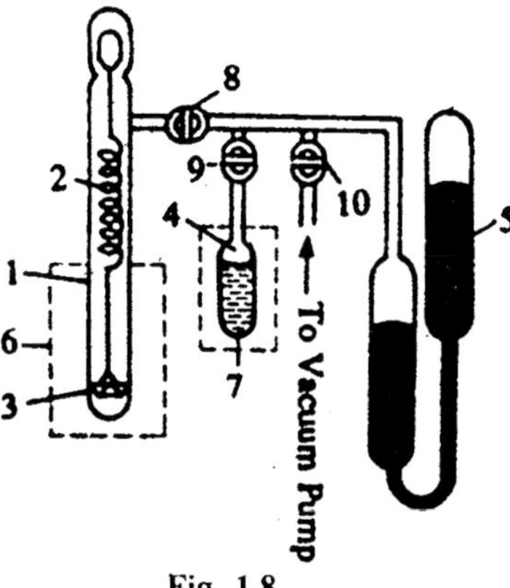

Fig. 1.8

The adsorbent is made to suspend on helical quartz spring 2 in tube 1. This part of the tube is kept in thermostat. When a gas or vapour is admitted into the apparatus, the weight of the adsorbent grows owing to adsorption and the quartz spring stretches. The elongation of the spring, preliminarily calibrated by means of weights, shows the mass of the adsorbed substance. The equilibrium pressure is usually measured with the aid of McLeod mercury manometers and U-shaped manometer 5. When studying the adsorption of a vapour, it is sometimes convenient to establish the equilibrium pressure by placing the source of a vapour-ampule 4 with the liquid adsorbate into thermostat 7 whose temperature determines the pressure of the vapour in the system. The weight method has been considerably improved and automated in vacuum installations with electromagnetic balances.

VARIOUS ADSORPTION ISOTHERMS

The various types of adsorption isotherms are :

I. *Classical Freundlich Adsorption Isotherm :* In 1909, Freundlich proposed an empirical equation and was known as Freundlich adsorption isotherm. This equation is as follows :

$$x/m = kp^{1/n} \quad ...(1)$$

where x is amount of adsorbate, m is the amount of adsorbent, p is the pressure, k and n are two constants depending upon the nature of the adsorbent and adsorbate, and n being less than unity.

Equation (1) is applicable to the adsorption of gases an solids.

In case of solution, equation (1) takes the form

$$x/m = kc^{1/n} \quad ...(2)$$

where c is the concentration of the solute in gm moles per litre.

Equations (1) and (2) predict the effect of pressure (or concentration) on the adsorption of gases (or solution) at constant temperature in a quantitative manner.

Teat of Frenndlich's Adsorption Isotherm : Taking logarithms of equations (1) and (2), we get

$$\log \frac{x}{m} = \log k + \frac{1}{n} \log p \quad ...(3)$$

and

$$\log \frac{x}{m} = \log k + \frac{1}{n} \log c \quad ...(4)$$

If log x/m is plotted against log p or log c, a straight line should be obtained as shown in Fig. 7. The slope of the line will give the value of 1/n and the intercept on the Y-axis gives the value of log k, *i.e.*,

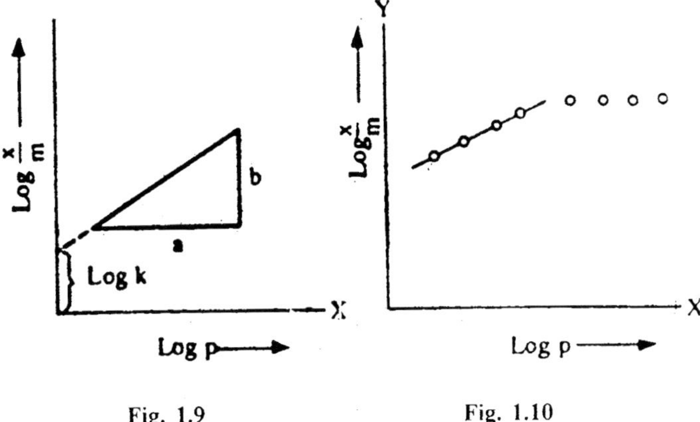

Fig. 1.9 Fig. 1.10

Thus by using equations (3) and (4), the values of k and n can be calculated from the graph (Fig. 1.9).

Analysis of the graph (Fig. 1.9) shows that as p increases, x/m also increases and, thus, the Freundlich's equation indicates no limit to this increase. But experimental values, when plotted, show some deviations from linearity especially at low pressures. This is seen in Fig. 1.10. If we compare theoretical and experimental curves (Fig. 1.9) and (Fig. 1.10), the two agree over a certain range of pressure only. Thus, Freundlich's equation has a limitation that it is valid over a certain range of pressure only.

Limitations of Freundlich's Equation

(1) It is valid over a certain range of pressure only.

(2) The constants k and n vary with the temperature.

(3) Freundlich adsorption equation is a purely empirical formula without theoretical foundation.

II. *Langmoir Adsorption Isotherm* : It has already been stated that Freundlich adsorption isotherm holds good for a certain range of pressure only. To solve this difficulty, Langmuir (1916) worked out an adsorption isotherm known as Langmuir's adsorption isotherm. The various assumptions are :

(a) The adsorbed layer on the solid adsorbent is assumed to be unimolecular in thickness. This view - is widely accepted for adsorption at low pressure or at moderately high temperature. However, the adsorbed molecules can hold other gas molecules by van der Waal's forces, so that multimolecular layers are possible. Such behaviour is apparent only at relatively low temperatures and at pressure approaching the saturation value. *But Langmuir only considered the formation of unimolecular layer while deriving this relation.*

(b) The adsorption is taking place on the fixed sites and there is no interaction between the adsorbed molecules on the surface. One site adsorbs one molecule. When the whole surface is completely covered by a unimolecular layer of the gas, further adsorption is not possible and indicates a maximum of saturation of adsorption.

(c) The process of adsorption is a dynamic process which consists of two opposing processes :

(i) *Condensation process :* It involves the condensation of the molecules of the gas on the surface of the solid.

(ii) *Evaporation process :* It involves evaporation of the molecules of adsorbate from the surface of the adsorbent.

When adsorption starts, the whole adsorbent surface remains bare and so the initial rate of condensation is maximum. As the surface becomes gradually covered, the rate of condensation becomes smaller and smaller. On the contrary, the initial rute of evaporation (desorption) of the condensed molecules is smallest at the beginning of adsorption, but increases as the surface becomes more and more covered.

Ultimately, when the equilibrium is reached, the rate of the condensation becomes equal to the rate of evaporation. It means that the number of gas molecules condensing on the given surface is equal to the number of molecules evaporating away per unit time from the same surface, *i.e.* the arrangement of the adsorbed molecule on the surface is unidirectional.

(d) Gas behaves ideally.

(e) Surface is uniform energetically.

Derivation : On the basis of above postulates, Langmuir deduced the equation describing the quantitative relationship between the pressure and the amount of gas adsorbed at constant temperature. Suppose n is the number of molecules of the gas striking one square cm of the surface per second. Let a be the fraction of the molecules condensing on the surface, Then, an is the total number of molecules which condense on the surface. This condensation is not taking place on the whole surface but it is taking place at only $n\alpha$ $(1 - \theta)$ sq. cm, where θ sq. cm is the fraction of the area already covered by the gas molecules and 1 sq. cm is the total surface area.

$\therefore$ Rate of condensation of gaseous molecules on the surface

$$= (1 - \theta)\,\theta n \qquad ...(5)$$

One knows that:

Rate of evaporation $\propto$ Area of surface covered.

$$\propto \theta$$

or Rate of evaporation $= A\theta$

where k is the proportionality constant. When equilibrium is set up, the rate of condensation is equal to the rate of evaporation, *i.e.*

$$A\theta = (1 - \theta)\,\theta n \qquad ...(6)$$

or $$k\theta + \theta\alpha n = \alpha n$$

or $$\theta = \frac{\alpha n}{1 + \alpha n} \qquad ...(7)$$

From, kinetic theory of gases, it follows that

Number of molecules $\propto$ pressure of the gas striking the surface

or $$n \propto p$$

or $$n = \beta p \qquad ...(8)$$

where β is the proportionality constant.

Now $$\frac{k + \alpha n}{\alpha n} = \frac{k}{\alpha n} + 1 \qquad ...(9)$$

$$= \frac{k}{\beta p \alpha} + 1 \qquad \left\{\begin{matrix}\text{From eqution (8)} \\ \beta p = n\end{matrix}\right\}$$

$$= \frac{1}{k_1 p} + 1 = \frac{1 + k_1 p}{k_1 p} \qquad ...(10)$$

where $k_1 = \left(\frac{\alpha\beta}{k}\right)$ is amptjer constant. Eq. (10) can be written

$$\frac{k + \alpha n}{\alpha n} = \frac{1 + k_1 p}{k_1 p} \qquad ...(11)$$

or $$\frac{\alpha n}{k + \alpha n} = \frac{k_1 p}{1 + k_1 p}$$

Comparing equations (7) and (11), we obtain

$$\theta = \frac{k_1 p}{1 + k_1 p} \qquad ...(12)$$

If it is supposed that one molecule thick layer of the gas is formed on the surface, then

$$\frac{x}{m} \propto \theta \qquad ...(13)$$

or
$$\frac{x}{m}\, k_2\theta \qquad ...(14)$$

where k_2, is another proportionality constant.

Equation (13) implies that the amount of gas adsorbed per unit mass of adsorbent is proportional to fraction of the surface covered. Substituting the value of 0 from equation (12) into the equation (14), we obtain

$$\frac{x}{m} = \frac{k_2 k_2 p}{1 + k_1 p} \qquad ...(15)$$

or
$$\frac{1}{\frac{x}{m}} = \frac{1 + k_1 p}{k_2 k_1 p}$$

or
$$\frac{p}{\frac{x}{m}} = \frac{1}{\frac{x}{m}} = \frac{1}{k_1 k_2} + \frac{p}{k_2} \qquad ...(16)$$

Equation (16) is known as *Langmuir's adsorption isotherm.*

A plot of $\frac{p}{x/m}$ against p should be a straight tine.

Another form of equation (16) can be obtained by introducing the term V_m which is equal to the volume of adsorbate required to complete a unimolecular layer, *i.e.*, to saturate the surface. The fraction, θ of the surface covered is then equal to V/V_m where V is the volume adsorbed at a given pressure p. Hence equation (12) becomes as

$$\frac{V}{V_m} = \frac{k_1 p}{1 + k_1 p}$$

or
$$\frac{p}{V} = \frac{1}{k_1 V_m} + \frac{p}{V_m} \qquad ...(16A)$$

Equation (16A) is another form of the Langmuir equation.

Discussion : Three different cases may arise :

Case I: When pressure of the gas is very low, k_1p is negligible as compared to unity. It implies that θ, the fraction covered by absorption, is quite small. In such a special case, equation (15) becomes as

$$\frac{x}{m} = k_1 k_2 p \qquad ...(17)$$

or $$\frac{x}{m} \propto p \qquad ...(18)$$

Thus, under low pressure, *the amount of the gas adsorbed per unit quantity of adsorbent is directly proportional to the pressure.* This has been confirmed by experimental observation.

Case II. When pressure is very large, k_1p becomes larger than unity. In such a special case equation (15) becomes as

$$\frac{x}{m} = \frac{k_1 k_2 p}{k_1 p} \qquad (\because k_1p >> 1)$$

or $$\frac{x}{m} = k_2 \qquad ...(19)$$

This equation shows that at high pressure, the amount of adsorbed gas is independent of pressure.

Case III. At low pressure, equation (18) is

$$\frac{x}{m} \propto p \text{ or } \frac{x}{m} = \text{constant} \times p$$

At high pressure, equation (19) is

Therefore, at moderate pressures, Langmuir adsorption equation becomes as

$$x/m = \text{constant} \times p^{1/n}$$

or $$x/m = kp^{1/n} \quad ...(20)$$

Equation (20) is the Freundlich adsorption equation (1). In equation (20), 1/n lies between zero and unity. Some typical shapes of Langmuir's curves are illustrated in Fig. 1.11.

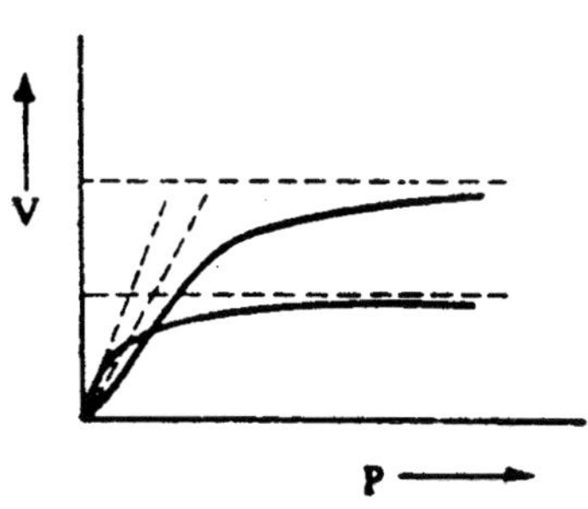

Fig. 1.11

As pressure is increased or temperature is decreased, additional layers are formed. This has led to the modern concept of multi-molecular adsorption.

Test of the Langmuir Adsorption Isotherm

From equation (16), we have

$$\frac{p}{x/m} = \frac{1}{k_1k_2} + \frac{p}{k_2}$$

A plot of $\frac{p}{x/m}$ versus p should give a straight line. The slope of this is $\frac{1}{k_2}$ and the intercept on the .y-axis gives $\frac{1}{k_1k_2}$ (Fig. 1.12).

In certain cases, the experimental curves are not straight. This may be due to the following reasons :

(i) non-uniformity of surfaces.

(ii) formation of multiple layers in some cases.

(iii) partial adsorption, and

(iv) some chemical reaction of the adsorbate with the adsorbent.

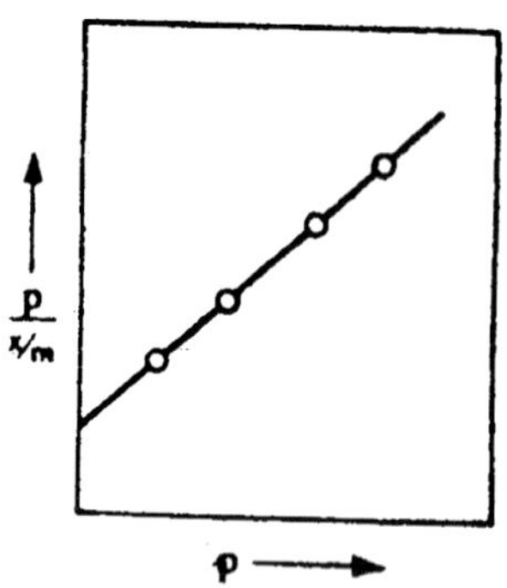

Fig. 1.12

Successes of the Theory

(i) The mechanism of adsorption presented by Langmuir explainschemical adsorption or chemisorption.

(ii) Langmuir's theory is more satisfactory than the Freundlich's equation while explaining physical adsorption of gases on different adsorbents whenever saturation is approached.

Limitations. The Main Limitations are

(i) Langmuir postulated that a saturated ,value of adsorption is independent of temperature. But experiment shows that it is actually falling off with rising emperatures.

(ii) Langmuir assumed' that an adsorption film on a plane surface will never be over a molecule thick. In actual practice, much thicker films have been reported.

(iii) This theory cannot explain all the five types of adsorption isotherms.

III. *The B.E.T. Equation* : In 1815 *de Sanssure* suggested that the adsorbed gas or vapour is in the form of a thick compressed polymolecular layer. This concept was formulated quantitatively by *Euken* and *Polanyi* a century-later. In contrast to the original views of *de Saussure, Polanyi, Brunauer Emmet* and *Teller* extended the *Langmnir's* approach to the multiple molecular layer adsorption and their equation is known as the B. E. T. equation. B.E.T. equation represents the first effective attempt to explainphysical adsorption from monolayer regions through the multiple. *Postulates of B.E.T. Equation :*

(i) The adsorbed layer may be polymolecular in thickness..

(ii) Langmuir's assumption applies to every layer.

(iii) There is a dynamic equilibrium between successive layers. The rate of evaporation from the first layer is equal to the rate a/ condensation on the preceding layer.

(iv) The heat of adsorption in each layer (excepting the first one) is involved in each of the evaporation processes.

(v) After the first layer, the heat of adsorption is equal to latent heat of condensation of vapour (=L).

(vi) The derivation is based on the same kinetic picture as represented ay Langmulr.

(vii) Condensation forces are the principal forces in adsorption.

Derivation of B.E.T. Equation : On the basis of above postulates, B.E.T. equation can be derived (Fig. 1.13).

Fig. 1.13 : The B.B.T. model.

Let S_0, S_1, S_2,......S_i represent the surface area of adsorbent covered by 0. 1, 2,......, i layers of the adsorbed molecules. As So must remain constant at equilibrium, the rate of condensation on the bare surface is equal to the rate of evaporation of desorption from the first layer. Thus,

$$a_1pS_0 = b_1S_1e^{-E_1/RT} \quad ...(21)$$

where a_1 and b_1 are constants, E_1 is the heat of adsorption of the first layer, T is the temperature and p is the pressure.

For the equilibrium in successive layers, we can write

$$a_2pS_1 = b_2S_2\, e^{-E_2/RT} \quad ...(22)$$

$$a_3pS_2 = b_2S_3e^{-E_3/RT} \quad ...(23)$$

....

$$a_i p S_{i-1} = b_{iS} i e^{-E_i/RT} \quad ...(24)$$

where E_2, E_3, E_4, ... E_i represent the heats of adsorption of 2, 3,......ith layer. Total surface area A of the adsorbent can be written as :

$$A = \sum_{i=0}^{\infty} S_i \quad ...(25)$$

Total volume absorbed, V, is given as

$$V = V_0 \sum_{i=0}^{\infty} i\, S_i \quad ...(26)$$

where V_0 denotes the volume of the gas adsorbed on one cm* of the adsorbed surface when it is covered by a unimolecular layer of the adsorbed gas. From Eqs. (25) and (26), we get

$$\frac{V}{A} = \frac{V_0 \sum_{i=0}^{\infty} iS_i}{\sum_{i=0}^{\infty} S_i}$$

or
$$\frac{V}{AV_0} = \frac{\sum_{i=0}^{\infty} iS_i}{\sum_{i \propto 0}^{\infty} S_i} = \frac{V}{V_m}(\text{say}) \quad ...(27)$$

where V_m (=A Vo) is the volume of the gas adsorbed when the entire surface of the adsorbent is covered by a unimoleciilar layer of the adsorbed gas. In order to carry out sum mation of eq. (27), *Bronauer, Emmet* and Teller made important assumptions that

$$\text{(i)} E_2 = E_3 = E_4 = ... = E_i = E_L \quad ...(28)$$

$$\text{(ii)} \quad \frac{b_2}{a_2} = \frac{b_2}{a_3} = ... = \frac{b_i}{a_i} = g \quad ...(29)$$

where E_L is the heat of liquefaction and g is constant. We will now express S_1, S_2, S_3, ... S_i in terms of S_0. From equation (21) we have

$$b_1\, S_1\, e^{-E_1/RT} = a_1 p S_0$$

or
$$S_1 = \left(\frac{a_1}{b_1}\right) \frac{p}{e^{-E_1/RT}} S_0$$

or
$$S_1 = \left(\frac{a_1}{b_1}\right) p e^{E_1/RT} S_0 = y\, S_0 \quad ...(30)$$

were $$y = \left(\frac{a_1}{b_1}\right) pe^{E_1/RT} \quad ....(31)$$

Also from equation (22),

$$b_2 S_2 e^{-E_2/RT} = a_2 pS_1$$

From equation (28), we have

$$E_2 = E_L$$

$$\therefore \quad b_2S_2b_2 S_2 e^{-E_L/RT} = a_2 pS_1$$

or $$S_2 = \left(\frac{a_2}{b_2}\right) \frac{p}{e^{-E_L/RT}} = S_1 = \left(\frac{a_2}{b_2}\right) pe^{E_L/RT}S_1$$

From equatiun (29). we have

$$\frac{b_2}{a_2} = g \text{ or } \frac{1}{g} = \frac{a_2}{b_2}$$

$$\therefore \quad S_2 = \left(\frac{p}{g}\right) e^{E_L/RT} S_1 = xS_1 \quad ...(32)$$

where $$x = \left(\frac{p}{g}\right) e^{E_L/RT} \quad ...(33)$$

Eliminating S between Eqs. (30) and (32), we get

$$S_2 = xyS_0,$$

Similarly, it can be written as

$$S_3 = x^2y\ S_0$$

$$S_4 = x^3y\ S_0$$

....

$$S_i = x^{i-1}y\ S_0$$

$$= \frac{x_i}{x} yS_0 \quad \left[\because \frac{x^4}{x} = x^{i-1}\right]$$

$$= x^i \left(\frac{y}{x}\right) S_0 = x^i cS_0 \quad ...(34)$$

where $c = \frac{y}{x} = \frac{a_1 g}{b_1} e^{(E_1 - E_L)/RT}$ ...(34) [From eqs. (31) and (33)].

Equation (27) can be written as

$$\frac{V}{V_m} = \frac{\sum_{i=0}^{\infty} iS_i}{\sum_{i=0}^{\infty} S_i} = \frac{\sum_{i=0}^{i=\infty} ic\,x^i\,S_0}{\sum_{i=0}^{i=\infty} cx^i\,S_0} \quad \text{[From (33A), Eq. } S_i = c\ xi\ S_0]$$

$$\text{or } \frac{V}{V_m} = \frac{cS_0 \sum_{i=0}^{\infty} ix^i}{S_0\left[1 + c\sum_{i=0}^{\infty} x^i\right]} \quad ...(35)$$

$$\text{But} \quad \sum_{i=1}^{\infty} i\,x^i\ \frac{x}{(1-x)^2} \quad ...(36)$$

$$\text{and} \quad \sum_{i=1}^{\infty} x^i\ \frac{x}{(1-x)} \quad ...(37)$$

Combining equations (35), (36) and (37), we get

$$\frac{V}{V_m} = \frac{c\dfrac{x}{(1-x)^2}}{\left[1 + c\dfrac{x}{(1-x)}\right]}$$

$$\text{or} \quad \frac{V}{V_m} = \frac{cx}{(1-x)\left[1+(c-1)x\right]} \quad ...(38)$$

$$\text{or} \quad V = \frac{V_m cx}{(1-x)\,[1+(c-1)x]}$$

Rearranging equation (38), we get

$$\frac{x}{(1-x)V} = \frac{1}{cV_m} + \frac{(c-1)x}{cV_m} \quad ...(39)$$

$$\text{where} \quad x = \frac{p}{p_0} \quad ...(40)$$

Equation (39), is known as B.E.T. equation. In equation (40). p is the equilibrium presture of the gas over the surface and p_0 is the saturated vapour pressure of the gas at experimental temperature.

B.E.T. Equation forn layers : Following relationship is obtained in place of equation (38) :

$$\frac{V}{V_m} = \frac{cx}{1-x}\left[\frac{1-(n+1)\,x^n + nx^{n+1}}{1+(c-1)\,x - cx^{n+1}}\right] \quad ...(41)$$

Equation (l)is the B.E.T. equation for n layers.

B.E.T. Equation and Laagmuir equation : When n = 1, equation (41) reduces to

$$\frac{V}{V_m} = \frac{cx}{1-x}\left[\frac{1-(n+1)\,x+x^2}{1+(c-1)\,x - cx^2}\right]$$

$$= \frac{cx(1-x)^2}{(1-x)\,[1+cx-x-cx^2]} \quad [\because (1-x)^2 = 1-2x+x^2]$$

$$= \frac{cx\,(1-x)}{(1-x)+cx\,(1-x)} = \frac{cx(1-x)}{(1-x)\,(1+cx)} = \frac{cx}{1+cx}$$

or $$\frac{V}{V_m} = \frac{cx}{1+cx} \qquad ...(42)$$

From equation (40), we have

$$x = \frac{p}{p_0} \qquad ...(43)$$

Substituting equation (43) in equation (42). we get

$$\frac{V}{V_m} = \frac{c\dfrac{p}{p_0}}{1+c\dfrac{p}{p_0}}$$

or $$\frac{p}{V} = \frac{p_0}{cV_m} + \frac{p}{V_m} \qquad ...(44)$$

This is Langmuir equation (16) if the usual P_0. c and V_m.

Properties of the B.E.T. Equation

$$\frac{x}{(1-x)V}\;\frac{1}{cV_m} + \frac{(c-1)\,x}{c\,V_m} \qquad ...(45)$$

Equation (39) is the general expression of a straight line (y = c + mx.) In order to test the validity of equation (39), a curve is drawn between x/(l – x) V and x. This has been found to be a straight line. Its slope is $\frac{(c-1)}{c\,V_m}$ whereas the intercept on the ordinate is $1/cV_m$. From these two quantities the value of V_m can be determined. As the number of moles of the gas in this volume is known and the area of cross section for a single molecule is available, it is possible to calculate the area of the adsorbing surface.

By this method, values of the surface areas that are self consistent are as follows :

Gas	N_2	O_2	Ar	Kr	n-C_4H_{10}
Area ($Å^2$/molecule)	16.2	14.1	13.8	19.5	18.1

The values given in the above table are close to the calculated ones from the liquid densities at the boiling points and are, in this respect, reasonable for a multilayer adsorption situation.

(ii) From the experimental point of view, the B.E.T. equation is easy to apply, and the surface areas so obtained are reasonably consistent. The equation in fact has become the standard one for practical surface area determinations, usually with nitrogen at 77°K as the adsorbate, but in general with any system giving type II isotherm.

(iii) B. E. T. equation also explain three of the five isotherm types described in Fig. 14. Thus fore large, *i.e.*, $E_1 >> E_L$, it reduces to the Langmuir equation, and for small c values, type III isotherms result, as illustrated in Fig. 1.14. However, the adsorption of relatively inert gases such as nitrogen, argon, etc., on polar surfaces generally gives c values around 100, corresponding to type II isotherms. For such isotherms, the approximate form of equation (45) works quite well in the usual region of fit of the B.E.T. equation a "one point" method of surface area determination thus follows.

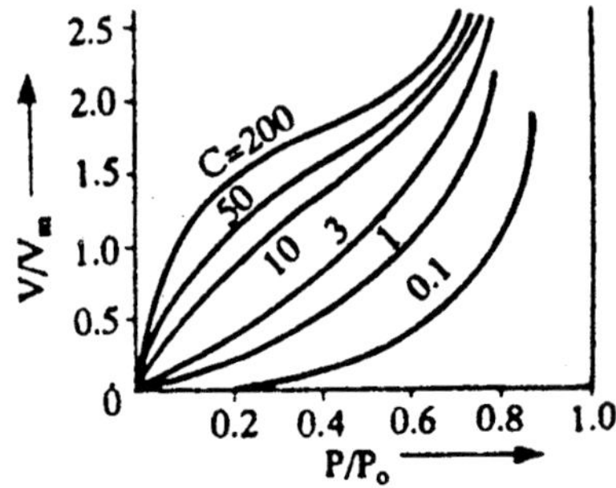

Fig. 1.14

$$\frac{V}{V_m} = \frac{1}{(1-x)}$$

Failures of B.E.T. Equation.

(i) B.E.T. equation fails below a relative pressure p/p_0 of 0-05 and it also fails when it is above 0.35.

(ii) The assumption that the adsorbate has liquid properties is not correct.

(iii) Coordination number of molecules in the higher layers also adds the criticism to the B.E.T. equation in another way.

Thus, the treatment of B E.T. equation is approximate and needs farther modification.

Modification of B.E.T. equation : In order to correct certain approximation which were made in the derivation of B.E.T. equations and to give a better fit to type II isotherms, it is assumed that multilayer formation is limited to n layers and not to the infinity layers. It means that the number of adsorbed layers cannot exceed a finite number, n. and the summation of equation (45) cannot be carried out to infinity and we then obtain,

$$\frac{V}{V_m} = \frac{cx}{(1-x)}\left\{\frac{1(n+1)\ n^n + nx^{n+1}}{1+(c-1)\ x - x^{n+1}}\right\} \qquad ...(46)$$

The value of n may be considered to be the width of pores, capillaries and surface defects which limit the maximum number of layers even at saturation pressure. If n = l, equation (46) gives Langmuir's adsorption isotherm. If n = ∞, then gives B.E.T. equation. From Fig. 1.15 it follows that by choosing the appropriate valve, the amount of adsorption predicted at large p/p_0 values is reduced and a better fit to data can usually be obtained.

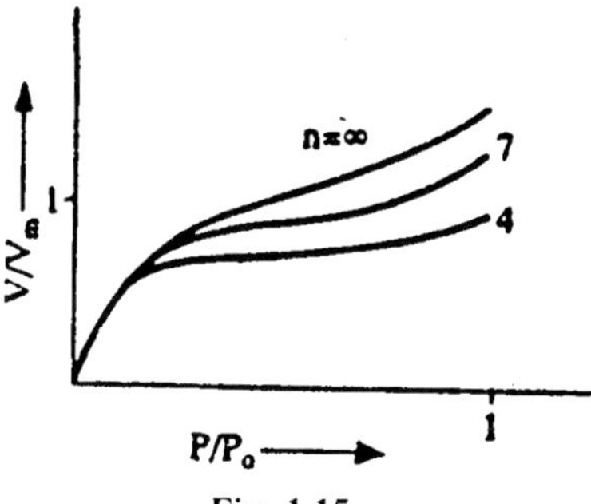

Fig. 1.15

DETERMINATION OF SURFACE AREA

Introduction

Before discussing the methods for measuring surface area, it may be well to define what is meant by the surface area of a porous solid. Quite clearly, a porous solid may be said to have two different types of areas. One of these is made up of the external, the geometric or the *outer surface area* of the porous particles. The other type is usually called the "*inner surface*" and is made up of surface of the walls of the capillaries, crevices and cracks in the porous catalyst particles.

Sometimes the ratio between the total surface area and the outer surface area needs to be stated. This ratio is usually known as the "*roughness factor*" of *the* solid. Such roughness factor may extend all the way from the value of unity for perfectly smooth solids upto values of several hundred or several thousands for very porous materials.

The specific surface area is denned as the surface area per unit mass (expressed as m^2/g). Various methods for the determination of surface area of solids arc as follows:

1. *Harkins and Jura Method :* By assuming that the same type of equation is applicable to the adsorption of gases on solids that has been found applicable to correlating the surface spreading force of absorbed films on liquids with the area occupied by adsorbed molecules. Harkins and Jura deduced that area of a solid can be obtained from the following equation:

$$\log\left(\frac{p}{p_0}\right) = B - \frac{A}{\upsilon^2}$$

where A and B are constants, and v is the value of the gas adsorbed at pressure p; p_0 is the liquefaction pressure of the gas. By plotting log p against l/υ^2, the slope (S) of the curve obtain ed has been shown to the related to the area A of the surface by the equation

$$A = kS^{1/2} \qquad ...(1)$$

where A- is a universal constant which can be evaluated by an independent method.

In some very ingenious experiments, Harkins and Jura also provided an independent means of evaluating k by exposing a finely devided solid such as TiO_2 to a sufficient pressure of water vapour to form four or five statistical adsorbed layers, and then immersing in liquid water this sample got coated with several layers of adsorbed water. They were then able to obtain from the evolved heat of immersion a direct measure of the surface area of the powder without any assumption as to the molecular cross-section of the water molecule. They merely divided the heat of immersion by 118.5 ergs, the value for the normal surface energy per square cm of liquid water to obtain a value for the number of square cm of area in the sample. Using this surface area for the powder they were then able to evaluate the constant of equation (1). For other solids they could apply equation (1) by assuming that the constant k was independent of the type of surface. Proceeding in this way they obtained surface area values for six separate solids with their nitrogen adsorption isotherms and compared them with the areas that were obtained by plotting the adsorption data according, *i.e.*, B.E.T. method.

2. *Benton and White Method :* Benton and White (1931) noticed a sharp break in the S-shaped isotherm for the adsorption of nitrogen at --191.5° on an iron catalyst at about 120 m.m. pressure. This apparently corresponds to a complete monolayer. It is evident that the product of the number of molecules in the monolayer and the molecular crosssection would give the surface area. This idea was further developed by Brauner who applied their B.E.T. equation to surface determinations. The isotherm may be put in the following form

$$\frac{x}{(1-x)\,V} = \frac{1}{V_m c} + \frac{(c-1)x}{V_m c}$$

where all letters are having the usual significance. The plot of the left hand .side of this equation against x would give V_m and c. The plot is often linear at pressures x less than about 0.3, and this linear portion will, in general, extend to both sides of the pressure corresponding to a monolayer. In general, the monolayer point would correspond to $x \approx 0.1$, when $c \approx 100$ and to $x \approx 0.5$ for $c = 1$.

It also becomes necessasy to find the area covered by each adsorbed molecule so as to get the value for the surface area of the adsorbent. Emmett and Teller regarded that the area, A of each adsorbed molecule may be given by the relation

$$A = 4.866\left(\frac{M}{4\sqrt{2}\,Nd}\right)^{2/3}$$

wncre M refers to the molecular weight of the gas, d the density of the liquefied or solidified adsorbate and N Avogadro's number. For argon and carbon dioxide at –183°C. the area has been found to be about 17 A^2, for NK_3 at –36°C it has been found to be about 13 A^2. For measurement of surface area, nitrogen is commonly used as the absorbate at liquid nitrogen temperature (–196°C). Nitrogen is having a cross-sectional area 16.2 A_2.

It is to be remembered that the areas obtained by the use of adsorbates other than nitrogen have been found to be different in many cases from those obtained by means of nitrogen. Thus, Harris and Emmett reported that for CS_2 the area might be only one-third to one-half as large as that calculated by the nitrogen adsorption method. In the same way, the areas obtained for butane and argon have been found to be different by a factor of 1.5 and 1.2. respectively. The reason for the discrepancies has been attributed to the larger molecules being screened out of some of the pores of the adsorbent, or to irregularities in packing of various molecules on the surface of the solid.

3. *B. E. T. Method* : Brunauer, Emmett and Teller derived an equation that has proved very useful in interpreting multilayer gas adsorption isotherms and in yielding information as to the surface area of solid catalysts. Their equation may be written in the form :

$$\frac{x}{V(1-x)} = \frac{1}{V_m c} + \frac{(c-1)x}{V_m c} \quad \text{[see Equation (45)]}$$

where x is the relative pressure of the adsorbate,

V is the volume of the gas adsorbed at x,

V_m is the volume of the gas required to form a monolayer on the solid, and c is a constant which depends on temperature, on the heat of the liquefaction of the adsorbate and the heat of adsorption in the first layer.

Compare with the general equation of a straight line

$$y = \text{intercept} + \text{slope } x.$$

It means that a straight line should be obtained if $\frac{x}{(1-x)V}$ is plotted against x. The slope of this line is

$$\text{slope} = \frac{(c-1)}{cV_m}, \qquad ...(2)$$

and intercept at y-axis is

$$\text{Intercept} = \frac{1}{cV_m} \qquad ...(3)$$

On adding Eqs. (1) and (2), we get

$$\text{Slope} + \text{Intercept} \ \frac{(c-1)}{cV_m} + \frac{1}{cV_m} + \frac{1}{cV_m} = \frac{c-1+1}{cV_m} = \frac{c}{cV_m}$$

$$\text{or (Slope + Intercept)} = \frac{1}{V_m}$$

$$V_m = \frac{1}{(\text{Slope} + \text{Interept})} \qquad ...(4)$$

If one molecule of an adsorbent occupies an area o, the total numbers of molecules present in a volume will occupy an area

$$S = \frac{\sigma V_m N}{22400} \qquad ...(5)$$

since the total number of molecules in volume V_m is $\frac{NV_m}{22400}$

Calculate the volume of V_m from equation (4) and then substitute in equation (5) to get the value of S, the surface area of solid.

B.E.T. surface areas have been found to agree quite reasonably with values calculated from electron micrographs. The B. E. T. method provides a relatively easy way to evaluate the surface area.

The monolayer volume is usually found out by using the BET volumetric adsorption apparatus (Fig. 1.16). The principle is simple. The pressure, volume and temperature of a quantity of adsorbate can be measured by the manometers M_1 and M_2, the burette B, and thermometers T_1 and T_2, respectively. The amount of gas present can be calculated. The gas is then brought in contact with the adsorbent sample (S) kept in the liquid nitrogen bath C. As soon as equilibrium is attained after adsorption, the amount of gas left in the gas phase would be calculated.

The difference between the amounts of gas presefpt initially and finally would give the absorbate 'lost' from the gas phase to the adsorbed phase. The accurate determination of the amount of the gas unadsorbed at equilibrium has been found to depend on a correct calibration of the '*dead space*' *i.e.*, the free space surrounding the adsorbent sample. This dead space volume is generally determined by using helium whose adsorption is negligible at liquid N, temperature. The true adsorption values are then corrected for the dead-space volumes.

4. *Point B Method :* In this method, the relative pressure p/p_0 is plotted against the volume of gas absorbed.

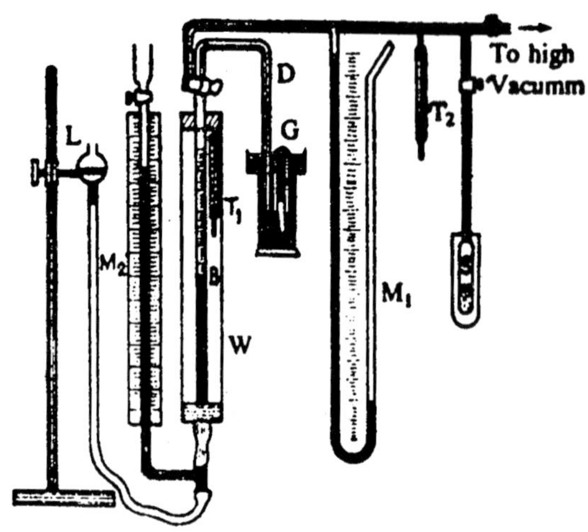

Fig. 1.16 : Vauum line for gas adsorption measurements.

From the graph, the adsorbed volume necessary to yield a monolayer of gas on the surface is determined. This can be done by reading directly the amonnt, V_b, adsorbed corresponding to the first inflextion point (Point B). It is assumed that the adsorbate covers the solid as a monolayer at this point.

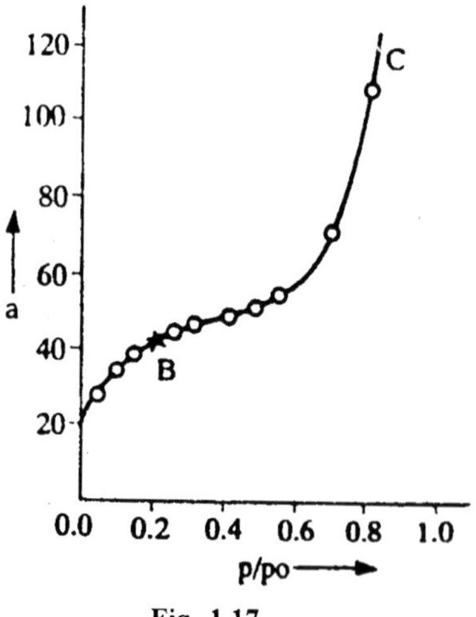

Fig. 1.17

Finally, the area per gm of the adso r-bent is calculated by substitution of the relevent data in the equation.

$$S = \left(\frac{P' V_b}{RT_0} \right) NA \qquad ...(6)$$

where P' = 1 atmosphere

T_0 = 273°K

R = Gas constant

A = Area occupied on the surface by a single molecule.

The main drawback of this method is that this method cannot be applied to all types of gas adsorbates and solids.

5. *From the Parmeability to Fluids* : The volume of a fluid passing in unit time (dV/dt cm^3/sec) through S cm^3 of a porous plug of length L is approximately given by the Kozeni—Carman equation :

$$\frac{dV}{dt} = \frac{(p_1 - p_2)\, S}{\eta\, L\, S_0} \; \frac{\epsilon^3}{k(1 - \epsilon)^2} \qquad ...(7)$$

where $p_1 - p$ = The driving pressure difference.

η = The viscosity of the fluid.

ϵ = The relative volume of voids, and

k = A numerical constant which is usually assumed to be equal to five (a pure number).

As all the quantities of equation (7) can be measured, one can measure S_0 (cm^{-1}) and from this, one can measure area of unit volume of the solid phase by applying the following equation :

$$S = \rho A_6$$

where ρ is the density of Ihe solid.

Limitations of the Method : The various limitations are as follows :

(i) The plug may be a felt of fibres, a compacted powder and so on, but should not contain any pores or voids with one entrance only; a pore is registered only if the fluid enters it from one and leaves it at the opposite end.

(ii) Surface roughness generally lowers the experimental values of dV/dt and this may cause an additional falsification of results.

(iii) Equation (7) was derived on the assumption that the gas-flow was laminar. If the pore diameter is small in comparison with the free path of the gas molecules (*i.e.*, when the pressures p_1 and p_2 are very small), then these molecules fly across the pores rather than roughly parallel to their axes. and another term must be added to the right-hand side of the equation.

6. *From the Electrical Potential of the Adsorbed layer :* If a metal electrode like silveror platinum is placed in a solution like sulphuric acid with which it does not react, a potential is developed which may be measured by means of a sensitive galvanometer or vacuum tube volt meter that draws very little current. Now if a small amount of current is made to flow through the system (of the order of micro amperes per square centimetre), the potential rises to a new steady state value. The plot of potential versus lime during the interval immediately after the start of current flow was nearly linear and of the form:

$$-E = kq + \text{constant}$$

where q denotes the amount of active meterial on the cathode surface or current time. The value of A: should vary from one system to the next only in proportion to the surface area and the ratio of k for two electrodes should give the ratio of the specific surface areas. Joncich and Hackerman obtained areas for platinised platinum by applying the above method very close to those given by the BET gas adsorption method.

7. From the Rate of Dissolution. We know that a very thin layer of liquid in contact with a soluble solid very soon becomes saturated with the latter, *i.e.*, acquires the concent-ration C_0 equal to the solubility of the solid. After that, the rate of dissolution is determined by the rate of diffusion of the solute (which is proportional to the difference $C_0 - C$, if C is the concentration far from the solid), to the inverse thickness of the diffusion layer and to the area of the solid-liquid interface. Let m be the mass dissolved at time t. Then dmfdt is the rate of dissolution. If this derivative is measured for, say, a well polished cube of a solid material (sample 1) and for a powder of the same substance (sample 2), then $(dm/dt)_1 : (dm/dt)_2 = A_1 : A_2$, *i.e.*, the ratio of the rates of dissolution is equal to the ratio of the two areas. The

geometrical area A_1 of a cube is readily obtained ; hence, also the geometrical area A_2 of the powder can be found.

The two most doubtful assumptions on which this method is based are:

(i) The thickness of the diffusion layer is identical in the two samples, and

(ii) the surface region of the powder is as perfect as its core.

If the above assumptions are ever satisfied, then Ag is the area of the boundary between the saturated film and the unsaturated solution so that it ought to be significantly smaller then the area derived from the gas adsorption measurements.

8. *From the Heat of Wetting* : In this method, 1 g of a powder, whose surface area is A_0, is immersed in a liquid. Then, A_0 cm^2 of the gas-solid interface disappear and A_0 cm^2 of the liquid-solid interface form. If the two total surface energies per unit area are U,, and U_{13}, then the energy change in immersion process is A_0 (U_{23} – U_{13}) and the heat of wetting Q is said to be equal to this product (with a negative sign as exothermal heat is considered positive), *i.e.*,

$$-Q = A_0 (U_{23} - U_{13}) \qquad ...(8)$$

From the above equation. A_0 can be estimated. In an earlier work, a silica gel containing 3 – 6 per cent water was used.

9 *Radioactive Tracer Method* : In 1922, F. Paneth devised a method to determine the surface area of crystalline powders with the aid of radioactive atoms. By exchanging tracer atoms of lead with lead in the surface of a crystalline precipitate of lead sulphate, one can determine the number of lead ions on the surface of the crystals, and knowing the area occupied by one lead ion, one can find the total area of the powder. The area occupied by one ion of a substance on a surface can be calculated from the distances between ions in a crystal lattice of a soid. This quantity (l^2) may be obtained from the following equation :

$$l^2 = \frac{M}{aN\rho}$$

where M is the mass of one molecule, a is the number of gram-atoms per mol of a solid, N is the A vogadro's number and p is the density of substance.

In this method, a powder of lead sulphate is agitated with a solution containing radioactive lead. Due to the exchange of ions, an exchange equilibrium sets in. Noting the change in the activity of the solution, one can establish the kinetics of the exchange reaction. Most of the exchange reactions follow the first order kinetics. Thus, the degree of exchange in the time t after the beginning of the exchange reaction can be found quite easily from the obvious relation:

$$x = \frac{a_0 - a_1}{a_0 - a_\infty}$$

where a_0 is the initial specific activity of the radioactive substance, a_t is the specific activity in time t after the beginning of the exchange reaction and $a\infty$ is the specific activity of this substance after equilibrium sets in.

One can find the mass of the substance capable of participating in the exchange reaction with the aid of the following equation :

$$\frac{m_{surface}}{M_{solution}} = \frac{a_0 - a_\infty}{a_\infty} \qquad ...(9)$$

where mmrfaei is the mass of the substance on the surface of the solid capable of taking part in the exchange reaction and muwiw is the mass of this substance in the solution. The mass of the substance in the solution can be found by ordinary chemical analysis. Hence it is easy to determine from eq. (i) the number of ions on the surface (the quantity $m_{surface} = \frac{N_A}{A}$ where A is the mass of one gram ion) and knowing the dimensions of ions, it is simple to find the total surface area of the crystals.

Importance of Surface Area

Surface area has been an important parameter in almost all physical and chemical processses which are involving powdered or porous solids. For example, catalysts used in dehdrogenation are having activities that are directly proportinal to the total surface area. Mesurcments of surface area provide much information about the composition of the surface of a catalyst or an adsorbent. Knowledge of surface area has been found to be also very useful in following the changes in catalysts during use, sintcring and impregnation.

The efficiency of adsorbents such as silica gel, activated alumina etc. in dehumidification of air and other gases and also in drying of liquids like oils and hydrocarbons, largely depends on their surface area. The extent of surface available in activated carbon has been a necessary information in large scale solvent recovery in many industries. Measurement of surface area has been thus the first step in any physical or chemical process using adsorbents or catalysts.

HEAT OF ADSORPTION

Introduction : Adsorption is an exothermic process. In adsorption, a decrease in the surface energy takes place which appears as heat and is known as heat of adsorption. Thus, *the amount of heat which is evolved during adsorption is known as heat of adsorption.*

This heat of adsorption mainly depends upon the nature of gas.

Types of Heats of Adsorption : There are two types of heat of adsorption such as :

(a) *Integral heat of adsorption :* When a gas is admitted to an adsorbent io an evacuated vessel and x grams or moles of it are adsorbed, then a heat Q_t is evolved. It is called the integral heat of adsorption. It is generally expressed in Kcal or in Joules.

(ii) *Differential heat of adsorption :* If the above vessel cotaining x gm of adsorbent is evacuated again and a slightly different amount of the gas is admitted so that the adsorbed amount becomes $x + \Delta x$ or $x - \Delta x$, the heat evolved is $Q_i + \Delta Q_i$ or $Q_i - \Delta Q_i$. The ratio ΔQ_t, Δx, as long as A x is small compared with x, is the differential heat of adsorption, qd. It is measured in Kcal/g or kilojoules/mole, etc.

Measurement of Heat of Adsorption

1. *Calorimetric Determination :* In these measurements one needs to determine the heat evolved when a definite mass of gas is adsorbed.

Calorimeters for measurement of the heat are of two main types:

(i) Isothermal.

(ii) Non-isothermal,

Let us discuss these one by one.

(i) *Isothermal :* The isothermal calorimeter most widely used for gas adsorption is the ice calorimeter of the Bunsen type.

The gas to be adsorbed is led into the centre of the adsorbent which is kept in the calorimeter, and the heat produced melts a corresponding amount of ice and causes a movement of a mercury thread in a capillary of the Bunsen's ice calorimeter.

Bunsen's ice calorimeter is specially suitable for the measurement of small amounts of heat evolved slowly.

The main advantage of the Bunsen's ice calorimeter is that the heat capacity C of the calorimeter and its contents need not be known.

(ii) *Non-isothermal* : In the non-isothermal methods, the adsorbent container plus the adsorbent is utilized as the working substance of the calorimeter. The temperature change is then measured by means of a thermocouple or a resistance thermometer.

2. *Calculation of Heat of Adsorption by Clansius-Clapeyron Equation* : The heat of adsorption can be calculated from the adsorption isotherms at two different temperatures T_1 and T_2. It is known as the isosteric heat qi and defined by the equation:

$$q_i = T_0(V - v)\left(\frac{\partial p}{\partial T}\right)_x \quad ...(1)$$

where $$T_0 = \frac{T_1 + T_2}{2}$$

T = A variable temperature,

V = Volume of a unit mass of gas (Usually, 1gm molecules)

v = Volume of an identical mass in the adsorbed state, and

p = The equilibrium gas pressure above the adsorbent containing x mass units of the gas or vapour.

In the above calculation, $\frac{\partial p}{\partial T}$ is taken at a constant adsorbed amount. Usually v may be neglected in comparison to V, and V (if a mole is selected as the unit of mass) may be taken as approximately equal to $\frac{RT_0}{p}$; hence equation (1) becomes as:

$$q_i \approx RT_0\left(\frac{\partial ln p}{\partial T}\right)_\alpha \quad ...(2)$$

where R = The gas constant.

Equations (1) and (2) are analogous to the Clapeyron equation for the latent heat of evaporation (λ). However, λ is independent of the amount evaporated while q_i depends on x.

The proof of the equation (1) is not significantly different from that of the Clapeyron equation.

Order of Magnitude of the Heat of Adsorption : For physical adsorption, the heats of adsorption are of the order of heats of vapourisation. This is generally less than 10 Kcal/mole.

In chemisorption, heats of adsorption are 10 to 100 Kcal/mole which indicate that forces are similar to those involved in chemical reactions.

ADSORPTION ISOBARS

Adsorption data may be presented in several ways. One of these is at constant pressure in the form of adsorption isobar. A typical isobar is shown in Fig. 18 where x/m is the weight of material adsorbed per unit weight of adsorbent, and T is the absolute temperature. The amount of adsorption is large at low temperatures and decreases rapidly with increasing temperature. This is characteristic of all adsorption systems; only temperature scale shifts from system to system. At extremely high temperatures, the amount of adsorption is reduced drastically and may be almost undectable.

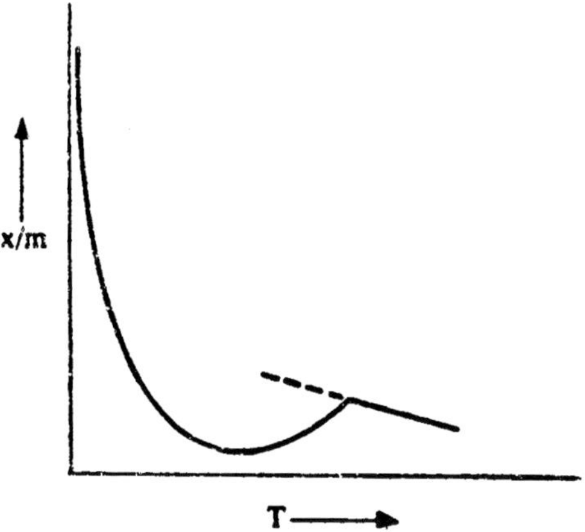

Fig. 1.18

According to Fig. 1.18, after the initial decrease a region of increased amount of adsorption may occur at intermediate elevated temperatures.

The designation of chemisorption or activated adsorption, is frequently applied to this region. An increase in the amount adsorbed with increasing temperature is believed to reflect the chemical forces between adsorbate and adsorbent. However, the increased adsorption, may be reversible, or it may not occur and the adsorption at elevated temperatures may be still irreversible. Consequently, the designation of chemisorption on this basis is not always satisfactory.

CHEMISORPTION

In chemisorption, the adsorption molecules are held to the surface by *valence forces* of the same nature as those which bind atoms together in molecules. These forces are, much stronger than those in van der Waal's adsorption (physical adsorption), and the heats evolved are of the same order as those liberated in chemical reactions; values of 10 to 100 K cal per mole being more common. Chemical adsorption is often characterised by taking place at elevated temperatures. It is often an activated process. It may be dissociative, non-dissociative, or reactive in nature. For example, when hydrogen molecules are adsorbed by tungsten, the bonds between the hydrogen atoms are broken and the resulting adsorbed atoms are considerably more reactive than are free hydrogen molecules.

A number of special features of chemisorption may now be considered briefly since they are of great importance in connection with the kinetics of surface reactions.

1. *The Unimolecular Layer* : On the surface of a substance, there are free valencies. When the gas molecules come in contact with the surface, each valence is satisfied by one gas atom and a bond is formed, liberating a large amount of energy which may be used up in dissociating the gas molecules. After a surface has become covered with a single layer of adsorbed molecules it is essentially saturated so that additional chemisorption cannot take place; a complete chemisorbed layer is thus a unimolecular layer.

   The formation of a unimolecular layer in chemisorption was emphasized by Langmuir and a number of other workers. This has been confirmed by a number of studies such as :

   (a) *Earlier studies* : A careful study of the 'adsorption of hydrogen on tungsten has been made by J.K. Roberts. If a tungsten surface were perfectly smooth and the 1.0 plane were exposed, the number of surface atoms would be 7.8 $\times$ 10^{14} per square cm; if the 100 planes were exposed the number of atoms would be 5.5 $\times$ 10^{14} per square cm. Roberts found that the number of hydrogen molecules that could be adsorbed was 4.4 $\times$ 10^{14}. This result is consistent with the hypothesis of a unimolecular layer, as is possible, hydrogen is adsorbed atomically, one atom being attached to each surface tungsten atom; number of atoms adsorbed is 8.8 $\times$ 10^{14} which is very close to the number of surface atoms.

(b) *Leed Technique* : The technique of low energy electron diffraction (Leed) provides useful information about the manner in which a chemisorbed layer arranges itself. For example

(i) Oxygen which is chemisorbed on (100) planes of nickel yields a (2 $\times$ 1) lattice-or mesh of oxygen atoms.

(ii) Carbon monoxide gives a (1 $\times$ 1) mesh of chemisorbed CO molecules.

(iii) Hydrogen, which is chemisorbed, yields the pattern of (1 $\times$ 2).

(iv) The chemisorbed atoms may change their organization with the change in the degree of coverage. For example, carbon monoxide, which is adsorbed on (100) faces of Pb, is bonded to specific sites having a coverage of about half a monolayer beyond which there occurs a switch to an adsorption layer that is not of registry with the crystal lattice.

(c) *Spectroscopy* : The main tool used in chemisorption is IR spectroscopy. For example when $^{15}N_2$ was adsorbed on a silica supported nickel surface, a band at 2128 at cm^{-1} was observed which was shifted to 2160 cm^{-1} when $^{15}N - {}^{14}N$ was used. The slight shift was attributed to the fact that dinitrogen molecule was not largely dissociated into atoms on the surface. The surface structure was assumed to be Ni $- N = N^+$ and the force constants of 3 $\times$ 10^5 dyne/cm and 19.1 $\times$ 10^5 dyne/cm were calculated for the Ni – N and N-N bonds, respectively.

Another interesting example is that when a mixture of CO and NO was adsorbed on various metal surfaces, their IR spectra showed a band at 2260 cm^{-1} which was attributed to the chemisorbed isothiocyanate, M – NCO.

(d) *Flash Desorption* : This is one of the most powerful techniques for studying both adsorption and adsorption rates. By this technique it becomes possible to do calculation of how much adsorption should have taken place in the time allowed if the sticking probability were unity. This technique involves the following steps:

(i) In this technique a clean filament or surface (usually of a metal) is exposed to a steady Sow of a gas at a known low pressure. The reason for keeping the low pressure is that even non-activated adsorption can take some minutes for complete monolayer coverage to be achieved.

(ii) After the adsorption, the surface is heated so that the adsorbed gas is evolved which increases the gas pressure in the system. This increase in pressure predicts to know how much actually was adsorbed and hence of sticking probability.

If the surface is a filament, the heating is done electrically and if there is a flat crystal surface, heating is done by an incident light beam. Now if the heating is done to a high temperature quickly all adsorbed gas is removed indiscriminately. Oft the other hand, if the heating is gradual, various separate successive desorptions are observed.

In Fig. 19 there is a series of desorption spectra for various surface coverages of CO which is adsorbed on (100) planes of tungsten. The carbon monoxide which is desorbed at low temperatures corresponds to a state in which there is a metal carbonyl like W – CO binding. This state has an apparent activation energy of about 15 Kcal/mole. The CO which is desorbed at higher temperatures corresponds to β_1, β_2, and β_3 states; these have desorption activation energies ranging upto 90 Kcal/mole. In the p. state, the C – O bond is much weakened and there is a partial dissociation into C and O.

From Fig. 1.19, it is evident that each type of adsorbed species produces a peak in the desorption spectrum, *i.e.*, the plot of rate of desorption (dn/dt) versus temperature in Kelvin degree.

2. *Kinetics of Chemisorption :* (Activation Energies). The variation in potential energy of a molecule of adsorbate which is approaching the surface is shown in Fig. 1.20. In this figure, P is representing physical adsorption where curve C chemisorption. At the point B (or A) where the two types of curves are intersecting, there may occur a change from one type of adsorption to another with no change of energy. This intersecting point will determine the nature of chemisorption.

If the curves are crossing at A, no activation energy is required. In such cases, chemisorption would take place at low" temperatures. Examples are chemisorption of hydrogen on tungsten, nickel, etc. But if the curves are crossing at B, an activation energy, E_A Would be required and the chemisorption would occur at higher temperatures.

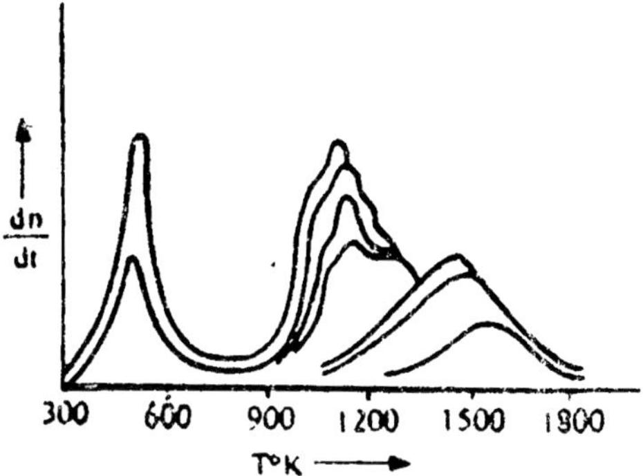

Fig. 1.19. Plain desorption spectra of CO from clean (100) planes of tungsten.

3. Heat of Chemisorption. In chemisorption, the heat of adsorption varies with the degree of surface coverage. This has been illustrated in Fig. 20 in which the heats of adsorption of hydrogen on various metals such as W, Fe, Ni and Rh are shown.

In order to understand the variable heat of chemisorptions, two explanations are to be followed.

First cause. The surface may be heterogeneous. *i.e.*, it is not homogeneous. It means that a site-energy distribution is involved. This distribution is responsible for variable heat of chemisorption. If the differential distribution function is exponential in Q, the resulting a (P, T) is known as the Freundlich isotherm, *i.e.*,

$$a\ (P, T) = AP^c \qquad ...(19)$$

where a denotes average surface coverage, and c is generally less than unity and is therefore written as l/n. The linear form of equation (19) is

$$\log v = (\log v_m\ A) - {}^{\cdot}n \log P. \qquad ...(20)$$

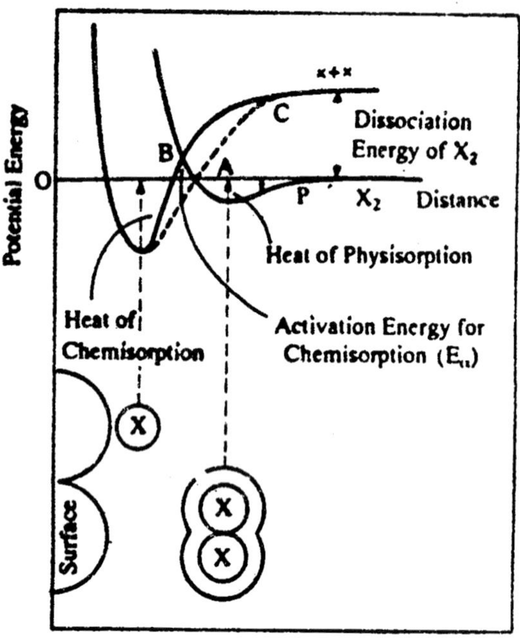

Fig. 1.20 : Potential energy curves for physical and chemical adsorption.

Very few examples are known which obey the equation (20). Examples obeying this equation are the adsorption of nitrogen and of hydrogen on tungsten powder.

Equation (19) is defective as it predicts a at infinite pressure which is not the case. Therefore, equation (19) is only useful in the middle range of an adsorption isotherm.

In order to extend the range of equation (19) to the whole adsorption isotherm, equation (19) was modified as follows :

$$a = \frac{AP^c}{1 - AP^c} \qquad ...(21)$$

Again, the above equation could not explain the variable heat of chemisorption along the whole adsorption isotherm.

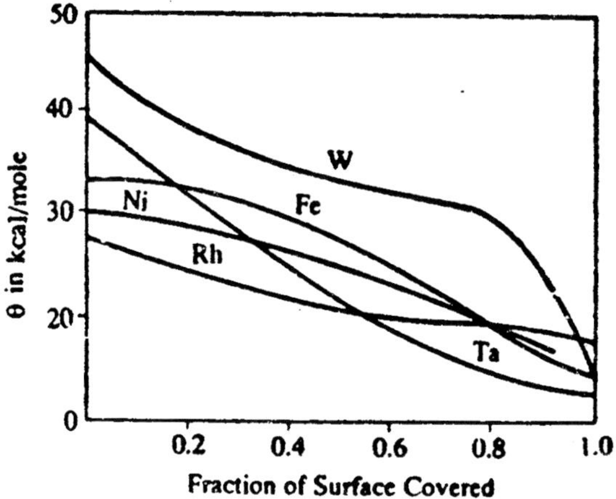

Fig. 1.21 : Heats of adsorption on various metals.

Temkin made an attempt to explain the variation in heat of chemisorption by suggesting the following relation :

$$a = \left(\frac{RT}{Q_0\alpha}\right) ln\ P + \text{constant} \qquad ...(22)$$

where $Q = Q_6(l - \alpha a)$.

Again, equation (22) may be useful for fitting the middle region of an adsorption isotherm. An example is the adsorption of hydrogen on a tungsten filament.

An important point to remember is that it is not possible to distinguish between the various equations as discussed above.

Second cause. Another cause of a variable heat of chemisorption is that of adsorbate-adsorbate interaction.

In physical adsorption, there are attractive van der Waal's forces acting between adsorbate molecules.

These attractive forces are generally very weak in comparison to chemisorption energies and it appears that in chemisorption, *repulsion effects* may be more important.

SURFACE FILMS

1. *Introduction* : Enough evidences have been accumulated in the recent past to show that when a slightly soluble substance is kept m a liquid-air interface, it may spread out to a thin and in most cases monomolecular film known as a *surface film*. This may be regarded as an extreme case of surface adsorption.

In 1860, Benjamin Franklin, after making some observations on the spreading of oils over the surface of the pond at Clepam Common, estimated that the thinnest layers of oil that could be formed were "2.5 nm" thick. Much later. Pockels and Ragleigh in 1891 discovered that some sparingly soluble substances would spread over the surface of a liquid to form films exactly one molecule thick *i.e.* unimolecular film or monolayer.

The above studies done by Benjamin and, Pockels and Rayleigh did not provide much information about the surface films. However, the exact study of films was started when Langmiur in 1917 gave a scientific device to calculate the surface pressure.

1. *Surface Pressure* : It is simply another way of expressing the lowering of surface tension caused by a surface film. On one side of the film is a clean water surface with tension γ_0. and on the other side a water surface covered to a certain extent with molecules of the substance forming the film, with lowered tension, γ. The surface pressure, F, is simply the negative of the change in surface tension.

$$F = -\Delta\gamma - \gamma_0 - y \qquad ...(1)$$

Different substances in unimolecular films display a great variety of *surface area vs. surface pressure* (F–A) isotherms. Sometimes the film follows a two-dimensional gas, sometimes a two-dimensional liquid or solid. In addition, there are other types of mondlayers which do not have exact analogs is the three dimensional world. However, their existence can be revealed by the occurrence of discontinuities in the F-A diagram. If a surface film is behaving as an ideal two dimensional gas, there can be an equation similar to the three-dimensional

$$PA + n^{\sigma}RT \qquad ...(2)$$

If an excluded area b^{σ}, a two dimensional analog of the van der Waal's excluded volume correction b, is considered, then equation (2) becomes as

$$F (A - n^{\sigma} b^{\sigma}) = n\sigma RT \quad ...(3)$$

The film or surface has the units of dyne-centimetre and can be measured directly.

3. Measurement of Surface Pressure

Langmuir's Method : In 1917, Irving Langmuir devised a method for measuring directly the surface pressure extorted by surface film on liquids. The apparatus used by him is known as *Langmuir film balance.*

The film balance has been considerably refined since the crude model used by Langmuir, and, in many laboratories, has been made into a precision instrument capable of measuring film pressures with an accuracy of hundredths of a dyne per centimetre. A modern form of a Langmuir film balance is shown in Fig. 1.22.

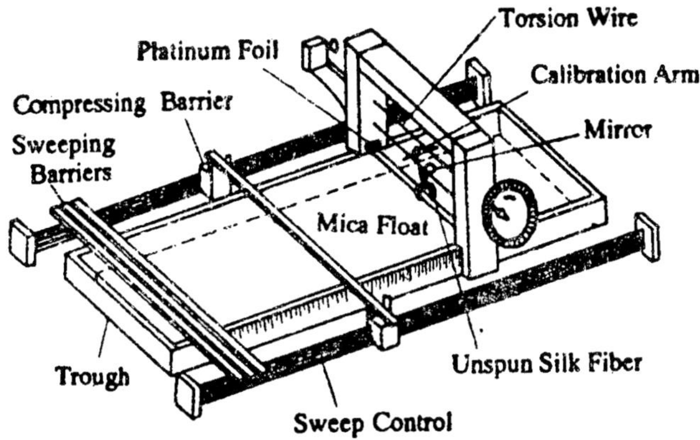

Fig. 1.22 : A modem form of a Langmuir film balance is shown.

Construction : It consists of following parts :

(i) *Fixed barrier :* This may be a strip of mica, and it floats on the surface of the water and is suspended from ? torsion wire.

(ii) *Compressing barrier :* This is a floating barrier. At the ends of the floating barrier, strips of platinum foil or waxed threads are attached. The strips are lying upon the water surface and connect the ends of barrier to the side of the trough, thus preventing leakage of surface films past the float.

(iii) *Sweeping barrier :* It is a movable barrier which rests upon the sides of the trough and is in contact with the water surface . A number of movable barriers are provided for sweeping the surface clean. The sweep barriers may be raised or lowered by means of a rack operated by a square drive rod.

(iv) *Trough* : The trough is a shallow rectangular tray 2 or 3 ft long and perhaps 1 ft wide, made of brass, stainless steel, glass or Teflon. The tray, if made of metal or glass, must be coated with paraffin, lacquer etc. to ensure a high contact angle.

(v) *Air thermostat* : For precise work, the film balance is placed inside an air thermostat, and all the controls are operated from the outside.

Working : In a typical experiment, a tiny amount of insoluble spreading substance is introduced onto a clean water surface. For example, a dilute solution of stearic acid in benzene might be used; benzene evaporates rapidly, leaving a film of stearic acid. Then, the sweeping barrier is advanced towards the compressing barrier. The surface film exerts a surface pressure on the float, pushing it backward. The torsion wire, attached to a calibrated circular scale, is twisted until the float is returned to its original position. The required force divided by the length of the float is the force per unit length or surface pressure.

Limitations of the method : The various errors in this method are as follows :

(i) If too much material has been used or if spreading is slow, the monolayer may not be fully formed and there may be patches of unspread material floating on the surface.

(ii) Care must be exercised so that no leakage is occurring past the sweep or float barriers, particularly at high film pressures.

(iii) If the film material is added as a solution in a volatile solvent, the addition must be slow and such that none of the solution reaches the edges of trough before evaporation of the-solvent.

4. *Structure of Surface Film* : The type of F–A isotherm observed depends on the structure of me compound which is being spread on the water. However, it is not possible to ascertain the exact conformation and packing of the molecules in the surface layer. In the case of molecules having polar end groups and long hydrocarbon chains, the hydrophilic end group (polar end) is in the water whereas the hydrophobic chain (hydrocarbon) is

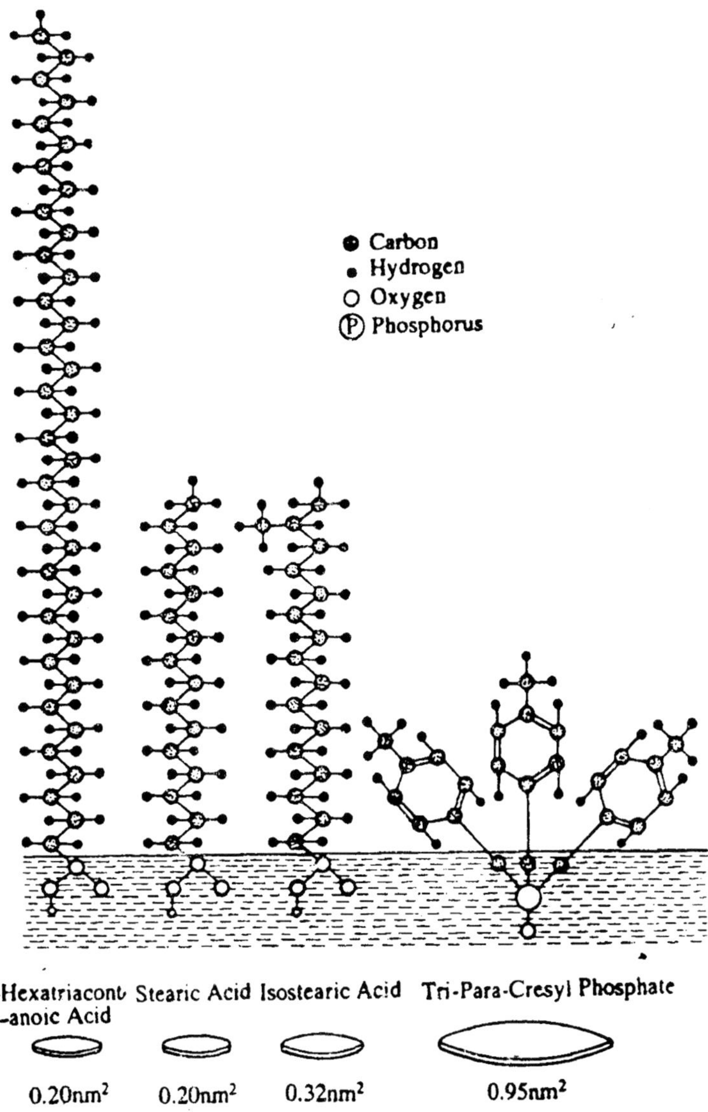

Fig. 1.23 : Molecules of film-forming substances at a water-air interface are oriented with their polar groups in the water (broken lines) and their non-polar portions in the air. Crosssectional areas of molecules are appearing at bottom.

in the air. This conclusion was reached by Langmuir for close packed surface films of all the normal fatty acids from C_{14} to C_{38}. In Fig. 1.23 the structures of stearic acid ($C_{17}H_{35}COOH$), n-hexatriacontanoic acid ($C_{35}H_{71}COOH$), isostearic acid and triparacresyl-phosphate are shown in the surface orientation that occurs in closet packing.

As the length of the hydrocarbon chain decreases, the solubility increases, owing to the increasing influence of the carboxylic group, and the effect on the surface tension decreases, *i.e.*, the molecules tend to concentrate less in the surface. The terms hydrophobic (water-repelling) and hydrophilic (water attracting) are often used to describe the functional groups.

5. *The Analogy between Surface Films and Gases* : The curves in Fig. 6 represent the effect of temperature on the surface pressure area surveys for myristic acid, $CH_3(CH_2)_{12}$ COOH, at low surface pressures and very high areas. The curves are strongly reminiscent of the pressure volume isotherms for a real gas near its critical temperature, and surface films behave in some respects as "two dimensional gases". Thus for the lower curve. BC represents the compression of the isolated .individual surface molecules (discontinuous or gaseous phase,) DE the compression of the continuous monomolecular film .(continuous or liquid phase), while CD represents as intermediate situation with small islands of surface film in equilibrium with the isolated individual molecules (liquid-gas equilibrium). The upper curve may be compared with an ideal gas isotherm and follows an equation analogous? To the ideal gas law

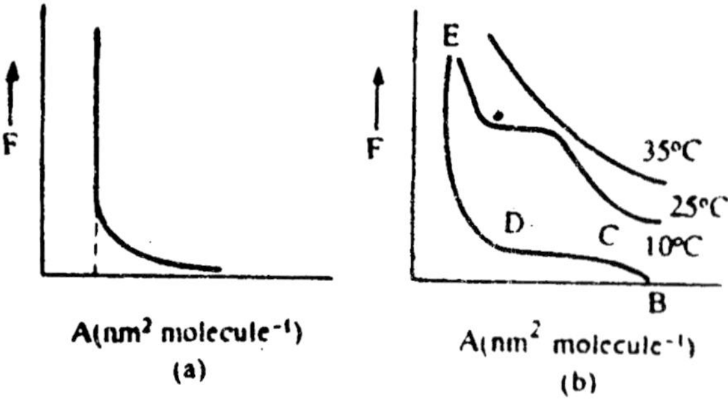

Fig. 1.24

$$fA = kT$$

where k = Boltzmann constant.

6. *Applications of Surface films* : A concrete application of insoluble monolayers is their use in the retardation of evaporation. Particularly in arid regions of the world, the water level of lakes and reservoirs may change as much as 90 cm in one month due to evaporation. In order to retard the evaporation, a monolayer of a suitable substance is deposited on the surface of water in a lake or a reservoir. However, the monolayer material must have the following properties :
   (i) It must spread easily.
   (ii) It must be self-healing because surface ripples will disrupt the monolayer.,
   (iii) It must be in expensive-which means, effectively capable of forming good film from naturally occurring mixtures.
   (iv) It must be non-toxic and free from other deleterious effects on aquatic life.

ADSORPTION FROM SOLUTION

Introduction : Adsorption of solutes from solutions can occur on various solids to different extents, which is the same as for gases. It may in general be traced to two effects:

(i) Due to decrease in the interfacial tension through adsorption of a solute and

(ii) Due to solid surface acquiring electrostatic Charge in a solvent. This charged surface of the adsorbent then attaches oppositely charged ions from the solution.

This type of adsorption is of three types :

1. *Positive adsorption* : In this type, the solute alone is adsorbed and the concentration of the solution gets decreased. An interesting example is that when activated charcoal is kept in contact with the dilute solution of acetic acid, a part of the acid is adsorbed by the charcoal and the concentration of the acid decreases. This type of adsorption follows Freundlich equation.
2. *Negative adsorption* : In this type, the solvent is adsorbed and the concentration of the solution is increased and an interesting

example is that when blood charcoal is added to potassium chloride solution, the concentration of the solution gets increased. This type of adsorption is not very common.

3. *Electrostatic Adsorption* : Many solids are known which on coming in contact with water acquire an electrostatic charge. This may be positive due to the attachment of H^+ ions or *negative* due to the attachment of OH^- ions to the surface of solid. These acquired charges on the surfaces will have the tendency to attract oppositely charged ions of solutes from the solutions. This is termed as *electrostatic adsorption* and, if possible, would occur over and above mechanical adsorption.

   An interesting example of electrostatic adsorption is silica powder which acquires a negative charge on coming in contact with water. If this silica powder having negative charge is shaken with positively charged ferric hydroxide sol and then filtered, the filtrate will be colourless, illustrating the phenomenon of electrostatic adsorption.

4. *Gibbs adsorption equation* : This equation represents an exact relationship between the adsorption and the change in the surface tension of a solvent due to the presence of a solute. This equation was first derived by *J. Willard Gibbs* (1878) and afterward independently by *J.J. Thomson* (1888).

The dG for a two component system is given by

$$dG = -S\,dT + Vdp + \mu_1 dn_1 + \mu_2 dn_2 + \gamma dA. \qquad ...(1)$$

where γ is the surface tension, dA. is the increase in surface area, S is the entropy, p is the pressure, V is the volume and dG is the change in Gibbs free energy. The last term γdA in eq. (1) is being introduced to compensate the increase in free energy owing to an increase in the area of exposed surface. By integrating eq. (1) at a constant temperature, pressure, surface tension and chemical potential of the component, we obtain the expression

$$G = \mu_1 n_1 + \mu_2 n_2 + \gamma A. \qquad ...(2)$$

where n_1 and n_2 are the number of moles of the solvent and solute respectively.

The complete differential of equation (2) yields

$$dG = \mu_1 dn_1 + \mu_2 dn_2 + n_1 d\mu_1 + n_2 d\mu_2 + \mu dA + Ad\gamma \qquad ...(3)$$

Comparing Eqs. (1) and (3), the result is

$$SdT - Vdp + Ad\gamma + n_1 d\mu_1 + n_2 d\mu_2 = 0. \qquad ...(4)$$

At constant temperature and constant pressure, equation (4) simplifies to

$$n_1 d\mu_1 + n_2 d\mu_2 + Ad\gamma = 0 \qquad ...(5)$$

We can imagine the system under consideration to be made up of two portions:

(i) *Surface phase :* It involves the portion of the system affected by surface process and therefore, equation (5) holds true only for it.

(ii) *Bulk phase :* The remainder of the solution, which is unaffected by surface forces, is known as bulk phase and, therefore, Gibbs-Duhem equation holds for this only. This equation is

$$n_1^0 d\mu_1 + n_2^0 d\mu_2 = 0 \qquad ...(6)$$

where n_1^0 and n_2^0 represent the number of moles of solvent and solute in the bulk phase respectively.

On multiplying equation (6) by $\frac{n_1}{n_1^0}$ and subtracting from equation (5), we obtain the expression

$$Ad\gamma + \left(n_2 - \frac{n_1 n_2^0}{n_1^0}\right) d\mu_2 = 0$$

or

$$-\frac{d\gamma}{d\mu} = \frac{n_2 - \frac{n_1 n_2^0}{n_1^0}}{A} \qquad ...(7)$$

where n_2 represents the number of moles of solute associated with n_1 moles of solvent in the surface phase and $\frac{n_1 n_2^0}{n_1^0}$ is the corresponding quantity in the bulk phase. It, therefore, follows that the quantity $\frac{n_2 - \frac{n_1 n_2^0}{n_1^0}}{A}$ is the excess concentration of the solute per unit area of the surface and is usually designated by the symbol Γ. Thus, eq (7) becomes as

$$\Gamma = \frac{d\gamma}{d\mu_2} \qquad ...(8)$$

where Γ is independent of n_1 and is dependent only on the nature of the surface phase, and not on its amount. Γ is also called the surface concentration of solute per unit area of interface.

For a solution,

$$\mu_2 = \mu_2^0 + RT\, ln\, a_2 \qquad ...(9)$$

where a_2 is activity of the solute. By differentiating eq. (9), we get

$$d\mu_2 = RT\, d\, ln\, a_2 \qquad ...(10)$$

assuming μ_2^0 as constant.

On substituting equation (10) in equation (8), we obtain

$$\Gamma = -\frac{1}{RT}\frac{d\gamma}{d\, ln\, a_2}$$

or

$$\Gamma = -\frac{a_2}{RT}\frac{d\gamma}{da_2}\left[\because d\, ln\, a_2 = \frac{da_2}{a_2}\right] \qquad ...(11)$$

Equation (11) is known as Gibbs adsorption equation.

Discussion of Gibbs Adsorption Equation : From equation (11), we have

(i) When $\frac{d\gamma}{dc}$ is –ve, the adsorption is positive. It means that further addition of the solute lowers the surface tension of the solution.

(ii) When $\frac{d\gamma}{dc}$ is positive, the adsorption is negative. It means that further addition of the solute increases the surface tension of solution.

The Gibbs Equation : Experimental Results. Surface tensions for the interface between air and aqueous solutions generally display one of the three forms indicated schematically in Fig. 1.25. The discussion about these three curves is outlined as follows:

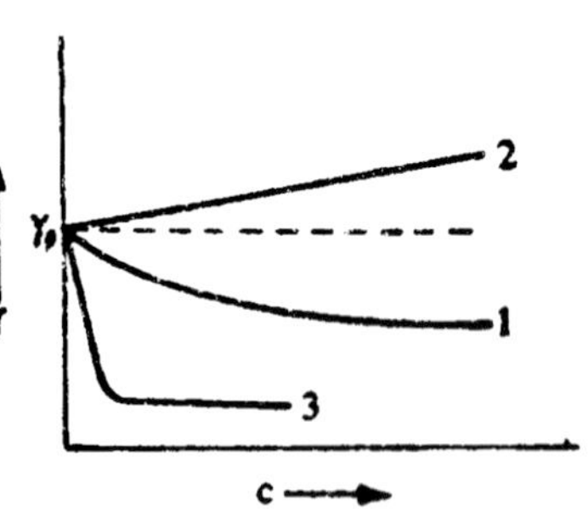

Fig. 1.25

(i) Curve 1 in Fig. 1.25 is the type of behaviour characteristic of most un-ionised organic compounds. The type of behaviour indicated by curve 1 indicates positive adsorption of the solute.

Since $\frac{d\gamma}{dc}$ and $\frac{d\gamma}{d}$ *ln* c are negative, T must be positive. The curve 1 corresponds to relatively dilute solutions.

(ii) Curve 2 is typical of inorganic electrolytes and highly hydrated organic compounds. The positive slope for curve 2 indicates a negative surface excess or a surface depletion of the solute. Note that the magnitude of negative adsorption is also less than that of positive adsorption.

(iii) The type of behaviour indicated by curve 3 is shown by soluble amphipathic species, especially ionic ones. The break in curve 3 is typical of these compounds; however, this degree of sharpness is observed only for highly purified compounds. If impurities are present, the curve will display a slight dip at the point.

Verification of the Gibbs Equation : Gibbs published his results on heterogeneous equilibrium in 1875 but his work was appreciated only at the turn of this century when experimental techniques were available to verify his results. The various methods used for doing the verification of Gibbs equation are as follows :

Domain and Barker (1911) Method

They studied the adsorption of nonylic acid solution from aqueous solution at the liquid-air interface. In this method, a long pipe is taken which contains, an aqueous solution of the nonylic acid. Through this solution, air or a hydrocarbon is bubbled. In order to calculate the total surface area, the number of bubbles and their dimensions are calculated. The foam carried by the bubbles is collected and analysed.

Then, the value of P is calculated by using equation

$$\Gamma = \frac{w_1(C_s - C_b)}{S} \qquad ...(12)$$

where S is the total surface area of the bubbles, C_s is the surface layer concentration, w_1 gm is the weight of the solvent in w gm of the solution and w gm is the weight of the solution in the foam after experiment.

The values of Γ calculated by using equation (12) are found to be many times greater than the theoretical values calculated from Eq. 11.

The Microtome Method of Mcbain (1933)

This method was used by Mcbain and coworker who employed a *microtome* which consisted of a sharp blade mounted on a carriage that rested on rails. The carriage could be propelled at high speed.

In this method, a trough is taken which contains the solution. This trough is coated with the hydrocarbon so that the liquid bulged about 0.05 to 0.1 mm above the upper level of the vessel without over-flowing. The surface layer of the liquid is cut off by means of a rapidly moving microtome blade slightly below the surface. By this method a thin layer of solution was scooped out and retained in a silver-reservoir in the blade. A slice of about 0.1 mm would be taken from about 1 m^2 of surface so that a few grams of solution were obtained. If C is the concentration of the solution and ΔC is the difference in the concentration between the solution and that of the microtome sample (both C and ΔC are expressed as gram solution per gram of water), then we get

$$\Gamma = \left(\frac{\Delta C}{A}\right)\left[\frac{w}{(1+C+\Delta C)}\right]$$

where A is the area of the surface sampled and w is the weight in grams of the sample.

When the microtome method was applied to aqueous solutions of p-toluidine, n-hexanoic acid and phenol, agreement to within about 10 per cent was found between the Gibbs equation and experiment.

The microtome method was also applied to aqueous sodium chloride solution for which $\frac{d\gamma}{dc}$ is positive. But in this case the predicted surface deficiency of salt was found. Alternatively, one can consider that a layer of pure water was present, of depth T given by

$$\tau = \frac{1000\,\Gamma}{m}$$

where m is the molality. These τ values are of the order of a few angstroms, and decrease with increasing salt concentration.

Bensen Method

This method is similar to the first method.

In this method, bubbles of air are passed through an aqueous solution of amyl alcohol. The foam carried by the bubbles is collected and analyzed. The surface concentration was found to 0.0394 N. This value was larger than the original value 0 0375 N. [Calculated from Gibbs adsorption equation].

The Tracer Method (1954)

This method was developed by Salley, Dixon and coworkers.

In this method, the solute to be studied is labelled with a radioisotope the ^{14}C or ^{35}S. Both ^{34}C and ^{35}S are emitting weak beta radiations. In order to detect and measure the intensity of these radiations, a detector is placed close to the surface of the solution as shown in Fig. 2. As the range of such beta emitters is small, the measured radioactivity corresponds to that of the surface region plus only a thin layer of solution.

When the above method was applied to ^{35}S—labelled Aerosol OTN anionic agent (di-n-octyl) sodium sulphosuccinate. $C_8H_{17}OOCCH_2CH(NaSO_3)—COOC_8H_{17})$, an interesting result was obtained which revealed that the measured surface excesses (D agreed with those calculated by means of Gibbs equation only if it was assumed that the surface adsorbed species was the undissociated acid which was formed due to the hydrolysis of the sodium salt.

In place of ^{14}C and ^{35}S, one may employ ^{3}H (tritium) as a labelling species. The main advantage of using ^{3}H is that the beta particles emitted by it are so weak that there is no need for applying correction for the radioactivity coming from the bulk solution because it is too small.

Tajima and coworkers (1970) used tritium as a labelling species to study the adsorption of sodium dodecyl sulphate at the solution-air interface. The results agreed very well with those calculated from surface tension data but there is the difference from the case of Aerosol 0.1 N anionic reagent (as discussed above) labelled with ^{35}S, *i.e.*, the sodium dodecyl sulphate is the surface active species but its hydrolysis product is not the surface active species.

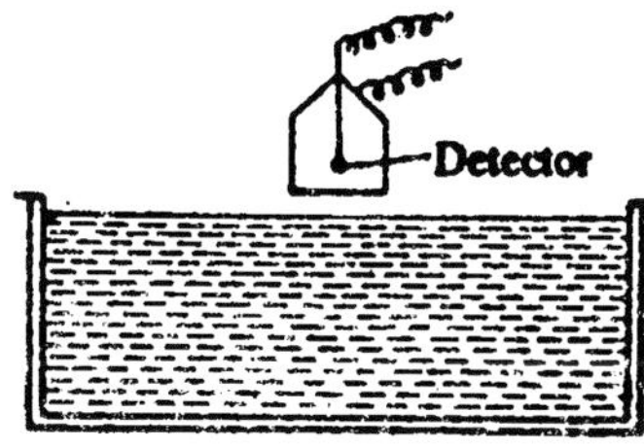

Fig. 1.26

Steiger and Aniansson (1954) applied the technique of the heavy atom recoil effect to measure surface concentrations.

Other examples of tracer method are as follows:

(i) Shinoda and Ito (1961) employed radiocalcium to determine the adsorption of calcium ions at surface of aqueous sodium dodecyl sulphate solutions.

(ii) Rehfeld (1969) determined the adsorption of tritiated sodium dodecyl sulphate at a polymer solution interface.

Ellipsometric Method

This method has been employed to measure the thickness of an adsorbed film from the ellipticity produced in light which is reflected from the film covered surface. Knowing this thickness, τ one can calculate Γ by applying the following relationship,

$$\Gamma = \frac{\tau}{V}$$

where V is the molecular volume which may be estimated either from molecular models or from the bulk liquid density.

Smith (1968) applied this method to study the adsorption of i-pentane on mercury and found the excellent agreement with the values obtained from other methods.

ALTERNATE DEFINITION OF SURFACE EXCESS

Suppose there are two bulk phases, a and p which are to be uniform upto an arbitrary dividing plane S, as shown in fig. 1. Let us restrict ourselves to plane surface so that C_1 and C_2 have been zero, and the condition of equilibrium does not impose any particular location for S.

If the section in Fig. 1.27 is of unit area in cross-section, and further if the phases were uniform upto S, amount of the ith component would be given by

$$xC_i^{\alpha} + (a - x)\, C_i^{\beta} \qquad ...(1)$$

Here the distance x and a have been relative to planes A and B located far enough from the surface region so that bulk phase properties prevail. The actual amount of component i present in the region between A and B would be given by

$$xC_i^{\alpha} + (a - x)\, C_i^{\beta} + \Gamma_i \qquad ...(2)$$

where Γ_i represents the surface excess per unit area. If it is positive, it implies an actual excess of the component is present and if negative, there is actually a surface deficiency. An alternative name for it has been *superficial density*.

For the case where phase β is gaseous. $C_i\beta$ may be neglected, and equations (1) and (2) become

$$xC_i^{\alpha} \text{ and } xC_i^{\alpha} + \Gamma_i$$

If a second arbitrary choice is now made for the dividing plane, namely, S' and distance x', it must follow that

$$xC_i + \Gamma_i' = xC_i + \Gamma_i \qquad ...(3)$$

as the same total amount of the ith component must be present between A and B regardless of how the dividing surface gets located. One then has

$$(\Gamma_i' - \Gamma_i)\ C_i = x - x'$$

so that

$$(\Gamma_i - \Gamma_1)/C_1 = (\Gamma_2' - \Gamma_2)/C_2 = ...$$

or, in general

$$(\Gamma'_i - \Gamma_i)/N_i = (\Gamma'_j - \Gamma_j)/N_j \qquad ...(4)$$

where N represents mole fraction or

$$\Gamma_j N_i - \Gamma_j N_j = T'_j N_i - \Gamma'_j N \qquad ...(5)$$

As S and S' are purely arbitrary in location, equation (5) would be true only if each side separately equals a constant

$$\Gamma_j N_i - \Gamma_i N_j = \text{constant.}$$

From equation (11) Art 16.13 it is apparent that if an increase in the concentration of a solute lowers the surface tension, Γ will be positive, whereas if an increase in the concentration of a solute increases the surface tension, Γ would be negative. The former and latter phenomena are termed as positive and negative adsorption, respectively.

Inorganic salts when dissolved in water give rise to negative adsorption, while the dissolution of organic solutes gives rise to positive adsorption.

A detailed picture demonstrating how concentrations might vary across a liquid-vapour interface is depicted in Fig. 1.28. The dividing line is drawn so that the two areas shaded i full strokes are equal, and the surface excess of the solvent would be zero. The area shaded with dashed strokes which is lying to the right of the dividing surface, minus the smaller similarly shaded area to the left of the dividing surface, would correspond in this case to positive surface excess of solute.

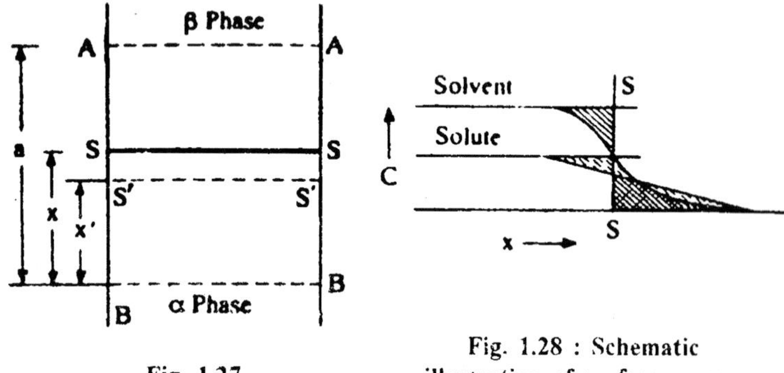

Fig. 1.27

Fig. 1.28 : Schematic illustration of surface excess.

ADSORPTION BY POROUS SOLIDS

Pores in real solids are the rule rather than the exception. Solids that have evolved gas during their formation, either geologically or industrially, or that have been formed by compaction of powers are sure to contain crevices. The game is true of solids made by dehydration of gelatinous precipitates, etc. A special class of porous solids is the zeolites, natural or synthetic, which have pores of accurately known molecular dimensions. They have the general formula $M_{x/n}$ $(AlO_2)_x$ $(SiO_2)_y$ zH_2O, where n is the valency of the cation, usually Ca^{2+}, Na^+, or K^+; and are widely used as selective adsorbents ("molecular sieves") and ion exchangers.

Classification of Pores by Width

The effect of porosity on the course of the absorption isotherm depends on the pore dimensions, so that it is convenient to classify them into three groups. *Macropores* have effective widths above 50 nm; *mesopores* fall in the range 2 nm < w < 50 am; micropores are those of width below 2 nm. This classification is recommended by IUPAC (the International Union of Pure and Applied Chemistry). Macropores have little effect on sorption, but smaller ones lead to type IV and type V isotherms, unless thy are very small, in which case type I isotherms result. The phenomena of hysteresis are associated with the existence of mesopores. At low relative pressures adsorption and desorption follow the same curve, but at a quite sharply defined value of P/P_0 the two branches begin to diverge, always in the same direction. The desorption requires lowering P below the value at which adsorption occurred—*i.e.*, the desorption branch lies to the left of the adsorption branch (type IV isotherm). Also, the value of P/P_0 at which the loop closes appears to be characteristic of the adsorbate and independent of the adsorbent. When comparisons are available, it also seems that adsorption on a porous solid is greater than that on the same solid per unit total area when it is pore-free.

Adsorption Hysteresis of Mesopore Width

The dominant theory of the origin of this hysteresis is that, since the adsorbed material is in a liquid-like state, menisci will form in the pores, and the corresponding Laplace pressure leads to actual *additional condensation* to liquid, filling up the pore. The pressure P at which condensation occurs is related to the vapour pressure of bulk liquid through the Kelvin equation, whose derivation starts by equating the chemical potentials of liquid and vapour phases; *i.e.*, at constant r

$$V_{vap}\, dP_{vap} = V_{liq}\, dP_{liq} \qquad ...(1)$$

But P_{vap} and Pus differ by the Laplace pressure, which leads (on assuming ideal gas behaviour and neglecting V_{vap}) compared with Vvap) to the familiar

$$ln\, \frac{P'}{P_0} = -\frac{2\sigma\bar{\upsilon}}{RTr_m} \qquad ...(2)$$

where r_m is the mean radius of curvature of the meniscus, $(r_1 + r_2)/2$, and a and P are the surface tension and molar volume of liquid absorbate. Consider adsorption at successively increasing P_{exp}. Adsorption proceeds normally, monolayer and multilayer on all accessible surfaces, external and within pores alike, as long as the amount of liquid adsorbed anywhere on a surface with the corresponding r_m is negligible. However, when some part of the surface has an r_m with P'/P_2 above unity over sufficient area for adsorption thereon to be measurable, liquid adsorbate will form there. As P_{exp} is increased, more and more of the pores—*i.e.*, those with larger and larger rm—fill with liquid until all the gas being added to increase P_{exp} has no place to go and the upper flat part of the type IV to V isotherm is reached.

Now consider desorption as P_{exp} is reduced. Each pore is filled with liquid and has a meniscus with radius of curvature r_m. The liquid will evaporate *i.e.*, desorb—only as P_{exp} reaches that P'. When, as at first, all pores are empty save for the same per area coverage as external surface, the gas molecules may "see" a meniscus of different rm from that which the same pore has when full. If so, hysteresis will occur. The form of the loop will depend on the distribution of pores as to both size and shape. (This formulation is known as the "ink bottle theory" because a shape of pore often postulated is narrower at its opening than in its interior space, leading to wide hysteresis loops.) The most extreme case of hysteresis would be encountered if the "pores" were formed by plane parallel slabs of separation if. No capillary condensation occurs until it happens suddenly when P_{exp}/P_0 reaches unity, and no desorption could occur until P_{exp} falls to $P_0 \exp\left(\frac{-2\sigma\overline{V}}{r_m RT}\right)$.

This theory has been elaborated to take into account the contact angle between condensate and pore wall and the continuous nature of the change in r_m for each pore as it fills or empties. A second direction of elaboration has been consideration of the pore distributions expected for both random and ordered packing of various sizes and shapes of particles of adsorbent. Instead of pursuing the topic in more detail, we turn to the use of the experimental isotherms to obtain pore-size distributions.

Although either the adsorption or desorption branch of a hysteresis loop may be used to obtain V_m the total volume of pores having an effective r_m above a given value, a complicating factor exists whose nature is easier to visualize by considering desorption. Suppose amounts v_i, + v_2, etc., are desorbed at values of $P_1 > P_2 >$, etc., corresponding to pore widths $w_1 > w_2 >$. etc. It is the liquid condensate that desorbs. The pore surface at width w_1 is not bare but remains covered with an adsorbed film of thickness corresponding to the thickness of the adsorbed film on external surface ($r_m = \infty$). It is not too difficult to correct w_t for this effect, but the amount desorbed *in the entire system* to reduce when the pressure is lowered to P_{1+i} is added to that from liquid condensed on pores of width W_{i+1}.

Distribution of "Hydraulic Radii" (Model-less)

These methods using the Kelvin equation in their base all involve some model for the pores. The "hydraulic radius" is defined as the ratio of volume to surface. Starting at the top of a hysteresis loop and desorbing a volume v_1 down to $P/P_0 = x_1$ gives the volume of adsorbate in the cores of group 1 pores, which can be expressed as volume of liquid adsorbate and is set equal to the core volume of the pores themselves. The adsorption branch of the loop from s_1 to $P/P_0 = 1$ can be used to obtain the corresponding surface area through a graphical integration of

$$\sigma\, dA = \Delta\mu\, dn = -RT\, ln\, P/P_0\, dn \qquad ...(3)$$

This equation is thermodynamic in the sense that the right-hand and left-hand sides both represent work done in capillary condensation. On the left is that of surface energy corresponding to surface lost when the pore fills. On the right is the change in free energy of the adsorbate going from a gaseous to a liquid state.

Next consider the volume desorbed when P is lowered to x_2. Part of it is core volume of group 2 pores, and part comes from reducing the ordinary thickness of monolayer-multilayer adsorption from t_1 to t_2. But the surface of mesopores undergoing this loss is already known, and the external surface is neglected, so v_2 can be obtained. The area of this group of pores is obtained in the same way as for group 1. The hydraulic radius of the pores of the second group is just v_2/A_2. As the process is continued, a value of x is reached such that the subtraction of the amount corresponding to desorption from the walls of all preceding groups to reduce thickness from t_{j-1} to t_j leaves zero volume for capillary loss. This marks the closure of the hysteresis loop.

In case where the same data are processed by different methods the general shape of the differential distributions is similar, but the model (peak) values are enormously different when pore dimensions are obtained from core dimensions by assuming some pore shape. It is argued that core volumes and surfaces have physical reality, but that the problem of real pore dimensions is yet to be solved.

Liquid Tensile Strength from Adsorption Hysteresis

We turn now to the once puzzling observation that the relative pressure at which the lower closure of hysteresis loops occurs is characteristic of the adsorbate and is independent of the pore structure of the adsorbent. Since the liquids wet the solids, the menisci in the pores are concave. Hence the Laplace pressure magnitude $2\sigma/r$, is negative—*i.e.*, a tension. Applying the Kelvin equation gives the magnitude of the tension as a function of relative pressure :

$$\tau = -\frac{RT}{V_L}\, ln \frac{P}{P_0} \qquad ...(4)$$

When P falls enough to increase τ beyond the tensile strength of the liquid, condensation cannot occur, and the loop closes. Experimental data on the tensile strength of liquid nitrogen where the critical closure is at P/P_0 = 0-42 for a great variety of adsorbents (τ + 402 bar) are not available to test this hypothesis, but less abundant data with other adsorbents give reasonably satisfying results.

Adsorption in Micropores

A further group of phenomena can occur in solids having an appreciable volume of micropores. The spaces barely admit one or at most two "layers" of molecules, and these are subject to the force-fields of both walls or all walls of the "pore". Extensive calculations have been made using potentials of the Lennard-Jones type, which show that, when the width of the space between parallel walls approaches molecular dimensions, the adsorption potential $\in$ is as much as 3 5 times as great as that for a comparable distance of the adsorbate from a single wall. The expected effect would be much as if a comparable "area" of high-energy surface were present—*i.e.*, a type I isotherm. That a limit is reached must follow from the limited volume of the micropores, and its value corresponds to the amount of adsorbate that could be accommodated in the liquid state. This adsorption is just added to the monolayer-multilayer adsorption on the external surface and capillary condensation in mesopores, if these are also present.

A striking confirmation of the correctness of this reasoning has been given. Powdered silica was studied by adsorption of N_2 at 77°K. It gave a type II isotherm with no hysteresis. After compression at 100 tons $in.^{-2}$, a type I isotherm was found. The interpretation is that the particles, shown by electron microscopy to be spherical with an average radius of ca. 2 nm, are non-porous, mild compression forces them to pace together with interstices in the mesopore range, and high compression reduces these interstices to micropore size. Similar results were obtained with powdered zirconia. Additional support is provided by the fact that isosteric heats of adsorption are much higher at low degrees of coverage for microporous solids than for the same system when the solid can be made non-porous.

The t-plot is a convenient way of revealing the presence of micropores. When they are present, the isotherm so plotted does not pass through the origin but, instead, intersects the n_{ads}, axis at the moles of adsorbate required to fill the micropores. Another scheme, known as the Dubinin-

Radushkevich (DR) equation and corresponding plot, is based on the idea that there is a distribution of values of W (micropore volume filled) as a function of the change in chemical potential RT ln P/P_0. The distribution is taken to be Gaussian (an empirical assumption). The resulting equation is

$$ln\, n_{ads} = ln\, \frac{W_0}{V} - K\left(ln\, \frac{P}{P_0}\right)^2 \qquad ...(5)$$

where W_0 is the total volume of micropores, and K is a constant of the system at constant temperature and has no consequential physical importance. Plotting ln or log adsorption in moles against $(ln\, P/P_0)^2$ or $(\log P/P_0)^2$ gives a straight line whose intercept at $P/P_0 = 1$ can be converted to W_0 by means of the molar volume of liquid adsorbate. In practice many DR plots are linear, but many deviate for P/P_0 much above 5×10^{-8}. Where comparisons exist, the values of W_0 are usually lower than those obtained by other methods.

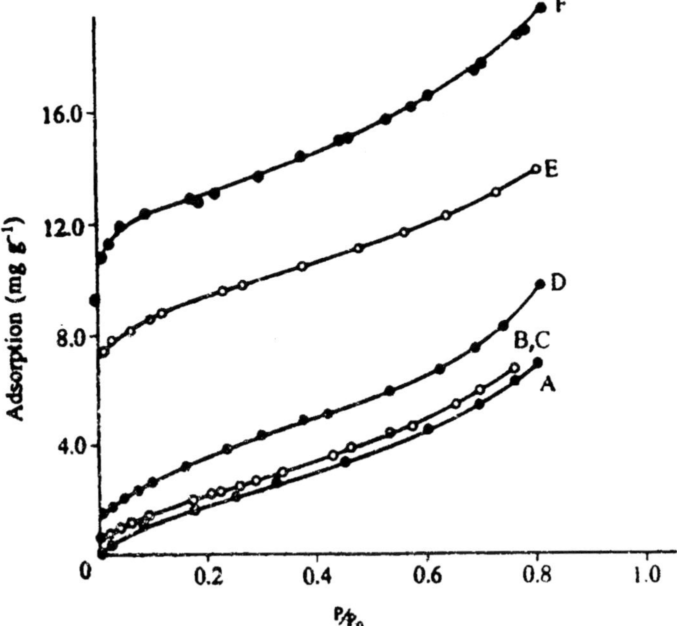

Fig. 1.29 : Adsorption of nitrogen on microporous carbon at 78° K with varying amounts of preadsorbed nonano. The quantity of preadsorption in milligrams per gram of carbon is A, 487; B. 299, C. 149; D. 427; F, 0.

An ingenious method for isolating the micropore contribution to a type II isotherm has been given as follows : A substance having large molecules is expected to be much more difficult to remove from micropores by evacuation at room temperature than from the external surface of the same solid. Consequently, if such a substance is preadsorbed to a given extent at 78°K and the sample is then pumped to constant weight at room temperature, some is left in the micropores, and subsequent adsorption of N_2 will be reduced. Progressive increase of the amount of preadsorption leads to a determination of total micropore volume. Fig. 1.29 shows a set of isotherms obtained for a carbon rendered microporous (by combustion) with nonano as the preadsorbate.

SURFACE TENSION AND SURFACE FREE ENERGY

The newly formed surface of a liquid, rapidly takes up an equilibrium conformation, whereas, the same is not true of a soft surface. The latter is likely to have a considerable range of values of surface free energy, varying from region to region on the surface, and also at anyone point. Unlike the surface of a liquid, the surface tension need not be the same in all directions. Let us suppose that the surface tension can be resoled into two directions at right angles, and that we can represent these partial surface tensions by γ^1 and γ^2. For an anisotropic solid, ir the area is increased in two directions by dA_1 and dA_2, as shown in Fig. 1.29, then the total increase in available, energy is given by the reversible work done against the stress γ^1 and γ^2 . Thus

$$d(AA^s)_{T,V,n} = \gamma^1 dA_1 + \gamma^2 dA_2 \qquad ...(1)$$

where A^s denotes the available energy per unit area. If $\gamma^1 = \gamma^2 = \gamma$ then

$$\gamma = \frac{d(AA^2)_{T,V,n}}{dA} = A^s + A\left[\frac{dA^s}{dA}\right]_{T,V,n} \qquad ...(2)$$

which can also be derived for an isotropic solid from Eq. (3) given below :

The available energy for an open system may be written

$$dA = -SdT - PdV + \gamma dA + \Sigma_i \mu_i dn_i \qquad ...(3)$$

and at constant T, V and n this yields

$$\gamma = \left(\frac{\partial A}{\partial A}\right)_{T,V,n} \qquad ...(4)$$

Then $$dA = d(A^sA) - A^s\,dA + AdA^s, \qquad ...(5)$$

which on substitution in equation (4) gives equation (2).

In the case of a solid, however. $\frac{dA^s}{dA \neq 0}$ as a general rule in fact it could only be so for an homotatic (ideal crystal-like) surface. Thus only if the surface achieved some uniform equilibrium state would $A^s = \gamma$, and in all other real cases A^s and y will be different from their equilibrium values and different from each other. It cannot be legitimate therefore to call γ the specific surface free energy.

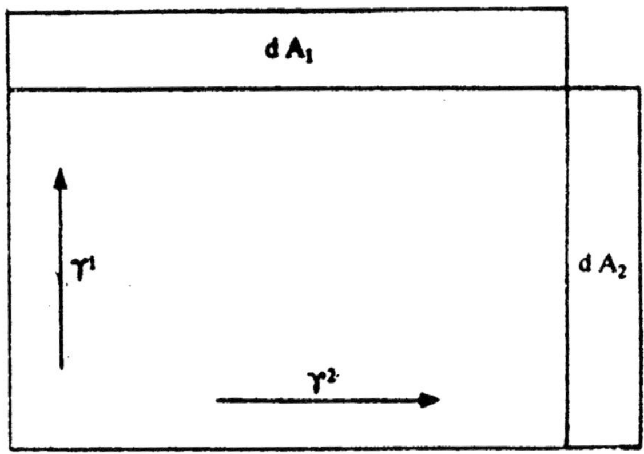

Fig 1.30 : Resolution of the surface tensions of an anisotropic solid in two directions.

This problem can also be seen to have further implications. If we integrate equation (3) under conditions of constant T and V then

$$A = \gamma A + \Sigma_i \mu_i n_i \qquad ...(6)$$

or

$$A^s = \gamma + \Sigma_i \mu_i \Gamma_t \qquad ...(7)$$

Thus even if the conditions of and deal surface could be maintained in mating $dA^s/dA = 0$, then $\Sigma_i \mu_i \Gamma_i = 0$ must also be satisfied. The reader ii recommended to cowuder this last point" again after reading the section dealing with the calculation of surface energy.

This type of consideration of the surface in relation to Gibbs free energy raises certain problems. If one starts with the equation

$$dG = -SdT + VdP + \gamma dA + \Sigma_i \mu_i dn_i \qquad ...(8)$$

then

$$\left[\frac{\partial G}{\partial A}\right]_{T,P,ni} = \gamma \qquad ...(9)$$

and therefore for an isotropic solid

$$\gamma = \frac{\partial(G^s A)}{\partial A} = G^s + A\left[\frac{\partial G'}{\partial A}\right]_{T,P,ni} \qquad ...(10)$$

which is analogous to equation (2). If, on the other hand, we start with

$$dG = -SdT + VdP - Ad\gamma + \Sigma_i\mu_i dn_i \qquad ...(11)$$

then

$$\left[\frac{\partial G}{\partial \gamma}\right]_{T,P,ni} = -A \qquad ...(12)$$

which if we expand analogously gives

$$\left[\frac{\partial(G^s A)}{\partial A}\right]_{T,P,ni} = -A\frac{\partial \gamma}{\partial A}$$

or

$$G^s = -A\left[\frac{\partial \gamma}{\partial A} + \frac{\partial G^s}{\partial A}\right]_{T,P,ni} \qquad ...(13)$$

which is not similar in form to equation (2). On the other hand integrating equations (8) and (11) at constant T and P gives

$$G = \gamma A + \Sigma_i\mu_i dn_i \qquad ...(14)$$

$$G = -\gamma A + \Sigma_i\mu_i dn_i$$

and therefore

$$G^s = \gamma + \Sigma_i\mu_i\Gamma_i$$

$$G^s = -\gamma + \Sigma_i\mu_i\Gamma_i \qquad ...(15)$$

The concept of surface tension applied to a solid has important implications in relation to the Laplace equation. Let us consider for a moment a nearly spherical crystal such that we may write

$$\Delta P = \frac{2\gamma}{r} \qquad ...(16)$$

The pressure differential ΔP will result in compression of the crystal. Thus if β is the compressibility, then we may write the approximate relation

$$\frac{\Delta V}{V} = 3\frac{\Delta r}{r} = -\Delta P\beta \qquad ...(17)$$

or

$$\Delta r = = 2\beta\gamma/3 \qquad ...(18)$$

This effect has been investigated for magnesium (II) oxide, using X-ray powder diffraction measurements. Values of Δr near the expected value of 0.06 nm, corresponding to an 0.1% change in lattice distance, were found for a 60 nm radius crystallite using a calculated value for γ of 6-573 Nm^{-1}. Reinvestigation of the situation by Guilliatt and Brett indicates that any adsorbed material such as water vapour produces lattice dilation, whereas in the absence of an adsorbed film the expected lattice contraction is observed, the relative magnitude of which increases with decreasing crystallite size, and is substantially in agreement with the theoretical predictions of Anderson and Scholtz. It is worth noting that surface dilation would imply a negative value for y in equation (18).

Shuttleworth set out to show that equating of surface tension and surface stress had very real conceptual problems for crystalline solids. He defined surface stress analogously to stress in bulk elasticity. If one imagines a cut is made perpendicular to the surface of the crystal and extending only a little way into it, then order for the surface to achieve an equilibrium configuration, and no additional stresses to appear in the bulk of the crystal, then a surface stress must be present, and could be achieved by local relaxation of the crystal structure. Since this surface stress will have at least the symmetry of the crystal face, then the surface tension can be taken to specify it when the surface has a three-fold (or greater) axis of rotational symmetry. In this case the normal stress components across all lines in the face are equal and all shear stresses are zero, so that the normal stress components are equal to the surface tension.

In a face-centred cubic crystal the (111), (100) and (110) faces have six-fold, four fold and two-fold axis of symmetry respectively. The shear component of the surface stress will be zero for the (111) and (100) faces, but not for the (110) face. Shuttleworth attempted calculations for (100) faces of inert gas crystals and alkali halide crystals at OK, expressing the surface energy as

$$U = U' + U'' \qquad ...(19)$$

where U' is the value derived from the surface energy of the crystal before any rearrangement of the surface atoms relative to ideal positions occurs, and U'' that due to the surface energy decrease on relaxation. He concluded that the surface stress was –130 mN m^{-1}. On the other hand Gibbs has shown that the surface tension must be positive as a condition for stability, and Dunning quotes a value when reviewing the work of Shuttleworth and Lennard-Jones and Dent. of 155 mN m^{-1}.

The mechanism by which surface stress could be relieved has been discussed by Herring and shown diagrammatically by Dunning. Suppose a cube of ideal crystal is subjected to a compressive surface stress, then its deformation Fig. 1.31(a) is equivalent to applying traction to each edge of the cube. This stress could be relieved by the presence of rows of dislocation just below the surface Fig. 1.31(b), since dislocations would have the effect of stretching a surface without increasing its area, or by vacancies actually in the surface Fig. 1.31(c). Such processes must involve increases in surface energy and the generation of surface heterogeneity.

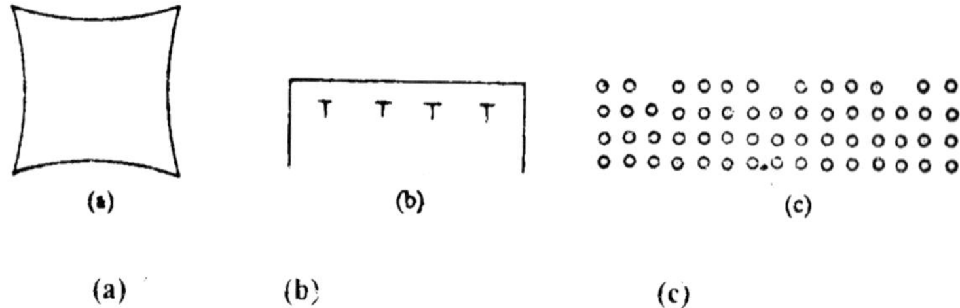

(a) (b) (c)

Fig. 1.31 : Herring's mechanism for the relief of surface stress by dislocations. (After Dunning).

Calculated surface energy values

Because of the impossibility of measuring surface tension values for solid surfaces, except in a few abnormal circumstances calculated surface energy values for solids take on a significance that they lack in the case of liquid interfaces. The early work in this field of particularly Lennard-Jones and Dent [12] before about 1960, was considerably limited in terms of what they could attempt, by severe computational difficulties. The advent of the modem computer changed this situation-and we can illustrate the impact that these made by looking first at the (100) face of sodium chloride crystals.

The Lennard-Jones and Dent model, although extremely elegantly treated, was restricted by the fact that they considered an ideal crystal, in which the ionic positions at the surface were identical to those achieved in the bulk crystal. This is obviously extremely improbable, and the first attempt to understand relaxation processes was due to Verwey. He assumed a bulk lattice spacing of 0.281 nm, and concluded that in the outermost layer the chloride ions moved out from the predicted ideal plane position to 0.286 nm from the plane of the ideal bulk crystal immediately beneath, and that the sodium ions moved inwards to 0.266 nm from the same plane, as illustrated in Fig. 1.32. Thus the plane of the outer chlorine ions was 0·020 nm farther out than the plane of the outer sodium ions, giving rise to a surface double layer. This differential effect is the result of the fact that the larger negative ions are more polarisable than the smaller positive ions, and that consequently there wilt be a larger induced electric dipole moment in the chloride ion than in the sodium ion. Thus the outer chloride ions will move so as to increase the distance of the positive end of the dipole from the 'plane of the sodium ions and decrease the distance of separation of the negative end.

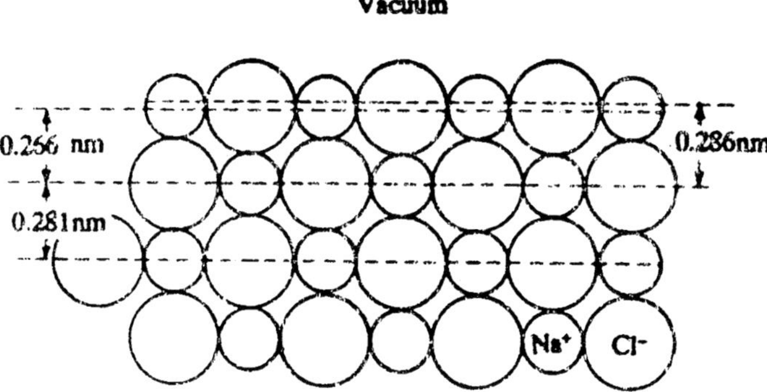

Fig. 1.32 : Verwey's single layer relaxation model of sodium chloride. In his calculations, compared with a bulk crystal layer separation of 0.281 nm, the outer sodium ions moved inwards by 0.015 nm and the outer chloride ions outwards by 0.005 nm. The circles represent approximate ionic radii.

There would seem no logical reason for supposing that only the outer plane should relax, and that some larger number of layers will in fact .show significant displacements. Benson et al., as part of a general study of relaxation in the surfaces of alkali halide crystals, showed the outer five layers were all significantly displaced from the ideal crystal position, and that only from the sixth layer in from the surface onwards was it fair to consider the crystal as bulk ideal crystal.

The method of calculation was to use numerical methods to minimise the total energy of the system by allowing ions in the outer five layers to move to new equilibrium positions. The interaction energy of two ions, i and j, was taken to be

$$u_{ij} = u_{ij}^{5} - e_i\,(r_{ij}.v_j)\,r_{ij}^{-3} + e_j\,(r_{ij}.\mu_i)\,r_{ij}^{-3}$$

$$(r_{ij}.\mu_i)\ (r_{ij}.\mu_j)\ r_{ij}^{-5} + (\mu_i - \mu_j)\ r_{ij}^{-2} \qquad ...(20)$$

where e and y. denote charge and dipole moment respectively and r_{ij} is the position vector of the ion i relative to the ion j, and

$$u_{ij}^{5} = e_i e_j r_{ij}^{-1} - c_{ij} r_{ij}^{-6} - d_{ij} r_{ij}^{-8} + b_{ij}\ \exp\ (-r_{ij}/\rho) \qquad ...(21)$$

is the Born-Meyer form of the potential energy function and represents the sum of coulombic, van der Waals and repulsive contributions. The other terms in (Eq. 20) are the energies of the charge-dipole and dipole-dipole interactions arising out of the polarisation of the ions, and the exponential term is the repulsive energy involving the 'hardness' parameter, ρ. Since the area occupied by an ion pair in the surface is $2a^2$, where a is the nearest neighbour separation in the bulk crystal, then the correction to the surface energy (compared with that of the ideal crystal) will be given by

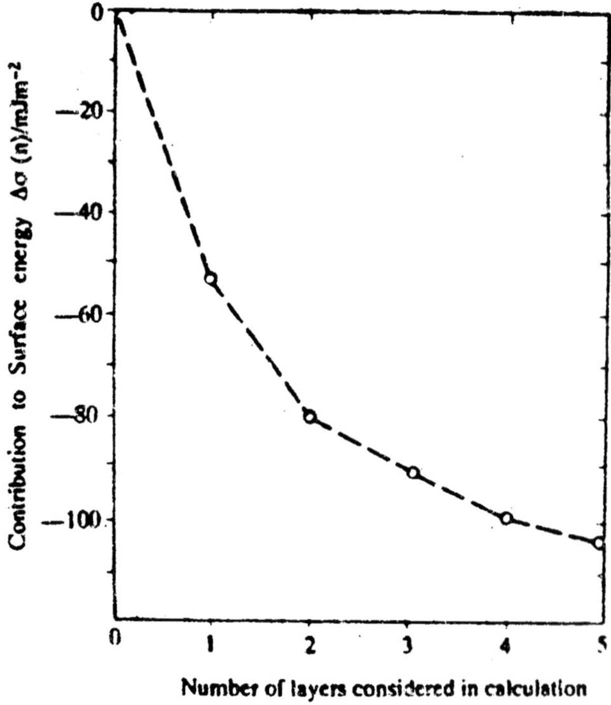

Fig. 1.33 : Values of the reduction In surface energy, $\Delta\sigma_{(100)}$, for the (100) face of NaCl, as a function of the number of layers assumed to relax.

$$\Delta\sigma_{(100)} + \Delta U_{m/n}/2a^2 \quad ...(22)$$

where $\Delta U_{m/n}$ is the reduction in the energy of the crystal brought about by relaxation. Thus the true surface energy, and will be related to that of an ideal crystal, $\sigma_{(100)}$, by

$$\sigma_{(100)} = \sigma^0_{(100)} + \Delta\sigma_{(100)} \quad ...(23)$$

$$= 210.9 - 107.4 = 103.5 \text{ mJ m}^{-2}$$

assuming the outer five layers relax. The significance of increasing the number of layers allowed to relax in the calculation can be seen in Fig. (1.33).

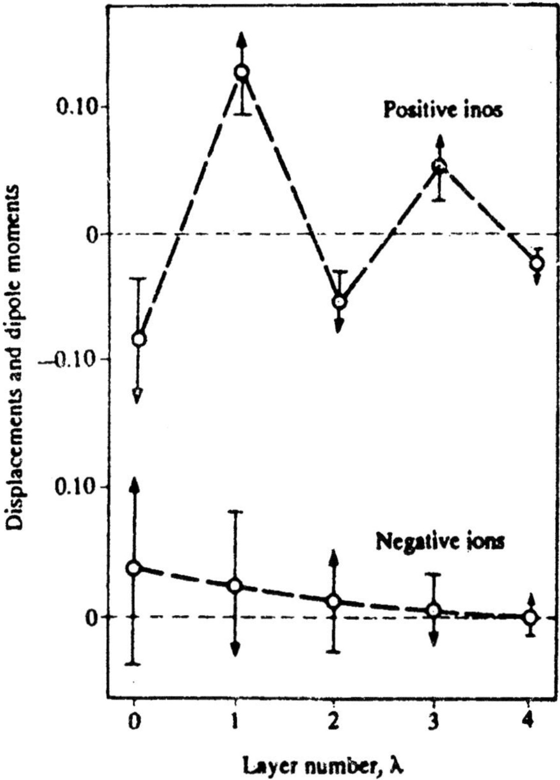

Fig. 1.34 : Equilibrium configuration of the first five layers, for the (100) face of NaCl. Displacements in units of a. Positive values indicate normal displacements outwards. The direction and magnitude of the induced dipole moments (Debye units) are indicated by the arrows, but for the negative ions they are scaled down by a factor of te.

Benson et al. data on the positional changes of the ions was represented by them as shown in Fig. 1.34 for the case where the outer five layers are allowed to relax. The most significant factor is that whilst the chloride ions are increasingly displaced away from the surface as the surface is approached from the bulk of the crystal, the displacement of the smaller sodium ions alternates. However, the degree of diaorder or distortion this relaxation process actually produces in the surface can be more readily seen in Fig. 1.35 in which the circles represent approximate values for the bulk crystalline ionic radii. It can be readily appreciated from the size of $\Delta\sigma_{(100)}$ the positional shifts of Fig. 1.35 that crystal surfaces must generally be very different from bulk crystal planes, and this would be expected to produce considerable behaviour from that predicted on the basis of ideal crystal geometry.

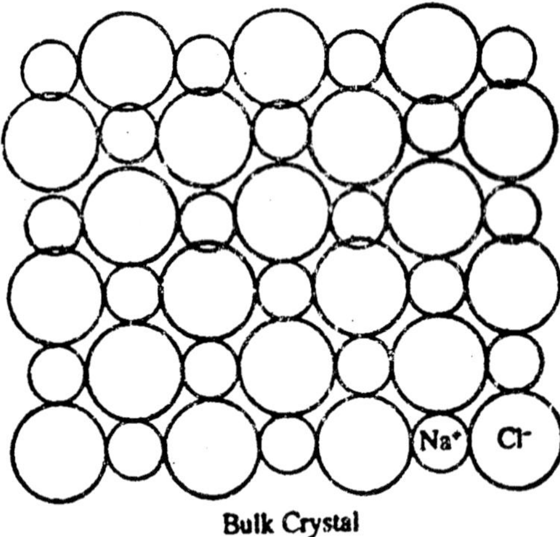

Fig. 1.35 : Surface relaxation of the (100) face of sodium chloride crystals. The circles represent approximate ionic radii. (From Benson et at).

Theoretical studies of relaxation at most crystal surfaces other than the alkali halides are still lacking. There is no real reason why any completely ionic crystals could not be treated in a similar way to that which Benson et al. have adopted, but for crystals exhibiting a degree of covalent character, silver iodide for example, a different approach is needed. The most probable route to solving such problems would seen to lie through the use of wave-mechanical methods, but is not clear at the moment how this could be dome, and the authors are not aware of any successful attempt. Crystals of intern gases held together by van der

Waals forces alone, can of course be dealt with in an analogous manner to that of Benson et al.

CAPILLARY CONDENSATION

The polymolecular adsorption is characterized by an S-shaped adsorption isotherm. However, it should be borne in mind that the curve of a similar shape may be obtained in adsorption that is complicated by *capillary condensation*. Let us consider this phenomenon in greater detail.

Capillary condensation is caused by the presence of fine pores in the adsorbent. Adsorptive vapours condense in such pores at pressures which are less than the pressure of saturated vapour over the plane surface because concave menisci are formed in capillaries as a result of merging liquid layers formed on capillary walls owing to vapour adsorption. Of course, concave menisci may originate only if the liquid formed wets capillary walls

The connection between radius r of a spherical meniscus which is formed in a capillary put into a liquid that wets its walls, and the pressure p of saturated vapour over the meniscus is given by Thomson's (Kelvin's) well-known equation whose derivation is presented in the text books of physics:

$$p = p_s \exp\left(-\frac{2\sigma V_{mol}}{rRT}\right) \qquad ...(1)$$

where p_s = pressure of saturated vapour over the plane surface of a liquid ;

σ = surface tension of a liquid;

V_{mol} = molar volume of a liquid;

R = gas constant ;

T = absolute temperature.

It should be noted that Eq. (1) is derived for a concave, spherical mensicus. For a cylindrical meniscus, one of whose main values of curvature is null. The equation assumes the following form :

$$p_{cyl} = p_s \exp\left(-\frac{\sigma V_{mol}}{rRT}\right) \qquad ...(2)$$

Hence, vapour pressure over a cylindrical meniscus is greater than that over a spherical one in a capillary of the same radius, *i.e.*,

$p_{cyl} > p$. This circumstance plays an important role in capillary condensation.

Thomson's equation is the main equation for calculations connected with the phenomena of capillary condensation. If p_s, the vapour pressure of a liquid, and R. The radius of an adsorbent capillary, are known, the equation may be used to calculate vapour pressure p_h above which condensation begins in capillaries. If p_s and p_h are given, the equation may be used to calculate the maximum radius of capillaries in which condensation will occur (this must be known in order to correctly select the adsorbent).

The condensation phenomenon should not be confused with physical adsorption. The elementary theory of capillary condensation does not take account of the specific action of surface forces. Capillary condensation differs from polymolecular physical adsorption also by the fact that the latter may occur on plane surfaces while capillary condensation cannot.

B. Deryagin and Z. Zorin studied the mechanism of capillary condensation by the optical method on a smooth glass surface. They have shown that a steep rise of the isotherm which characterizes capillary condensation begins for non-polar substances (CCl_4 and others) at p/p_s of about 0.98, and for polar substances (water, alcohols, nitrobenzene), at somewhat smaller relative pressures. These scientists also discovered that, when polar substances are being sorbed, there is a sharp transition from the adsorption layer to a liquid phase. This conclusion suggests coexistence of lens-shaped nuclei, *i.e.*, regions of a new liquid phase, and polymolecular adsorption layers of uniform thickness. The liquid phase is formed owing to the growth of these islands while the adsorption layer which surrounds them does not change noticeably. Conversely, the liquid phase in the surface condensation of non-polar substances is formed apparently as a result of the continuous thickening of the adsorption layer; this condensation is reversible.

Therefore, for polar substances, the difference between the adsorption polymolecular layer and the volume of liquid has the nature of phase distinctions, and polymolecular adsorption layers can be regarded as boundary phases. Conversely, the adsorption layer of vapours of non-polar substances cannot be regarded as a special phase which differs from the liquid phase because a continuous transition can exist between them and their coexistence is impossible.

In adsorption accompanied by capillary condensation, hysteresis is often observed when adsorption and desorption isotherms do not coincide.

This phenomenon was studied in detail by van Bemmelen and Zsigmondy for the adsorption of water by silica gel. The results of their experiments are presented schematically as a diagram in Fig. 1.36 where m, the mass of water adsorbed by silica gel, is plotted on the ordinate, and the equilibrium values of vapour pressure p, on the abscissa.

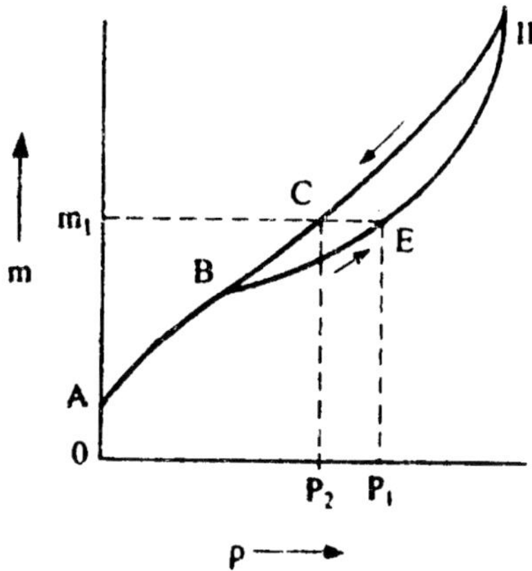

Fig. 1.36 : Hysteresis in capillary condensation.

At p = 0, silica gel still contains a small amount of water, and this is characterized by the OA segment. This is the water of crystallization which may be removed only by calcination. The adsorption isotherm is reversible only in the AB region. From point B, the isotherm becomes irreversible, *i.e.*, vapour pressure p_1 corresponds to the mass of moisture m_1 in adsorption while p_2 corresponds to the same mass in dehydration, and $p_1 > p_2$. This becomes clear when a line which is parallel to the abscissa and which intersects the hysteresis loop is plotted and perpendiculars are drawn from the intersection points to the pressure axis. Zsigmondy explained such a phenomenon by saying that capillary condensation occurred in the BED region while water evaporated from capillaries in the BCD region.

Air adsorbed by dry capillary walls prevents them from being watted when water is added to silica gel. As a result, contact angles which are formed here by a liquid with capillary walls in silica gel will apparently always be greater than the respective angles in evaporation when the walls are completely wetted with water. Hence, the menisci of a liquid that fills up a capillary will be also less concave in the first case than in the second, arid vapour pressure which corresponds to the same amount of liquid adsorbed by silica gel will be greater in hydration than in dehydration.

The curves BCD and BED have a certain inclination to the pressure axis because silica gel capillaries of different radii are filled up or emptied consecutively. The condensate fills narrow capillaries already at low pressure while considerably higher pressure is required for filling wide capillaries. Of course, an inverse relation is observed when water evaporates from capillaries.

The preliminary thorough removal of air from a porous adsorbent usually greatly reduces hysteresis. This seems to confirm the explanation that hysteresis is caused by the adsorption of air on capillary walls. However, there are also other explanations of this complicated phenomenon. In particular, hysteresis in capillary condensation may be explained by the shape of adsorbent pores. Suppose that an adsorbent has pores which are represented in Fig. 1.37. When a pore is conical an adsorption film with a concave surface is formed in it and the spherical surface has the greatest curvature in the narrowest part of the pore. At $p = p_s \exp[-2\sigma V_{mol}/(rRT)]$, vapour is saturated in respect to this surface and begins to condense. The liquid moves to the wider part of the pore, and r increases. For vapour to continue condensing, pressure p must grow (Fig. 1.37a). When p diminishes the liquid is desorbed from the capillary walls and the isotherm will follow the same way in the opposite direction, *i.e.*, capillary condensation in conical pores is quite reversible.

In cylindrical pores, which are closed at one end. *i.e.*. have the shape of a test tube (Fig. 1.37b). a spherical meniscus is formed at the closed end in adsorption. At $p = p_s \exp[-2a\ V_{mol}/(rRT)]$, capillary condensation occurs and the pores are filled up with liquid. However, unlike in the preceding case, the meniscus radius here does not change and therefore the pores are filled up at a constant value of p, to which the vertical part of the isotherm for capillary condensation corresponds (Fig. 1.37b). The desorption will occur in the opposite direction in the same way, *i.e.*. capillary condensation in cylindrical capillaries having one end closed is also quite reversible.

Lastly, in cylindrical pores which are opened at both ends (Fig. 1.37c). a spherical meniscus cannot be formed in adsorption. Condensation begins on the inner cylindrical meniscus of the film which covers the capillary walls at a pressure of $p_{cyl} = p_s \exp[-\sigma V_{mol}/(rRT)]$. As a result of condensation, the thickness of the film of a liquid increases while the pore radius decreases, and therefore a pore is filled with liquid at pressure p. The isotherm of capillary condensation, like in the previous case, has a vertical region (the isotherm in Fig. 1.37c). However, owing to the smaller curvature of the cylindrical surface of a meniscus in comparison with that of the spherical surface (when the capillary ladius is the same), the vertical region on the isotherm corresponds to higher values of vapour pressure.

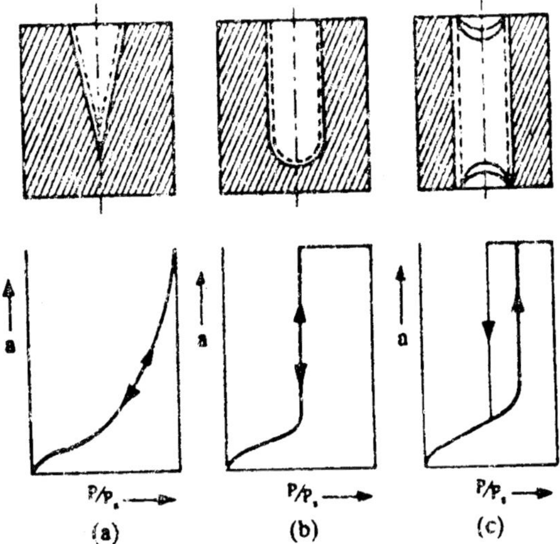

Fig. 1.37 : Diagram of capillary condensation in pores having a different shape : a–conical; b–cylindrical closed at one end; c–cylindrical opened at both ends.

After a pore is filled up, both of its ends have spherical menisci whose curvature decreases as vapour pressure increases. In desorption. The process occurs reversibly at first. *i.e.*, when small amounts of a liquid evaporate, spherical menisci with a growing curvature are pressed into capillary mouths. However, at $p = p_s \exp[-\sigma V_{mol}/(rRT)]$, these spherical menisci cannot burst open yet and the capillary at this pressure still remains filled up. Only when vapour pressure is reduced to $p = p_s \exp[-2\sigma V_{mol}/(rRT)]$. will the radius of the spherical meniscus be equal to that of the adsorption film in the cylindrical capillary, and will all the liquid filling up the capillary evaporate. Thus, the desorption curve will diverge from the adsorption one to give a characteristic loop of capillary-condensation hysteresis.

Pores of real adsorbents are not of the same size and shape. They are not filled up or emptied simultaneously. That is why the curves of the hysteresis loop are usually inclined towards the abscissa.

The recuperation (return for use in production) of volatile solvents which are lost in technological processes is based on the-phenomena of adsorption and mainly capillary condensation.

For example, let us consider the recuperation of a solvent from glues used in rubber production. In producing rubberized cloths, about 180 kg of rubber glue containing approximately 85 percent of high-quality benzine are usually spent on a roll of 300 metres. When the cloth is dried after being covered with glue, benzine is volatilized and mixes with air. Hence, an enormous amount of expensive benzine in short supply is lost.

To recuperate the volatile solvent, benzine vapours mixed with air are sucked off from driers when the cloth is being dried, and are fed by means of air pumps to the recuperator which consists of two adsorbers. Benzine vapours enter an adsorber which is filled with activated charcoal. The other adsorber is disconnected during this time. In the first adsorber where the vapour-air mixture has entered, adsorption and then capillary condensation of benzine vapours occur until the adsorbent is completely saturated with the volatile solvent as may be easily established if benzine vapours are no more retained by the charcoal layer. After saturation is attained, the first adsorber is disconnected from the supply tube and the second adsorber is connected to it. Hot steam is fed into the disconnected adsorber in order to evaporate and desorb benzine. Benzine vapour and steam are fed into a cooler and then into a separator where condensed benzine and water are separated as a result of the simple phase separation of these immiscible liquids. During this time, the second adsorber has adsorbed a sufficient amount of benzine and is disconnected from the supply tube in order to carry out the desorption process. The first adsorber is connected now to the tube again. This is how the continuous industrial process of recuperating a volatile solvent is effected.

The capillary condensation theory as an adsorption theory is limited first of all because it relates only to a small region of the isotherm, namely, to the region of pressures close to p_0. At the same time, it shows that when considering the sorption process as a whole, one must never forget the important role played by the condensation of vapour in bodies with fine pores, which include most of the adsorbents and catalysts used in practice.

WETTING PHENOMENA

Wetting phenomena are similar to the adsorption phenomenon. and they are also determined by the intensity of interaction between molecules of different substances.

Wetting and the contact angle : If the molecules of a liquid interact with the molecules of a solid to a greater extent than among themselves, the liquid spreads on the surface, or, as we usually say, wets it. The liquid spreads until it covers the surface of a solid or the liquid layer becomes monomolecular. Such complete wetting is observed, for example, when a drop of water is deposited on the surface of clean glass.

The liquid does not spread if its molecules interact with one another to a greater extent than with the molecules of a solid. Conversely, the liquid collects on the surface into a drop which would be almost spherical were it not for the action of gravity. A similar case is observed when a drop of mercury is deposited on any non-metallic surface.

Besides these two extreme cases, there may be intermediate cases of incomplete wetting when a drop forms with a solid surface an equilibrium angle, known as the *contact angle*, or the *wetting angle*; this depends on the ratio of the intensities of molecular forces which act, on the one hand. Between molecules of a liquid, and, on the other, between molecules of a liquid and of a solid.

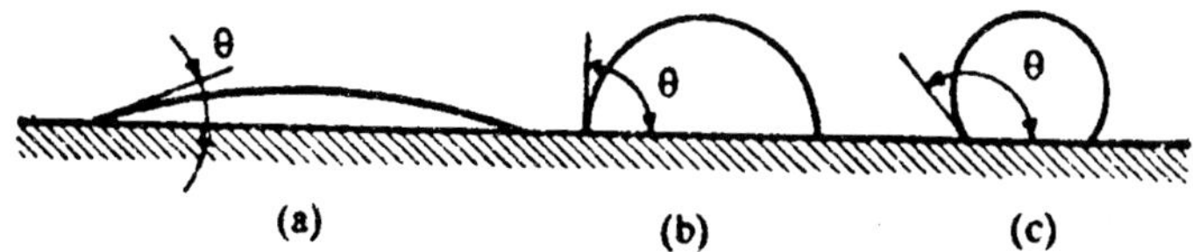

Fig. 1.38 : Different cases of incomplete wetting.
a–$\theta < 90°$; b–$\theta = 90°$; c–$\theta > 90°$

Fig. 1.38 represents drops which, on a solid surface, form an acute contact angle ($\theta < 90°$). a right contact angle ($\theta = 90°$), and an obtuse contact angle ($\theta > 90°$). The contact angle formed by a drop on the surface of a solid is always measured from the liquid side. Complete nonwetting. *i.e.*, when the contact angle is 180°, is hardly ever observed because forces of attraction, however small, always act between a liquid and a solid.

The values of contact angle formed by water on the surface of various solids in an air atmosphere are given below :

Quartz	Malachite	Galenite	Graphite	Talc	Sulphur	Paraffin
0°	17	47°	55-60°	69°	78°	106°

A solid is wetted by a liquid as a result of the action offers of surface tension.

Wetting is a process in which free energy decreases in a system consisting of three contacting phases.

Proceeding from the general -condition of minimum surface energy when the contacting media are in equilibrium, the loss of free surface energy as the liquid-solid interface is formed can be taken as a measure of wetting a body by a liquid. It follows that a given surface is wetted better by a liquid whose spread causes a decrease in the surface energy of a system by a greater quantity than that in the case of another liquid. Since wetting is accompanied by a decrease in surface energy, heat is liberated in the wetting process. The heat of wetting per square centimetre of a surface usually ranges from 10^{-3} to 10^{-5} cal. The heat of wetting (*i.e.*, heat of immersion) can serve as a characteristic of the ability of a liquid to wet the surface of a solid if the contact angle of wetting cannot be determined, for example, when powders are wetted by a liquid.

The wetting phenomenon can be observed also when, instead of air another liquid is taken that does not mix with the first one and has lower density. If each of the two liquids can wet the surface, there will apparently be competition between them that is similar to competition in the adsorption of two adsorptives. Wetting is determined by the ratio of molecular forces acting between molecules of each liquid, on the one hand, and between molecules of liquids and molecules of a solid, on the other, therefore, it is not difficult to see that, between the two liquids, the liquid whose value of polarity is closer to that of a solid will wet the surface. The liquid which wets the surface better is said to have great selective wetting in respect to the given surface.

Selective wetting was investigated by P. Rehbinder. Let us consider this phenomenon in greater detail. Suppose that the surface of a solid is in contact with polar water and some non-polar hydrocarbon. Then, the surface is said to be *hydrophilic* if water selectively wets the surface, *i.e.*, if the contact angle θ formed from the side of water is less than 90° and the value of $B = \cos\theta > 0$. Selective wetting by water is usually observed when the difference in the polarities between water and a solid is less than that between a non-polar hydrocarbon and a solid. Substances with a hydrophilic surface are characterized by strongly pronounced intermolecular interaction; these are quartz, glass, corundum, gypsum, and malachite, *i.e.*, silicates carbonates, sulphates, and oxides and hydroxide of metals. Cellulose is among the organic substances having a hydrophilic surface.

A surface is said to be *hydrophobia* or *oleophilic* if a solid is wetted better by a non-polar hydrocarbon, *i.e.*, if $\theta > 90°$ for water, and the value of $B = \cos \theta < 0$. According to Equation this can be observed only when $\sigma_{2,3} < \sigma_{1,3}$ or when $\sigma_{2,3} - \sigma_{1,3} < 0$. Selective wetting by a nonpolar hydrocarbon is observed when the difference in polarities between a hydrocarbon and a solid is less than that between water and a solid. Substances having a hydrophobic surface are all the hydrocarbons and other organic compounds with large hydrocarbon radicals, and inorganic compounds such as sulphides of heavy metals, talc, graphite, and sulphur.

When the contact angle is 90°, an intermediate case will be observed, selective wetting being absent.

If all the minerals are arranged in a series according to the growth of their hardness. the series, as Rebbinder has indicated, coincides with the series of the some minerals arranged according to their selective wettability by water. Minerals of high hardness, *i.e.*, quartz. corundum, and diamond, are very hydrophilic.

Practical importance of wetting : Wetting is important for successful effecting several technological processes. For example, in the textile technological process, the good wetting of fibre or textiles is a prerequisite of dyeing, bleaching, desizing, impregnating, laundering, and so forth. Wetting is significant in the effective use of insecticide-fungicide combinations because the leaves of plants and the wool of animals are always hydrophobic. Wetting is also important in printing. The mechanical treatment (cutting, drilling, polishing) of metals and non-metallic bodies is accelerated and facilitated when they are wetted by the appropriate liquids. It is also easier to bore oil wells in rocks when special boring solutions which contain wetting agents are used. In tinning, soldering, and welding, metals, and also in pasting together various, solids, it is necessary to wet their surfaces well. Selective wetting is the basis of ore concentration, *i.e.*, flotation. Let us consider, as an example, the role of wetting in such processes as laundering, impregnation, and floatation.

The purpose of laundering is to remove impurities, such as the yolk of wool, size, soot, dust, and proteins, from the surface of a solid which is usually a fibre or a textile. In laundering, the fibre—impurity interface is replaced by the interfaces between the fibre and the detergent solution, and between the impurity and the detergent solution. The processes on which laundering is based differ from selective wetting only by the fact that a solid impurity or a semi-solid impurity acts as the first liquid.

Let us consider the laundering process by taking the example of the removal of a liquid hydrocarbon (fat) from the surface of a textile by means of ordinary soap. The engineer's job is to reduce as much as possible surface tension at the interfaces between the detergent solution and the impurity, and between the detergent solution and the fibre. Tensions of these surfaces decrease after the adsorption of soap on the surfaces of fat and textile; of course, adsorption occurs in a way that the polar parts of soap molecules are turned towards water, and their non-polar parts, towards an impurity or a fibre. Pat then collects into a drop under the action of unchanged surface tension at the solid—impurity interface, and the drop may be easily removed from the fibre surface by even inconsiderable mechanical action.

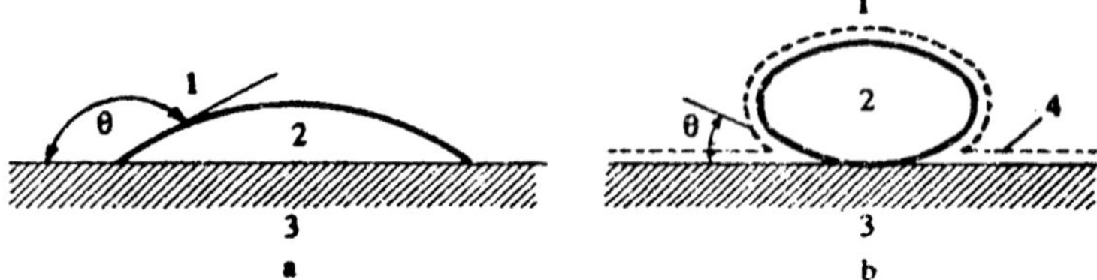

Fig . 1.39 : Diagram of the washing of a hydrocarbon in laundering by a liquid which wets the surface (a) and by a liquid which does not wet the surface (b): I–soapy solution; 2–textile; 3–hydrocarbon; 4–hydrohi lie detergent layer

Washing occurs, consisting in a sharp growth of B = cos θ (for water), *i.e.*, in a diminution of the contact angle. This is shown in Fig. 1.39.

In laundering, detergent 1, while being adsorbed both on the surface of textile 3 and on the surface of a hydrocarbon particle 2 contaminating the textile, forms hydrophilic soap layer 4 on them. This layer helps to separate the particles of an impurity from the textile because, if the surface being washed is better wetted by water under the conditions of selective wetting, it is worse wetted by a hydrocarbon. Moreover, the layer of hydrated, partially ionized soap molecules that is formed on the hydrocarbon drops makes the emulsion which has originated stable and thus helps to remove the impurity together with the detergent solution at the end of laundering.

The adsorbing soap molecules can orient their polar groups towards the fibre, and their non-polor hydrocarbon radicals, into the detergent solution, on the surface of a bleached hydrophilic textile owing to the polarity of cellulose. It would seem that the surface should become hydrophobic in this case, reducing the laundering effect. However, when sufficiently soap solutions are used, after the first molecular layer has originated, the second soap layer whose molecules are oriented in the opposite direction, *i.e.*, their polar groups are in the detergent solution, is formed on the textile surface which becomes hydrophilic.

Rehbinder believes that sufficient mechanical strength and viscosity of hydrated adsorption layers of a detergent are also a prerequisite for detergency. On the one hand, such layers at the interface between the detergent solution and air promote foaming which is important in laundering. On the other, when stable hydrated adsorption layers are formed around particles of fat, impurities washed off are emulsified and will not settle again on the fibre.

The phenomena of wetting and non-wetting are also the basis of the notation process, *i.e.*, a method of concentrating minerals which is now widely used. This method is based on different wetting of particles, which are being separated, by water. To make it clear, let us consider the behaviour of sufficiently small hydrophobic and hydrophilic mineral particles at the water—ait and water–oil interfaces.

Hydrophilic particles are wetted by water and are drawn into it under the action of surface tension at the water--air or water-oil interface. Besides the force of surface tension, gravity abacus on the particle As a result, the particle passes into the aqueous phase and sinks.

Fig. 1.40 : Non-wetting of the capillary of a hydrophobicized textile by water

Water does not wet hydrophobic particles, and the partiale may remain at the interface under the action of surface tension at the water–– air or water-oil interface, provided the particle is not too large and gravity is not greater than the flotation force. Both of these cases are schematically illustrated in Fig. 1.41. Of course, when a mineral is ground to the required extent of dispersion, the size of particles at which they will remain on the surface can always be selected because, in crushing, gravity decreases in direct proportion to the cube of the radius of the particle whereas the flotation force decreases in direct proportion to the radius. However, an excessively great degree of dispersion may be harmful since small particles are subjected to intensive Brownian motion, and this reduces the probability of their attachment at the water–air or water–oil interface.

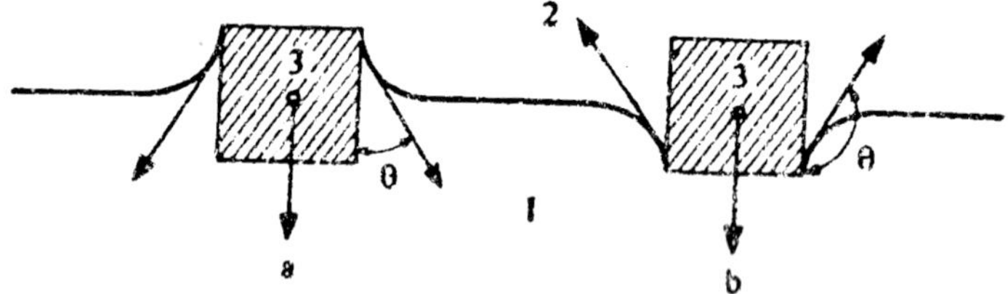

Fig. 1.41 : Separation of hydrophilic (a) and hydrophobic (b) particles by flotation: 1–water; 2–air or oil; 3–solid

The flotation concentration of mineral ores is based on the fact that sulphur compounds of metals in the ore are more hydrophobic than barren rock, such as quartz. The separation of ore by flotation is almost never effected by simply introducing ground ore into water whose surface borders on air or oil. In such form, the flotation process is too ineffective. At present, froth flotation is widely used. It consists in the introduction of air bubbles into the mineral suspension, *i.e.*, the flotation pulp. When bubbles rise upwards, they accumulate on their surface the ore particles on which water forms a large contact angle. As a result, mineralized froth is collected on the pulp surface. The froth is removed from the pulp surface as an ore concentrate by means of gravity or with special rakers. Particles of barren rock that are well wettable by water do not adhere to the bubbles, but settle to the bottom and form notation wastes, or "tailings".

The optimum size of mineral grains in notation is 0.15-0.01 mm. However, mineral particles may be larger (0.5-1.0 mm) in the notation of pit coal and native sulphur. The weight ratio of ore to water in the pulp is usually in the range of 1:4 to 1:2.

APPLICATIONS OF ADSORPTION

The phenomenon of adsorption has found many applications in the industries. Some of the important applications are described as follows:

1. *High Vacuum* : In this method, activated charcoal is being used to create high vacuum in the vessel. This method, is due to the *Tait* and *Dewar* (1874). In the method a bulb is exhausted by an ordinary exhaust pump. This bulb is then connected with another bulb containing charcoal. By immersing the charcoal in the liquid air, the air in the bulb is adsorbed by the charcoal and thus creates the high vacuum, *i.e.*, the pressure is generally reduced to 1/34000 of the original pressure. In some cases, 2 × 10–7 mm pressure has been obtained by using this method.
2. *Gas Masks* : During World War I charcoal was used in the preparation of both the British and American gas masks. The charcoal adsorbed all toxic gases and vapours and allowed only pure air to pass through the pores of it. For this purpose, the charcoal must possess the following characteristics:
   (a) The charcoal must possess high adsorptive capacity.
   (b) It should adsorb all the toxic gases immediately, *i.e.*, in a very small time period.
   (c) It should be able to reduce the concentration of toxic gases from 1000 ppm to 1 ppm in less than 0.1 sec.

   The activated coconut charcoal was found to be the best adsorbent.
3. *Softening of Hard Water* : In permanent process for the softening of hard water, the hard water is made to pass through a column packed with sodium aluminium silicate (zeolite). Ca^{2+} and Mg^{2+} ions, which are responsible for hardness, get adsorbed on zeolite with a simultaneous release of sodium ions:

$$Na_2Al_2Si_4OM + CaCl_2 \rightarrow Ca(Al_2Si_4O_{12}) + 2NaCl$$

$$Na_2Al_2O_{12} + MgSO_4 \rightarrow Mg(Al_2Si_4O_{12}) + Na_2SO_4$$

The exhausted permuted is regenerated with 10% solution of sodium chloride.

$$Mg, Ca(Al_2Si_4O_{12}) + 2NaCl \rightarrow Na_2(Al_2Si_4O_{12}) + (Ca, Mg)Cl_2$$

The hard water can also be softened by synthetic ion exchange resins. There are two types of ion-exchange resins.

(i) *Cation exchange resins* : These are large organic molecules with sulphonic acid group (–SOgH). The resins are converted into sodium salt by treating it with NaCl. This sodium salt is then used for softening hard water by ion exchange reaction.

$$RSO_3{}^-Na^+ + Ca^{2+}(Mg^{2+}) \rightarrow (RSO_3)_2\ Ca(Mg) + 2Na^+$$

The exhausted resins are then regenerated by treating it with 20% sodium chloride solution.

(ii) *Anion exchange resins* : These are also large organic molecules having active amino group ($-NH_2$), which ionize in water to give

$$RNH_2 + H_2O \rightarrow RNH_3 + OH^-$$

The anion exchange reaction can be represented by

$$RNH_2 + OH^- + X^- \rightarrow RNH_3X + OH^-$$

where $X^- = Cl^-$, HCO_3^-, CO_3^{2-}, SO_4^{2-}, etc. In practice, water is demineralized by passing through two columns containing cationic and anionic exchange resins respectively.

4. *Drying Gases* : The adsorptive force of silica gel and alumina for water is very great.

   It, therefore, acts as a good drying agent. Both silica gel and alumina have been used in the dehydration and purification of CO_2, O_2, N_2, He and Cl_2, Silica gel is employed in drying air for blast furnaces.

5. *Decolourisation* : Animal charcoal has been used to remove colouring matter from coloured solution. For example, the decolourisation of sugar can be done by passing its solution over animal charcoal. The colouring material is retained on the charcoal and the solution (after passing over the charcoal) obtained will be colourless.

6. *Refining of Petroleum and Vegetable Oils* : Fuller's earth and silica gel are now-a-days used in large quantities for refining petroleum and vegetable oils.

7. *Catalysis* : Most of the catalysed reactions are affected through adsorption of reactants on solid surfaces of catalysts. Thus,

adsorption plays an important role in heterogeneous catalysis. Examples are:

(i) the use of iron in the synthesis of ammonia by Haber's process.

(ii) The use of nickel in the hydrogenation of oils.

8. *Chromatographic Analysis*

Principle : It is known that the rate of adsorption varies with a given adsorbent for different materials. This principle of selective adsorption is used in chromatographic analysis.

Chromatographic analysis is a process by means of which a mixture of substances is separated into its various components passage through a column of a suitable adsorbent. Because many of the early applications were with coloured 'substances, the word chromatography was used.

Process : In this method, the mixture to be separated is dissolved in a suitable solvent and allowed it to pass through a tube containing the adsorbent. The component which has greater adsorbing power is adsorbed in the upper part of column. The next component is adsorbed in the lower portion of the column which has lesser adsorbing power than the first component.

This process is continued. As a result, the materials are partially separated and adsorbed in the various parts of the column. After the proper separation is complete, the components can be recovered in their pure form by mechanically separating the column and extracting with proper solvents. This process of desorption is called elution. Various applications are:

(i) Separating the components found in the solution produced by extracting a green leaf with petroleum ether.

(ii) Separating the carotenes by using adsorbing column of powdered sugar.

Variation in Chromatographic Technique : A number of variations have now been developed in the original column chromatography.

(a) *Partition chromatograpy :* In this technique, a partition of the solute is carried out between two immiscible solvents, one of which is fixed on a fixed column and other containing the solute is percolating through the column.

(b) *Gas chromatography :* It is a special modification of partition chromatography in which the second solvent is a gas.

(c) *Paper chromatography* : In this technique, the packed column is replaced by a filter paper strip.

9. *Dyeing* : Most of the dyes arc adsorbed on the surface of cloth. A mordant added during the dyeing process helps in the adsorption of the dye.

10. *Qualitative Analysis* : Example of this is the lake test for Al^{3+}, in which the $Al(OH)_3$ particles are detected due to the adsorption on the dye by them.

11. *Prevention of Evaporation of Water* : In countries facing scarcity of water a layer of stearic acid is adsorbed on the surface of water reservoirs. This prevents the evaporation of water.

12. *In Curing Diseases* : It has been seen that a number of drugs are adsorbed on the germs and kill them or these are adsorbed on defective tissues and kill them.

13. *Concentration of Ores* : In the froth flotation process, the ore particles are adsorbed on the air-oil interface, while impurities remain in the water.

14. *Adsorption Indicators* : Sometimes, particularly in the titration of halides or of silver, a new type of useful indicator is employed. These indicators were first introduced by K.

    Fajan (1923–24) and are known as adsorption indicators because the indicator is adsorbed by the precipitate at the end point. During the process of adsorption the indicator undergoes certain change which produces a change in the colour of the solution.

Examples of Adsorption Indicator

(i) *Acid dyes* : Fluorescein, eosin which are used as their sodium salts.

(ii) *Basic dyes* : Those of rhodamine series which are employed as their halogen salts.

Theory of Adsorption Indicators : The action of adsorption indicators is based upon the following two facts:

(a) Finely divided precipitates tend to adsorb on their surfaces ions present in the solution. Consequently the particles become electrically charged, either positive (if cations are adsorbed) or negative (if anions are adsorbed).

(b) That the precipitated salt tends to adsorb only ions common to itself. Thus precipitate of AgCl tends to adsorb either silver or chloride ions (whichever is available in the solution in excess) in preference to ions such as sodium or nitrate.

Consider the titration of $AgNO_3$ solution with a solution of NaCl. The precipitated AgCl adsorbs chloride ions which are in excess and common to AgCl, This may be termed as primary adsorbed layer and will be held by secondary adsorption of oppositely charged ions in solution. As soon as the equivalence point is reached, no chloride ions are available but silver ions are present in excess together with nitrate ions. Therefore, precipitate of silver chloride will adsorb Ag+ ions as primary adsorbed layer and nitrate ions will be held by secondary adsorption. These adsorption effects are represented below:

$(AgCl)Cl^- \mid Na^+$ $\qquad$ $(AgCl)\ Ag^+ \mid NO_3^-$

If fluorescein is also present in the solution, at the equivalence point the adsorbed silver ions unite with the negative fluorescein ions which are much more strongly adsorbed than the nitrate ions and the resulting compound silver fluoresccinate reveals its presence by its reddish-pink colour. Fluorescein in the original solution imparts a greenish yellow colour.

SOLVED EXAMPLES

Example 1:

Langmuir gave the following values for the adsorption of methane on mica at 90°K.

P	*13-4*	*11-1*	*9-6*	*8-55*	*7-4*	*6-68*	*5-85*
x/m	*850*	*80-4*	*76-9*	*71-60*	*67-9*	*64-20*	*61-20*

By means of these data verify graphically the validity of Langmuir''s isotherm for the given system.

Solution:

The values of $\frac{P}{(x/m)}$ are calculated from the data (in question).

P	13.4	11.1	9.6	8.55	7.4	6.68	5.85
$\frac{P}{(x/m)}$	0.1576	0.1381	0.1265	0.1194	0.1090	0.1040	0.956

The calculated values $\frac{P}{(x/m)}$ are plotted against P in Fig. 1.42.

It is clear from the Fig. (1.42) that the dependence of $\frac{P}{(x/m)}$ on P satisfies Langmuir's isotherm very well.

$$\text{Slope of this line} = \frac{0.1576 - 0.1090}{13.4 - 7.4} = \frac{0.0686}{6}$$

$$= 0.0081$$

$$\text{But Slope} = \frac{1}{k_2}$$

$$\because \quad \frac{1}{k_2} = 0.0081$$

$$\text{or} \quad k_2 = 123.45$$

Interception of the Y-axis.

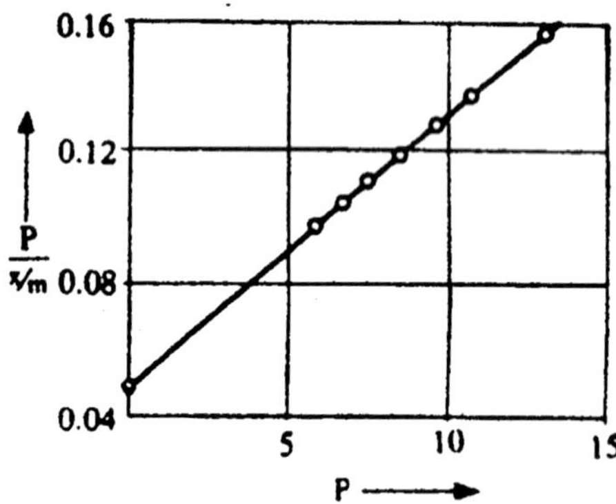

Fig. 1.42

$$= 0.0484.$$

$$\text{But intercept} = \frac{1}{k_1 k_2}$$

$$\text{or} \quad \frac{1}{k_1 k_2} = 0.0484$$

$$\text{or} \quad k_1 k_2 = \frac{1}{0.0484}$$

$$\text{But} \quad k_2 = 123.45$$

$$\therefore \quad k_1 \times 123.45 = \frac{1}{0.0484}$$

or $$k_1 = \frac{1}{123.45 \times 0.0484} = 0.1674$$

Example 2:

Test graphically the applicability of the Langmuir isotherm to the following data referring to the adsorption of a gas on charcoal.

Pressure (p)	*100*	*200*	*500*	*900*
x/m	*1-56*	*1-97*	*2-29*	*2-41*

From your graph, calculate the value of k_1 *and* k_2

Solution:

P	100	200	500	900
$\frac{P}{(x/m)}$	64.10	101.5	218.4	373.5

Plot the graph (Fig. 1.43)

Slope is,

$$\frac{284}{730} = \frac{1}{k_2}$$

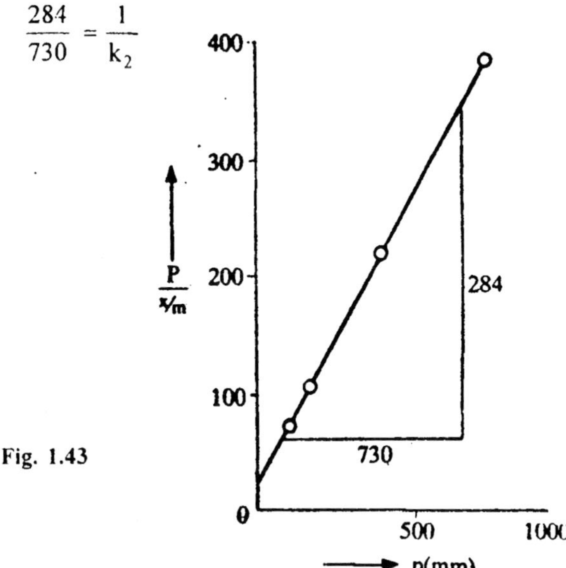

Fig. 1.43

Surface Chemistry

$\therefore k_2 = 2.57 \text{ mg g}^{-1}$

Intercept on the $\frac{P}{(x/m)}$ axis is

or $$25 = \frac{1}{k_1 k_2}$$

or $$k_2 = \frac{1}{25 \times 2.57}$$
$$= 1.56 \times 10.2 \text{ mm}^{-1}$$

Example 3:

Freundlich gave the following data for the adsorption of acetic acid on blood charcoal:

c	*0.0181*	*0.0616*	*0.2677*	*0.8817*	*2.785*
x/m	*0.457*	*0.801*	*1.55*	*2.84*	*3.76*

Obtain the constant k and n in the Freundlich equation

$$x/m = kc^{l\ n}$$

Solution:

Freundlich equation is

$$\frac{x}{m} = kc^{1/n} \qquad ...(1)$$

Taking logarithm of equation (1).

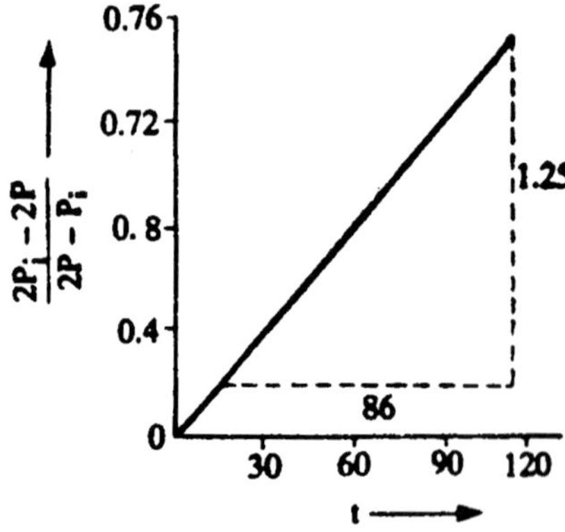

Fig. 1.44

$$\log \frac{x}{m} = \log k + \frac{1}{n} \log c$$

$= \log c\ \bar{2}.2577\ \bar{2}.7896\ \bar{1}.9453\ 0.4448$

$\log (x/m)\ \bar{1}.6693\ \bar{1}.9036\ 0.1903\ 0.3945\ 0.5752$

Plot log c against log (x/m).

Slope of the line $= \frac{1}{n}$

$$\frac{1}{n} = \frac{0.5}{1.17} = \frac{1}{2.35} \quad \text{or} \quad n = 2.35$$

Also, intercept on the Y-axis is given by

$$\log k = 0.425 \text{ or } k = 2.66$$

Example 4:

The following data have been obtained for the adsorption of nitrogen on silica at 77° K. P_0 is the vapour pressure of liquid nitrogen at this temperature.

P/P_0	*0.05*	*0.15*	*0.25*	*.04*	*0.6*	*0.8*
ml adsorbed per gm of silica	*30*	*38*	*42.5*	*48*	*55*	*108*

Calculate the surface area of silica in terms of square metres per gram by B.E.T. (point B) method.

Assume the area of nitrogen molecule as 16.2 A^{o2}.

Solution:

P/P_0 is plotted against ml adsorbed by 1 gm (Fig. 1.45).

Point B corresponds to the volume which is the volume necessary to yield mono-layer of gas on the surface.

Thus,

V_B = 40 ml = 0.040 litre, A = 16.2Å^2, (given)

R = 0082, N = 6.02×10^{23}, T_0 = 273K.

Substitute these values in the following equation, we get

$$A = \left(\frac{P' V_b}{RT_0}\right) NS \qquad ...(1)$$

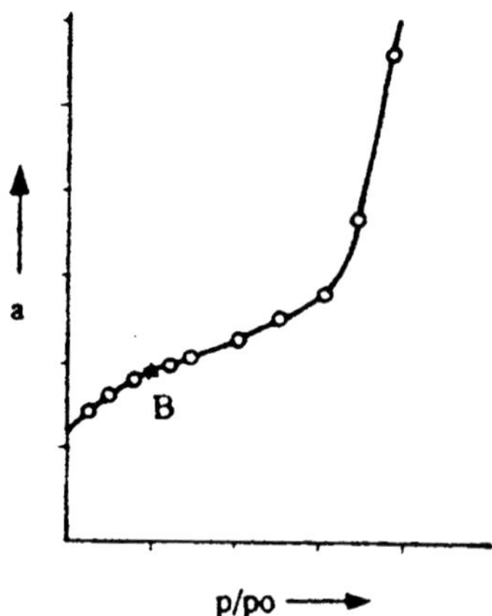

Fig. 1.45

$$\text{Area} = \left(\frac{1 \times 0.040}{0.082 \times 273}\right) 6.02 \times 10^{23} \times 16.2 \ A^{o2}$$

$$\text{Area} = \frac{0.040 \times 6.02 \times 10^{23} \times 16.2}{0.082 \times 273 \times 10^{20}} \text{ metre}^2 \text{ gm}^{-1}$$

$$= 174 \text{ metre}^2 \text{ gm}^{-1}$$

Example 5:

The following data for the adsorption of aqueous acetic acid on charcoal were obtained by Labowitz:

C_0	C_e	m
0.503	0.434	3.96
0.252	0.202	3.94
0.126	0.0899	4.00
0.0628	0.0347	4.12
0.0314	0.0113	4.04
0.0157	0.00333	4.00

In the above table C_0 is the molarity of acetic acid in solution before addition to charcoal. C_e is the molarity of acetic acid remaining in solution at equilibrium and m is the number of grams of charcoal.

In all these cases the volume of the solution in contact with charcoal was 200 ml. Show that these data fit the Freundlich adsorption isotherm.

$$\frac{x}{m} = k\,C_e^{1/n}$$

where x = number of grams of acetic acid adsorbed.

Evaluate the constants k and n.

Solution:

Let x = number of grams of adsorbed CH_3COOH

$$= (C_0 - C_e) \text{ mole litre}^{-1} \times 0.200 \times 60.0 \text{ gm mole}^{-1}$$

$$\frac{x}{m} = k\,C_e^{1/n}$$

$$\log \frac{x}{m} = \log k + \frac{x}{m} \log C_e$$

Plot log (x/m) vs log C_e. Get straight line. Intercept for C_e = 1 (log C_e = 0) is log k. Slope = l/n.

C_0	C_e	x	x/m	log(x.m)	log C_e
0.503	0.434	0.824	0.209	–0.680	–0.362

The other five cases are treated similarly. Intercept for log C_e = 0 is

$$\log k = -0.552 = 9.448 - 10$$

or $$k = 0.28$$

Slope = 0.335 = l/n or n = 2.82.

2

EQUATIONS AND TRANSPORT PHENOMENA IN GASES

COLLISION DIAMETER

When two molecules approach one another due to attractive forces, there is a distance of closest approach beyond which the molecules cannot set closer. The repulsive forces become most predominant than the attractive forces, at and beyond this distance. Thus, it is obvious that there is never a physical contact between the molecules. Nevertheless, a collision is said to occur under this situation and the distance between the centres of the molecules when they are closest is called the collision diameter.

It is denoted by σ (sigma). It is not the actual diameter of the molecules. However the actual diameter of the molecule has no significance in the collisions of the molecules and it is the collusion diameter which is considered in all calculations.

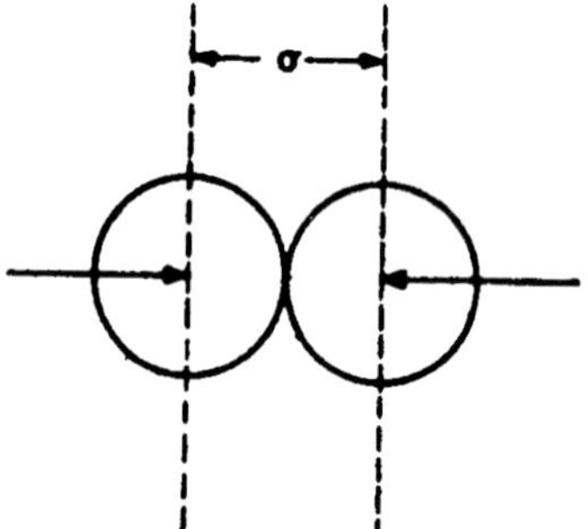

Fig. 2.1 : Collision diameter of molecules.

It is possible to calculate molecular diameters of gases from the knowledge of their viscosities or thermal conductivities. The molecular diameters of some common gases are shown as below:

BAROMETRIC FORMULA

The effect of external fields can be neglected in most considerations of PVT behaviour of gases on a laboratory scale. In particular, the pressure can be considered to be uniform throughout the system. But when large-scale systems are considered, the earth's atmosphere, for example, the effect of gravity must be taken into account. In the case of liquids, gravity, being the cause of hydrostatic pressure, shows itself on a laboratory scale.

The effect of gravity on fluids (both gases and liquids) can be represented by the following model. A vertical column of fluid (Fig. 2.2) of cross-sectional area A experiences a constant gravitational field which exerts a force g per unit mass (neglecting the variation of g with altitude). The hydrostatic pressure at any point in the fluid is determined by the total weight of fluid pressing down from above. More precisely, the pressure P at any altitude z equals the weight of fluid above z divided by the area A.

The relationship between P and z is found by considering an infinitesimal slab of fluid between z and z + dz (shaded in Fig. 2.2). The corresponding pressures are denoted by P and P + dP, respectively. At equilibrium, the net upward force. PA – (P + dP) A, must exactly balance the weight of the slab, d g A dz:

$$PA - (P + dP).\ A = dg.A.dz$$

$$\text{or } dP = -\ d.\ g.\ dz \qquad ...(1)$$

where, d is the density of the fluid when under a pressure P. The minus sign reflects the decrease in pressure with increasing altitude.

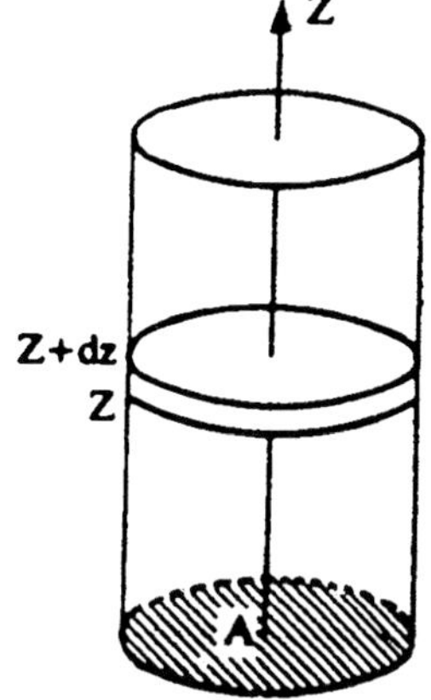

Fig. 2.2 : Column of Fluid in Gravitational Field.

For Liquids : We knows that density of liquid (d) is independent of pressure. Therefore, the pressure at height z is given by

$$\int_{P_0}^{P_z} dP = -\int_0^z d.g.dz$$

$$\text{or} \qquad P_z - P_0 = d.g.dz \qquad ...(1A)$$

where, P_z is the pressure of the column of height z and P_0 is the pressure at the bottom of the column.

For Gases : When equation (1) is applied to gas, the dependence of density on pressure must be taken into account. Assuming that the gas is ideal

$$d = MP/RT \qquad ...(2)$$

From equation (1) and (2), we get

$$dP = -\frac{MP}{RT}. g\, dz$$

$$\frac{dP}{P} = -\frac{MP}{RT} dz \qquad ...(3)$$

Integrating equation (3) between $P = P_0$

when $z = 0$, and $P = P_z$ when $z = z$,

$$\log \frac{P_z}{P_0} = -\frac{Mg}{RT} z$$

or

$$P_z = P_{(0)}\, e^{-Mzg/RT} \qquad ...(4)$$

where, P_0 represents the pressure at sea level. This is the well known barometric distribution law, giving the dependence of pressure on altitude for a hypothetical atmosphere which is in equilibrium at a constant temperature.

Two alternative forms of Eq. 4, are also known which are commonly used. These are as follows :

(a) In terms of density gas. As the density of a gas is directly proportional to the pressure, Eq. (4) may be written as follows :

$$d = d_0\, e^{-Mzg/RT} \qquad ...(4B)$$

(b) In terms of number of particles per unit of volume.

$$\because \quad PV = nRT \therefore PV = \frac{N}{N_A} RT$$

or

$$PN_A = \frac{N}{V} RT = N' RT \quad \text{or } P \propto N'$$

From the above expression, it follows that the pressure of gas is directly proportional to the number of particles per unit volume. Therefore, we can write

$$N' = N_0'\, e^{-Mgz/RT}$$

or

$$N' = N_0'\, e^{-Mgz/KT} \qquad ...(5)$$

Eq. (5) is nothing but an expression of Boltzmann distribution law which describes the distribution of molecules in various energy levels with respect to some reference level.

Discussion

Equations (4) and (5) do not apply to the earth's atmosphere, which is neither at equilibrium, because of winds, nor isothermal, since temperature also drops with altitude. The barometric formulae [Eqs. (3) and (4)] are however fairly accurate in the stratosphere (altitudes 10 to 32 km) which has a constant temperature of about – 55°C. The condition of the atmosphere as a whole is more accurately approximated by constant entropy and density rather than by constant temperature.

MEAN FREE PATH

According to the kinetic theory the molecules of gas are moving with very large velocities at ordinary temperature. Since the molecules exert no force on one another except during collision, they move in straight lines with constant speed between two successive collisions. The path traversed by any molecule between two successive collisions may be called the free path and the average of all such free paths as the mean free path. If λ_1, λ_2, ... λ_n are the successive free paths traversed in total time t, then we must have

$$\lambda_1 + \lambda_2 + \lambda_3 + \ldots \lambda_n + = \overline{C}\ t \qquad \ldots(1)$$

where $\overline{C}$ is the average speed of a molecule. If N is the total number of collisions suffered, *i.e.*, the free path traversed in time t, and λ is the mean free path, then we can write

$$\lambda = \frac{\lambda_1 + \lambda_2 + \lambda_3 \ldots \_ + \lambda_n}{N} = \frac{\overline{C}t}{N} \text{ [Using eq. (1)]} \qquad \ldots(2)$$

It is apparent that if the molecules were point masses, *i.e.*, if the molecules occupied no volume, no collisions would occur and the mean free path would be infinite. But molecules have finite volumes and, therefore, will collide with; each other during their random motion.

The larger the molecules is, then, the more collisions will occur and shorter will be the mean free path. Also, the more molecules present in the gas, the greater will be the number of collisions. Thus, the mean free path will depend on both the molecular size and the density of matter present.

Calculation of the Mean Free Path λ

Let us consider a gas having n molecules per ml. To simplify the calculations we assume that :

(i) Only the molecule under consideration is in motion while the remaining molecules are at rest.

(ii) The sphere of influence of the molecule has a diameter σ. In other words, it means that the molecules can collide with those molecules the centres of which lie at a distance of σ or less Fig. 2.3(a, b).

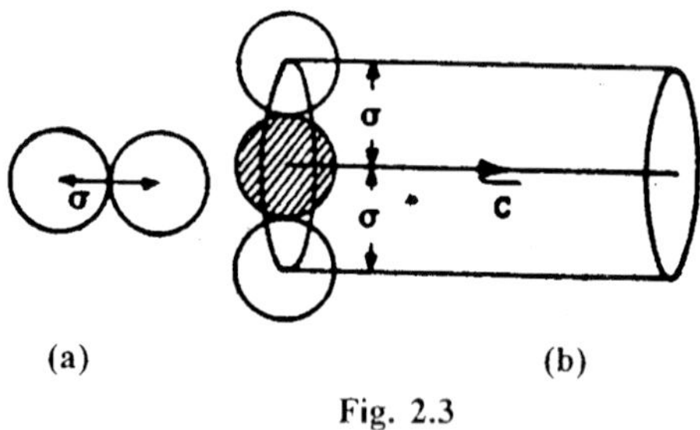

Fig. 2.3

If $\overline{C}$ is the average velocity of a molecule in one second it will collide with all the molecules whose centres lie within a cylinder of radius σ and length $\overline{C}$ [Fig. (2)]. Therefore,

The volume of the cylinder = $\pi\sigma^2\overline{C}$.

Then, the number of collisions made by the moving molecule in one second is given by

$$Z_1 = \pi\sigma^2\overline{C}n$$

As the distance traversed by the molecule in one second is c, therefore, the mean free path is given by

$$\lambda = \frac{\text{Total distance traversed in one second}}{\text{Number of collisions suffered by the molecule in one sec.}}$$

$$= \frac{\overline{C}}{\pi\sigma^2\overline{C}n} = \frac{1}{\pi\sigma^2 n} \qquad ...(3)$$

Equation (3) has been derived by assuming that one molecule under consideration is moving where as all others are at rest which does not represent the actual state of affairs. Therefore, Maxwell assumed that all the molecules are moving with all possible velocities in all possible directions and found the result by applying the distribution law of molecular speed. The exact result obtained by him is

$$\lambda = \frac{1}{\sqrt{2}\pi\sigma^2 n} \qquad ...(4)$$

If m is the mass of the molecule, then

$$\rho = mn$$

where, ρ is the density of gas. Then, the expression for the mean free path in terms of density becomes

$$\lambda = \frac{m}{\sqrt{2}\pi\sigma^2 \rho} \qquad ...(5)$$

From expression (5), it follows that the mean free path ;is inversely proportional to the density of gas. Equations (4) and (5) can be used to determine the mean free path only when the molecular diameter σ is known. A knowledge of viscosity of the gas also enables us to determine λ, the mean free path.

EQUATION OF STATE

Every gas there exists a relation between its pressure, volume and absolute temperature and this relation is known as *equation of state.*

$$PV = RT. \qquad ...(1)$$

Equation (1) is known as equation of state for ideal gases.

As most of the real gases show deviations from ideal behaviour, it means that equation (1) needs modification. The first attempt was made by van der Waal and he deduced the following equation :

$$\left(P + \frac{a}{V^2}\right)(V - b) = RT \qquad ...(2)$$

where a and b are constants. Again, equation (2) is not true for all real gases. Thus, equation (2) needs further modification.

EFFECT OF HEIGHT ON DISTRIBUTION

When In P is plotted against height z (Eq. 4). a straight line is obtained whose slope is –Mg/RT. From the nature of curve, it is evident that pressure decreases as we go above the ground level.

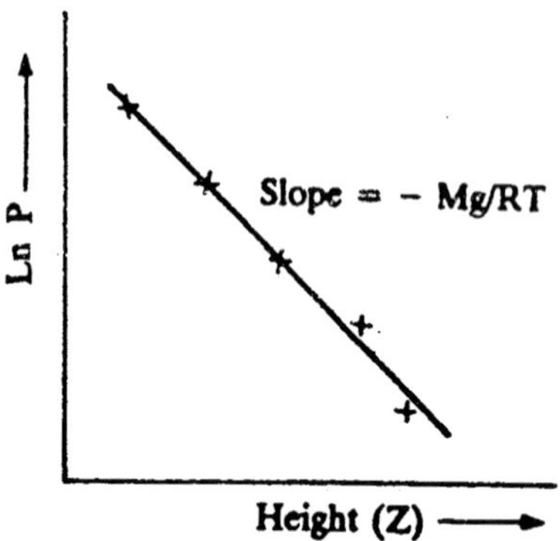

Fig. 2.4 : Plot of ln P against height z.

BAROMETRIC FORMULA BY TAKING INTO ACCOUNT THE VARIATION OF ACCELERATION DUE TO GRAVITY WITH ALTITUDE ABOVE THE EARTH'S SURFACE

We know
$$\frac{dP}{P} = -\frac{Mg}{RT}dz \qquad ...(6)$$

The acceleration due to gravity is given as follows :

$$g = Gm_E/r^2 \qquad ...(7)$$

where G = Gravitational constant,

m_E = mass of the earth,

r = Distance from the centre of the earth.

If r_E refers to the radius of the earth, then the altitude above the earth's surface

$$z = r - r_E \qquad ...(8)$$

On substituting Eqs. (7) and (8) into Eq. (6), we get

$$\frac{dP}{P} = -\frac{MGm_E dz}{RTr^2} = \frac{MGm_E dz}{RT(z+r_E)^2} \qquad ...(9)$$

On integrating the above equation, we get

$$\int_{P_0}^{P_z} \frac{dP}{P} = -\frac{MGm_E}{RT}\int \frac{dz}{(z+r_E)^2}$$

$$\ln\frac{P_z}{P_0} = \frac{MGm_E}{RT}\left(\frac{1}{z+r_E} - \frac{1}{r_E}\right)$$

DERIVATION OF THE BAROMETRIC FORMULA TAKING INTO ACCOUNT THE VARIATION OF TEMPERATURE WITH ALTITUDE

This type of condition can be seen in the lower part of the atmosphere where temperature gets decreased with altitude. Thus, it is possible to write

$$T = T_0 - az$$

where T_0 = Temperature of the surface of the earth,

T = Temperature at the altitude, and

a = A positive constant.

From Eq. (3), we have

$$\frac{dP}{P} = -\frac{MG\,dz}{RT} = -\frac{Mg\,dz}{R(T_0 - az)}.$$

Suppose $T_0 - az = y$ so that $dy = -a\,dz$ and $dz = -dy/a$. Hence on integration, we get

$$\int_{P_0}^{P_z} \frac{dP}{P} = -\frac{Mg}{R} \int \frac{dz}{T_0 - az} = -\frac{Mg}{R} \int_{y_0}^{y} -\frac{dy/a}{y}$$

or
$$\ln\left(\frac{P_z}{P_0}\right) = \frac{Mg}{Ra} \ln\left(\frac{y}{y_0}\right) = \frac{Mg}{Ra} \ln\left(\frac{T_0 - az}{T_0}\right)$$

MOLECULAR CHAOS

From the particle nature of matter, we now come to the conclusion that, "All matter consists of tiny particles called molecules which are capable of independent existence".

The particles of gases and liquids are in continuous motion and travel on the average into the speed of the order of a few miles per hour. So they possess energy of motion which is also named as Kinetic energy. These particles (molecules) are separated by empty spaces called voids. These particles move in straight lines till they collide against other molecules of the gas or with the walls of the vessel containing the gas. As a result of collisions, they get deflected from their original paths and their velocities also keep on varying. Assuming the gas molecule to be rigid spheres the result of their collisions of different types may be as shown in Fig. 2.5.

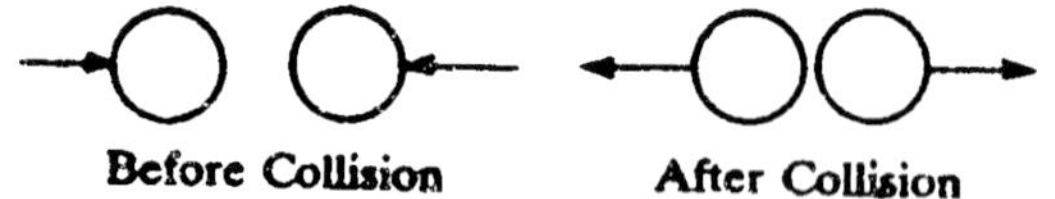

Fig. 2.5 : Head-on Collision

(a) *Head-on Collision :* Here the molecules collide when they approach other with different speeds and from different directions. Both the speeds and the directions of the molecules are changed after collision Fig. 2.5.

(b) *Collision at an Angle :* Here the kinetic energy of the molecules is not lost during collision. Only the total energy is redistributed, Fig. 2.6(b) and 2.6(c).

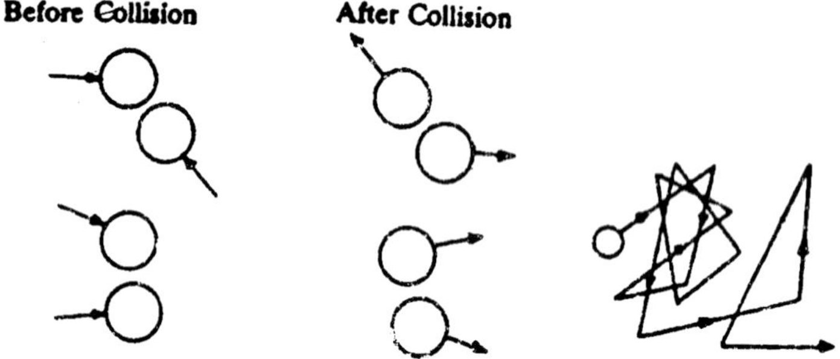

Fig. 2.7 : Zigzag motion of molecules resulting from collisions.

Fig. 2.6(b) & (c) : Collision at an angle.

It may also be stated that kinetic energy of molecules is not lost during collision, but the total energy of molecules is redistributed. For example, if v_1 and v_2 be the velocities of colliding molecules 1 and 2 before collision and v_2 and v_4 be the velocities of these molecules after collision respectively,

$$\frac{1}{2} m_1 v_2^2 + \frac{1}{2} m_2 v_2^2 = \frac{1}{2} m_1 v_3^2 + \frac{1}{2} m_2 v_4^2,$$

where, m_1 and m_2 are the masses of the two molecules.

Thus in a gas we have a zig-zag and hapazard movement of molecules travelling in all directions and with different speeds. This gives rise to molecules disorder which is also called molecular choas.

COLLISION NUMBER AND COLLISION FREQUENCY

According to kinetic theory of gases, the molecules of a gas are constantly moving in different directions with different velocities and hence they keep on colliding with one another. The number of collisions which a molecule makes with other molecules in one second is called collision number. The number of collisions which take place in one second among the molecules present in one centimeter cube (1 cc) of the gas is called collision frequency.

On the basis of kinetic theory of gases, it can be shown that in a gas containing n identical molecules per cc, the number of collisions which a single molecule will under go with other molecules in one second (*i.e.* collision number N_c) is given by

$$Nc = \sqrt{2}\pi\overline{C}\sigma^2 n \qquad ...(1)$$

where, $\overline{C}$ = average velocity of the gas molecules in cm/sec.,

σ = molecular diameter in cm.,

and n = number of molecules/cc of the gas (as already mentioned).

[The expression for N_c can be derived as follows :

Consider a particular molecule A moving in a particular direction as shown in Fig. 2.8. If the average speed of the molecule is $\overline{C}$ cm/sec it will travel a distance of $\overline{C}$ cm in one second. Further, if only A is supposed to move and all other molecules are supposed to be stationary. A will collide in 1 sec with all the molecules whose centres lie within the cylinder of length $\overline{C}$ cm as shown in Fig. 2.8. Volume of the cylinder of length $\overline{C}$ cm and radius equal to the molecular diameter = $\pi\sigma^2\overline{C}$.

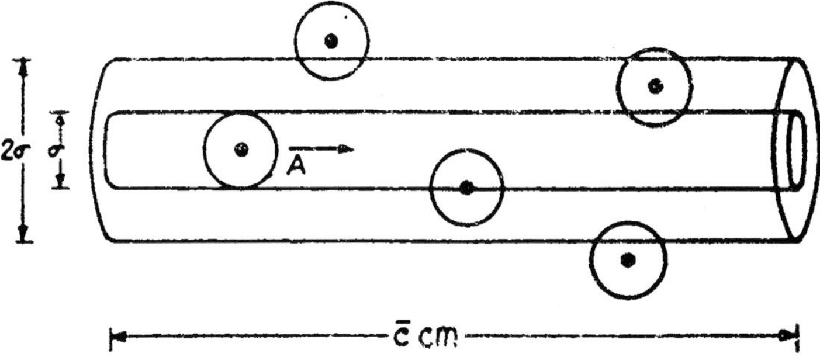

Fig. 2.8 : Movement of molecule A assuming other molecules to be stationary.

If n is the number of molecules/cc, then the number of molecules present in the cylinder $\pi\sigma^2\overline{C}n$. Hence, the number of collisions which the molecule should make in 1 sec with the other molecules in the cylinder would be $\pi\sigma^2\overline{C}n$.

However, in the above derivation it has been supposed that only molecule A moves and other molecules are stationary. This means that the relative speed of A has been taken to be $\overline{C}$ cm/sec.

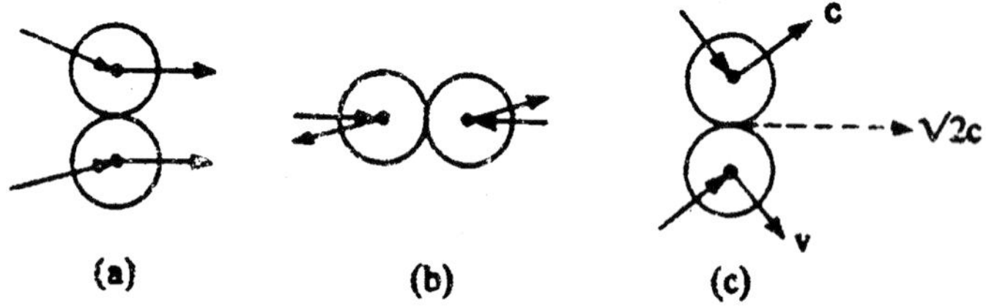

Fig. 2.9 : Types of molecular collisions.

However, as all the molecules are moving with the speed v cm/sec, all types of collisions will occur, ranging from glancing collisions where the relative speed may be zero to the head on collisions where the relative speed may be $2\overline{C}$ as shown in Fig. 2.9

(a) Relative velocity = 0

(b) Relative velocity = $2\overline{C}$.

(c) Relative velocity = $\sqrt{2}\overline{C}$.

On the average, the molecules may move at right angle to each other after collision (Fig. 2.9c). Hence the relative speed will be = $\sqrt{2}\overline{C}$. Thus although the molecule A travels a distance of v cm in 1 sec. It collides with other molecules with a relative speed of $\sqrt{2}\overline{C}$.

Thus taking $\sqrt{2}\overline{C}$ in place of $\overline{C}$, the number of collisions which the molecule makes in 1 sec with other molecules would be $\sqrt{2}\pi\sigma^2\overline{C}n$.

Hence the total number of collisions which all the n molecules present in 1cc of the gas will undergo in one second must be n times the value of N_c *i.e.*, should be equal to

$$(\sqrt{2}\pi\overline{C}\sigma^2 n) \times n = \sqrt{2}\pi\overline{C}\sigma^2 n^2 \qquad ...(2)$$

Further, since each collision involves two molecules, the number of molecular collisions occurring in one cc of the gas in one second will be one half of the above number *i.e.*, will be equal to

$$\frac{1}{2} \times \left(\sqrt{2}\pi\overline{C}\sigma^2 n^2 \right) = \frac{1}{\sqrt{2}} \pi\overline{C}\sigma^2 n^2 \quad ...(3)$$

This is the collision frequency of the gas and is usually represented by Z. Hence

$$Z = \frac{1}{\sqrt{2}} \pi\overline{C}\sigma^2 n^2 \quad ...(4)$$

Thus $Z \propto$ average velocity of the gas molecules ($\overline{C}$)

$\propto$ square of the molecular diameter (σ^2)

$\propto$ Square of the number of molecules/ cc (n^2)

Further from the kinetic theory of gases, it is found that the average velocity is given by

$$\overline{C} = \left(\frac{8}{\pi} \frac{RT}{M} \right)^{1/2} \quad ...(5)$$

where R is gas constant, T is absolute temperature and M is the molecular weight of the gas. Substituting this value in the expression for collision frequency we get

$$Z = \frac{1}{\sqrt{2}} \pi \left(\frac{8}{\pi} \frac{RT}{M} \right)^{1/2} \sigma^2 n^2 \quad ...(6)$$

or $\quad R = 2\sigma^2 n^2 \sqrt{\pi RT/M}$

This is another very common form for the expression for collision frequency.

Effect of Temperature and Pressure

Since with increase of temperature, the average velocity of the gas molecules increases and with increase of pressure, the number of molecules per cc of the gas increases, hence with increase of temperature of with increase of pressure, the collision frequency increases. However, it is interesting to mention that the value of collision frequency is so high that even under ordinary conditions of temperature and pressure, the molecules experience 10^{25} to 10^{28} collision per cc per second.

Collision Number and Mixture of Gases

For a mixture of two gases a and b, the collision frequency is given as follows:

$$Z_{ab} = (\sigma_a + \sigma_b)^2 \left(\frac{\pi RT}{2\mu}\right)^{1/2} n_a n_b \quad ...(7)$$

where, n_a and n_b are the number of a and b per unit volume, σ_a and σ_b are the corresponding diameters and μ its reduced mass which is defined as follows :

$$\mu = \frac{M_a M_b}{M_a + M_b} \quad ...(8)$$

Eq. (7) may be deduced from Eq. (4). Suppose both a and b have the same diameter d and molecular weight M. Then using Eq. (4), we get

$$Z_{ab} = \frac{1}{\sqrt{2}} \pi \overline{C} \sigma^2 (n_a + n_b)^2 \quad ...(9)$$

Subtraction of the number of collisions involving just a molecules or b molecules will give the number of collisions between a and b molecules. Hence

$$Z_{ab} = \frac{1}{\sqrt{2}} \pi \overline{C} \sigma^2 (n_a + n_b)^2 - \frac{1}{\sqrt{2}} \pi \overline{C} \sigma^2 n_a{}^2 - \frac{1}{\sqrt{2}} \pi \overline{C} \sigma^2{}_b{}^2$$

$$= \frac{2}{\sqrt{2}} \pi \overline{C} \sigma^2 n_a n_b = \sqrt{2}\, \pi \overline{C} \sigma^2 n_a n_b \quad ...(10)$$

If one recognises the different diameters and molecular weights of molecules a and b, we may write as follows :

$$\sigma = \frac{\sigma_a + \sigma_b}{2}, \ \mu = \frac{M_a M_b}{M_a + M_b} \text{ and } \overline{C} = \sqrt{\frac{8RT}{2\pi\mu}} \quad ...(11)$$

On substituting Eq. (11) into Eq. (10), we get

$$Z_{ab} = (\sigma_a + \sigma_b)^2 \sqrt{\frac{\pi RT}{2\mu}}\, n_a n_b \quad ...(12)$$

Eq. (12) is same as Eq. (7). Equation (7) is important in the calculation of reaction rates since a chemical reaction between two molecules can occur only when they collide.

LIMITATIONS OF VAN DER WAALS EQUATION

Inspite of the success achieved by van der Waals equation appreciable deviations have been observed at too low temperatures or too high pressures and specially temperatures' near the critical temperature of the gas. The reason is that the values of a and b vary with temperature, van der Waals equation is empirical in nature.

The values of van der Waals constants have been found to be different for different gases and hence depend on .the nature of the gas and are such that when substituted in the equation give the PV – P relationship which agrees with the experimental observations.

The van der Waals equation is only one of many equations of state which have been proposed over years, though it should be pointed out that all subsequent equations have made use of the two fundamental postulates of van der Waals, *i.e.*, molecules have finite size and interact with each other.

CALCULATION OF THE BOYLE'S TEMPERATURE FROM VAN DER WAAL'S EQUATION

By definition, Boyle temperature may be defined as the temperature at which the gas obeys Boyle's law, *i.e.*, the value of PV remains constant for an appreciable range of pressure from zero pressure. Mathematically, *Boyle point* may be expressed as the temperature at which,

$$\lim_{P \to 0}\left[\frac{\partial (PV)}{\partial P}\right] = 0$$

The van der Waals equation for n moles of the gas may be put as follows:

$$P = \frac{nRT}{V - nb} - \frac{n^2 a}{V^2}$$

On multiplying throughout by V, we obtain

$$PV = \frac{nRTV}{V - nb} - \frac{n^2 a}{V} \qquad \text{(Note this step)}$$

$$\therefore \left[\frac{\partial (PV)}{\partial P}\right]_T = \left[\frac{nRT}{V - nb} - \frac{nRTV}{(V - nb)^2} + \frac{n^2 a}{V^2}\right]\left(\frac{\partial V}{\partial P}\right)_T = 0 \quad \text{(at}$$

the Boyle temperature)

As $\left(\frac{\partial V}{\partial P}\right)_T$ is always negative (*i.e.*, it is not equal to zero), it means that the expression in square brackets on the right hand side is equal to zero. Hence

$$\frac{nRT}{V-nb} - \frac{nRTV}{(V-nb)^2} + \frac{n^2a}{V^2} = 0$$

or $$nRTV^2(V-nb) - nRTV^3 + n^2a(V-nb)^2 = 0$$

or $$n^2a(V-nb)^2 = -nRT[V^2(V-nb) - V^3]$$

or $$na(V-nb)^2 = -RT(V^2 - nbV^2 - V^3) = nbRTV^2.$$

$$RT = \frac{a}{b}\left(\frac{V-nb}{V}\right)^2 = \frac{a}{b}\left[1-\frac{nb}{V}\right]^2$$

As at the Boyle point, $T = T_B$

$$\therefore \quad T_B = \frac{a}{Rb}\left[1-\frac{nb}{V}\right]^2$$

As when $P \to 0$, the volume V will be infinitely large so that $nb/V \to 0$.

$$\therefore \quad T_B = \frac{a}{Rb}$$

MODIFIED FORM OF THE VAN DER WAAL'S EQUATION

The equation of van der waal be written as

$$P\left(1+\frac{a}{PV^2}\right).V\left(1-\frac{b}{V}\right) = RT$$

$$PV = RT\left(1+\frac{a}{PV^2}\right)^{-1}\left(1-\frac{b}{V}\right)^{-1}$$

or $$PV = RT\left(1-\frac{a}{PV^2}\right)\left(1-\frac{b}{V}\right)$$

(neglecting higher powers)

$$PV = RT\left(1+\frac{b}{V}-\frac{a}{PV^2}\right) \text{ (neglecting } -ab/PV^3)$$

But $$V = RT/P$$

$$\therefore PV = RT\left(1+\frac{Pb}{RT}-\frac{aP}{R^2T^2}\right) = RT\left[1+p\left(\frac{b}{RT}-\frac{a}{R^2T^2}\right)\right]$$

i.e., $$PV = RT(1+AP)$$

where $$A = \frac{b}{RT} - \frac{a}{R^2T^2} = \frac{b}{RT}\left[1-\frac{a}{bRT}\right]$$

$$= \frac{1}{8}\frac{RT_c}{P_c} \cdot \frac{1}{RT}\left[1 - \frac{27}{64}\frac{R^2T_c^{\,2}}{P_c}\frac{8P_c}{RT_c} \cdot \frac{1}{RT}\right]$$

or $$A = \frac{1}{8}\frac{T_c}{P_c}\frac{1}{T}\left[1 - \frac{27}{8}\frac{T_c}{T}\right] \quad ...(1)$$

In the above derivation, we have used the van der Waal's constants a and b in terms of critical constants.

$$a = \frac{27}{64}\frac{R^2T^2_c}{P_c} \text{ and } b = \frac{1}{8}\frac{RT_c}{P_c} \quad ...(2)$$

THE DIETERICI EQUATION

In 1899 Dieterici proposed an empirical equation in the form

$$P = \frac{RT}{V - b} \cdot e^{-a/RTV}$$

However, the theoretical basis of the above equation was later developed by Jeans. In this derivation the volume correction was evidently the same as that in van der Waal's equation whereas for the correction of pressure the exponential factor $e^{-a/RTV}$ was introduced. In order to explain this pressure correction, Jeans gave the following explanation :

" *A molecule in coming to the wall from the interior has to overcome the forces of attraction and thereby attains a potential energy higher than that possessed by a molecule in the bulk*"

In consequence, the density of molecules near the wall will be less than that in the interior. If n and n_0 represent of molecules per c.c. at the walls and in the interior, then, according to the distribution law,

$$n/n_0 = e^{-A/RTV} \quad ...(1)$$

where A represents the excess energy per mole at the walls.

If d and d_0 represent the densities of the gas at the walls and in the interior, then

$$n/n_0 = d/d_0 = P/P_0 \quad ...(2)$$

where P and P_0 denote the pressure of the gas at the walls and in the interior. Combining Eqns. (1) and (2), we get

$$P/P_0 = e^{-A/RTV}$$

or $$P0 = Pe^{A/RT}$$

Remembering that P_0 is the ideal pressure, the equation of state is

$$Pe^{A/RT}(V - b) = RT$$

or

$$P = \frac{RT}{V - b}.e^{-A/RTV}$$

Jeans realised that A also depends upon the volume. Therefore, the above equation modifies to

$$P = \frac{RT}{V - b}.e^{-a/RTV} \quad ...(3)$$

Equation (3) is known as Dieterici Equation. On expanding, equation (3) may be put as

$$P = \frac{RT}{V - b}\left[1 - \frac{a}{RTV} + \frac{1}{2}\left(\frac{a}{RTV}\right)^2 - ......\right]$$

$$= \frac{RT}{V - b} - \frac{a}{V(V - b)} \text{ (neglecting higher powers)} \quad ...(4)$$

When pressure is very low, the volume becomes very large, *i.e.*, $V - b \approx V$, Therefore, equation (A) becomes as

$$P = \frac{RT}{V - b} - \frac{a}{V^2} \quad ...(5)$$

Equation (5) is the same as that of van der Waal's equation. Thus, at low pressure the *Dieterici equation* becomes the same as that of the van der Waal's equation. The extent of validity of the *Dieterici equation* may be observed by comparing the values of P_c/b. the critical coefficient and the Boyle's temperature with experimental results. Let us calculate these values one by one.

(a) *Vc/b Ratio* : Putting a/RT = C in equation (3), we get

$$P = \frac{RT}{V - b}e^{-C/V}$$

Differentiating this equation with respect to volume V at constant temperature, we get

$$\left(\frac{\partial P}{\partial V}\right)_T = -\frac{RT}{(V - b)^2}e^{-C/V} + \frac{RT}{V - b}.\frac{C}{V^2}e^{-C/V} = -\frac{P}{V - b} + P,\frac{C}{P^2}$$

The above equation on differentiating with respect to volume V at constant temperature T gives rise to

$$\left(\frac{\partial^2 P}{\partial V^2}\right)_T = -\frac{1}{(V-b)}\cdot\left(\frac{\partial P}{\partial V}\right)_T + \frac{p}{(V-b)^2}$$

$$+\frac{C}{V^2}\left(\frac{\partial P}{\partial V}\right) - \frac{2PC}{V^3} = \left(\frac{\partial P}{\partial V}\right)_T\left[\frac{C}{V^2} - \frac{1}{V-b}\right]$$

$$+ P\left[\frac{1}{V-b^2} - \frac{2C}{V^3}\right]$$

At the critical point, both the first and the second differential coefficients would be zero. Hence,

when $\left(\frac{\partial P}{\partial V}\right)_T = 0, \frac{P_c}{V_c - b} = \frac{P_c C}{V_c^2}$

or $\frac{C}{V_c^2} = \frac{1}{V_c - b}$ ...(6)

and when

$\left(\frac{\partial^2 P}{\partial V^2}\right)_T = 0, \frac{1}{(V_c - b)^2} = \frac{2C}{V_c^3}$ or $\frac{2C}{V_c^3} = \frac{1}{(V_c - b)^2}$

$\therefore$ $V_c/2 = V_c - b$ or $V_c = 2b$,

i.e, $V_c/b = 2$, or $V_c = 2b$ ...(7)

From eq. (7), the value of V_c is 2b. However, the experimental value is also 2b. This shows that *Dieterici equation* is satisfactory.

(b) Critical coefficient, $\left(\frac{RT_c}{V_c P_c}\right)$

At the critical temperature T_c, $C = a/RT_c$ ...(8)

Now from Eq. (6) above,

$$C = \frac{V_c^2}{(V_c - b)} = \frac{4b^2}{2b - b} = 4b$$

From Eq. (8), we get

$\therefore$ $\frac{a}{RT_c} = 4b$ or $T_c = \frac{a}{4bR}$ ...(9)

The critical pressure,

$$P_c = \frac{RT_c}{V_c - b}\cdot e^{-a/RT_c V_c}$$

$$= \frac{a}{4b} \frac{1}{2b-b} . e^{-4b/2b} = \frac{a}{4b^2} e^{-2} \quad ...(10)$$

So the critical coefficient,

$$\frac{RT_c}{P_c V_c} = \frac{a}{4b} . \frac{1}{2b} . \frac{4b^2}{a} e^2 = \frac{1}{2} e^2 = 3.695$$

Again, the experimental value of the critical coefficient is 3.6. This shows that the equation of Dieterici is satisfactory.

(c) *Boyle Temperature T_B :* Multiplying Eqn. (3) by V, the Dieterici equation becomes as

$$PV = \frac{RTV}{V-b} . e^{-a/RTV}$$

Then
$$\left[\frac{\partial(PV)}{\partial P}\right]_T = \left\{\left(\frac{RT}{V-b} - \frac{RTV}{(V-b)^2}\right). e^{-a.RTV} + \frac{RTV}{V-b} . \frac{e}{RTV^2} e^{-a.RTV}\right\}\left(\frac{\partial V}{\partial P}\right)_T$$

We know, $\partial V/\partial P \neq 0$, and in the minimum of *Amagat's curves,*

$$\left[\frac{\partial(PV)}{\partial P}\right]_T = 0$$

$$\therefore \quad \frac{RT}{V-b} - \frac{RTV}{(V-b)^2} + \frac{RTV}{V-b} . \frac{a}{RTV^2} = 0$$

or
$$\frac{RTV}{V-b}\left[\frac{1}{V} - \frac{1}{v-b} + \frac{a}{RTV^2}\right] = 0$$

or
$$\frac{a}{RTV^2} = \frac{1}{V-b} - \frac{1}{V} = \frac{b}{V(V-b)}$$

or
$$RT = \frac{a(V-b)}{bV}$$

At the Boyle point, T_B, the minimum lies on the PV axis; *i.e.*, P $\rightarrow$ 0, $[\partial(PT)/\partial P] = 0$, and V is very large so that $V - b \approx V$

$$\therefore \quad RT_B = \frac{a}{b} . \frac{V-b}{V} \approx \frac{a}{b}$$

But from Eq. (9), $RT_c = a/4b$.

Hence $T_B/TC = 4.0$

However, the experimental values of T_B/TC is 2.98. This shows that the equation of Dieterici is not wholly satisfactory and its limitations are the same as that of the van der Waal's equation.

For sake of convenience we are now making a comparison of the deduced values from the Dieterici equation with the experimentally observed and those obtained from van der Waal:

Table 2.1

	van der Waal's	*Dieterici*	*Experimental (average)*
Vc/b	3.0	2.0	2.0
RTc/PcVc	2.65	3.696	3.6
TB/TC	3.375	4.0	2.98

Reduced equation of State (Dieterici). By putting,

$$\pi = P/P_c,\ \phi = V/V_c,\ \theta = T/T_c.$$

The above values in Eq. (8), we get

$$\pi P_c = \frac{R\theta T_c}{\phi V_c - b}\, e^{-a/R\theta V_c \phi V_c}$$

Substituting the critical values from Eqs. (7), (9) and (10), we get

$$\pi e^{-2} = \frac{\theta}{2\phi - 1}\, e^{-(2/\theta\phi)}$$

or $$\pi(2\phi - 1) = \theta\ e^{2-(2/\theta\phi)}$$

The above equation is the required reduced equation of state.

THE BERTHELOT EQUATION

In 1899 Berthelot proposed an empirical equation which is as follows:

$$\left(P + \frac{a}{TV^2}\right)(V - b) = RT \qquad ...(1)$$

The Berthelot equation is the same as that of the van der Waal's except that the pressure correction is a/TV^2 instead of a/V^2. However, Berthelot further modified his equation in the light of same experimental results. According to him, the value of the b should be equal to the volume occupied by the liquid super-cooled at absolute zero of temperature, *i.e.*, $V_0 = b$ where V_0 is the volume at absolute zero. He determined the value of V_0, by extrapolating the Cailletet and Mathias curves to absolute zero. Berthelot obtained that the value of V_c/V_0 is approximately four, *i.e.*,

$$V_c/V_0 = 4$$

But

$$V_0 = b$$

$$\therefore \quad V_c/b = 4$$

$$\text{or} \quad b = 1/4 \ V_c \qquad \text{...(2)}$$

For the other two constants a and R of the equation, he accepted the experimental values which were

$$a = \frac{16}{3} P_c V_c^2 T_c$$

and

$$R = \frac{32}{9} \frac{P_c V_c}{T}$$

Since $b = 1/4\ V_c$, we have $T_c^2 = a/6bR$ ...(3)

Equation (1) may be transformed to ...(4)

$$PV = RT + Pb - \frac{a}{TV} + \frac{ab}{TV^2} = RT + Pb - \frac{a}{TV}$$

$$PV = RT + Pb - \frac{aP}{RT^2} \qquad \left[\because V = \frac{R}{P}\right]$$

$$PV = RT\left[1 + \frac{Pb}{RT} - \frac{aP}{R^2T^3}\right] = RT\left[1 + \frac{P}{T}\left(\frac{b}{R} - \frac{a}{R^2T^2}\right)\right]$$

Substituting a, b and R by the critical constant values given in Eqs. (2) and (3), we get

$$PV = RT\left[1 + \frac{P}{T}\left(\frac{V_c}{4} \cdot \frac{9T_c}{32P_cV_c} - \frac{16}{3}P_cT_cV_c^2 \ \frac{81T_c^2}{(32P_cV_c)^2} \cdot \frac{1}{T^2}\right)\right]$$

$$= RT\left[1 + \frac{9}{128}\frac{PT_c}{TP_c}\left(1 - \frac{6T_c^2}{T^2}\right)\right] \qquad \text{...(5)}$$

Equation (5) is very useful for the determination of densities, heat capacities and in the evaluation of free energy changes, etc.

On differentiating Eq. (3) with respect to P, we get

$$\frac{\partial(PT)}{\partial P} = RT \cdot \frac{9}{128} \cdot \frac{T_c}{TP_c}\left(1 - \frac{6T_c^2}{T^2}\right) \qquad \text{...(6)}$$

At the Boyle point, $\frac{\partial(PV)}{\partial P} = 0$. hence equation (6) becomes as,

$$\frac{T_c^2}{T_B} = \frac{1}{6}$$

or
$$\frac{T_B}{T_c} = \sqrt{(6)} = 2.45$$

The value 2.45 is less than the experimental value.

Reduced Equation. The reduced form of the Berthelot's equation may be obtained from Eq. (5) which is as follows:

$$PV = RT\left[1 + \frac{9}{128}\frac{PT_c}{TP_c}\left(1 - \frac{6T_c^2}{T^2}\right)\right]$$

$$\pi\phi\, P_cV_c = R\,\theta\, T_c\left[1 + \frac{9}{128}\cdot\frac{\pi}{\theta}\left(1 - \frac{6}{\theta^2}\right)\right]$$

or
$$\pi\phi = \theta\,\frac{RT_c}{P_cV_c}\left[1 + \frac{9}{128}\cdot\frac{\pi}{\theta}\left(1 - \frac{6}{\theta^2}\right)\right]$$

or
$$\pi\phi = \left[\frac{32\theta}{9} + \frac{\pi}{4}\left(1 - \frac{6}{\theta^2}\right)\right] \quad ..(7)$$

Equation (7) is the reduced form of Berthelot's equation.

THE EQUATION OF KAMMERLING ONES

In 1913, Kammerling and Ones proposed a more satisfactory expression for the equation of state which may be written as

$$PV = A + \frac{B}{V} + \frac{C}{V^2} + \frac{D}{V^4} + \frac{E}{V^6} + \ldots\ldots \quad ...(1)$$

were A, B, C, D, etc. are known as first, second, third, fourth etc. virial co-efficients. These co-efficients remain constant at a given temperature. Equation (1) may also be written as

$$PV = 1 + \frac{B'}{V} + \frac{C'}{V^2} + \frac{D'}{V^4} + \ldots\ldots \quad ...(2)$$

On the other hand, Holborn and others used a virial equation in which the product PV is expressed in a power series of the pressure as,

$$PV = A_1 + B_1P + C_1P^2 + D_1P^3 + \ldots\ldots \quad ...(3)$$

When we compare Eq. (2) and Eq. (3), we observe the following important points :

(i) The value of A_1 is RT.

(ii) The value of second virial co-efficient is different in the two equations and becomes of major importance in these equations.

(iii) The values of higher virial co-efficients are again different in the two equations and become significant only at high pressures.

When different power terms of equations (2) and (3) are compared, we get

$$A_1 = RT,\ B_1P = RT\ B'/p,\ C_1P^2 = C'/V^2.\ RT \qquad ...(4)$$

On comparing Eq. (4) with (1), we get that A = A1 = RT. In this equation, the second virial co-efficient is important whereas other virial coefficients of higher powers of 1/V become significant only at high pressures.

Suppose we write the van der Waals equation as

$$P = \frac{RT}{V-b} - \frac{a}{V^2} = \frac{RT}{V}\left(1 - \frac{b}{V}\right)^{-1} - \frac{a}{V^2} \qquad ...(4A)$$

or
$$PV = RT\left[1 + \left(b - \frac{a}{RT}\cdot\frac{1}{V} + \frac{1}{2}\left(\frac{b}{V}\right)^2 + \ldots\ldots\right]$$

$$\approx RT\left[1 + \left(b - \frac{a}{RT}\right)\frac{1}{V}\right] \qquad ...(5)$$

On comparing Eq. (5) with Eq. (1) we get the second virial co-efficient.

$$B = bRT_B - a$$

At the Boyle temperature, B = 0. *i.e.*,

$$bRT_B - a = 0$$

or
$$T_B = a/(bR)$$

Again the Berthelot equation,

$$PV = RT + \frac{9}{128}\frac{RT_c}{P_c}\left(1 - \frac{6T_c^2}{T^2}\right)P$$

Hence the virial coefficient,

$$B = \frac{9}{128}\cdot\frac{RT_c}{P_c}\left(1 - \frac{6T_c^2}{T^2}\right)$$

THE BEATTIE-BRIDGEMAN EQUATION OF STATE

The Beattie-Bridgeman's equation is

$$P = \frac{nRT(1-\epsilon)}{V^2}(V + nP) - \frac{n^2A}{V^2} \quad ...(1)$$

where $B = B_0\left(1 - \frac{nb}{V}\right) A = A_0\left(1 - \frac{na}{V}\right)$ and $\epsilon = \frac{nC}{VT^3}$

The equation of state (1) can be written in the virial form

$$\frac{PV}{n} = RT + \frac{n\beta}{V} + \frac{n^2\gamma}{V^2} + \frac{n^2\delta}{V^3} \quad ...(2)$$

where $\theta = RTB_0 - A_0 - RC/T^2$,

$$\gamma = - RTB_0b + A_0a - \frac{RB_0C}{T} \text{ and } \delta = \frac{RB_0bc}{T^2}$$

Equation (2) is expanded in terms of itself,

$$\frac{V}{n} = \frac{RT}{P} + \frac{\beta}{RT} + \left[\frac{\gamma}{(RT)^2} - \frac{\beta}{(RT)^3}\right]$$

$$P + \left[\frac{\delta}{(RT)^3} - \frac{3\beta\gamma}{(RT)^4} + \frac{2\beta^3}{(RT)^5}\right] P^2 \quad ...(3)$$

Equation (3) gives PV/n in terms of the order of P^3. A less exact form would be obtained by replacing n/V by P/Rt in each term on the right side of equation (2).

$$\frac{V}{n} = \frac{RT}{P} + \frac{\beta}{RT} + \frac{\gamma}{(RT)^2} P + \frac{\gamma}{(RT)^2} P^2 \quad ...(4)$$

Equation (2) would probably give a better representation of the density of gases than equation (3) provided we redetermined the values of parameters A_0, a, B_0, b and c for this form of equation. To do this we would need to resmooth all of the compressibility data to give densities at each temperature for evenly spaced set of values of P/RT. Thus, in place of equation (1), we would write

$$\frac{V}{n} = \left(\frac{RT}{P} + B\right)(1-\epsilon) - \frac{A}{RT} \quad ...(5)$$

where $A = A_0\left(1 - \frac{aP}{RT}\right) B = \left(1 - \frac{bP}{RP}\right)$

and $$\in = \frac{C}{T^3}\frac{P}{RT}$$

Thus, we have two sets of the equation of state parameters : one for equation (1) or (2) and one for equation (4) or (5). Unfortunately, the values of parameters for equation (1) have not yet been determined and we are forced to use those determined for equation (2). Sufficient accuracy is obtained in many thermodynamic calculations if we drop the last two terms of equation (4) and write

THE CLAUSIUS EQUATION

In the van der Waal's 'a' was assumed to be a constant. However, 'a' varies with temperature. In order to allow for the variation of 'a' with temperature, Clausius (1800) proposed the following equation which involves the assumption that the molecular attraction factor is inversely proportional to the temperature.

$$\left[p + \frac{a}{T(V+c)^2}\right](V-b) = RT \qquad ...(1)$$

The Clausius equation four constants a, b, c and R. The quantity 'c' may be put equal to kb where k is universal constant.

As we have done earlier, the Boyle's temperature should be given by

$$T_B{}^2 = \frac{a}{Rb} \text{ and } T_B{}^2 = 27\frac{(1+k)\,T_c{}^2}{8}$$

If T_B and T_C are assumed to have the experimental value of 2.5, it follows that k = 0.85

It can also be proved that $RT_c/P_cV_0 = 3.15$

This value is a slight improvement of the result derived from the van der Waal's equation on the whole.

" Clausius equation does not represent a great advance and since it suffers from the disadvantage of involving four constants, it has not come into the general use.

Let us consider various molecules, each of mass m and root mean square velocity c. Suppose the positional coordinates of a given molecule be x, y and z. Let X, Y and Z be the three components of the net external forces acting on the molecule. Then, one can write

$$X = m\frac{d^2x}{dt^2},\ Y = m\frac{d^2y}{dt^2}$$

and $$Z = m\frac{d^2z}{dt^2}$$

On multiplying the above equations by x, y and z respectively, we get

$$xX = mx\frac{d^2x}{dt^2},\ Yy = my\frac{d^2y}{dt^2}$$

and $$zZ = mz\frac{d^2z}{dt^2} \qquad ...(1)$$

We know $$\frac{d}{dt}\left(x\frac{dx}{dt}\right) = x\frac{d^2x}{dt^2} + \left(\frac{dx}{dt}\right)^2$$

or $$x\frac{d^2x}{dt^2} = \frac{d}{dt}\left(x\frac{dx}{dt}\right) - \left(\frac{dx}{dt}\right)^2 = \frac{1}{2}\frac{d}{dt}\left(\frac{dx^2}{dt}\right) - \left(\frac{dx}{dt}\right)^2 \qquad ...(2)$$

Similarly, we can prove that

$$y\frac{d^2y}{dt^2} = \frac{d}{dt}\left(y\frac{dy}{dt}\right) - \left(\frac{dy}{dt}\right)^2 = \frac{1}{2}\frac{d}{dt}\left(\frac{dy^2}{dt}\right) - \left(\frac{dy}{dt}\right)^2 \qquad ...(3)$$

and $$z\frac{d^2z}{dt^2} = \frac{d}{dt}\left(z\frac{dz}{dt}\right) - \left(\frac{dz}{dt}\right)^2 = \frac{1}{2}\frac{d}{dt}\left(\frac{dz^2}{dt}\right) - \left(\frac{dz}{dt}\right)^2 \qquad ...(4)$$

Substituting Eqs. (2), (3) and (4) in Eq. (1) and adding

$$Xx + Yy + Zz = \frac{m}{2}\frac{d}{dt}\left\{\frac{d}{dt}\left(x^2 + y^2 + zh^2\right)\right\}$$

$$- m\left\{\left(\frac{\partial x}{dt}\right)^2 + \left(\frac{\partial y}{dt}\right)^2 + \left(\frac{\partial z}{dt}\right)^2\right\}$$

$$= \frac{m}{2}\frac{d}{dt}\left\{\frac{d}{dt}\left\{\frac{d}{dt}\ x^2 + y^2 + z^3\right) - mc^2 \qquad ..(5)$$

where $$C^2 = \left(\frac{\partial x}{dt}\right)^2 + \left(\frac{\partial y}{dt}\right)^2 + \left(\frac{\partial z}{dt}\right)^2$$

If we now consider all the molecules, the sum $x^2 + y^2 + z^2$ should be independent of time t, *i.e.*, its derivative would be zero. Thus, this expression vanishes in equation (5). Therefore, this equation becomes as

$$Xx + Yy + Zz = mc^2 \qquad \text{....(6)}$$

Taking all the molecules, we have then

$$\Sigma (Xx + Yy + Zz) = - \Sigma mc^2$$

or $$-\frac{1}{2} \Sigma (Xx + Yy + Zz) = \frac{1}{2} \Sigma mc^2 = \frac{1}{2} N mc^2 \qquad \text{...(7)}$$

where, N is the total number of molecules. The term on the left-hand side of equation (7) was named by Clausius as virial of the system. As the term on the right-hand side of Eq. (7) denotes the total kinetic energy of translation of the molecules of the gas, it means that the total kinetic energy of the gas is its virial. Eq. (7) is known as the virial theorem of Clausius.

Derivation of van der Waal's Equation. When we consider the real gases, there will be forces for impact on the molecule due to wall collisions and intermolecular forces of attraction. Thus, the virial form of Eq. (7) may be written as

$$\frac{1}{2} N mc^2 = -\frac{1}{2} \Sigma (Xx + Yy + Zz) \text{ wall} - \frac{1}{2} \Sigma (Xx + Yy + Zz) \text{ int}$$

The last term on the right side determines the virial for the intermolecular forces present.

But $$-\frac{1}{2} \Sigma (Xx + Yy + Zz) = 3/2 \text{ PV}$$

$$\therefore \quad \frac{1}{2} N mc^2 = \frac{3}{2} PV - \frac{1}{2} \Sigma (Xx + Yy + Zz) \text{ int}$$

But $$\frac{1}{2} mc^2 = \frac{3}{2} kT = 3PV - \Sigma (Xx + Yy + Zz) \text{ int}$$

or $$PV = N kT + \frac{1}{3} \Sigma (Xx + Yy + Zz) \text{ int} \qquad \text{...(8)}$$

If ϕ denotes the interaction energy between a given pair of molecules at a distance r joining their centres, then

$$\Sigma (Xx + Yy + Zz) \text{ int} = - r\frac{d\phi}{dr}$$

Substituting this value in Eq. (8), we have

$$PV = N kT = -\frac{1}{3}\sum r\frac{d\phi}{dr}. \qquad \text{...(9)}$$

In order to carry out the summation of the last term in eq. (9), consider n, the number of molecules per cc. in the bulk, *i.e.*, n = N/V). Thus, according to Boltzmann, the number of molecules n, at a distance r from a given molecule in $n_r = n\ e^{\phi/kT}$. k where k is the Boltzmann's constant. If we assume radial distribution, the number of molecules present in a shell of thickens dr at a distance r from the given molecule is given by $n_r . 4\pi r^2 dr$. For every pair of molecule, the interaction is $-r d\phi/dr$ and hence the total interaction of all molecules of the system with given molecule is

$$\int_0^\infty n_r\ 4\pi r^2 dr \left(-r\frac{d\phi}{dr}\right)$$

$$= -\int_0^\infty n.e^{-\phi/kT}\ 4\pi r^3 d\phi = -\frac{4\pi N}{V}\int_0^\infty e^{-\phi/kT}\ r^3 d\phi.$$

If we consider al the N molecules of the system, the total interaction would be

$$-\sum r\frac{d\phi}{dr} = -\frac{2\pi N^2}{V}\int_0^\infty e^{-\phi/kT}\ r^3 d\phi.$$

On integrating the above equation by parts, we get

$$-\sum r\frac{d\phi}{dr} = -\frac{2\pi N^2}{V}\left(-kT\left\{r^3 e^{-\phi/kT}\right\}_0^\infty + 3\ kT\int_0^\infty e^{-\phi/kT}\ r^2 dr\right)$$

$$= \frac{2\pi N^2 kT}{V}\left(\left\{r^2\right\}_0^\infty - 3\int_0^\infty e^{-\phi/kT}\ r^2 dr\right)$$

where $\underset{r\to\infty}{\mathrm{Lt}}\ \phi = 0$

or $$-\sum r\frac{d\phi}{dr} = \frac{2\pi N^2 kT}{V}\left(\int_0^\infty r^3\ dr - 3\int_0^\infty e^{\phi/kT}\ r^2 dr\right)$$

$$= \frac{6\pi N^2 kT}{V}\int_0^\infty\left(1 - e^{-\phi/kT}\right) r^2 dr.$$

On substituting abvoe expression for real gases in (9).

$$PV = NKT + \frac{2\pi N^2 kT}{V}\int_0^\infty\left(1 - e^{-\phi/kT}\right) r^2 dr \qquad ...(10)$$

If we are considering 1 gm-mole of gas, then

$N = N_0$ and $N_0 k = R$;

Hence equation (10) becomes as

$$PV = RT + \frac{2\pi N_0^2 kT}{V}\int_0^\infty\left(1 - e^{-\phi/kT}\right) r^2 dr \qquad ...(11)$$

Equation (11) is the rigorous equation for an equation of state for real gases, van der Waal's made the following assumptions :

(i) The molecules are considered to be rigid spheres of diameter σ.

(ii) The attractive forces between the molecules are considered to be weak and their value decreases with increases in distance.

(iii) When molecules are very close, the molecules experience an intense repulsive force. This repulsive force begins from a distance $r = \sigma$ and $\phi \to \infty$ as r becomes less than σ

Under the above mentioned conditions,

$$\int_0^{\infty}\left(1 - e^{-\phi/kT}\right) r^2 dr = \int_0^{\sigma}\left(1 - e^{-\phi/kT}\right) r^2 dr + \int_{\sigma}^{\infty}\left(1 - e^{-\phi/kT}\right) r^2 dr$$

When $r < \sigma$. $\phi \to \infty$,

$$\therefore \quad \int_0^{\infty}\left(1 - e^{-\phi/kT}\right) r^2 dr = \int_{\sigma}^{\infty} r^2 dr + \int_0^{\sigma}\left(1 - e^{-\phi/kT}\right) r^2 dr = \frac{1}{3}\sigma^2 + \int_{\sigma}^{\infty} \frac{\phi}{kT} r^2 dr$$

Substituting the above equation in Eq. (11), we get

$$PV = RT + \frac{2\pi N_0^2 kT}{V}\left[\frac{\sigma^3}{3}\frac{\phi}{kT} r^2 \, dr\right]$$

$$= RT + \frac{RT}{V}\left[\frac{2\pi N_0 \sigma^3}{3} + 2\pi N_0^2 \int_{\sigma}^{\infty} \frac{\phi}{kT} r^2 \, dr\right]$$

$$PV = RT + \frac{RT}{V}\left(b - \frac{a}{RT}\right) \qquad ...(12)$$

where $b = \frac{2}{3} + \pi N_0 \sigma^2$ and $a = 2\pi N_0^2 \int_{\sigma}^{\infty} \phi \, r^2 \, dr$

Equation (12) is the van der Waal's equation which is derived from the virial theorem. This equation has been corrected upto second term.

Alternative Derivation of van der Waal's Equation by Using Virial Theorem : A rigorous deduction of the equation of state is possible from a consideration of the virial theorem of Clausius. An alternative analytical representation for real gas behaviour is provided by the virial equation of state. The dependence of P on compressibility factor isotherms suggests a power-series of the form.

$$z, (P, T) = \frac{PV}{RT} = 1 + \frac{b(T)}{RT} P + \frac{c(T)}{RT} P^2 + ... \qquad ...(1)$$

The representation of the equation of state exhibits explicitly approach to ideality in the limit $P \to 0$.

Multiplying throughout by RT in equation (1), we have

$$PV = RT + b(T)\,P + c(T)\,p^2 + \ldots \qquad \text{....(2)}$$

Since molar volume V decreases monotonically as P increases, an alternative form for the above expression is

$$PV = RT\left(1 + \frac{B(T)}{V} + \frac{C(T)}{V^2} + \ldots\right) \qquad \text{...(3)}$$

For the last form of the equation of state, ideality is approached in the limit $V \to \infty$. Equation (2) or (3) is known as the virial equation of state (Kammerling-Ones, (1901). The function b(T), c(T), or B(T), C(T), are known respectively, as the second virial co-efficient, third virial co-efficient, and so on. (The first virial co-efficient is simply RT or 1, respectively).

It is of interest to relate the van der Waal's equation to the virial expansion (eq 3) for the equation of state. Write

$$P = \frac{RT}{V - b} - \frac{a}{V^2} \qquad \text{...(4)}$$

Multiplying equation (4), by V, we get

$$PV = \frac{RTV}{V - b} - \frac{a}{V} \qquad \text{...(5)}$$

Use the expression

$$(1 - x)^{-1} = 1 + x + x^2 + \ldots \qquad (x < 1)$$

in the form

$$\frac{V}{V - b} = \left(1 - \frac{b}{V}\right)^{-1} = 1 + \frac{b}{V} + \frac{b^2}{V^2} + \ldots \qquad \text{...(6)}$$

The expansion is valid provided $b/V < 1$, and converges rapidly when $b/V << 1$. The latter condition, and sometime seven the former, breaks down in the case of dense gases or liquids. Substituting eq. (6) into (5), we obtain van der Waal's equation in virial form

$$PV = RT\left[1 + \frac{b - \left(\frac{a}{RT}\right)}{V} + \frac{b^2}{V^2} + \frac{b^2}{V^3} \ldots +\right] \qquad \text{...(7)}$$

The second virial coefficient is given by

$$B(T) = b(T) = b - \frac{a}{RT} \qquad ...(8)$$

where as higher viribal co-efficients ($n \geq 3$) are simply b^{n-1}, for example

$$c(T) = b^2 \qquad ...(9)$$

From the alternative form of the virial expansion [equation (2)] expressed as series in P, the third virial co-efficient is,

$$c(T) = \frac{2ab}{R^2T^2} - \frac{a^2}{R^3T^3}$$

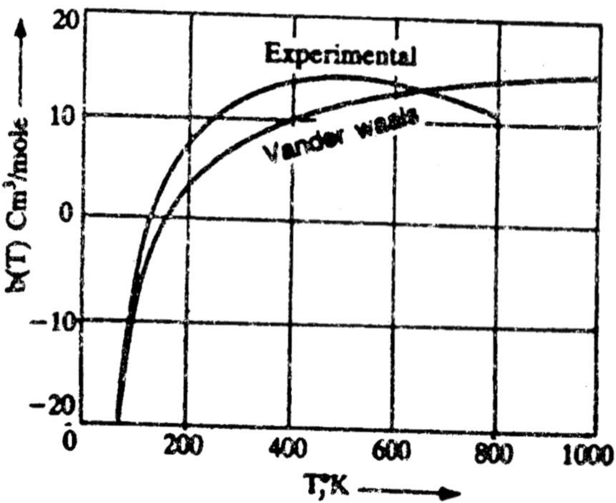

Fig. 2.10 : Second Virial Coefficient for Neon.

In Fig. (2.10), second virial co-efficient for neon is compared with (b) (T) calculated from equation (9). The van der Waals equation is evidently able to reproduce semiquantitatively the temperature dependence of the second virial co-efficient. It shows that b(T) is negative and steep at low temperature, positive and flatter at high temperature. It does not, however, show that b (T) decreases again at higher temperature nor does it give the correct limiting value as $T \to \infty$. For the third and higher virial co-efficient, the van der Waals equation is entirely inadequate. Using equation (9), the Boyle temperature for the van der Waal's equation is given by

$$T_B = a/Rb$$

But we know,

$$T_c = 8a/27Rb \text{[See van der Waal's equation]}$$

$$\frac{T_B}{T_C} = \frac{27}{8} = 3.375$$

Some representative values are :

He, 3.65: H_2, 3.21;

Ar, 2.73 : N_2, 2.56;

NH_3, 2.13: CH_4, 2.58:

MAXWELL'S LAW OF DISTRIBUTION OF VELOCITIES

The Maxwell's law of distribution of velocities establishes that in a steady state the number of molecules with a given velocity remains constant. By the term steady state it does not mean that all the molecules retain their velocities unchanged. However, it only means that if some molecules change their velocities due to collisions, etc., an equal number of other molecules acquire the original velocity of the molecules that have undergone a change thereby, keeping the overall position the same.

The treatment outlined below is based on that first given by J. Clerk Maxwell (1860). He made the following assumptions :

(i) The gas consists of molecules with all possible velocities ranging from 0 to ∞.

(ii) When the gas is in the steady state, its density almost remains uniform throughout.

(iii) Though the velocities of individual molecules are changing yet definite number of molecules have velocities between definite ranges. This is sometimes mentioned as the steady state of the gas.

Proof:

Suppose the number of molecules present per c.c of the gas is n. Consider a molecule whose velocity is c. Let u, v, w be its components along three rectangular axes (x, y, and z). Then,

$$c^2 = u^2 + v^2 + w^2 \qquad ...(1)$$

If it is assumed that the values of u. v and w for any molecule ar completely independent of each other, then it means the probability, that the u component lies between u and u + du is a function of u alone, *i.e.*, f(u) du. Similarly, y component is a function of f(v) dv and w a function of f(w) dw. The probability W that the three components of the molecular velocity shall simultaneously lie between u and du, between v and v+dv, and between w and dw, respectively is then given by

$$W = f(u)\ f(v)\ f(w)\ du\ dv\ dw \qquad ...(2)$$

Suppose the individual components are varied by the infinitesimal amounts δu, δv δw, maintaining the total velocity c as constant. This is equivalent to making a small change in the direction of motion without affecting the speed, *i.e.*, δc is zero. The condition that δc, and hence δc^2, is zero is obtained from equation (1) ; thus one can write

$$\delta(c^2) = \delta(u^2 + v^2 + w^2)$$

$$2c\delta c = 2u\delta u + 2v\delta v + 2w\delta w$$

or $$u\delta u + v\delta v + w\delta w = 0 \qquad [\because \delta c = 0] \qquad ...(3)$$

The motion of the molecule is considered to be completely random, *i.e.*, no direction being preferred over any other. Therefore, it follows that the functions f(u), f(v) and f(w) (which determine the number of molecules with components in given ranges) will remain constant, provided c is constant, *i.e.*, in mathematical language, the variation in product f(u) f(v) f(w) will be zero, *viz.*,

$$\delta[f(u)\ f(v)\ f(w)] = 0$$

$$f'(u)\ f(v)\ f(w)\ \delta u + f(u)\ f'(v)\ f(w)$$

$$\delta v + f(u)\ f(v)\ f'(w)\ \delta w = 0 \qquad ...(4)$$

where f' (u) is a derivative of f(u) with respect to u. *i.e.*, df(u)/du, and so on. Now divide equation (4) by f(u) f(v) f(w) to get

$$\frac{f'(u)}{f(u)}\delta u + \frac{f'(v)}{f(v)}\delta v + \frac{f'(w)}{f(w)}\delta w = 0 \qquad ...(5)$$

Multiply equation (3) by and arbitrary factor x and then add the resulting quantity to equation (5), giving

$$\left(\frac{f'(u)}{f(u)} + xu\right)\delta u + \left(\frac{f'(v)}{f(v)} + xv\right)\delta v + \left(\frac{f'(w)}{f(w)} + xw\right)\delta w = 0 \qquad ...(6)$$

For a given velocity c, the variations δu, δv and δw are completely arbitrary. It means that each of the quantities in the brackets of equation (6) must be zero, *i.e.*,

$$\frac{f'(u)}{f(u)} + xu = 0 \qquad \text{or} \qquad \frac{f'(u)}{f(u)} = -xu \qquad ...(7)$$

As f '(u) is the first derivative of f(u), it means that f '(u)/f(u) is equivalent to d in f(u). Thus, equation (7) becomes as

$$d \ln f(u) = -xu$$

Integrating the above equation,

$$\ln f(u) = -x\,u^2/2 + \ln A \qquad ...(8)$$

where ln A is the integration constant. Equation (8) may be written in the form

$$f(u) = Ae^{-xu2/2} \qquad ...(9)$$

For sake of convenience, quantity x/2 in equation (9) is replaced by quantity $1/\alpha^2$, resulting the new equation as

$$f(u) = Ae^{-u2/\alpha 2} \qquad ...(10)$$

Treating the other terms in equation (6) in an analogous manner, it follows that

$$f(v) = Ae^{-v2/\alpha 2} \text{ and } f(w) = Ae^{-\omega 2/\alpha 2} \qquad ...(10\ A)$$

Substituting equation (10) and (10 A) in (2), we get

$$W = A^3e^{-(u2 + v2 + w2)\ \alpha 2}\,du\,dv\,dw$$

$$= A^3e^{-c2\ \alpha 2}\,du\,dv\,dw \qquad ...(11)$$

In order to make direct use of equation (11) it is necessary to evaluate A and α; this can be done in the ensuing manner. As the velocity components can possess can values ranging from $+\infty$ to $-\infty$, it means that the probability of a value of u between these limits must be unity. In other words, the integral of f(u) du between $+\infty$ and $-\infty$ must be equal to unity, *i.e.*, using equation (10),

$$s\int_{-\infty}^{+\infty} Ae^{-u^2/\alpha^2}\,du = 1 \qquad ...(12)$$

Integrating above equation (12), we get

$$A\,\pi^{1/2} \propto = 1 \qquad ...(13)$$

$$A = 1\pi^{1/2} \propto \qquad ...(14)$$

Substituting equation (14) in (11), we get

$$W = \frac{1}{\pi^{3/2}\,.\,\alpha^3} e^{-c^2/\alpha^3}\,du\,dv\,dw \qquad ...(15)$$

It would be convenient for this purpose to change the cartesian coordinates to the polar coordinates. The volume element du dv dw would then be equal to $c^2 \sin\theta \, d\theta \, d\phi \, dc$. Hence, equation (15) becomes as

$$W = \frac{1}{\pi^{3/2} . \alpha^3} e^{-c^2/\alpha^3} c^2 \, dc \sin\theta \, d\theta \, d\phi \qquad ...(16)$$

In order to obtain the fraction of the total number of molecule, *i.e.*, $W = dn_c/n$, having velocities between c and c + dc, irrespective of the direction, it is necessary to integrate Eq. (16) with respect to θ between the limits zero and π, and with respect to φ between the limits zero and 2π, thus including all possible directions. It follows, then, that

$$\frac{dn_c}{n} = \frac{1}{\pi^{3/2} \alpha^3} e^{-c^2/\alpha^2} c^2 dc \int_0^{\pi} \sin\theta \, d\theta \int_0^{2\pi} d\phi$$

$$\frac{dn_c}{n} = \frac{1}{\pi^{3/2} \alpha^3} e^{-c^2/\alpha^2} c^2 dc \, . \, 2 \, . 2\pi$$

$$\left(\because \int_0^{\pi} \sin\theta \, d\theta = 2 \text{ and } \int_0^{2\pi} d\phi = 2\pi \right)$$

$$\frac{dn_c}{n} = \frac{4\pi}{\pi^{3/2} \alpha^3} e^{-c^2/\alpha^2} c^2 \, dc$$

$$= \frac{4\pi}{\pi^{1/2} \alpha^3} e^{-c^2/\alpha^2} c^2 \, dc \qquad ...(17)$$

The significance of ∝ may be seen by expressing the mean square velocity $\bar{c}^2$ in the form

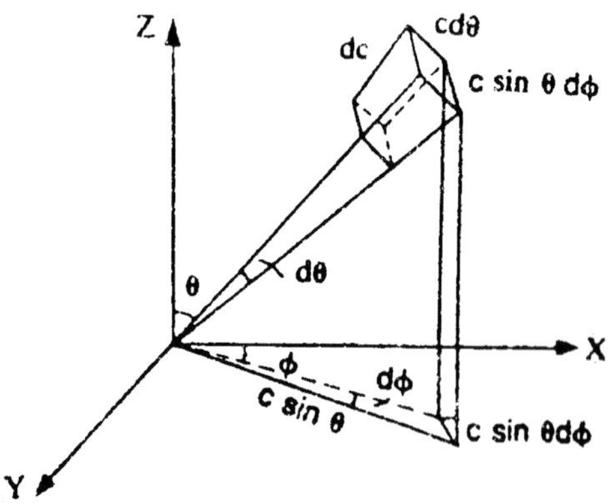

Fig. 2.11

$$\overline{c}^2 = \frac{\int_0^\infty c^2 dn_c}{n} \qquad ...(18)$$

Substituting equation (17) in (18). we get

$$\overline{c}^2 = \frac{4}{\pi^{1/2}\alpha^3}\int_0^\infty e^{-c^2/\alpha^2} c^4\, dc \qquad ...(19)$$

$$= \frac{4}{\pi^{1/2}\alpha^3} \times \frac{3\pi^{1/2}\alpha^5}{8} = \frac{3}{2}\alpha^2$$

or $$\alpha^2 = 2\overline{c}^2/3 \qquad ...(20)$$

We also know, PV = 1/2 $mN\overline{c}^2$: for a mole of gas, N is the Avogadro's number and PV is then equal to RT, and so

$$RT = \frac{1}{2} mN\overline{c}^2$$

or $$\overline{c}^2 = 3\ RT/mN \qquad ...(21)$$

Substituting equation (21) in (20), we get

$$\alpha^2 = \frac{2}{3}.\frac{3RT}{mN} = \frac{2RT}{mN}\frac{2kT}{m} \qquad \left(\because k = \frac{R}{N}\right)$$

or $$\frac{1}{\alpha^2} = \frac{m}{2kT} \qquad ...(22)$$

Substituting equation (22) in (17), we get

$$\frac{dn_c}{n} = \frac{4}{\pi^{1/2}}\left(\frac{m}{2kT}\right)^{3/2} e^{-mc^2/2kT} c^2\, dc \qquad ...(22A)$$

$$= \frac{4}{\pi^{1/2}}.\pi 3/2\left(\frac{m}{2kT}\right)^{3/2} e^{-mc^2/2kT} c^2\, dc$$

$$= 4\pi\left(\frac{m}{2kT}\right)^{3/2} e^{-mc^2/2kT} c^2\, dc \qquad ...(23)$$

or $$\frac{1\,dn_c}{n\,dc} = 4\pi\left(\frac{m}{2kT}\right)^{3/2} e^{-mc^2/2kT} c^2 \qquad ...(24)$$

$$= 4\pi\left(\frac{mN}{2\pi NkT}\right)^{3/2} e^{-mc^2N/2kTN} c^2$$

$$= 4\pi \left(\frac{M}{2\pi RT} \right)^{3/2} e^{-Mc^2/2RT} c^2 \qquad ...(25)$$

where M (= mN) is the molecular weight of the gas and r (= kN) is the gas constant. If E represents the kinetic energy of 1 mole or molecules having the velocity c, then

$$E = \frac{1}{2} Mc^2 \qquad ...(26)$$

Differentiating equation (26), we get

$$dE = \frac{1}{2} M\, 2c\, dc = Mc\, dc$$

Multiplying above equation by c, we get

$$c\, dE = Mc^2\, dc \qquad ...(27)$$

From Eq. (26), we get

$$c = (2E/M)^{1/2} \qquad ...(28)$$

Substituting the value of c in the left side of eq. (27) we get

$$(2E/M)^{1/2}\, dE = Mc^2\, dc \qquad ...(29)$$

or

$$(2E)^{1/2}\, dE = M^{3/2}\, c^?\, dc$$

Substituting equation (29) in (25), we get

$$\frac{1}{n} \frac{dn_c}{dE} = \frac{2\pi}{(\pi RT)^{3/2}} \cdot e^{-E/RT} E^{1/2} \qquad ...(30)$$

The equations (22A), (23), (24), (25) and (30) are different forms of the Maxwell's law of distribution of molecular velocities.

TRANSPORT PHENOMENA IN GASES

Introduction : If the properties of a gas vary from one point to another, then in general a flow of some associated quantities like energy, mass, etc., will take place through the gas. Such processes are known as transport phenomena.

Types : There are three types of transport phenomenon :

(i) If the temperature of the gas is not uniform, heat conduction will take place from regions of high temperature to regions of low temperature.

(iii) If the mean velocity of the gas is not everywhere the same, forces will be exerted by each portion of the gas on adjacent portions tending to eliminate these velocity differences a process giving rise to the phenomenon of viscocity.

(iii) If the composition is not everywhere the same, then the process of diffusion takes place.

General Expression for the Transport Phenomena in Gases

Let us consider a system which is in equilibrium or in the steady state for which the Maxwell-Boltzmann distribution law is valid. If the system is disturbed at some places and the disturbance is transmitted throughout the system, the system is no longer in equilibrium and this disturbed system will not follow the Maxwell-Boltzmann law but some other law which may be more complicated. But for sake of simplicity, we will assume that such systems will obey the Maxwell-Boltzmann's law.

Suppose we make the superimposed disturbance in the z-direction, *i.e.*, the molecules at different distances in z-direction, possess different velocities, or different temperatures or different pressures, all of which disturb the normal equilibrium state of the system. As such a disturbance possesses different values at different distances along the z-axis, it is expressed by saying that the disturbance possesses a gradient along z-axis. If G denotes this disturbance, then the gradient is dG/dz.

Suppose we consider any imaginary plane A parallel to xy plane, which lies at a distance z along the z-axis. Now the disturbance carried to this plane A is due to the collisions with molecules which are arriving at this plane from planes both above and below it. Suppose λ is the mean free path of the molecules.

Then, any molecule which reaches A and strikes a molecule here must have had its previous collision at a point B which lies at a distance of $\lambda \cos \theta$ from the plane A. This molecule and such other molecules coming from above and below the plane A and striking this plane will transfer their disturbances here.

If a molecule above A possesses a greater disturbance than below A, the disturbances (T_1) imparted to A on collision will be given by

$$T_1 = \left(G_A + \lambda \cos \theta \frac{dG}{dz} \right) \quad \text{...(1)}$$

where, G_A is the value of disturbance on the plane A. Similarly, at any moment from a point below A and striking the plane A will impart; a disturbance (T_2)

$$T_2 = \left(G_A - \lambda \cos\theta \frac{dG}{dz}\right) \qquad ...(2)$$

Now as these two disturbances are in opposite directions, the net disturbance transferred to A is equal to the difference between the two, *i.e.*,

$$\Delta T = T_1 - T_2 = \left(G_A + \lambda \cos\theta \frac{dG}{dz}\right) - \left(G_A - \lambda \cos\theta \frac{dG}{dz}\right)$$

$$= 2\lambda \cos\theta \frac{dG}{dz} \qquad ...(3)$$

We will calculate the number of molecules ($v_{c\theta\phi}$) coming at an angle θ and $\theta + d\theta$ and ϕ and $\phi + d\phi$ and having velocity lying between c and c + dc from above A and striking the unit area of the plane A. This given by

$$v_{c\theta\phi} = \frac{(N)(c\cos\theta)}{V} \frac{\sin\theta\, d\theta\, \theta\phi}{4\pi} \frac{dN_c}{N}$$

$$= \frac{c}{4\pi} \sin\theta \cos\theta\, d\theta\, d\phi\, dn_c \qquad ...(4)$$

where $\quad \frac{dN_c}{V} = dn_c$

Integrating Eq. (4) with respect to ϕ between limits 0 and 2π, we get

$$v_{c\theta} = \frac{c}{4\pi} \sin\theta \cos\theta\, d\theta\, dn_c\, [\phi]_0^{2\pi} = \frac{c(2\pi)}{4\pi} \sin\theta \cos\theta\, d\theta\, dn_c \qquad ...(5)$$

Each of these molecules will impart a disturbance given by Eq. (3). Hence the total disturbance carried is given by

$$\Delta_{\theta,c} = \Delta T . v_{c\theta} \qquad ...(6)$$

Substituting Eqs. (2) and (5) in (6), we get

$$\Delta_{\theta,c} = \frac{c.2\pi}{4\pi} \sin\theta \cos\theta\, d\theta\, dn_c\, 2\lambda \cos\theta \frac{dG}{dz}$$

$$= c\lambda \sin\theta \cos^2\theta\, d\theta\, dn_c \frac{dG}{dz} \text{ per sec.} \qquad ...(7)$$

Integrating Eq. (7) for θ between limits 0 and π/2.

$$\Delta_c = \frac{1}{3} c\lambda \, dn_c \, \frac{dG}{dz} \text{ per sec.} \qquad ...(8)$$

Integrating with respect to c between 0 and ∞, we get

$$\Delta_c = \frac{1}{3}\lambda \frac{dG}{dz} \int_0^{\infty} c\, dn_c = \frac{1}{3}\lambda \frac{dG}{dz} . \frac{n}{1} \int_0^{\infty} c \frac{dn_c}{n} = \frac{1}{3} n \lambda \frac{dG}{dz} \bar{c}$$

...(9)

where $\bar{c} = \int_0^{\infty} c \frac{dn_c}{n}$ $\bar{c}$ is the average speed of the molecules. We will now apply general result [Eq. (9)] to particular cases of viscosity, thermal conductivity, and diffusion.

(1) *Viscosity :* Viscosity is due to transport momentum, hence G may be taken to represent momentum. Let us consider momentum along the x-axis. Then,

$$G = mu \qquad ...(10)$$

where, u us the component along x-axis and m is mass of the molecule. Equation (10) may be put as

$$\frac{dG}{dz} = m \frac{du}{dz} \qquad ...(11)$$

where, du/dz stands for the velocity gradient. Substituting equation (11) in (9), we get

$$\Delta = \frac{1}{3} m \lambda n \bar{c} \frac{du}{dz} \qquad ...(12)$$

In this case, Δ stands for the transfer of momentum per second, *i.e.*, it is equal to the rate of change of momentum, *i.e.*, force. Thus, equation (12) becomes as

$$\equiv \text{Force} \equiv \frac{1}{3} mn\bar{c}\, \lambda \frac{du}{dz} \qquad ...(13)$$

But the viscous force is given by

Δ ∝ Area on which the force acts × the velocity gradient

$$\Delta \,\alpha\, A \frac{du}{dz} \text{ or } \Delta = \eta A \frac{du}{dz} \qquad ...(14)$$

where, η is the co-efficient of viscosity. If A is unity and du/dz = 1, then the force Δ = η and this force is, by definition, the coefficient of viscosity. Hence Eq. (13) becomes as follows :

$$\eta = \frac{1}{3} m\, n\, \bar{c}\, \lambda \qquad ...(15)$$

We know average velocity,

$$\bar{c} = \left(\frac{8\ RT}{M\pi}\right)^{1/2} \qquad ...(16)$$

and

$$\lambda = \frac{1}{\sqrt{2\pi\sigma^2 n}} \qquad ...(17)$$

Substituting Eqs. (16) and (17) in Eq. (15),

$$\eta = \frac{1}{3}\, mn\, \frac{1}{\sqrt{2\pi\sigma^2 n}}\left(\frac{8\ RT}{\pi M}\right)^{1/2} = \frac{1}{3} m \frac{1}{\sqrt{2\pi\sigma^2}}\left(\frac{8\ RT}{\pi M}\right)^{1/2} \qquad ...(18)$$

But mass of one molecule $= \dfrac{\text{Molecular weight}}{\text{Avogadro's number}}$

or

$$m = M/N \qquad ...(19)$$

$$\eta = \frac{1}{3}\frac{M}{N}\frac{1}{\sqrt{2\pi\sigma^2}}\left(\frac{8\ RT}{\pi M}\right)^{1/2} = \frac{2(RTM)^{1/2}}{3(\pi)^{3/2}\, N\sigma^2} \qquad ...(20)$$

where, σ is the diameter of the molecule. From equation (20) it follows that a knowledge of Avogadro's number (N) and the determination of viscosity η enables us to find out the molecular dimensions (σ).

Further, we know that the van der Waal's constant 'b' is four times the actual volume of the molecule, *i.e.*,

$$b = 4 \times \left(\frac{4}{3}\right)\pi r^3 \times N$$

But molecular diameter, $(\sigma) = 2r$

or

$$r = \frac{\sigma}{2}$$

$$\therefore \qquad b = 4 \times \left(\frac{4}{3}\right)\pi\left(\frac{\sigma}{2}\right)^3 n = \frac{2}{3}\pi N\sigma^3 \qquad ...(21)$$

Multiplying equations (20) and (21) and rearranging,

$$\sigma = \frac{\theta}{4}\eta\, b\sqrt{\left(\frac{\pi}{RTM}\right)} \qquad ...(22)$$

From equation (22) it follows that the value of van der Waals constant will give us the magnitude of the molecular diameter.

Effect of Temperature

From Eq. (20), it follows that viscosity is proportional to the square root of the absolute temperature. However, it has been observed experimentally that the increase in viscosity is somewhat higher than that predicted by this expression. The reason for this deviation is that there exists intermolecular attraction which was not considered in the kinetic theory. Sutherland gave a satisfactory empirical relation between viscosity and temperature. His relation is as follows :

$$\eta = k\sqrt{\frac{T}{\left(1+\frac{C}{T}\right)}} \qquad ...(22A)$$

where, k and c are constants. Here C is sometimes called Sutherland constant,

1. Effect of Pressure

From Eq. (18), it follows that viscosity is independent of pressure. Experimentally, it has been found to be so. When the pressure is so low that the mean free path becomes comparable with the dimensions of the apparatus, the collision of molecules are primarily with the walls, and under such a condition, Eq. (20) is not valid.

Alternative Derivation of Eq. (15)

Suppose a gas is moving in XY plane in such a way that there occurs a mass motion of the gas parallel to XY plane but no motion along the z-axis. Suppose an imaginary plane AB is considered. the layers of the gas above AB are moving with greater velocity. While the layers of the gas below AB are moving which a smaller velocity in the same direction. The tendency of the molecules in the layer above is AB is to accelerate the motion of molecules in the layer below AB.

On the other hand, the tendency of the molecules of the layer above AB is to retard the motion of the molecules of the layer above AB. Due to this fact there arises a difference in velocities on the two sides of AB. IN other words a velocity gradient is established. Due to this velocity gradient a viscous drag exists between the two layers or different layers of the gas tend to destroy the relative motion between them. This property of the gas is called viscosity. The fundamental law of viscosity is that the magnitude of the viscous force Δ acting between two layers is proportional to the area A of cross section of the layer and the velocity gradient du/dz, *i.e.*,

$$\Delta = \eta A \frac{du}{dz}$$

where η is a constant, known as coefficient of viscosity.

Now the molecules moving towards the surface AB are only those which on the average lie within the mean free path λ. If u is the mass velocity of the gas molecules along the plane AB and du/dz is the velocity gradient in the upward direction perpendicular to AB, the velocities of the gas molecules along CD and EF would be

$$\left(u + \lambda \frac{du}{dz}\right) \text{ and } \left(u - \lambda \frac{du}{dz}\right) \text{ respectively.}$$

Suppose n is the number of molecules per c.c and c is their average velocity with which they are moving constantly in all possible directions. Then, the number of molecules crossing per unit area of AB layer downwards in second is n $\bar{c}$/6 while an equal number, *i.e.*, n $\bar{c}$/6 is crossing upwards.

If m is the mass of the molecule, then the total mass crossing unit area of AB per second either side is 1/6 m n $\bar{c}$. Therefore, the momentum carried downwards by the molecules crossing unit area of AB per second from the plane CD would be equal to mass × velocity, *i.e.*,

$$= \frac{1}{6} m n \bar{c}\left(u + \lambda \frac{du}{dz}\right)$$

Similarly, the momentum carried uqwards

$$= \frac{1}{6} m n \bar{c}\left(u - \lambda \frac{du}{dz}\right)$$

Net momentum transferred per second downwards

$$= \frac{1}{6} m n \bar{c}\left(u + \lambda \frac{du}{dz}\right) - \frac{1}{6} m n \bar{c}\left(u - \lambda \frac{du}{dz}\right)$$

$$= \frac{1}{3} m n \bar{c}\ \lambda \frac{du}{dz}$$

But this net transfer of momentum per second is Δ. Therefore,

$$\Delta = \frac{1}{3} m n \bar{c}\ \lambda \frac{du}{dz} \qquad \text{...(A)}$$

But the viscous force Δ is given as follows :

$$\Delta = \eta\, A\, \frac{du}{dz}$$

If A is unity and $\frac{du}{dz} = 1$, then the force = η and this force, by definition, is the coefficient of viscosity. Hence, Eq. (A) becomes as follows :

$$\eta = \frac{1}{3} m\, n\, \bar{c}\, \lambda \qquad ...(B)$$

The above equation is same as Eq. 15.

Thermal Conductivity in Gases

In this case if we may assume G as representing the mean kinetic energy E, of a molecule at any point in the gas so that E is a function of z, *i.e..*, the different layers of the gas are at different temperatures, *i.e.*,

$$\frac{dG}{dz} = \frac{dE}{dz} = m\, C\, v\, \frac{dT}{dz} \left[\because C_v = \frac{dE}{dT} \right] \qquad ...(23)$$

where Cv stands for the specific heat of gas at constant volume, and dT/dz is the temperature gradient. On substituting Eq. (23) in (9), we get

$$\Delta = \frac{1}{3}\, m\, n\, \lambda\, Cv \frac{dT}{dz} \bar{c} \qquad ...(24)$$

In equation (24), Δ is the total flow of energy across unit area of the plane in unit time and this energy is in the form of heat. If K is the coefficient of thermal conductivity, then

$$K = \frac{\Delta}{dT/dz} \text{(by definition)} \qquad ...(25)$$

Substituting equation 24) in (25), we get

$$K = 1/3\ m\ n\ \lambda\ Cv\ \bar{c}$$

Alternative Derivation of Eq. 26

This can be deduced in the same way as in the case of viscosity of gases. The only difference is that the molecules are considered as carriers of heat energy instead of momentum. Suppose the mass of the gas is at rest while CD and EF are the hot and cold layers of the gas respectively as shown in Fig. 2.12.

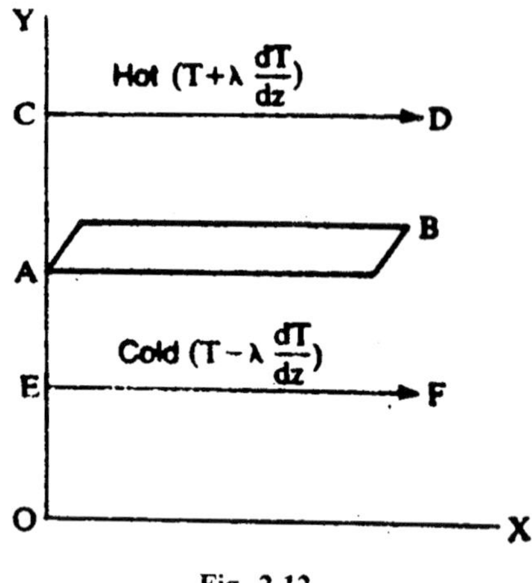

Fig. 2.12

The molecules coming from the higher temperature side CD and passing down-ward the plane AB will have greater kinetic energy than those molecules which are coming from low temperature side and passing through AB on the upward side. It means that the average kinetic energy of the molecules is increasing while that above is decreasing. In simple words it means that the temperature below AB is increasing while above AB is decreasing. Thus, the conduction is due to the transport of energy.

Suppose AB is a layer at temperature T and dT/dz is the temperature gradient. Now the molecules moving towards the surface AB will be only those which on the average lie within the mean path, λ. Thus, the temperature of CD and ER layers would be $\left[T + \lambda \frac{dT}{dz}\right]$ and $\left[T - \lambda \frac{dT}{dz}\right]$ respectively.

Suppose n is the number of molecules per c.c. and $\bar{c}$ is their average velocity due to thermal agitation with which they are moving in all possible. directions. Now the number of molecules, which are crossing unit area of AB downwards in the second, would be $n\,\bar{c}/6$ and same number would be crossing upwards. If m is the mass of molecule, then the total mass crossing unit area of AB per second either side would be $1/6\ m\ n\ \bar{c}$.

Hence, total heat 6 carried by all the molecules which are moving are moving downwards and crossing the layer AB per unit area per second would be as follows :

$$= \text{mass} \times \text{specific heat} \times \text{temperature}$$

$$= \frac{mn\bar{c}}{6} \times Cv \times \left(T + \frac{dT}{dz}.\lambda\right)$$

Similarly, total heat carried by all the molecules which are moving upwards and crossing the layer AB per second would be as follows

$$= \frac{mn\bar{c}}{6} \times Cv \times \left(T - \frac{dT}{dz}.\lambda\right)$$

Therefore, the net transfer of heat per unit area per second would be

$$\Delta = \frac{mn\bar{c}}{6} Cv \left(T + \frac{dT}{dz}.\lambda\right) - \frac{mn\bar{c}}{6} Cv \left(T - \frac{dT}{dz}.\lambda\right)$$

$$= \frac{mn\bar{c}}{6} Cv \frac{2.\,dT}{dz}.\lambda = \frac{1}{3} mn\bar{c}\,\lambda.\frac{dT}{dz}.Cv$$

The coefficient of thermal conductivity K of a gas is defined as the quantity of heat flowing per unit time per unit temperature gradient and is given as follows :

$$\Delta = K\frac{dt}{dz} \qquad \text{or} \qquad K = \frac{\Delta}{dT/dz}$$

$$K = \frac{\frac{1}{3}mn\bar{c}\,\lambda.\frac{dT}{dz}.C_v}{dT/dz} = \frac{1}{3} mn\bar{c}\lambda C_v \qquad ...(26)$$

But

$$\lambda = \frac{1}{\sqrt{2}\pi\sigma^2 n} \text{ and } \bar{c} = \left(\frac{8RT}{\pi M}\right)^{1/2}$$

$$\therefore \qquad K = \frac{1}{3} mn \left(\frac{8RT}{\pi M}\right)^{1/2} \times \frac{1}{\sqrt{2}\pi\sigma^2 n} \times C_v$$

$$= \frac{mCv}{3\sqrt{2}\pi\sigma^2} \times \left(\frac{8RT}{\pi M}\right)^{1/2} \qquad ...(26)$$

On comparing Eqs. (26) with (15), we get

$$K = \eta\, Cv$$

This relation does not agree with the experimental data. According to the theoretical consideration, $K/\eta\, Cv$ must be unity but it has been found to be equal to $\in$ whose value varies from 1 to 2.5. Chapman deduced the following relation :

$$\frac{K}{\eta C_v} = \in = \frac{(9\gamma - 5)}{4} \qquad ...(27)$$

where $\gamma = 1.66$ for monoatomic gases; $\in = 2.5$

$\gamma = 1.4$ for diatomic gases; $\in = 1.9$

$\gamma = 1.33$ for triatomic gases; $\in = 1.75$

Diffusion in Gases

If G refers to concentration or pressure, then

$$\frac{dG}{dz} = \frac{dn}{dz} \qquad ...(28)$$

Substituting Eq. (28) in (9), we get

$$\Delta = \frac{1}{3} n \eta \bar{c} \frac{dn}{dz} \qquad ...(29)$$

$$\text{But Diffusion coefficient} = \frac{\Delta}{dn/dz} \qquad ...(30)$$

Substitution of Eq. (29) in (30, we get

$$\text{Diffusion coefficient} = \frac{1}{3} n \eta \bar{c} \qquad ...(31)$$

But
$$\lambda = \frac{2}{\sqrt{2}\,\pi \sigma^2 n}$$

$$\therefore \text{Diffusion coefficient} = \frac{1}{3} n \bar{c} \frac{1}{\sqrt{2}\,\pi \sigma^2 n} = \frac{1}{3\sqrt{2}} \frac{\bar{c}}{\pi \sigma^2}$$

But
$$\bar{c} = \sqrt{\left(\frac{8RT}{\pi M}\right)}$$

$\therefore$ Diffusion coefficient,

$$D = \frac{1}{\sqrt{2}\pi\sigma^2} \sqrt{\left(\frac{8RT}{\pi M}\right)} = \frac{2}{3(\pi)^{3/2} \sigma^2} \sqrt{\left(\frac{RT}{M}\right)} \qquad ...(32)$$

Alternative Derivation of Eq. 31

Suppose a mass of gas is moving between parallel planes AB and CD. Suppose the concentration (number of molecules per c.c.) increases in vertical direction from AB to CD through the through the intermediate plane XY. Therefore, the concentration of gas above XY is greater than that below XY. Thus, to maintain an equilibrium, the molecules of the gas will be crossing the XY and AB to CD and vice versa due to thermal agitation. Thus, this diffusion of gas molecules through the intermediate plane may by assumed to the transport of mass.

C ----D

X-----Y

A----B

If n is the concentration at the plane XY and dn/dt is the rate of change of concentration in vertical direction (also called concentration gradient), then the concentration at plane CD will be

$$= n + \lambda \frac{dn}{dz}$$

and the concentration at plane AB will be

$$= n - \lambda \frac{dn}{dz}$$

where, λ is the distance between CD and XY or AB and XY.

But molecules are moving in all possible directions due to thermal agitation.

Therefore, it can be assumed that 1/3 of the total number of molecules are moving along any axis or 1/6th of the molecules along any axis in one particular direction.

Thus, the number of molecules crossing plane XY downwards per unit area per second would be as follows :

$$= \frac{1}{6} n \bar{c} \left(n + \lambda \frac{dn}{dz} \right)$$

and the number of molecules crossing plane XY upwards per unit area per second would be as follows :

$$= \frac{1}{6} n \bar{c} \left(n - \lambda \frac{dn}{dz} \right)$$

Thus, the net number of molecules crossing unit area per second of plane XY in the downward direction would be as follows :

$$\Delta = \frac{1}{6} n \bar{c} \left(n + \lambda \frac{dn}{dz} \right) - \frac{1}{6} \bar{c} \left(n - \lambda \frac{dn}{dz} \right) = \frac{1}{3} n \bar{c} \lambda \frac{dn}{dz}$$

But Diffusion coefficient $= \dfrac{\Delta}{dn/dz}$

$$\therefore \text{ Diffusion coefficient } \frac{\frac{1}{3} n \bar{c} \lambda \frac{dn}{dz}}{\frac{\Delta}{dn/dz}} = \frac{1}{3} n \bar{c} \lambda \qquad \text{...(33)}$$

DEGREES OF FREEDOM

The degrees of freedom of a dynamical system may be defied as *the total number of independent co-orainates required to specify its position and configuration. For example* :

(i) In monoatomic gases like helium, argon, krypton, etc., molecule consists of only one atom. It means that a molecule can be represented by a point in space without assigning any internal structure to it. Therefore, there will be only translatory motion which can take place in any direction in space and can be resolved parallel to three axes X, Y and Z of the cartesian co-ordinate system. Thus, a monoatomic molecule requires there co-ordinates to define its position and hence possesses three degrees of freedom (Fig. 2.13a).

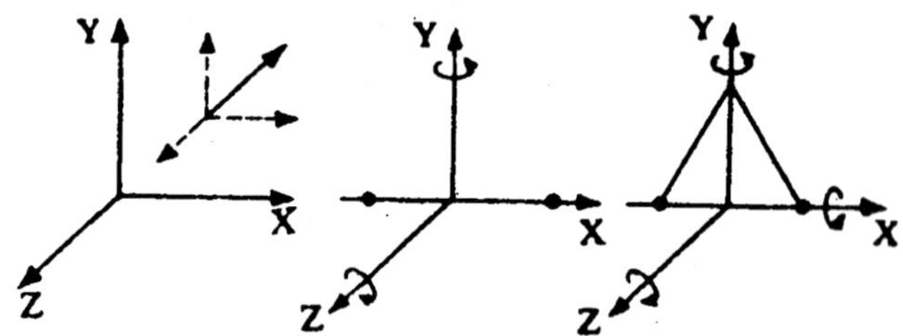

Fig. 2.13

(ii) In diatomic gases like hydrogen oxygen, etc., the molecule consists of two atoms which are joined rigidly to one another like a dumb-bell (Fig. 2.13b). Such a molecule, besides its translatory motion, can rotate. This rotatory motion can be resolved, like translatory motion, into three components about any three mutually perpendicular axes through a point fixed in it. But the rotational motion about an axis along the rigid rod will be negligible as compared to those about the other two axes. Thus, a diatomic molecule will have two rotational motions. Now a diatomic molecule will possess five degrees of freedom three due to translatory motion and two due to rotatory motion. A diatomic molecule also possesses two degrees of freedom for its vibratory motion. Hence the total number of degrees of freedom for a diatomic molecule will be serve.

(iii) A polyatomic molecule (like CO_2, etc) can rotate about three mutually perpendicular axes (Fig. 2.13c). Thus, the state of motion of a polyatomic molecule can be described by six coordinates and has six degrees of freedom, three due to translatory motion, and three due to rotatory motion. Besides this there will be (3n – 6) degrees of freedom for vibratory motion of a polyatomic molecule.

LAW OF EQUIPARTITION OF ENERGY

This law is due to Maxwell and can be stated as follows : "The total kinetic energy of a dynamical system consisting of a large number of particles in thermal equilibrium is equally divided among all its degrees of freedom and the energy associated with each degree of freedom is 1/2 kT where k is the; Boltzmann's constant and T is the absolute temperature of the system."

The average kinetic energy of the molecule of a monoatomic gas is given by 3/2 kT, where k is the Boltzmann's constant. The value 3/2kT represents the translational kinetic energy per molecule. Therefore, the kinetic energy of translation per molecule is given by

$$\text{Average kinetic energy} = \frac{1}{2} m V_x^2 + \frac{1}{2} m V_y^2 + \frac{1}{2} m V_z^2 \quad ...(3)$$

where, m is the mass of molecule and v_x, v_y and v_z are the components of velocity along three axes. According to the theorem of equipartition of energy, each term should contribute the same amount to the total energy per molecule, *i.e.*,

$$\frac{1}{2} m V_x^2 = \frac{1}{2} m V_y^2 = \frac{1}{2} m V_z^2 \quad ...(2)$$

Substituting equation (2) in (1), we get

$$\frac{1}{2} m V_x^2 + \frac{1}{2} m V_x^2 + \frac{1}{2} m V_x^2 = \frac{3}{2} kT$$

or

$$\frac{3}{2} m V_x^2 = \frac{3}{2} kT$$

$$\frac{1}{2} m V_x^2 = \frac{1}{2} kT \quad ...(3)$$

Similarly, we can prove that

$$\frac{1}{2} m V_y^2 = \frac{1}{2} kT$$

and $$\frac{1}{2} m V_z^2 = kT \quad ...(4)$$

From equations (3) and (4), we conclude that the kinetic energy per molecule in each degree of freedom is 1/2 kT. Similarly, it can be proved that the average energy per molecule will be 1/2 kT for each degree of freedom of rotational and vibrational motion. It means that if a molecule having n degrees of freedom will have total average energy of nkT/2. It follows that the average kinetic energy per degree of freedom will be given by :

Average kinetic energy per gm molecule per; degree of freedom

$$= \frac{1}{2} kT \times N$$

$$= \frac{1}{2} NkT = \frac{1}{2} RT \qquad [\because Nk = R] \quad ...(5)$$

where, N is the Avogadro's number and R is a gas constant.

Proof:

Suppose we consider a system having f degrees of freedom. Let q be any co-ordinate associated with; one of the degrees of freedom, and U_q be the corresponding velocity component. Then, the kinetic energy associated with this velocity component will be given by $1/2mU_q^2$ where m is the mass of the molecule. In order to find the number of molecules having components between U_q and $U_q + dU_q$, consider a zone of cells in the phase space of 2f dimensions. According to Maxwell's law of distribution of velocities, the number of molecules having velocity components between U_q and $U_q + dU_q$, will by given by

$$NU_q dU_q + N\left(\frac{m}{2\pi kT}\right)^{1/2} e^{-E_q/kT} \quad ...(6)$$

where N is the Avogadro's number and E_q is the total energy of the molecule possessing the velocity component U_q and is given by

$$Eq = \text{potential energy} + \text{kinetic energy} = \epsilon' + \epsilon_q \quad ...(7)$$

where ϵ' is the potential energy which is independent of velocity ;component U_q, but depends only on position. The average kinetic energy per molecule associated with velocity component U_q is given by

$$\overline{\epsilon_q} = \frac{\int_{-\infty}^{+\infty} \epsilon_q N\left(\frac{m}{2\pi kT}\right)^{1/2} e^{-E_q/kT}\, dU_q}{\int_{-\infty}^{+\infty} N\left(\frac{m}{2\pi kT}\right)^{1/2} e^{-E_q/kT}\, dU_q} \qquad ...(8)$$

Substituting equation (7) in (8), we get

$$\epsilon_q = \frac{\int_{-\infty}^{+\infty} \epsilon_q N\left(\frac{m}{2\pi kT}\right)^{1/2} e^{-(\epsilon' + \epsilon_q)/kT}\, dU_q}{\int_{-\infty}^{+\infty} N\left(\frac{m}{2\pi kT}\right)^{1/2} e^{-(\epsilon' + \epsilon_q)/kT}\, dU_q}$$

$$= \frac{\int_{-\infty}^{+\infty} \epsilon_q e^{-\epsilon'/kT} e^{-\epsilon_q/kT}\, dU_q}{\int_{-\infty}^{+\infty} e^{-\epsilon'/kT} e^{-\epsilon_q/kT}\, dU_q}$$

But ϵ' is velocity independent and therefore its value will both change with dU_q. Thus, equation (9) becomes as

$$\therefore \epsilon_q = \frac{\int_{-\infty}^{+\infty} \epsilon_q e^{-\epsilon_q/kT}\, dU_q}{\int_{-\infty}^{+\infty} e^{-\epsilon_q/kT}\, dU_q}$$

But $\qquad \epsilon_q = \frac{1}{2} mU_q^2$

$$\therefore \epsilon_q = \frac{\int_{-\infty}^{+\infty} \frac{1}{2} mU_q^2\, e^{-mU_q^2/kT}\, dU_q}{\int_{-\infty}^{+\infty} e^{-mU_q^2/2kT}\, dU_q}$$

$$= \frac{\frac{1}{2} m \left\{\sqrt{\frac{\pi}{2}}\left(\frac{2kT}{m}\right)^{1/2}\right\}}{\left\{\sqrt{\left\{\left(\frac{2\pi kT}{m}\right)\right\}}\right\}}$$

$= \frac{1}{2}$ kT [From the values of standard integral]. ...(11)

From equation (11), it follows that the average kinetic energy per molecule with each degree of freedom is 1/2 kT which is the law of equipartition of energy.

SIGNIFICANCE OF MAXWELL'S LAW

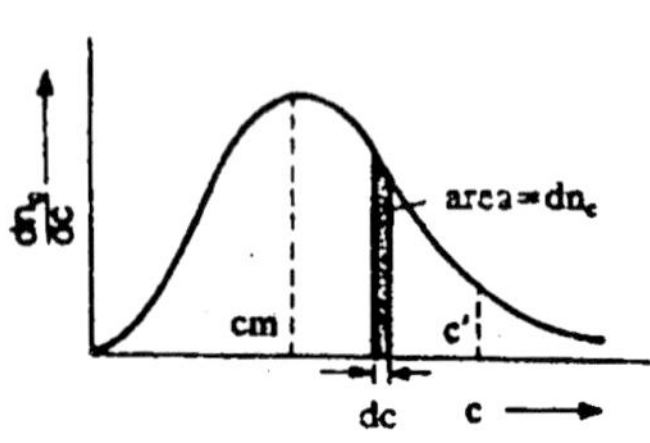

Fig. 2.14 : Maxwell's distribution function.

Fig. 2.15 : Distribution function at different temperatures $T_1 < T_2 < T_3$

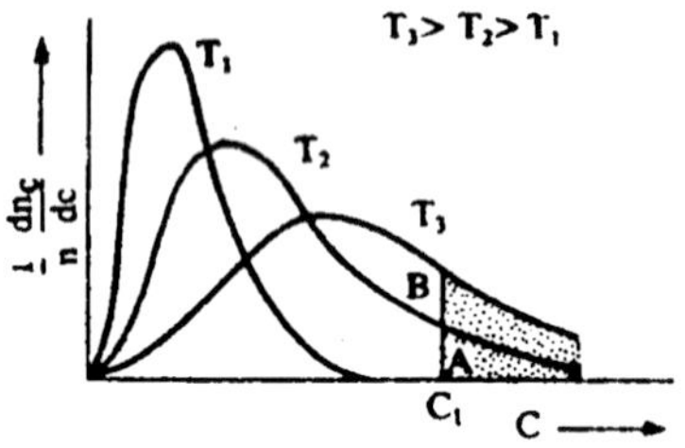

$$\frac{dn_c}{dc} = 4\pi n\left(\frac{m}{(2\pi kT)}\right)^{3/2} c^2.e^{\frac{-mc^2}{2kT}}$$

In the above equation the ratio dn_c/dc is the Maxwell distribution function of molecular velocities: it represents the number of molecules per unit range of velocity. This distribution can be graphically represented at any given temperature (T) by evaluating dn_c/dc for different values of c. the curve obtained would be of the form as given in Fig. 2.14. It is seen that with increase in c, the curve slowly rises, reaches a maximum and then slopes down.

Similar curves are obtained if $1/n.\ dn_c/dc$ be plotted against c (Fig. 2.15), in which the furcation of the total number of molecules in a velocity range c and c + dc would be available.

An examination of these curves reveals the following :

(i) The number of molecules having very low velocity (Lt $c \to 0$) or very high velocities (Lt $c \to \infty$) would be very small.

(ii) The number of molecules within a velocity range c and c+dc is obtained from the shaded area (Fig. 2.15), which is the product of the ordinate and variation of velocity range dc.

The number or molecules with velocities less than (say c') equals the area under the curve to the left of c'. The entire area under the curve of course corresponds to all the molecules.

(iii) The curve has a maximum. The velocity corresponding to this peak represents the velocity possessed by the majority of molecules. This velocity is called the most probable velocity, denoted by C_m.

(iv) With variation of temperature, separate distribution curves are obtained. At higher temperature, there are wider distribution of velocities. The percentage of molecules having higher velocity is increased. The maxima shift to the right and the curves are flattened with rise in temperature. The magnitude of C_m will also increase. The areas under all the separate curves are equal.

The number of molecules having velocities greater than c_1 is given by the area on the right of AB (Fig. 2.14). With rise in temperature this number will increase as the area on the right of AB increases.

(v) Calculation of the most probable velocity. At a given temperature, the condition which would satisfy the external point of the distribution curve is

$$d\left(\frac{dn_c}{dc}\right) = 0$$

This distribution equation is

$$\frac{dn_c}{dc} = 4\pi n\left(\frac{m}{(2\pi kT)}\right)^{3/2} c^2 e^{\frac{-mc^2}{2kT}}$$

At a constant temperature,

$$\frac{dn_c}{dc} = A_1\, c^2\, e^{\frac{-mc^2}{2kT}},$$

where $\quad A_1 = 4\pi n\left(\frac{m}{(2\pi kT)}\right)^{3/2}$

Hence $\quad d\left(\frac{dn_c}{dc}\right) = A_1 \frac{d}{dc}\left(c^2 . e^{\frac{-mc^2}{2kT}}\right) = 0$

i.e., $\quad A_1 c^2 . \left(\frac{-2cm}{2kT}\right) e^{\frac{-mc^2}{2kT}} + A_1\, 2c.\, e^{\frac{-mc^2}{2kT}} = 0$

or $\quad 2c\, e^{\frac{-mc^2}{2kT}} \left(1 - \frac{mc^2}{2kT}\right) = 0$

There are three obvious possibilities,

$$\text{(i) } c = 0, \text{ (ii) } e^{\frac{-mc^2}{2kT}} = 0, \text{ when } c = \infty;$$

and $$\text{(iii) } \left(1 - \frac{mc^2}{2kT}\right) = 0, \text{ when } c = \sqrt{\frac{2kT}{m}}$$

The first two possibilities correspond to the minima: When $c \to 0$ and when $c \to \infty$, $dn_c \to 0$.

The third condition satisfies the maximal point. The velocity corresponding to this is therefore the most probable velocity, *i.e.*,

$$c_m = \sqrt{\frac{2kT}{m}} = \sqrt{\frac{2kT}{m}} \quad ...(31)$$

AVERAGE VALUES

The Maxwell distribution can be profitably used in estimating average values of the molecular properties which are functions of velocity. If q be such a property, then its average $(\bar{q})$ is obtained by summing up the products of q and dn_c for all values of c from zero to infinity and dividing the sum by the total number of molecules (n). That is,

$$\bar{q} = \frac{1}{n}\int_0^\infty q\, dn_c = \frac{1}{n}\int_0^\infty q \cdot 4\pi n \left(\frac{m}{2\pi kT}\right)^{3/2} \cdot c^2\, e^{\frac{-mc^2}{2kT}}\, dc \quad ...(32)$$

For example, the kinetic energy is a function of velocity. The average kinetic energy $(\bar{\epsilon})$ of a molecule will be

$$(\bar{\epsilon}) = \frac{1}{n}\int_0^\infty \epsilon .\, dn_c$$

We shall use this method here to compute the average and the root mean square velocities.

Average velocity, C_α : The average velocity is given by

$$C_\alpha = \frac{1}{n}\int_0^\infty c\, dn_c = \frac{1}{n}\int_0^\infty c . 4\pi n \left(\frac{m}{2\pi kT}\right)^{3/2} . c^2\, e^{\frac{-mc^2}{2kT}}\, dc$$

$$\text{or } C_\alpha = 4\pi \left(\frac{m}{2\pi kT}\right)^{3/2} \int_0^\infty c^3 e^{-bc^2}\, dc, \left(\text{where } b = \frac{m}{2kT}\right)$$

$$= 4\pi \left(\frac{m}{2\pi kT}\right)^{3/2} \frac{1}{2b^2}, \text{ [Standard value]}$$

$$= 4\pi \left(\frac{m}{2\pi kT}\right)^{3/2} . \frac{1}{2} \times \frac{(2kT)^2}{m^2} = \sqrt{\frac{8kT}{\pi m}}$$

The average velocity, $C_\alpha = \sqrt{\frac{8kT}{\pi m}} = \sqrt{\frac{8RT}{\pi m}}$ ...(33)

Root mean square velocity, $\sqrt{\bar{c}^2} = c.$

The mean square velocity,

$$\bar{C}^2 = \frac{1}{n}\int_0^\infty c^2 . 4\pi n \left(\frac{m}{2\pi kT}\right)^{3/2} C^2 e^{\frac{-mc^2}{2kT}} dc$$

$$= 4\pi \left(\frac{m}{2\pi kT}\right)^{3/2} \int_0^\infty c^4 . e^{-bc^2} dc, \left(\text{where } b = \frac{m}{2kT}\right)$$

$$= 4\pi \left(\frac{m}{2\pi kT}\right)^{3/2} \times \frac{3}{8}\sqrt{\frac{\pi}{b^5}} \qquad \text{(Standard value)}$$

$$= 4\pi \left(\frac{m}{2\pi kT}\right)^{3/2} \times \frac{3\sqrt{\pi}}{8} \times \left(\frac{2kT}{m}\right)^{5/2} = \frac{3kT}{m}$$

$$\therefore c = \sqrt{\bar{c}^2} = \sqrt{\frac{3kT}{m}} = \sqrt{\frac{3R}{M}} \qquad ...(34)$$

From equation (32), (33) and (34), we find

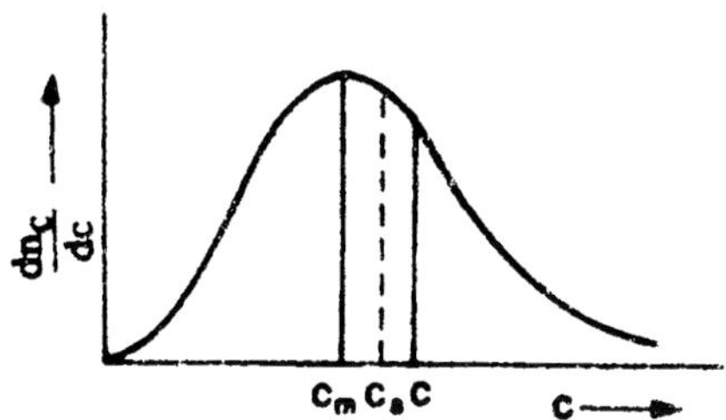

Fig. 2.16

$$c_m = \sqrt{\frac{2kT}{m}}$$

$$c_\alpha = \sqrt{\frac{8kT}{\pi m}} = \sqrt{\frac{2.55kT}{m}}$$

$$c = \sqrt{\frac{3kT}{m}}$$

$$\therefore c_m : c_\alpha : c = 1 : 1.128 : 1.224$$

MAXWELL'S DISTRIBUTION FOR KINETIC ENERGY

Since kinetic energy $\in = 1/2\ mc^2$, it is quite easy to transform the Maxwell's distribution of velocities into the distribution of kinetic energy.

$$\frac{1}{2}mc^2 = \in;\ c^2 = \frac{2\in}{m};\ c = \left(\frac{2\in}{m}\right)^{1/2};$$

$$d\in = mc\ dc = m \times (2\in/m)^{1/2}\ dc$$

or $\quad dc = (2m\in)^{-1/2}\ d\in$

Hence Maxwell's distribution (changing dn_c to $dn\in$) will be

$$dn_c = 4\pi n\left(\frac{m}{2\pi kT}\right)^{3/2} c^2\ e^{\frac{-mc^2}{2kT}}\ dc$$

$$\therefore \quad dn_\in = 4\pi n\left(\frac{m}{2\pi kT}\right)^{3/2} . \left(\frac{2\in}{m}\right) e^{\frac{-\in}{kT}} . (2m\in)^{-1/2}\ d\in$$

$$dn_\in = = 2\pi n\left(\frac{1}{\pi kT}\right)^{3/2} \in^{-1/2} e^{\frac{-\in}{kT}}\ d\in \qquad ...(35)$$

This is Maxwell's distribution for kinetic energy.

It is often necessary to know that fraction of molecules in a gas having kinetic energies exceeding a given value $\in_1$. Suppose, the molecules having energies greater than $\in_1$ is $n_{\in 1}$. Then,

$$n_{\in 1} = \int_{\in_1}^{\infty} dn_\in$$

From Eq. (35),

$$\frac{n_{\in 1}}{n} = \frac{2}{\sqrt{\pi (kT)^{3/2}}} \int_{\in_1}^{\infty} \in^{1/2}\ e^{\frac{-\in}{kT}}\ d\in$$

Suppose $\in = kTx^2$,

so that $\quad \in^{1/2} - (kT)^{1/2}\ x$ and $d\in = kTd\ (x^2)$.

$$\frac{n_{\in 1}}{n} = \frac{2}{\sqrt{\pi}} \int_{\sqrt{\in_1/kT}}^{\infty} x.e^{-x2}\ d\left(x^2\right)$$

$$= -\frac{2}{\sqrt{\pi}} \int_{\sqrt{\in_1/kT}}^{\infty} x\ d\left(e^{-x_2}\right)$$

$$= -\frac{2}{\sqrt{\pi}}\left[\left\{x . e^{-x_2}\right\}_{\sqrt{\in_1/kT}}^{\infty} - \int_{\sqrt{\in_1/kT}}^{\infty} e^{-x^2}\ dx\right]$$

$$\frac{n_{\epsilon 1}}{n} = 2\left(\frac{\epsilon_1}{\pi kT}\right)^{1/2} e^{\frac{-\epsilon_1}{kT}} + \frac{2}{\sqrt{\pi}} \int_{\sqrt{\epsilon_1/kT}}^{\alpha} e^{-x^2}\, dx$$

When $\epsilon_1 >> kT$, the second integral term in the right hand side is almost zero. In these circumstances,

$$\frac{n_{\epsilon 1}}{n} = 2\left(\frac{\epsilon_1}{\pi kT}\right)^{1/2} e^{\frac{-\epsilon_1}{kT}} \qquad ...(36)$$

It may be noted that the quantity on the right side varies rapidly with temperature.

An approximate energy distribution. The energy distribution may be simplified with some approximations. Restricting the molecular motion to a plane, we need consider only two rectangular components of the velocity. Thus, we have,

$$dn_{xy} = nA^2\, e^{-b\left(c_x^2 + c_y^2\right)}\, dc_x.dc_y \;\; nA^2\, e^{-bc^2}\, dc_x.dc_y$$

where $A^2 = \frac{m}{2\pi kT'}\; b = \frac{m}{2kT}$,
n = total number of molecules.

Changing to polar co-ordinates, we have

$$dn = nA^2\, e^{-bc2}\,.\, c\, dc\,.\, d\theta,$$

where θ may have values between 0 and 2π.

Further $\epsilon = \frac{1}{2} mc^2$

$$c\, dc = \frac{1}{m}\, d\epsilon$$

$\therefore$ The number of molecules having energy ϵ,

$$dn_{\epsilon} = n\left(\frac{m}{2\pi kT}\right) e^{-\epsilon/kT}\,.\,\frac{1}{m} d\epsilon.\left(2\pi\right) = n.\,\frac{1}{kT}.\, e^{-\epsilon/kT}\, d\epsilon$$

Hence, on integration,

$$\frac{n_{\epsilon}}{n} = \int_0^{\infty} \frac{1}{kT}\, e^{-\epsilon/kT}\, d\epsilon$$

or $$\frac{n_{\epsilon}}{n} = e^{-\epsilon/kT} \qquad ...(37)$$

This is the fraction of the total number of molecules possessing energy in excess of ϵ.

EXPERIMENTAL VERIFICATION OF MAXWELL'S DISTRIBUTION LAW

Two methods are outlined below:

First Method

Stern in 1926 determined experimentally the actual distribution of velocities of the silver atoms and observed that the values were spread over a range, in general agreement with the requirements of the distribution law. Letter, this method was improved by T. L. Costa, H. D. Symth and K. T. Compton (1927) to determine the shape of the velocity distribution curve.

Apparatus

It consisted of two toothed discs on a common axis (Fig. 2.17). A beam of molecules (H_2 or O_2 or N_2 or CCl_4) was so passed that when the discs were stationary, the beam passed through the gaps between the teeth on to a radiometer vane, the deflection of the later giving a measure of the number of molecules striking it.

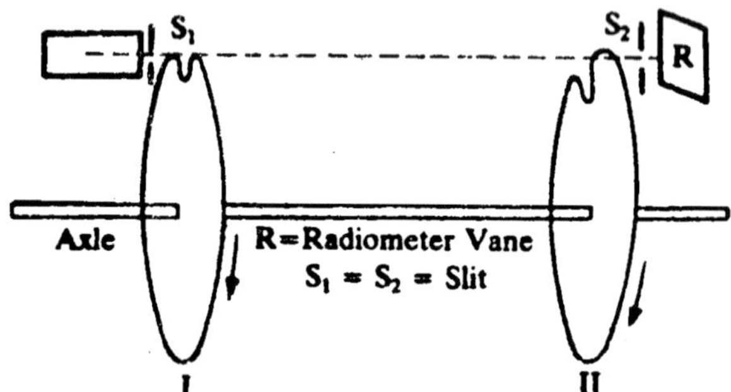

Fig. 2.17

Working

The discs were set in rotation. A molecule passing through a gap in the first will pass through a gap in the second only if the time required to travel the distance between the discs is equal to an integral multiple of the time necessary for the discs to rotate from one gap to the next. From a knowledge of the speed of the discs, therefore, the velocity of the molecules passing through can be determined, and the number possessing the velocity ;is given by the deflection of the radiometer vane. By making measurements with the discs rotating at various speeds, it is possible to obtain a velocity distribution curve. This curve is found to be in agreement with the Maxwell velocity distribution.

Second Method

An excellent method for the verification of the Maxwell-Boltzmann law of distribution of speeds has been given by Estermann, Simpson and Stern. A schematic diagram of their apparatus is shown in Fig. 2.18.

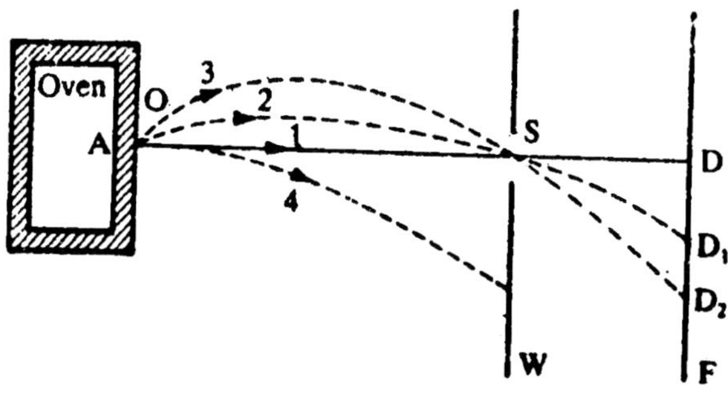

Fig. 2.18

Apparatus

Cesium atoms from the oven O emerge from the opening A. These atoms pass through a horizontal linear slit S in a screen W. A hot tungsten filament F is held parallel to the slit S and can be moved up and down. The filament is surrounded by a negatively charged metal cylinder which has not been shown in the diagram. The whole apparatus is enclosed in ;an evacuated chamber (10^{-8} mm. of Hg). The opening A and slit S are horizontal.

Working

In the absence of gravity, the cesium atoms from oven O will strike the wire at D because O, S and D at the same horizontal level. In the presence of gravity, the path of cesium atoms will follow the parabolic paths as shown by lines 1, 2, 3 and 4.

The cesium atoms along the paths 1, 2, and 3 reach at D, D_1 and D_2 respectively, where as the atoms going along the path 4 does not reach the wire.

When cesium atom strike the wire F, they undergo ionisation and re-evaporate. These ionised atoms will be collected by a negatively charged detecting cylinder surrounding the tungsten filament F. The magnitude of the current indicates the intensity of the atoms at various positions. The detector is moved at various positions along the filament to detect the positions where the atoms after passing through the slit S strike and undergo ionisation. The vertical height of the detector represents the magnitude of the velocity and the ionisation current indicates the number of atoms striking the wire at a particular point. Then, a graph is drawn between the vertical height (speed of the atoms) of the detector along X-axis and the ionisation current along the Y-axis. The velocity distribution obtained from the graph is found to be in agreement with the Maxwell velocity distribution.

SOLVED EXAMPLES

Example 1:

Calculate the pressure in torr of a barometer on a flying rocket at an altitude of 20 km (Assuming the pressure to be 760 torr at sea level and mean temperature – 23° C and mean temperature –2°C and using the average molecular weight of air (80% N_2, 2% O_2).

Solution:

$$P_0 = 760 \text{ torr, } h = 20 \text{ km} = 20\ (10^5) = 2 \times 10^6 \text{ cm}$$

$$T = -\ 23°C = 250 \text{ K,}$$

$$M = 0.8 \times 28 + 0.2 \times 32 = 28.8$$

$$\therefore\ P = P0\ e^{-Mgz/RT]}$$

or $$P = 760 \times e^{-[28.8 \times 980.66 \times 2\ 106/8.314 \times 107 \times 250]}$$

$$= 760 \times e^{-2.7176} = 760 \times 0.0660308 = 50.183408 \text{ torr.}$$

Example 2(a):

Express the van der Waals equation in the virial form as a power series in 1/V and derive and expression for the Boyle temperature.

Solution:

Van der Waal's equation for one mole of a gas is

$$\left(P + \frac{a}{V^2}\right)(V - b) = RT$$

$$\therefore\ P = \frac{RT}{V-b} - \frac{a}{V^2} = \frac{RT}{V(1-b/V)} - \frac{a}{V^2}$$

$$\therefore \quad PV = \frac{RT}{1-b/V} - \frac{a}{V} = RT\left(1-\frac{b}{V}\right)^{-1} - \frac{a}{V}$$

Since b << V, w can use the binomial theorem to expand the quantity

$\left(1-\frac{b}{V}\right)^{-1}$ obtaining

$$PV = RT\left(1+\frac{b}{V}+\frac{b^2}{V^2}+\frac{b^3}{V^3}+\ldots\right)-\frac{a}{V}$$

Taking the term -a/V inside the bracket, we get

$$PV = RT\left(1+\frac{b}{V}-\frac{a}{VRT}+\frac{b^2}{V^2}+\frac{b^3}{V^3}+\ldots\right)$$

$$= RT\left(1+\left(\frac{b-a/RT}{V}\right)+\frac{b^2}{V^2}+\frac{b^3}{V^3}+\ldots\right) \quad \ldots(1)$$

Comparing this equation with the virial equation of state, viz.,

$$PV = RT\left(1+\frac{B_2(T)}{V}+\frac{B_3(T)}{V^2}+\frac{B_4(T)}{V^3}+\ldots\ldots\right).$$

we see that $B_2(T) = b - \frac{a}{RT}$;

$B_3(T) = b^2$;

$B_4(T) = b^3$, etc.

Since the van der Waals constant b is very small, the terms involving b_2, b_3, etc., can be neglected so that the van der Waal's equation (i) can be written in the virial form as

$$PV = RT\left(1+\frac{b-(a/RT)}{V}\right)$$

Since at the Boyle temperature, the second virial coefficient is zero, *i.e.*,

$$\frac{b-(a/RT_B)}{V} = 0.$$

Hence, $T_B = \frac{a}{Rb}$ for a gas obeying van der Waal's equation of state.

Example 2(b):

Show that under conditions of low pressures (and hence low densities), the Dieterici equation of state reduces to the van der Waals equation of state.

Solution:

In the Dieterici equation,

$$P = \frac{RT}{V-b} e^{-a/RTV}$$

Suppose, $x = a/RTV$ so that the exponential can be written as e^{-x}. Expanding it as a power series (assuming that $x << 1$,) we have

$$e^{-x} = 1 - x + \frac{x^2}{2!} - \frac{x^3}{3!} + \dots\dots$$

Hence, $$P = \frac{RT}{V-b}\left(1 - \frac{a}{RTV} + \frac{a^2}{2R^2T^2V^2} - \frac{a^3}{6R^3T^3V^3} + \dots\right)$$

$$= \frac{RT}{V-b} - \frac{a}{V(V-b)} + \frac{a^2}{2RTV^2(V-b)} - \dots\dots$$

(neglecting the higher powers)

As $b << V$,

$\therefore$ $bV << V^2$.

Thus, bV can be neglected as compared to V^2.

Hence, $$P = \frac{RT}{V-b} - \frac{a}{V^2}$$

or $$\left(P + \frac{a}{V^2}\right)(V-b) = RT$$

This is van der Waals equation for 1 mole of the gas.

Example 3(a):

At N.T.P., the viscosity of hydrogen is 8.4 × 10^{5} poise and the average velocity of the molecules is 1.7 × 10^{5} cm. per sec. Calculate the mean free path and the molecular diameter. (ρ = 9 × 10^{5}).

Solution:

We know, $$\eta = \frac{1}{3} m n \bar{c} \lambda = \frac{1}{3} \rho \bar{c} \lambda$$

where ρ is the density

or $$\lambda = \frac{3\eta}{\bar{c}\rho} = \frac{3 \times 8.4 \times 10^{-5}}{1.7 \times 10^5 \times 9 \times 10^{-5}} = 1.6 \times 10^{-5} \text{ cm.}$$

Also, we know $$\eta = \frac{1}{\sqrt{2}\pi\sigma^2 n}$$

$$\text{or } \sigma = \left(\frac{1}{\sqrt{2\pi\, n\, \lambda}}\right)^{1/2} = \left(\frac{1}{\sqrt{2\times 3.14\times \frac{6.02\times 10^{23}}{2400}\times 1.6\times 10^{-4}}}\right)^{1/2}$$

$$= 2.24\times 10^{-5} \text{ cm}$$

Example 3(b):

Calculate the molecular diameter of oxygen. Given $\eta' = 1.92 \times 10^{-4}$ at 0^oC,

Solution:

$$\text{We know, } \sigma = \frac{9}{4}\eta b \sqrt{\left(\frac{\pi}{RTM}\right)}$$

$$= \frac{9}{4}\times 1.92\times 10^{-4}\times 31.2\times \sqrt{\left(\frac{3.14}{8.4\times 10^{7}\times 273\times 32}\right)}$$

$$= 2.7\times 10^{-8} \text{ cm} = 1.7 \text{ A}^0$$

Example 4:

Calculate the mean free path of a gas by taking the diameter of a molecule as 2×10^{-8} cm. At N.T.P. one mole of a gas occupies 22.4 liters and Avogadro's number is 6.02×10^{23}

Solution:

$$\text{Here } n = \frac{6.02\times 10^{33}}{22.4\times 1000} = 2.7\times 10^{19} \text{ molecules.c.c.}$$

$$\therefore \lambda = \frac{1}{\sqrt{2\pi\sigma^2 n}} = \frac{1}{\sqrt{2\pi\left(2\times 10^{-8}\right)^2\times 2.7\times 10^{19}}} = 2.1\times 10^{-5} \text{ cm.}$$

Example 5:

Calculate the molecular weight of a gas if its pressure is falling to one-half of its value in a vertical distances of 1 km at 27^oC.

Solution:

$$P = P_0/2,\ z = 1 \text{ km} = 1000 \text{ m} = 1000\times 100 \text{ cm}$$

$= 100000$ cm,

$g = 980.66$ cm/sec^2, $T = 273 + 27 = 300$ K

On substituting these values in the following equation, we get

$$P = P_0\, e^{-Mgz/RT}$$

$$\frac{P_0}{2} = P_0\, e^{-M(980.66) \times (100000)/(8.314 \times 107 \times 300)}$$

$$2.3.03 \log 0.5 = -M(980.76) \times (100000)/(8.314 \times 10^7 \times 300)$$

or $$M = \frac{2.303 \times 0.3010 \times 8.314 \times 10^7 \times 303}{980.66 \times 100000} = 1.7630849.$$

Example 6:

Calculate the atmospheric pressure at an hill station whose height above the sea level is 2250 m if the pressure at the ground level is 1 atm and temperature is 25° C, assuming that there exist no complications such as turbulence or temperature gradients. ($M_m = 29$ g mol^{-1}).

Solution:

From the barometric formula,

$$\ln \frac{P_0}{P_z} = \frac{Mgz}{RT}$$

Now, $M = 29$ g mol^{-1} $= 29 \times 10–3$ kg mol^{-1}

$g = 9.81$ ms^{-2}

$z = 22250$ m

$T = 25°C = (25 + 273)$ K $= 298$ K

$P_0 = 1$ atm

$$\therefore \log\left(\frac{1}{P_z}\right) = \frac{(29 \times 103 \text{kgmol}^{-1})(9.81 \text{m s}^{-2})(2250 \text{m})}{2.303 \times (8.314 \text{J K}^{-1} \text{mol}^{-1})(298)} = 0.1121$$

$\log P = -0.1121 = \bar{1}.8879$

Taking antilogs, $P = 0.7725$ atm

3

SOLUTIONS AND THEIR THEORIES

MEANING OF SOLUTION

It is a homogeneous mixture of two or more substances having uniform properties (such as density, refractive index, etc.) throughout. For example, if a sugar lump is dipped in a beaker of water, the lump disintegrates and within a short time disappears into the liquid phase. In this process, the molecules of the sugar leave the crystal structure of the solid and become uniformly dispersed throughout the water thus producing a complete mixing of the two substances. Thus, it is a solution of sugar in water.

Component

The substances making up a solution are called components of the solution. For example, the solution f sugar in water in an example of a two component system consisting one liquid phase.

Solvent and Solute

The component having the same physical state as the solution is termed as the solvent, and to he component solute. Thus, in the solution of sugar in water, solvent is water whereas solute is sugar.

There is no theoretical distinction between the terms solvent and solute, since the molecules of both are uniformly distributed throughout the solution. Consider, for example, a solution made by mixing equal volumes of ethyl alcohol and water. Either may, with equal justification, be considered to be dissolved in each other. *However, the component present in the larger amount is called solvent whereas the component present in the smaller amount is called the solute.*

TYPE OF SOLUTIONS

Since there are three states of matter, there are theoretically nine possible classes or types of solutions. Three types are possible when a liquid is the solvent, since the solute may be a as. a liquid or a solid. Similarly, three classes are possible when the solvent is a gas and three when the solvent is a solid. The various types of solutions with examples, are given in Table 3.1.

Table 3.1 : Various Types of Solutions with Examples

S.No.	*Solute*	*Solvent*	*Type of the solution*	*Examples*
1.	Gas	Gas	Gas-Gas	Any mixture of gases as in air.
2.	Gas	Liquid	Gas-liquid	Carbon dioxide in aerated bottles; mineral water
3.	Gas	Solid	Gas-Solid	Hydrogen adsorbed on palladium.
4.	Liquid	Gas	Liquid-Gas	Moisture in air when we have mist
5.	Liquid	Liquid	Liquid-Liquid	Alcohol in water, benzene in toluene
6.	Liquid	Solid	Liquid-Solid	Hg in gold
7.	Solid	Gas	Solid-Gas	Comphor in air, iodine vapour in air
8.	Solid	Liquid	Solid-Liquid	Sugar in water, common salt in water
9.	Solid	Solid	Solid solutions	Alloys like brass containing zinc in copper

Various methods for Expressing constrations of solutions

A large number of methods are known which are used to express the concentrations of solutions. Some of these methods are discussed as follows for a solution made up of two components A and B.

Mass Fraction

The mass fraction of a component in a solution is expressed as the mass of that component per unit mass of solution. Suppose w_A and w_B are the masses of components A and B respectively. Then, the mass fraction (W_A) of A can be expressed as

$$W_A = \frac{w_A}{w_A + w}$$

and mass fraction (W_B) of B can be expressed as

$$W_B = \frac{w_B}{w_A + w_B}$$

Mass percentage of component A will be equal to $W_A \times 100$. Similarly mass percentage of component B will be $W_B \times 100$.

Mole Fraction

It is the ratio of moles of one component to the total number of moles of component (solute as well as solvent) of the solution. Suppose, a solution is prepared from n_A moles of A and n_B moles of a B in a fixed quantity of the solution. Then

$$\text{Mole fraction of A} = \frac{\text{Moles of A}}{\text{Moles of A + Moles of B}}$$

or

$$x_A = \frac{n_A}{n_A + n_B}$$

and

$$\text{Mole fraction of B} = \frac{\text{Moles of B}}{\text{Moles of A + Moles of B}}$$

or

$$x_B = \frac{n_B}{n_A + n_B}$$

Let us apply the above definition of mole fraction to a solution having one mole of water and three poles of ethyl alcohol. Then,

$$x_{H_2O} = \frac{1}{1+3} = 0.25$$

$$x_{C_2H_5OH} = \frac{3}{1+3} = 0.75$$

Molarity

Molarity of a solution is defined as the number of moles of solute per litre of the solution. It is generally denoted by M. For example, a 0.1 M solution of NaCl means that one litre of such a solution contains 0.1 mole of NaCl.

If n_B moles of solute B are dissolved in V litres of solvent A, then molarity is expressed as:

$$M = \frac{n_B \text{ moles}}{\text{V litres}}$$

In laboratory, molarity is generally used to express concentrations of solutions. But the main drawback of this mode is that its values depend upon temperature due to expansion or contraction of the liquid.

Mole fractions and mass fractions are generally expressed in positive number while molalities are expressed in units of moles per dm^3 of solutions.

Molality

Molality of a solution is the number of moles of the solute per 1000 kg (1kg) of the solvent. It is generally denoted by m. Suppose n_B represents the number of moles of solute and w_A the number of grams of solvent Then, the molality of solution, m_B, is defined as follows:

$$m_B = \frac{1000}{w_A} n_B$$

The main advantage of molality over molarity is that the former quantity does to depend upon temperature.

A 1 m solution of cane sugar contains 1 mol of can sugar in 1000 g (1 kg) of water. A 5 m solution of H2SO4 means that it has bee prepared by dissolving 5 moles of H_2SO_4 in 1000 g (1 kg) of water.

Normality

The normality of a solution may be defined as the number of gram equivalents of solute per litre of the solution. For example, a 0.1 N $AgNO_3$ solution means that it contains 0.1 gram-equivalent of $AgNO_3$ per litre of the solution. The amount in gram-equivalent may vary from reaction to reaction.

Parts Per Million (p.p.m.)

This mode of expressing concentration is preferred for very dilute solutions. It may be expressed as follows:

$$\text{p.p.m. of a substance} = \frac{\text{Mass of the substance}}{\text{Total mass}} \times 10^6$$

For example, 1 g if KCl, when dissolved in a total mass of 10^6 g of water, will yield a solution containing 1 p.p.m. of KCl.

$$\text{p.p.m. of KCl} = \frac{\text{Mass of KCl}}{\text{Total mass}} \times 10^6 = \frac{1}{10^6} \times 10^6 = 1$$

VAPOUR PRESSURE OF A LIQUID

Suppose a pure liquid is placed in a beaker which is covered with a bell jar. A small fraction of molecules of liquid will always possess sufficient minimum energy so that they may escape from the liquid in the for of vapours and these will fill the space available to the. A fraction of these molecules will again return from vapour to the liquid state till at a certain temperature an equilibrium is attained between the vapour and liquid phases. The pressure exerted by the vapour in such a situation at a five temperature is termed as the vapour pressure of the liquid.

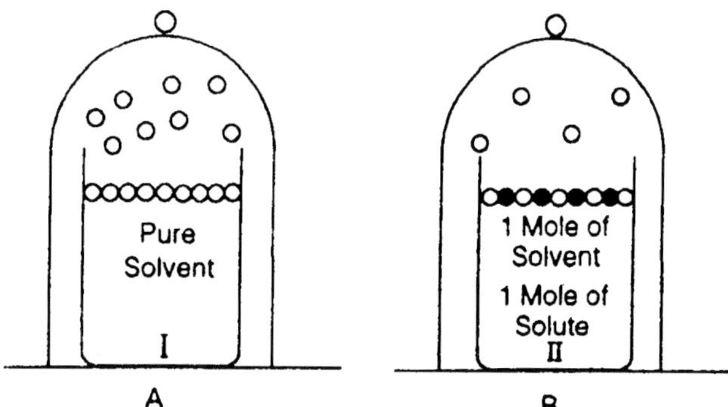

Fig. 3.1 : Decrease in the vapour pressure when a solute is added to a solvent: (i) evaporation of molecules from the surface of pure solvent. (ii) in a solution solute particles also occupy a part of the surface area and so reduce the number of solvent molecules at the surface that evaporate (escape is reduced).

LOWERING OF VAPOUR PRESSURE

In order to prepare a solution, a non-volatile solute is added to a solvent. It has bee found that the vapour pressure of solution is always less than that of pure solvent. We can understand this by considering Fig. 3.1. Let beaker I contains pure solvent whereas beaker II contains 1 mole of non-volatile solute and I mole of solvent. Due to evaporation of liquid solvent, liquid vapours will be present over the liquid phase in both beaker I and II. But the relative umber of solvent molecules present over the liquid surface of beaker II has been found to be less than the above I. The reason for this is that some of the non-volatile solute molecules are also present in the liquid surface of II. The presence of these molecules reduces the escaping surface. But evaporation of a liquid at any temperature below its boiling point depends upon the escaping surface of the liquid. Therefore, the vapour pressure of a solution I will be less than the vapour pressure of pure solvent. I.

Suppose P^o be the vapour pressure of pure solvent and P the vapour pressure of solution. The $P^o - P$ will be known as the lowering of vapour pressure.

If we now extend the consideration discussed as above to the case when solute is another volatile liquid or solid, the vapour phase above the liquid in beaker II will consist of vapours of both the components. It is also expected that partial vapour pressure of each component of the solution will depend upon its molar concentration of mole fraction in solution.

IDEAL SOLUTIONS

Raoult's law describes the behaviour of solutions in the same way as the ideal as law describes behaviour of gases. Ideal solutions are those which obey Raoult's law over the entire range of concentration. The properties of such ideal solutions are the average of the properties of this components in proportion to their mole fractions.

In an ideal solution of two components A and B, all the intermolecular forces between A and A, B and B, and A and B are alike, so that the escaping tendency of an A or B molecule would be independent of whether it is being surrounded by A molecules, B molecules or varying proportions of A and B molecules. Thus, the scaping tendency, as measured by the vapour pressure, of each component in this type of solution will remain the same as that in the pure component therefore Raoult's law is obeyed. Such a solution can only form if the components A and B are identical in structure and polarity.

On mixing the two components to form an ideal solution, no change in intermolecular forces between two component occurs and therefore the heat change on mixing, ΔE_{mixing}, in such ideal solutions will be zero. Also, in ideal solutions the volume of the solution will be equal to the sum of the volumes of the components before they are mixed. Therefore, it is evident that volume change on mixing , ΔV_{mixing} will be zero. Thus if we ix 40 ml of a solute with 60 l of a solvent, the total volume of the resulting ideal solution should be 100 l (*i.e.*, $\Delta V = 0$).

Fro the above discussion it is evident that an ideal solution should obey the following conditions:

(i) An ideal solution should obey Raoult's law over the entire range of concentration.

(ii) When an ideal solution is prepared from its components, there should be neither volume change ($\Delta V = 0$) nor enthalpy change ($\Delta H = 0$).

Ideal solutions are generally rare. However, few ideal solutions are known. For example, an ideal solution is the liquid mixture of bezene and toluene. These form early ideal solutions by mixing them in any proportion. The reason of this is that in these solutions the benzene-benzene attractions, the benzene-toluene attractions and toluene-toluene attractions are almost alike. The following are the other binary mixtures which form ideal solutions : ethyl bromide and ethyl iodide; chlorobenzene and bromobenzene; etc.

NON IDEAL SOLUTIONS

A no ideal solution does not obey Raoult's law ad its formation is accompanied by a volume change and enthalpy, *i.e.*, $\Delta V \neq 0$ and $\Delta H \neq 0$.

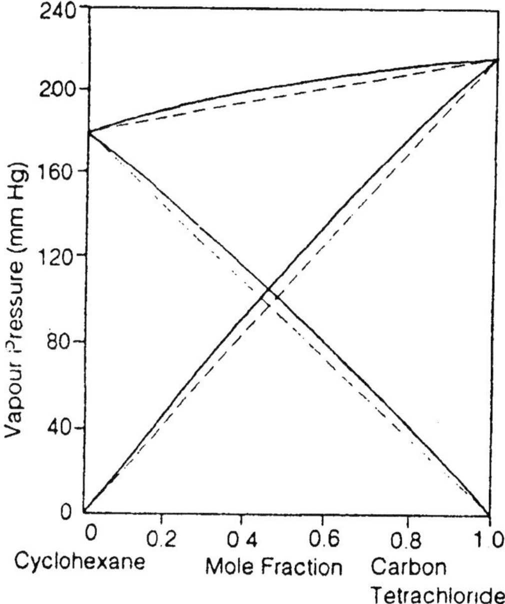

Fig. 3.2 : Real solutions showing small deviations from ideal behaviour. The dotted lines represent ideal behaviour.

Most of the solutions exhibit appreciable devications (positive or negative) from their ideal behaviour, *i.e.*, they deviate from Raoult's law. The deviation may be positive or negative. Non-ideal solutions may be divided into three types:

1. *Type I* : In the solutions of type I, small deviations have been observed from their ideal behaviour. The total pressures of such solutions have been found to remain to within the vapour pressures of the pure constituents. This behaviour has bee depicted in Fig. 3.2 in which broken lines are representing the ideal behaviour whereas dark lines are representing the real behaviour. A rare example of non-ideal solutions of type I is cyclohexane-carbon tetrachloride system.

2. *Type II* : The liquid pairs of type I exhibit large positive deviations. I the process of dissolving to form solutions, there occurs the absorption of heat, and the partial vapour pressure of each component in these solutions has been found to be greater than that predicted by Raoult's law.

The absorption of heat reveals that the solutions will be less stable than either of the pure components. Hence, the escaping tendency of the molecules, which is measured by the vapour pressures of the components, will be expected to be higher in solution than in either of the pure components.

The liquid pairs showing positive deviations will also show a slight increasing volume.

The positive deviations have bee exhibited by such liquid pairs for which the A-B attractive forces are weaker than the A -A or B-B forces.

Solutions exhibiting positive deviations are generally obtained by mixing a highly polar liquid with non-polar liquid.

The behaviour followed by solutions of type I is denoted in Fig. 3.3.

The liquid pairs exhibiting positive deviations are acetaldehyde-carbon disulphide, water-propyl alcohol, ethyl alcohol-chloroform and ethanol-cyclohexane mixtures.

Liquid pairs exhibiting negative devications give minimum boiling point azeotropes.

3. *Type III* : Liquid pairs exhibiting negative deviations are obtained when some bonding exists in the solutions which does not exist in either of the pure components. It means that this type of devication is exhibited

by such liquid pairs for which A–B attractions are stronger than A–A or B – B attractions. Thus, both A and B will have less tendency to leave the solution and thus the total vapour pressure would become less than the total partial vapour pressures of components. Such solutions exhibit increase in boiling points when solute is added to the.

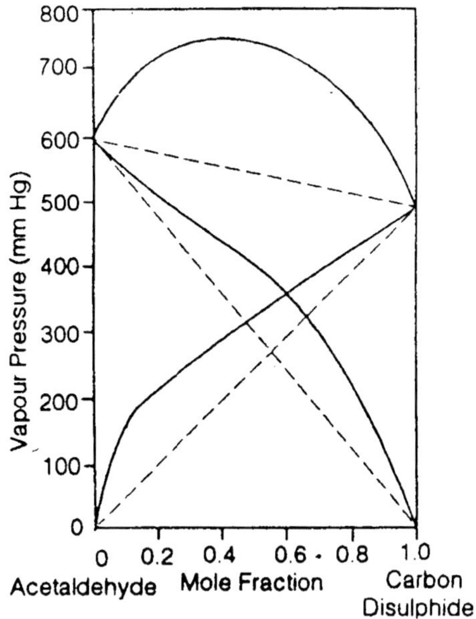

Fig. 3.3 : Positive deviations from ideal behaviour. The dotted lines represent ideal behaviour.

We are aware of the fact that the process of solution is accompanied by the absorption or evolution of heat, unless the components yield an ideal solution. Whenever evolution of heat occurs, the resulting solution exhibits a negative deviation from its ideal behaviour *i.e.,* the partial vapour pressure of each component in the solution would be less than that allowed by Raoult's law.

The evolution of heat accompanying the process of solution reveals that the solution is more stable than either of the pure components. Hence th escaping tendency of the molecules, which is measured by the vapour pressures of the components, would be less in solution than in either of the pure components.

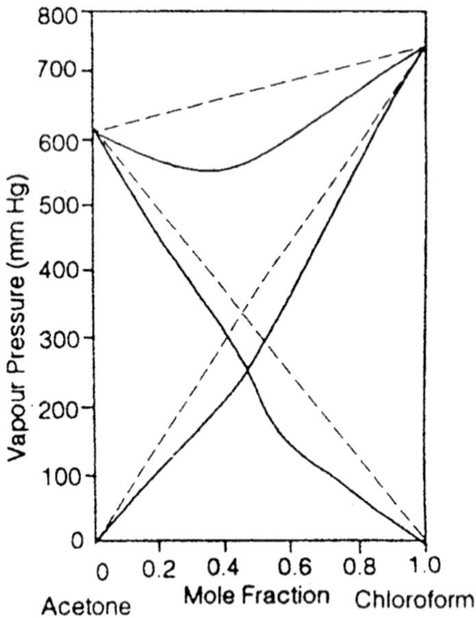

Fig. 3.4 : Negative deviations from ideal behaviour. The dotted lines represent ideal behaviour.

A few examples of liquid-pairs which exhibit positive and negative deviations from their ideal behaviour have been summarised in Table 3.2.

Table 3.2 : Non-Ideal Mixtures.

Mixtures showing negative deviations	Mixtures showing positive deviations
$(CH_3)_2CO + C_7H_5NH_2$	$(CH_3)_2CO + CS_2$
$CHCl_3 + C_6H_6$	$CCl_4 + CHCl_3$
$CHCl_3 + (C_2H_5)_2O$	$CCl_4 + C_6H_6$
$CH_3COOH + C_5H_5N$	$C_6H_6 + (CH_3)_2CO$
$H_2O + HCl$	$(CH_3)_2CO + C_2H_5OH$
$H_2O + HNO_3$	$H_2O + C_2H_5OH$
$CHCl_3 + (CH_3)_2CO$	$H_2O + CH_3OH$
	$CCl_4 + C_6H_5 . CH_3$

Solutions exhibiting negative deviations show maximum boiling point azeotroipes. These solutions also show decrease in volume on mixing alongwith evolution of heat. Examples of type III acetone chloroform, water-sulphuric acid, etc.

I the solutions exhibiting large negative deviation, the total vapour pressure curve shows the minimum for one intermediate composition. It is shown in Fig. 3.4. For example, mixtures of chloroform and acetone exhibit a negative deviation due to hydrogen boding Cl_3C---H...O = $C(CH_3)_2$.

RAOULT'S LAW APPLICABLE TO BINARY SOLUTIONS OF TWO LIQUIDS

Let us consider a binary solution of two liquids A and B whose mole fractions are x_A and x_B respectively. If P_A and P_B denote their respective partial vapour pressures above the solution, then these will be proportional to the respective mole fractions x_A and x_B in the solution. Therefore, we may write as follows:

$$P_A \propto x_A$$

and

$$P_B \propto x_B$$

Raoult investigated the vapour pressures of a number of binary solutions which are obtained by mixing volatile iscible liquids, like benzene and toluene, at constant temperature and concluded that in those cases, the above equations may take the following forms:

$$P_A = P_A^o \times x_A \qquad ...(1)$$

and

$$P_B = P_B^o \times x_B \qquad ...(2)$$

In the above relations, P_A^o and P_B^o denote the vapour pressures of pure components A and B respectively. Equations (1) and (2) describe the relationship between vapour pressure of a component and its mole fraction and this relation is known as Raoult's law. This may be enunciated as follows:

"The partial pressure of any volatile component of a solution of volatile liquids at any temperature is equal to the product of vapour pressure of the pure component and the mole fraction of that component in the solution."

Suppose the vapour behaves like an ideal gas. Then, by Dalton's law of partial pressures, the total pressures, P will be given as follows:

$$P = P_A^o x_A + P_B^o x_B \quad ...(3)$$

From Raoult's law it follows that the plot of P_A against x_A for a solution should give a straight line passing through the point P_A^o when x_A becomes unity. This is shown by broken lines in Fig. 435. Similarly, a plot of P_A against x_B should also give a straight line passing through P_B^o when x_B becomes unity. This is also shown by broken lines. The total vapour pressure, P, of the solution, at any composition, will be equal to the sum of P_A and P_B. This is show in Fig. 3.5. In this figure, the pressure P_A and P_B have been denoted by broken straight lines I and II respectively whereas the line III, which is obtained by joining the points P_A^o and P_B^o, denotes $P_A + P_B$. The solutions which obey Raoult's law are called ideal solutions.

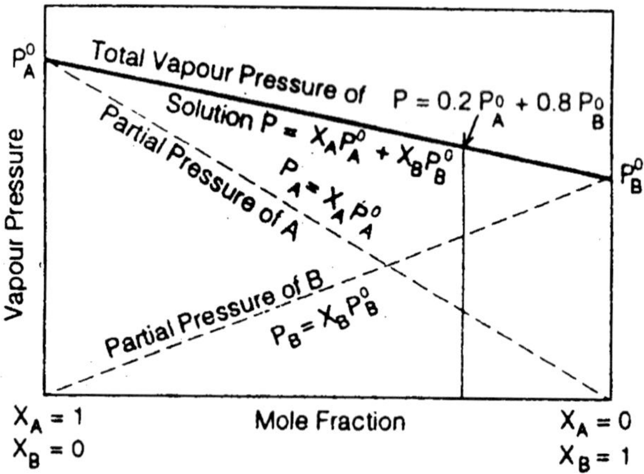

Fig. 3.5 : Vapour pressures of ideal solutions.

Raoult's law as applicable to a solution of a non-volatile solute: Suppose we consider a solution obtained by dissolving a non-volatile solute in a volatile solvent (*e.g.*, glucose in water). In such a solution, no contribution of vapour pressure of non-volatile solute to the total vapour pressure of solutions will be made. For such a solution, the total vapour pressure will be only due to the vapour pressure contribution of the solvent present in the solution. Hence, it is evident that the vapour pressure of the solution will be lowered if mole fraction of the solvent in a solution is decreased. Therefore, equation (3) may be written as follows:

$$P = P_A = P_A^o x_A \qquad ...(4)$$

For a binary solution, we know

or $$x_A + x_B = 1 \qquad ...(5)$$

On substituting the above value of x_A in equation (4), we get

$$P_A = P_A^o(1 - x_B)$$

or $$\frac{P_A}{P_A^o} = 1 - x_B$$

On rearranging the above equation, we get

$$1 - \frac{P_A}{P_A^o} = x_B$$

or $$\frac{P_A^o - P_A}{P_A^o} = 1 - x_B \qquad ...(6)$$

In the above equation, $P_A^o - P_A$ denotes the *lowering of vapour pressure* which depends upon the temperature changes whereas $(P_A^o - P_A)P_A^o$ denotes the relative lowering of vapour pressure for the solution which is independent of temperature changes. Thus, the Raoult's law for solutions of non-volatile solutes may be stated as follows:

"*The relative lowering of the vapour pressure of a solution is equal to the mole fraction of the non volatile solute provided solvent alone is volatile.*"

Limitation: Raoult's law cannot be applied to a mixture of the volatile liquids which do not form a solution.

Bunsen Absorption Coefficient

The solubility of a gas is usually determined by measuring the volume rather than the mass that dissolves. It is frequently expressed in terms of Bunsen absorption coefficient (α) which is defined as *the volume of the gas at STP (2373 K and 1 atm pressure dissolved by unit volume of the solvent at the given temperature under a partial pressure of 1 atmosphere of the as.* If V_0 is the volume of the gas that dissolves reduced to STP, V is the volume of solvent and p the partial pressure of the as in atmosphere, the absorption coefficient α, is given by

$$\alpha = \frac{V_0}{V_p}$$

Table 3 shows the Bunsen absorption coefficient (α) for some of the gases as 298 K in different solvents.

Table 3.3 : Bunsen Absorption Coefficient of Gases at 298 K

Solvent	He	H_2	N_2	O_2	CO	CO_2
Water	0.0087	0.0019	0.0014	0.0028	0.0025	0.088
Ethanol	0.0282	0.0820	0.1320	0.1450	0.1750	3.00
Benzene	0.0180	0.0658	0.1050	0.1630	0.1550	—
Acetone	0.0320	0.0660	0.1300	0.2070	0.1990	6.50

Henry's Law

Le Chatelier's principle predicts that with the increase of pressure the solubility of a gas should increase. Consider a system at equilibrium, containing a gas in contact with its solution in a give solvent. On increasing the pressure, the volume of the gas will be reduced and hence an increase in solubility will result from an increase of pressure.

William Henry in 1803 carried our a systematic investigation of the solubility of a gas in a liquid and observed the following law known as Henry's law. The law states *that the mass of a gas dissolved by a unit volume of a solvent at constant temperature is directly proportional to the pressure of the as with which it is i equilibrium.* If X_2 is the mole fraction of the gas dissolved by unit volume of the solvent at equilibrium pressure p, then

$$X_2 \propto p \qquad ...(2)$$

or

$$X_2 = K'_H p \quad \text{or} \quad p = K_H X_2 \qquad ...(3)$$

where K_H is a proportionality constant known as Henry's law constant. The magnitude of K_H depends on the nature of the as, solvent and the units of pressure.

Equation (3) is an equation of a straight line passing through the origin. Thus, a plot of solubility of th gas against the equilibrium pressure at a give temperature gives a straight line passing through the origin (Fig. 3.6). This reveals the validity of Henry's law.

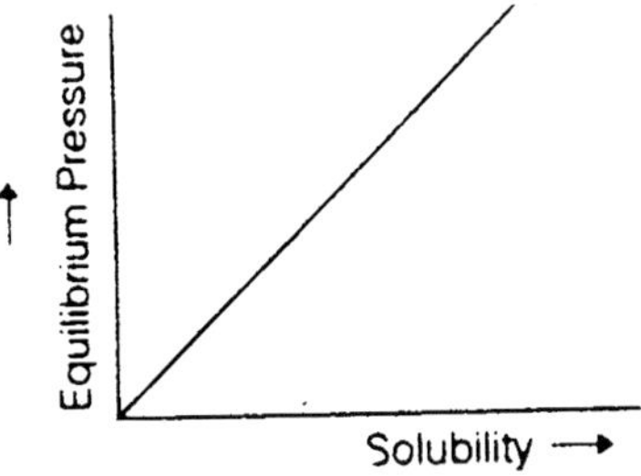

Fig. 3.6 : Variation of solubility of a gas with pressure.

Henry's law may be stated in another form also. The mass of the gas (m) dissolved per unit volume of the solvent is proportional to its concentration in solution (C_2), whereas the pressure p of the gas is given by $p = C_1RT$ (C_1 being its concentration in the as phase). Hence

$$K'_H = \frac{m}{p} = \frac{\kappa' C_2}{C_1RT}$$

At constant temperature, we have

$$\frac{C_2}{C_1} = K_1 \quad \text{(constant)}$$

or $$\frac{\text{Concentration of the as in liquid phase}}{\text{Concentration of the as in gaseous phase}} = K_1$$

In other words, the concentrations in the gaseous ad liquid phases bear a constant ratio to one another at constant temperature.

Again, if we regard the volume of the gas dissolved instead of mass or concentration, we have

$$pv = \frac{m}{M}RT \quad \text{or} \quad m = \frac{Mpv}{RT}$$

$$= kpv \quad \left(k = \frac{M}{RT}\right)$$

where v represents the volume of the as dissolved per unit volume of the solvent, M is the molar mass of the gas. Hence

$$K'_H = \frac{m}{p} = \frac{k\,pv}{p};$$

$$v = \frac{K'_H}{k} = \text{constant} \qquad ...(4)$$

Hence the Henry's law may also be stated as the volume of the gas dissolved by a solvent at a give temperature and is independent of pressure.

When several gases are simultaneously dissolved in a solvent, equation (3) is valid independently for each gas, p being the partial pressure of the gas considered. The Henry's law constant K_H would be different for different gases.

Limitations of Henry's Law

Henry's law is valid only for an ideal gas. For real gases the law holds if

(i) the pressure is low, at high pressure the law becomes less exact ad the proportionality constant shows a considerable variation;

(ii) the temperature is not too low;

(iii) the dissolved gas neither reacts with the solvent nor dissociates or associates in the solvent;

(iv) the solubility of the gas is low.

For example, Henry's law is not obeyed in case of solubility of HCl or NH_3 gas in water due to the chemical reactions, whereas it is obeyed by these gases in benzene as solvent.

RELATIVE LOWERING OF VAPOUR PRESSURE

The vapour pressure of a liquid is lowered when a non-volatile solute is dissolved in it and the lowering is proportional to the amount of solute dissolved.

Suppose the pure liquid has vapour pressure p and the solution has vapour pressure p_s, the lowering will be $p - p_s$.

"*The ratio of the lowering of vapour pressure to the vapour pressure of the pure solvent* $\frac{p - p_s}{p}$ *is known as relative lowering of vapour pressure.*"

Though the vapour pressure of a liquid increases rapidly with temperature, the relative lowering of vapour pressure is constant at all temperatures for a given dilute solution.

Raoult's Law

It states that: "*The relative lowering of vapour pressure is equal to the ratio of the number of molecules of the solute and the total number of molecules in the solution i.e., the molar fraction of the solute present in solution.*"

Mathematically it can be represented as:

$$\frac{p - p_s}{p} = \frac{n}{n + N}$$

where n and N are the number of moles of solute and the solvent respectively.

Suppose number of moles of solute = n

Suppose number of moles of solvent = N

$\therefore$ Number of g moles of solute in solution = $\frac{n}{n + N}$

Thus fraction of moles of solute in solution = $\frac{N}{n + N}$

Hence vapour pressure of solution will be proportional to both of them

i.e., $$p_s \propto \frac{n}{n + N} \quad \text{and} \quad p_s \propto \frac{N}{n + N}$$

But as the solution is very dilute n is very small, the value of $\frac{n}{n + N}$ becomes very small. So that fist proportionality can be neglected and hence we have only

$$p_s \propto \frac{N}{n + N}$$

or $$p_s = k\frac{N}{n + N} \text{ where k is constant.} \quad \text{...(i)}$$

Transforming (i) into an equation of pure solvent we put p in place of p_s and n = 0 and we get:

$$p = k \quad \text{...(ii)}$$

Substituting the value of k from (ii) in (i), we get:

$$p_s = p \times \frac{N}{n + N}$$

or $$\frac{p_s}{p} = \frac{N}{n + N}$$

Subtracting both the sides from 1 we get,

$$1 - \frac{p_s}{p} = 1 - \frac{N}{n + N}$$

or
$$\frac{p - p_s}{p} = \frac{n + N - N}{n +} = \frac{n}{n + N}$$

or
$$\frac{p - p_s}{p} = \frac{n}{n + N} \qquad ...(iii)$$

This is a Raoult's Law.

Applicability of Raoult's Law

The Raoult's law equation derived as above is very useful in determination of molecular mass of solute. It can be written as:

$$\frac{p - p_s}{p} = \frac{w / m}{\frac{w}{m} + \frac{W}{M}}$$

Thus knowing other terms in the equation, m, the molecular mass of solute can be calculated.

Thus the equation can be utilized in calculation the molecular mass of dissolved substance when the relative lowering of vapour pressure produced by a known weight of the solute in a known weight of solvent is known.

MEASUREMENT OF LOWERING OF VAPOUR PRESSURE

Berometric Method

Raoult measured the individual vapour pressures of a liquid and the solution by this method. He introduced the liquid or the solution into Toricellia vacuum of a barometer tube and measured the depression of the mercury level. The method is neither practicable nor accurate as lowering of vapour pressure has been too small.

Manometric Method

The vapour pressure of a liquid or solution can be conveniently determined with the help of a manometer (Fig. 3.7). The bulb B is charged with the liquid or solution. The air in the connecting tube is then removed with a vacuum pup.

If the stopcock is closed, the pressure inside is due only to the vapour evaporating from the solution or liquid. This method is generally used for aqueous solutions. The manometric liquid can be mercury or n-butyl phthalate which has low density and low volatility.

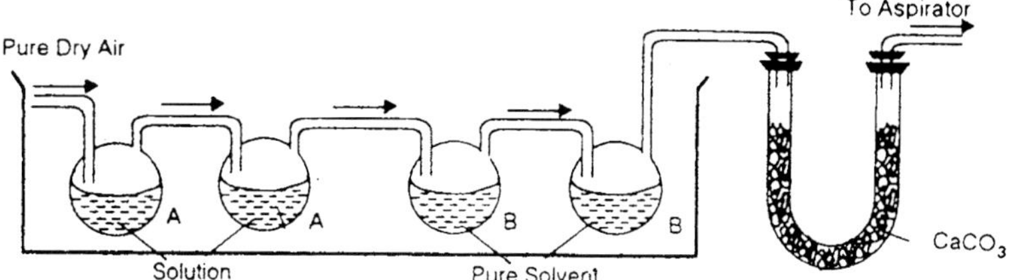

Fig. 3.7

Walker and Ostwald's Method

(i) A current of dry air is passed through two sets of bulbs A ad B containing the solution and the solvent respectively and placed in a constant temperature bath.

(ii) As the air passes through the solution it takes up with it the vapours of the solvent. The amount of vapour take up by the air is proportional to the vapour pressure p_s of the solution. When the air enters the bulbs B it takes up more solvent vapours for the vapour pressure p of the solvent is more than that of solution.

The amount of vapour take fro bulbs B is proportional to difference in the vapour pressure of solvent and the solution $(p - p_s)$. When the air comes out of the bulbs B, it is saturated with solvent and the amount of solvent present in it is proportional to p, the vapour pressure of the solvent.

(iii) The amount of solvent carried by air from the bulbs A and B can be known from the loss in weight of bulbs A and B respectively.

$\therefore$ Loss in weight of A is $\propto p_s$

Loss in weight of B is $\propto p - p_s$

Loss in weight of A + B is $\propto p$

Hence $\dfrac{\text{Loss in wt. of B}}{\text{total loss in wt. of A + B}} = \dfrac{p - p_s}{p}$

(iv) The total loss in weight of bulbs A and B can also be determined by finding out the increase in weight of $CaCl_2$ tube attached at the end of bulbs B. In that case:

$$\frac{\text{Loss in wt. of B}}{\text{Gain in wt. of CaCl}_2\text{ tube}} = \frac{p - p_s}{p}$$

Thus the relative lowering of vapour pressure can be calculated from the values of different weights and consequently molecular weight of solute is calculated.

OSMOSIS

When a solution is separated from its solvent by a semipermeable membrane, the solvent molecules pass through it into solution to have uniform concentration on both sides of the membrane.

"*The spontaneous flow of solvent into a solution or from a ore dilute to a concentrated solution through a semipermeable membrane is known as osmosis.*"

Illustration of Osmosis

Take two eggs of equal size whose outer shells have been removed. Put one of them in distilled water and the other in saturated salt solution. After few hours the egg placed in water swells up while the one in salt solution shrinks. It is due to the fact that in case of egg placed distilled water, the water enters the concentrated egg fluid while in other case it goes out of the egg into more concentrated salt solution to have uniform concentration in and out.

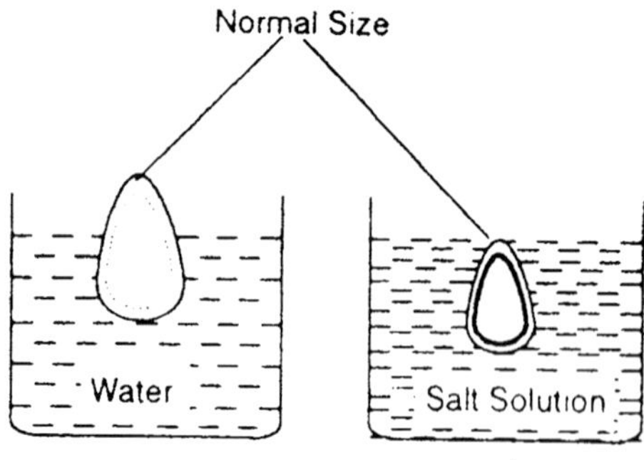

Fig. 3.8

Difference from Diffusion

(i) In osmosis the presence of semipermeable membrane is essential.

(ii) In osmosis it is only the solvent molecules which flow out whist in diffusion both the solute as well as solvent molecules flow out in opposite directions.

In osmosis the flow of solvent molecules start from the solution of lower concentration to that of higher concentration while in diffusion the molecules over form a region of higher concentration to those of lower concentration.

Osmosis differs from diffusion in the following respects:

Table 3.4

Osmosis	*Diffusion*
1. There is a flow of solvenet into the solution through a semipermeable membrane.	1. There is a flow of both the solvenet and the solute and no semipermeable membrane is required.
2. Solvent flows from the solution of lower concentration to solution of higher concentration.	2. Solution flows from higher concentration to lower concentration until an equilibrium in concentration is achieved.

Semipermeable Membrane

A membrane which allows the solvent but to the solute molecules to pass through it is known as semi-permeable membrane.

Examples:

(i) The membrane surrounding the plant and animal cells are almost semipermeable. In fact pig bladder has bee used as semi-permeable membrane in the past in different experiments.

(ii) A layer of phenol saturated with water acts as a semipermeable layer for a solution of calcium nitrate as the latter is not soluble in phenol.

(iii) The gelatinous precipitates of inorganic substance such as calcium phosphate and copper ferrocyanide are now commonly used as semipermeable membranes.

Of laboratory experiments copper ferrocyanide is referred and is constructed by depositing it in the porous walls of a battery pot.

Preparation

The pronous pot is first thoroughly cleaned by washing it with acid, water, alkali and finally with distilled water. The air bubbles enclosed in the pores are removed by forcing water through the pot under pressure. The pot is then filled with a 2.5% solution of copper sulphate and placed in a vessel containing solution of potassium ferocynide of same strength. A bottomless platinum cylinder is placed surrounding the pot and acts as anode.

On passing electric current, copper ions go out of the pot while ferocynide ions come into the pot. They meet some where in the walls of the pot to form a compact and stout membrane of copper ferocyanide.

$$2CuSO_4 + K_4Fe(CN)_6 \rightarrow \underset{\text{Copper ferrocyanide}}{Cu_2Fe(CN)_6} + 2K_2SO_4$$

When the membrane is being formed, the electrical resistance of the cell increase and finally reaches a maximum value. On completion of membrane, the current stops and the bell ceases ringing.

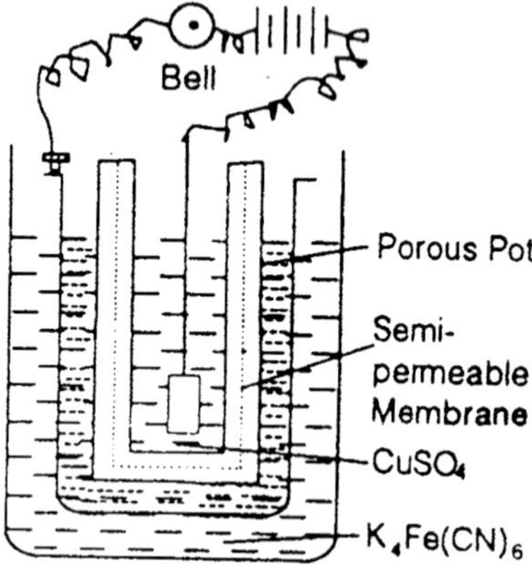

Fig. 3.9 : **Electrical deposition of semi-permeable membrane.**

RELATION BETWEEN LOWERING OF VAPOUR PRESSURE AND OSMOTIC PRESSURE

Consider a tube the lower part of which is fitted with a semipermeable membrane and containing the solution. It is immersed in a vessel containing the pure solvent and the whole arrangement is placed in larger outer vessel which is evacuated. The osmosis take place and the level of solution in the tube rises till the hydrostatic pressure developed o the solution prevents osmosis. The osmotic pressure of the solution is thus

$$P = h \times \rho \times g \qquad ...(1)$$

where P is osmotic pressure, h the height to which the solution rises in the where tube; ρ the density of the solvent for being *dilute* solution; g is the Acceleration due to gravity.

Now the pressure of vapours at the level of surface A of the solution must be same inside and outside the tube. If p is the vapour pressure of pure solvent and p_s vapour pressure of the solvent over solution, the difference between them is equal to the pressure of the vapour column of height h. This is

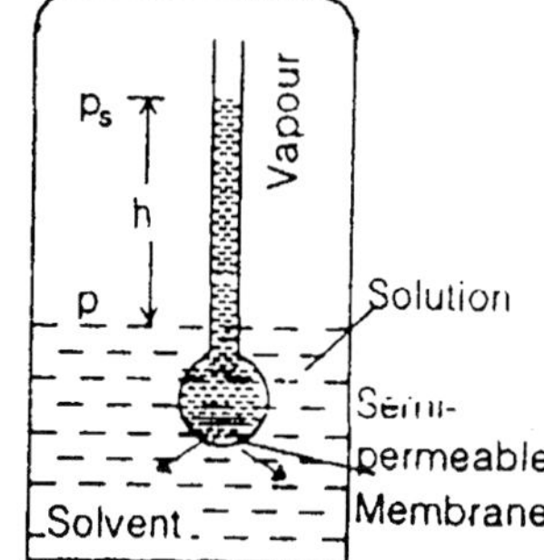

Fig. 3.10

$$p - p_s = p \times g \times d \text{...(ii)}$$

(where d is the density of the vapour)

Let M be the molecular ass of the solvent vapour, then the volume V occupied by Mg of vapours of pressure p and temperature, T is given by the gas equation:

$$pV = RT \quad \text{or} \quad V = \frac{RT}{p}$$

$$\therefore \quad \text{d, the density of vapour} = \frac{M}{V} = \frac{M}{RT/p} = \frac{pM}{RT}$$

or

$$d = \frac{pM}{RT} \qquad ...(iii)$$

Substituting the value of h and d from (i) and (iii) in (ii) we get;

$$p - p_s = \frac{P}{\rho g} \times g \times \frac{pM}{RT}$$

or

$$\frac{p - p_s}{p} = \frac{M}{RT\rho} \times P \qquad ...(iv)$$

or

$$p - p_s = \frac{Mp}{RT\rho} \times P$$

Hence the factor $\frac{Mp}{RT\rho}$ is constant for a solvent of molecular mass M, density ρ, vapour pressure p at temperature T.

$$p - p_s \propto P$$

Hence lowering of vapour pressure is directly proportional to osmotic pressure of solution.

Derivation of Raoult's Law Equation

Let n moles of solute be dissolved in volume V of the solution then according to V and Hoff's equation of solution:

$$PV = nRT$$

or $$P = \frac{nRT}{V} \quad ...(v)$$

Substituting the value of P from (v) in (iv) we get;

$$\frac{p - p_s}{p} = \frac{M}{R\rho T} \times \frac{nST}{V} = \frac{Mn}{\rho V}$$

But ρV is product of density and volume = Mass of solution, F

$$\therefore \quad \frac{p - p_s}{p} = \frac{Mn}{F} = \frac{n}{F/M} = \frac{n}{N}$$

where F/M is the number of moles of solvent in ass F of the solvent.

$$\therefore \quad \frac{p - p_s}{p} = \frac{n}{N} \quad ...(vi)$$

This is modified form of Raoult's law equation.

THEORIES OF OSMOTIC PRESSURE AND SUPERMEABILITY

Though we know that osmotic pressure is bought into existence only when the solution is separated fro the solvent by a semipermeable membrane, we still do not know how a semipermeable membrane acts.

1. Sieve Theory

Traube first suggested that the semipermeable membrane acts like a molecular seive whereby the molecules bigger than the solvent are retarded, while the solvent molecules filter through. Thus the solvent flows from a region of higher solvent concentration to one of lower concentration. But this theory raised eyebrows when it was seen that solute molecules even smaller than the resolvent were retarded by the membrane.

Later, when the theory of chemical interaction at the poles due to the polar groups of the protein molecules lining the pores became known, this theory of *molecular seiving* became popular.

Bigelow assumes that the membrane acts like a set of very fine capillary tubes. The walls of these capillaries are neither wetted by water nor by solution. Thus each capillary will have at its opposite ends water ad solution separated by a small gap. The vapour pressure other side will decide the flow of solvent molecules. As vapour pressure is greater on the water side, transfer of water will take place from solvent into solution. This theory has a general acceptance.

2. Chemical Theory

Amstrong proposed a chemical theory whereby the solvent was supposed to form a kind of loose chemical compound with the membrane, and was later spilt off again. But due to lack of experimental evidence this theory was rejected.

3. Preferential Solubility Theory

Another theory which speaks of preferential solubility was well received. It is supported by experimental proof and it states that solvent dissolves in the membrane, diffuse through ad is give off at the other end. When a mixture of nitrogen and hydrogen gas is passed through a heated palladium box, hydrogen is give off at the other end. This separation is achieved because H_2 dissolves in palladium, diffuses through ad is give off at the other end.

4. Kinetic Theory

The kinetic theory suggests that the osmotic pressure is due to bombardment of the molecules of solvent o the membrane. As the solution side carries solute molecules too, the bombardment per unit area of surface will be less. Hence the solvent molecules will diffuse slowly from this side than the solvent side resulting in an attempt to make the number equal.

5. Hydrostatic Theory

The hydrostatic theory suggests that the entrance of solvent into the solution is supposed to be due to the existence of an attractive force of the solvent for the solute. This might be due to variation in surface tension.

6. Vapour Pressure Theory

According to this view the supermeable membrane is a vapour sieve *i.e.*, the vapours of the solvent can only pass through it. As the vapour pressure of the pure solvent is higher than that of the solution, the solvent molecules can pass through the membrane to the solution side. The theory satisfactorily explains the phenomenon of osmosis.

7. Solution Theory

According to this theory put forward by Therrmite, membrane is permeable to those substances which dissolve in it and is impermeable to those substances which are insoluble in it. For example calcium nitrate is insoluble in phenol but is soluble in water and hence a layer of phenol slipped between calcium nitrate and water acts as semi-preamble membrane. This theory is widely accepted.

Why Exactly Does Osmosis Take Place?

The answer becomes very simple if we look at it thermodynamically. When a solute is dissolved in a solvent, the energy of the solvent molecules is reduced considerably because of the solute-solvent intractions. When this solution is separated from the pure solvent by a seipermeable membrane rapid movement of the solvent molecules across the barrier occurs in the direction of the solution. The hydrostatic pressure so developed ion the copartner containing the solution is enough to increase the free energy of the solvent molecules in the solution. When the free energy of the solvent molecules is the solution is restored to a value equal to that of the pure solvent, an equilibrium is achieved and osmosis stops. More the user of solute particles in the solution, greater is the osmotic pressure developed. Thus, osmotic pressure is one of the four colligative properties that a solution possesses (vapour pressure, rise in boiling point, depression of freezing point, being the others). Under ideal conditions, it is just like gas pressure, directly proportional to the absolute temperature and to concentration, and is independent of the chemical nature of the dissolved material.

OSMOTIC PRESSURE

When a solution is separated fro the pure solvent by a semipermeable membrane, a diffusion of solvent takes place through the membrane from the pure solvent into the solution. In case, if two solutions of different concentrations are separated by semipermeable membrane, the solvent molecules will move from the dilute solution to the ore concentrated solution side. *This spontaneous movement of solvent molecules through a seipermeable membrane from a region of dilute solution into a region of concentrated solution is termed as osmosis.*

If several solutes are present osmosis will take place if the semipermeable membrane is impermeable to any one of the various kinds of molecules or ions.

In order to demonstrate osmosis, a thistle funel, whose lower end is tied with a animal membrane, is filled with a sugar solution and the kept in a beaker which contains distilled water (Fig. 3.11). Due to osmosis, water will flow into the funel through the membrane. A considerable rise in level of the liquid in the thistle funel is noticed.

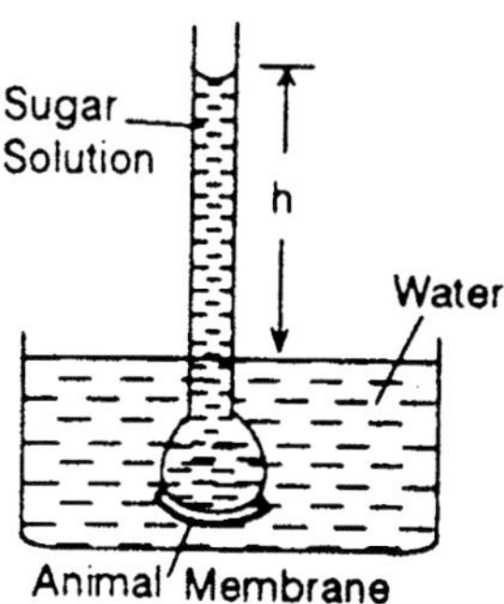

Fig. 3.11

As the liquid rises in the tube, a hydrostatic pressure is developed. This pressure increases the tendency for the solvent molecules to over from the solution back into the pure solvent and operates against the force causing osmosis. As a result, an equilibrium condition is finally reached in which the hydrostatic pressure is sufficient to prevent further diffusion. *That hydrostatic pressure acting on the solution side of the semipermeable membrane that is just sufficient to prevent osmosis is termed as the osmotic pressure of the solution.*

If a liquid rises to a height h, the

Osmotic pressure = hdg where d is the density of the solution.

Another definition of osmotic pressure : Suppose a solution is kept in a cup whose walls contain a seipermeable membrane. This cup is tightly closed by a rubber piston (Fig. 2.12). The, this cup is kept in a bigger beaker containing water (solvent).

Due to osmosis, the water will move from the beaker it of the cup through the semipermeable membrane. This tendency can be overcome by applying pressure on the solution by keeping increasing weights on the piston. As soon as a proper weight is placed, no osmosis takes place. *This excess pressure acting on the solution which prevents osmosis is known as osmotic pressure of the solution.*

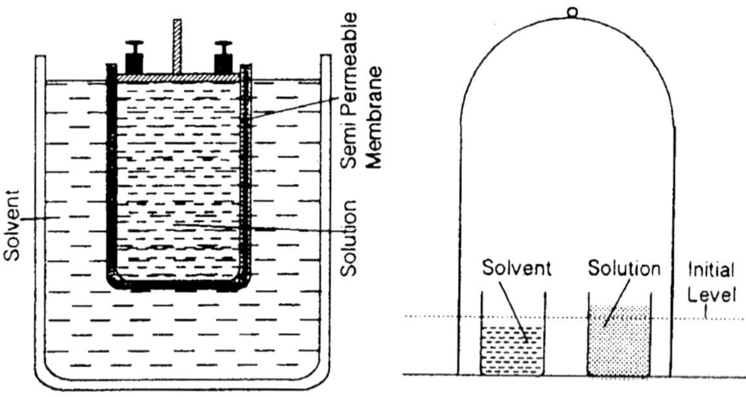

Fig. 3.12 Fig. 3.13

Another definition of osmotic pressure : Another definition of the osmotic pressure may be given in terms of vapour pressure. We know that the vapour pressure of a solution is lower than that of its solvent. Let us place two beakers (Fig. 3.13), one filled with a solution and other with solvent under reduced pressure as shown in Fig. 3.13. The vapour phase acts as a semipermeable membrane. The vapours of solvent from the beaker containing solvent will travel towards the beaker containing solution. The movement of vapour can be checked by applying external pressure o the solution so that the vapour pressure of the solution just becomes equal to that of solvent. Thus, the osmotic pressure may be defined as *the external pressure which must be applied o the solution in order to increase its vapour pressure to such a extent that it becomes equal to the vapour pressure of the solvent.*

VAN'T HOFF'S THEORY OF DILUTE SOLUTIONS

From measurements of osmotic pressure Van Hoff observed that certain laws which are obeyed by gases are also obeyed by dilute solutions. The Boyle's law, Charle's Law, Gas equation and Avogadro's hypothesis are also applicable to dilute solutions and are shown below:

(i) *Boyle Vant Hoff Law :* Pfeffer's results indicate that the osmotic pressure of solution is directly proportional to its concentration.

$$\therefore \qquad P \propto C \propto \frac{1}{V},$$

(where P, osmotic pressure; C, concentration in moles per litre; V, volume of solution containing 1 mole of solute)

$$PV = \text{constant (at constant T)}$$

I other words "*At constant temperature, the product of osmotic pressure and volume is constant.*"

This is exactly similar to Boyle's Law for gases.

(ii) *Pressure Temperature Law* : The results of osmotic pressure measurement indicate that if the concentration of solution is kept the same, the osmotic pressure varies directly as absolute temperature. The concentration we know is inversely proportional to volume and since the volume changes in liquids with rise of temperature are negligible, hence P µ T at constant volume.

In other words "*At constant volume, the osmotic pressure of a dilute solution is directly proportional to absolute temperature.*"

This is similar to Charle's law for gases.

(iii) *General equation for solutions* : From the above two laws:

$$P \propto \frac{1}{V} \text{ and also } P \propto T,$$

$$\therefore \qquad P \propto \frac{T}{V} \quad \text{or} \quad PV \propto T$$

Hence PV = ST, (where S is solution constant).

This equation is exactly similar to general gas equation and the value of S (.0821 litre-atoms) corresponds about exactly with R obtained for gases.

(iv) *Avogadro-Van Hoff Law* : For a given solution

$$P_1V_1 = ST_1$$

(where V_1 is the volume containing 1 mole of the solute).

For another solution,

$$P_2V_2 = ST_2$$

(where V_2 is the volume containing 1 mole of solute).

Now if $P_1 = P_2$ and $T_1 = T_2$; then $V_1 = V_2$.

In other words, *equal volume of solutions exerting same osmotic pressure at same temperature contain equal number of solute molecules.*"

This is similar to Avogadro's law of gases.

Van Hoff, on the basis of analogous behaviour of dilute solutions to gases as discussed above, put forward in 1885 the theory of dilute solutions called Van Hoff's theory of dilute solution. According to it:

"*A substance in solution behaves exactly like a gas and the osmotic pressure of a dilute solution is equal to the pressure which the solute would exert if it were a gas at the same temperature and occupying the same volume as the solution*".

In other words the theory may be stated as "The solute molecules in a dilute solution play the same role as is played by the gas molecules in a gas, the osmotic pressure being analogue of gas pressure."

MEASUREMENT OF OSMOTIC PRESSURE

Different methods are used in measuring the osmotic pressure:

(i) Pfeffer's method,

(ii) Morse and Frazer's method

(iii) Berkley and Hartley's method

(iv) Electronic Osmometre

But the one mostly employed in measuring the osmotic pressure is due to Berkely and Hartley.

1. Pfeffer's Method

Pfeffer's method (1817) : Pfeffer gave a direct method to measure osmotic pressure of solution. Here a porous pot (A) containing membrane of copper ferrocyanide in its wall is cemented to a glass tube (B) containing solution and attached to manometer (M). The porous pot is kept in pure solvent. The osmotic pressure exerted by the solution is given by the manometer. The method is of historical interest only and has been given up.

Disadvantages:

(i) The osmotic pressure developed in dilute solution is very great and bursts the semipermeable membrane used.

(ii) It takes a long time to register the final osmotic pressure.

2. Morse and Frazer's Method

An improvement of this method was made by H.N. Morse and J.C.C.W. Frazer ad their collaborators (1901-1923). They prepared

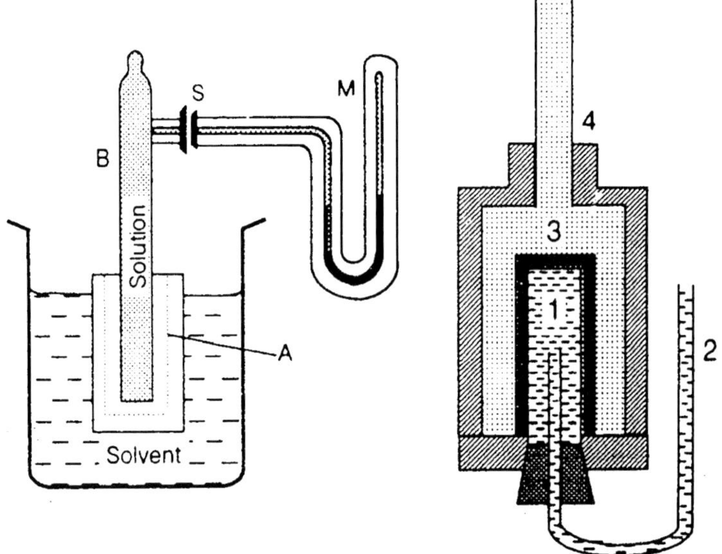

Fig. 3.14 Pfeffer's method. **Fig. 3.15 : Frazer's osmotic pressure apparatus**

sophisticated semi-permeable membranes of copper ferrocyanide by using an electric current. This made the membranes more tough ad they were capable of withstanding high pressures without leakage. The apparatus, as shown in Fig. 3.15, has two chambers. Chamber 1 which has the semipermeable membrane deposited on its walls is filled with water. Tube 2 is also filled with water. Chamber 3 is filled with solution. When osmosis begins, solvent flows from 1 to 3 increasing the hydrostatic pressure in vessel 3. This hydrostatic pressure developed, which is equal to osmotic pressure, is measured by a manometer attached to 4.

3. Berkley and Hartley's Method (1909)

This is the most simple, rapid and accurate method of measuring osmotic pressure. It is based on the fact that counter pressure applied o the solution so as to prevent osmosis is a measure of osmotic pressure.

(i) The apparatus consists of two concentric tubes, the inner one being that of porcelain having electrically deposited semipermeable membrane of copper ferrocyanide in it's walls. The two ends of the inner tube are connected to a capillary T on one side and dropping funnel D on the other. The outer tube is made of gun metal and is fitted with an arrangement for applying definite pressure.

(ii) In the angular space between the two tubes is introduced the solution whose osmotic pressure is to be measured while the inner tube is filled with water by means of dropping funnel upto a definite level T in the capillary tube.

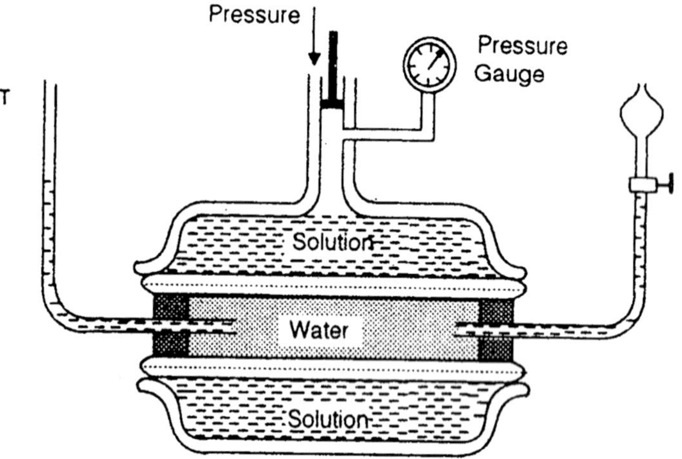

Fig. 3.16 : Berkley and Hartley's method.

(iii) Due to osmosis the water from the inner tube tends to pass into the solution which is indicated by the downward motion of the water meniscus in the capillary tube T. The external pressure is applied on the solution to prevent the flow of water and consequently lowering of meniscus. This pressure so applied is equal to osmotic pressure and is directly measured by means of pressure gauge attached to a piston.

Advantage

(i) The equilibrium is established ore quickly and hence *time required* for measurement of osmotic pressure is much smaller.

(ii) The strain on membrane is much less and hence there is *no chance* of its *bursting* out as in other methods.

(iii) The strength of solution does not change during measurements and hence is more accurate.

For solutions in non-aqueous solvents where suitable seipermeable membranes are available only with difficulty another method called Towned's porous disc method is quite useful. For biological fluid's however, De Varies plasmolytic method (1884) is very convenient.

4. Electronic Osmometer

Sorensen in 1917 first published the data of his measurements of osmotic pressure o protein solutions under carefully controlled conditions. His results and those of Starlin's on serum which was reproduced using collodion membranes and better designed modern osmometers, showed that a strict control of pH and salt concentration, and knowledge of the final concentration of protein are mandatory while determining the osmotic pressures of protein solutions. The osmometers which were used by Sorensen and others in the first half of 20th century though efficient, took several days for standardization. The osmotic event was rapid but the rise due to capillarity in the manometer tube required several days to reach an equilibrium value. The osmometers designed later were easy to handle and more accurate.

The manometers in these latter type of instruments contained organic liquids, paraffin, toluene or alcohols with which equilibrium could be attained in a very short time. The sample requirement also was low. But these instruments required a rigorous thermostatic control within 0.004°. Later, this problem was circumvented by the invention of an electronic osmometer by Rowe and Abrams in 1957. This could be operated without thermostatic control and the sample for determination was needed in a very small volume (only 0.5 ml). A detailed discussion of the apparatus is givė as follows;

An osmometer adapted for rapid measurements of osmotic pressure using small volumes of sample was designed as above by Rowe and Abrams in 1957. The U-tube has a semi-permeable membrane arranged in its arm B which holds the protein solution (sample) above it while the solvent lies beneath it. Arm 'A' also contains the same solvent. In the horizontal portion of the tube lies a very thin platinum foil which is connected further to a mechano-electronic transducer in circuit with a galvanometer. A controlled air pressure is continuously exerted on the protein solution.

When the tap is closed, the system if not in equilibrium, tries to attain it. The solvent passes through the membrane and the resulting pressure change displaces the platinum foil. This is indicated on the galvanometer scale. If the system is in equilibrium, no deflection can be observed in the galvanometer. The osmotic pressure exerted by the solution can be calculated from the formula,

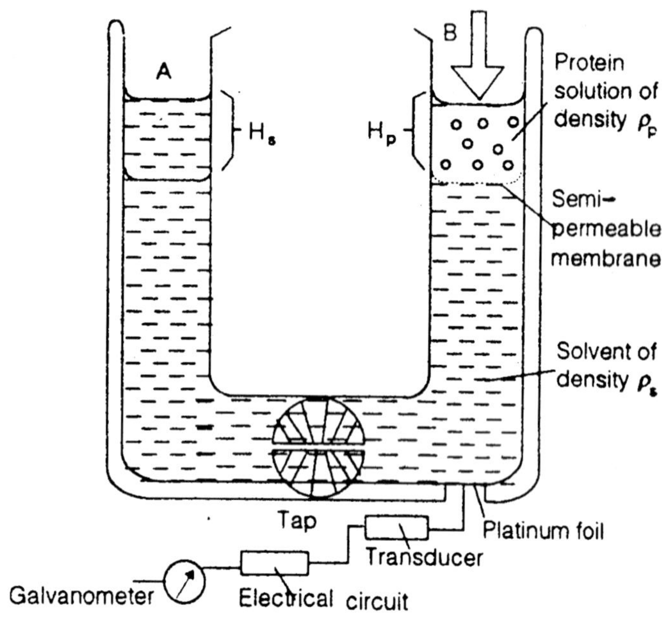

Fig. 3.17 : A diagrammatic cross-section of an electronic osmometer.

$$O.P. = P + H_p r_p - H_s \rho_s - H_t$$

where
P = pressure applied to protein solution,
H_p = height of column of protein above membrane,
H_s = height of column of solvent above membrane,
H_t = effect due to difference of surface tension between protein solution and solvent,
ρ_p = density of protein solution, and
ρ_s = density of solvent.

Molecular Weight From Osmotic Pressure

According to van Hoff, dilute solutions obey the general gas equation PV = ST where P = Osmotic pressure

V = Volume in litres containing 1 mole

S = Solution constant, .0821 litre-atm

T = Absolute temperature.

Thus from this equation

$$V = \frac{ST}{P} \qquad ...(9)$$

Let w g of solute be dissolved in litre of solution for determining osmotic pressure then the amount which will be present in V litres must be 1 mole (*i.e.*, mol wt. in g.)

or w g is present in 1 litre.

$\therefore$ M, the mol. wt. in g will be in = $\frac{M}{w}$ litres

This must be the volume $V = \frac{M}{w}$ ...(ii)

From equations (i) and (iii), we get

$$\frac{M}{w} = \frac{ST}{P} \quad \text{or} \quad M = \frac{S \times T \times w}{P}$$

or

$$M = \frac{.0821 \times T \times w}{P}$$

Thus, knowing w, T and P for the give solution, M, the mol. mass of substance can be calculated.

This method is, however, confronted with *difficulty* if the substance whose molecular weight is to be determined is an electrolyte. In such cases as the molecules dissociate the values of osmotic pressure actually observed and calculated from the solution equation (PV = ST) are not similar and hence the molecular weight calculated from osmotic pressure is not correct.

Isotonic Solutions

The solutions having same osmotic pressure are know as *isotonic solutions*. When such solutions are separated by a semipermeable membrane, no osmosis takes place.

We know for two solutions, $PV = P'V'$.

If the solutions are isotonic $P = P'$, then V must be same as V'. Hence the volumes of these solutions containing 1 mole of the respective substances must be same.

In other words: "*The isotonic solutions have same molar concentration.*"

For example : 5% solution of urea is isotonic with 15% grape sugar solution as the osmotic pressure exerted by these solution is same. It is due to the fact that their molar concentrations are equal (*i.e.*, $\frac{5}{60}$ and $\frac{15}{180}$).

The knowledge of isotonic solutions is very helpful in determining molecular weight. Thus if the molecular weight of one of the substance forming isotonic solutions be known that of the other can be calculated.

If an unknown solution, has lower osmotic pressure than the give known solution, the former is called *hypotonic solution but* in case the unknown solution has higher osmotic pressure it is called *hypertonic solution.*

MEASUREMENT OF BOILING POINT ELEVATION

There are several methods available for the measurement of the elevation of boiling point. Some of these are outlined below.

1. Landsberger-Walker method

This method was introduced by Landsberger and modified by Walker.

Apparatus : The apparatus used in this method is shown in Fig. 3.18 and consists of :

(i) An inner tube with a hole in its side and graduated in ml;

(ii) A boiling flask which sends solvent vapour into the graduated tube through a 'rosehead' (a bulb with several holes);

(iii) An outer tube which receives hot solvent vapour issuing from the side-hole of the inner tube;

(iv) A thermometer reading to 0.01 K, dipping in solvent or solution in the inner tube.

Procedure : Pure solvent is kept in the graduated tube and vapour of the same solvent boiling in a separation flask is passed into it. The vapour causes the solvent in the tube to boil by its latent heat of condensation. When the solvent starts boiling and temperature becomes constant, its boiling point is recorded.

Now the supply of vapour is temporarily cut off and a weighed pellet of the solute is dropped into the solvent in the inner tube. The solvent vapour is again allowed to pass through until the boiling point of the solution is reached and this recorded. The solvent vapour is then cut off, thermometer and rosehead raised out of the solution, and the volume of the solution read.

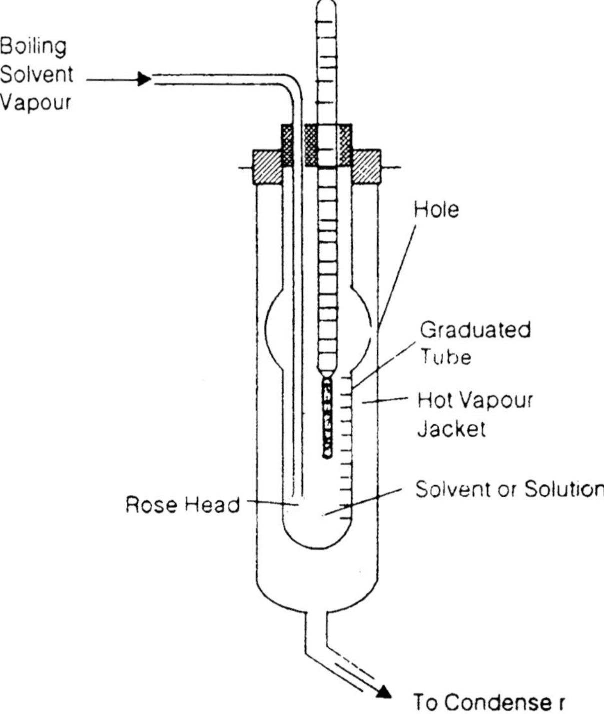

Fig. 3.18 : Landsberger-Walker apparatus.

From a difference in the boiling points of solvent and solution, the molecular weight of the solute can be found out by using the expression

$$m = \frac{1000 \times K_b \times w}{\Delta T \times W}$$

where w = weight of solute taken, W = weight of solvent which is given by the volume of solvent (or solution) measured in l multiplied by the density of the solvent at its boiling point.

2. Cottrell's Method

A method better than Landsberger-Walker method was devised by Cottrell (1910).

Apparatus : It consists of : (i) a graduated boiling tube containing solvent or solution; (ii) a reflux condense which returns the vaporised solvent to the boiling tube; (iii) a thermometer reading to 0.01 K, enclosed in a glass hood; (iv) A small inverted funnel with a narrow stem which branches into three jets projecting at the thermometer bulb.

Beckmann Thermometer (Fig. 3.19a) : It is a differential thermometer. It is designed to measure small charges in temperature and to the temperature itself. It has a large bulb at the bottom of a fine capillary tube. The scale is calibrated from 0 to 6 K and subdivided into 0.01 K. The unique feature of this thermometer, however, is the small reservoir of mercury at the top. The amount of mercury in this reservoir can be decreased or increased by tapping the thermometer gently. In this way the thermometer is adjusted so that the level of mercury thread will rest any desired point o the scale when the instrument is placed in the boiling (or freezing) solvent.

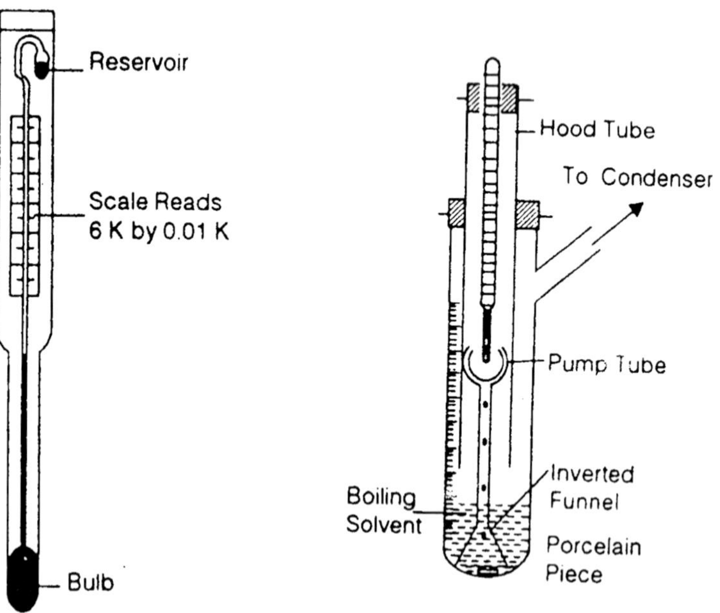

(a) : Beckmann thermometer reading to 0.01 K.

(b) : Cottrell's Apparatus.

Fig. 3.19

Procedure : The apparatus is fitted up as shown in Fig. 3.19b. Solvent is kept in the boiling tube with a porcelain piece lying in it. It is heated o a small flame (micro burer). As the solution starts boiling, solvent vapour arising from the porcelain piece pumps the boiling liquid into the narrow set.

Thus a mixture of solvent vapour and boiling liquid is continuously sprayed around the thermometer bulb. The temperature soon becomes constant and the boiling point of the pure solvent is recorded.

Now a weighed pellet of the solute is added to the solvent and the boiling point of the solution noted as the temperature becomes steady. Also, the volume of the solution in the boiling tube can be noted. The difference of the boiling temperature of the solvent and solute gives the elevation of boiling point. While calculating the molecular weight of solute the volume of solution is converted into mass by multiplying with density of solvent at its boiling point.

Depression in Freezing Point

Freezing point is the temperature at which solid and liquid states of a substance have the same vapour pressure. But the vapour pressure of solution is less than that of the solvent. Therefore, the freezing point of the solution will be lower than that of its solvent. The difference between the freezing points of the pure solvent and solution is called the depression in freezing point of the solution.

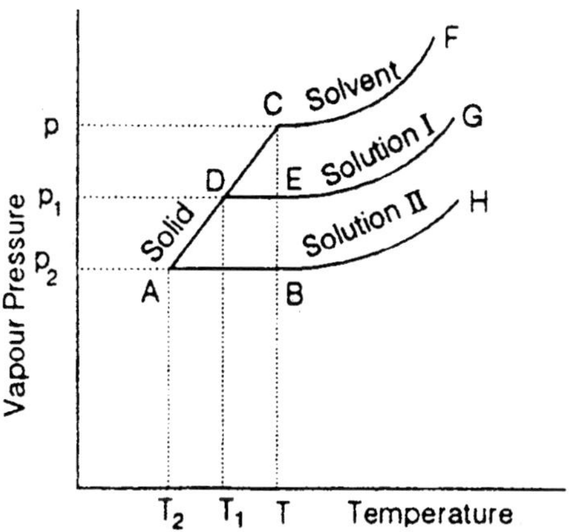

Fig. 3.20 : Depression in freezing point.

In order to understand the depression in freezing point, the curves between vapour pressure and temperature for solid solvent, liquid solvent and two solutions of different concentrations are plotted as show in Fig. 3.20.

In Fig. 3.20, T_f is the temperature at which the curve AC due to solid solvent intersects with the curve AE due to liquid solvent. Therefore. T_f is the freezing point of the solvent. Similarly, T_1 and T_2 are the freezing points of two solutions I and II respectively. For very dilute solutions, the curves are considered to be straight lines. From similar triangles ABC and DCE, we get

$$\frac{BC}{CE} = \frac{AB}{ED}$$

or
$$\frac{p - p_2}{p - p_1} = \frac{T - T_2}{T - T_1}$$

or
$$\frac{\Delta p_2}{\Delta p_1} = \frac{\Delta T_2}{\Delta T_1} \quad ...(1)$$

From the above relation, it follows that the lowering of vapour pressure is directly proportional to the depression of freezing point *i.e.*,

$$\Delta p \propto T_f \quad \text{or} \quad \Delta T_f \propto \Delta p \quad ...(2)$$

From Raoult's law, we have

$$\Delta p \propto x_B$$

$$\therefore \quad \Delta T_f \propto x_B \quad \text{or} \quad \Delta T_f = Kx_B \quad ...(3)$$

where K is a proportionality constant. The mole fraction x_B of solute is defined mathematically as:

$$x_B = \frac{\frac{w_B}{m_B}}{\frac{w_A}{M_A} + \frac{w_B}{M_B}} \quad ...(4)$$

where w_A = mass of solvent, w_B = mass of solute, and
M_A = molecular mass of solvent and
M_B = molecular mass of solute.

For dilute solutions, $\frac{w_B}{M_B} << \frac{w_A}{M_A}$, equation (4) becomes as follows:

$$x_B = \frac{\frac{w_B}{M_B}}{\frac{w_A}{M_A}} = \frac{M_A}{M_B} \times \frac{w_B}{w_A} = n_B \frac{M_A}{w_A} \quad ...(5)$$

In the above equation, n_B/w_A represents the molality of the solution if w_A, mass of the solvent, is taken in kilogram units. Therefore, equation (5) becomes as follows:

$$x_B = m \cdot M_A \qquad ...(6)$$

On substituting the above equation in equation (3), we get

$$\Delta T_f = K \cdot M_A \cdot m = k_f m \qquad ...(7)$$

where k_f (KM_A) is a ew constant called *molal freezing point depression constant* which relates the depression in freezing point for the solution with its molality.

In order to define k_f, put m = 1 in equation (7), we get

$$\Delta T_f = k_f$$

From the above relation, it follows that "*Molal freezing point depression constant for the solvent is numerically equal to the depression in freezing point for 1 molal solution.*"

The molality of a solution is defined mathematically as

$$m = \frac{1000\, w_B}{M_B w_A} \qquad ...(8)$$

On substituting equation (8) in (7), we get

$$\Delta T_f = k_f \frac{1000\, w_B}{M_B w_A} \qquad ...(9)$$

or

$$M_B = \frac{1000\, k_f \cdot w_B}{\Delta T_f \cdot w_A} \qquad ...(10)$$

Values of k_f for some solvents are given in Table 3.5.

Table 3.5 : Freezing Point Depression Constants for Some Solvents

S.No.	*Solvent*	*f.p. (K)*	*k_f(K/m)*
(i)	H_2O	273.0	1.86
(ii)	C_2H_5OH	155.7	1.99
(iii)	C_6H_6	278.6	5.12
(iv)	$CHCl_3$	209.6	4.70
(v)	CCl_4	250.5	31.8
(vi)	CS_2	164.2	3.83
(vii)	$C_4H_{10}O$ (Ether)	156.9	1.76

Equation (10) is of a great practical importance because it permits the calculation of molecular mass of solute (M_B) provided the remaining quantities k_f, w_B, ΔT_f and w_A are known.

Unit of K_f: It will be degree/molality or K/m or °C/m.

Measurement of Freezing Point Depression

Two methods given below are used:

1. Beckmann's Method

This is the cost *widely used method* and gives sufficient accurate results.

(i) The apparatus consists of a big tube A having a side tube for introducing the solute.

(ii) It is fitted up with stirrer and Beckmann's Thermometer. The latter can read even $\frac{1}{100}$th of a degree.

(iii) The tube is filled with a definite weight of the solvent, sufficient to dip the thermometer bulb and is suspended in another tube B wide enough to provide sufficient air space between them.

(iv) This whose system is placed in an outer vessel containing freezing mixture whose temperature is about 5° below the freezing point of the pure solvent.

(v) The space between the two test tubes serves as an jacket and prevents direct heat conduction and consequent super cooling.

(vi) On placing the tubes in the freezing mixture the temperature of the solvent in the inner tube gradually falls and due to *super cooling* even goes below the true freezing point of the solvent. On rapid stirring, however, the solid begins to separate and the mercury rises rapidly in the thermometer due to latent heat set free and finally become steady. The temperature is noted which is the freezing point of the pure solvent.

(vii) The inner tube is taken out to remelt the solvent and a known weight of solute is introduced into it. The tube is the placed back in its former place and the freezing point of the solution is determined as before. The difference in the two readings gives the depression of the freezing point. By substituting the value in the equation, the molecular weight of the solute can be calculated.

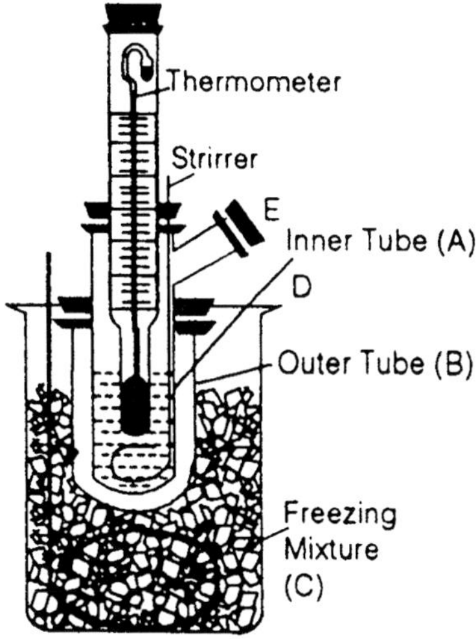

Fig. 3.21

2. Limitations of the Method

(i) Since the relation between molecular weight and depression of freezing point is derived from Raoult's law which is applicable to dilute solution only, *the concentration of solute in solution must be very low* otherwise abnormal values are obtained.

(ii) Since the depression of the freezing point is proportional to number of molecules of the solute, the method gives *abnormal value for substances which associate or dissociate* in solution. The observed molecular weight corresponds to true mol. wt. in case of compounds which either dissociate nor associate *i.e.*, non-electrolytes.

(iii) The method is not *applicable to volatile substance* for part of it may vaporize and due to which the concentration of the solution may chance and abnormal values may be obtained.

(iv) The substance should be perfectly soluble in solvent chosen and must remain in liquid phase during the experiment. The method thus *cannot be applied to insoluble or sparingly soluble substance.*

Calculation of Molecular Weight

Applying the expression

$$m = \frac{1000 \times K_f \times w}{\Delta T \times W}$$

We have $m = \dfrac{1000 \times 3.86 \times 0.124}{0.324 \times 25} = 59.83$

Thus the molecular weight (or relative molecular mass) of X is 59.83.

Rast's Camphor Method

This method due to Rast (1922) is used for determination of molecular weights of solutes which are soluble in molten comphor. The freezing point depressions are so large that an ordinary thermometer can be used.

Pure camphor is powered and introduced into a capillary tube which is sealed at the upper end. This is tied along a thermometer and heated in a glyceron bath (Fig. 3.22). The melting point of campho is recorded. The a weighted amount of solute and camphor (about 10 times as much) are melted in test tube with the open end sealed. The solution of solute in camphor is cooled in air. After solidification, the mixture is powdered and introduced into a capillary tube which is sealed. Its melting point is recorded as before.

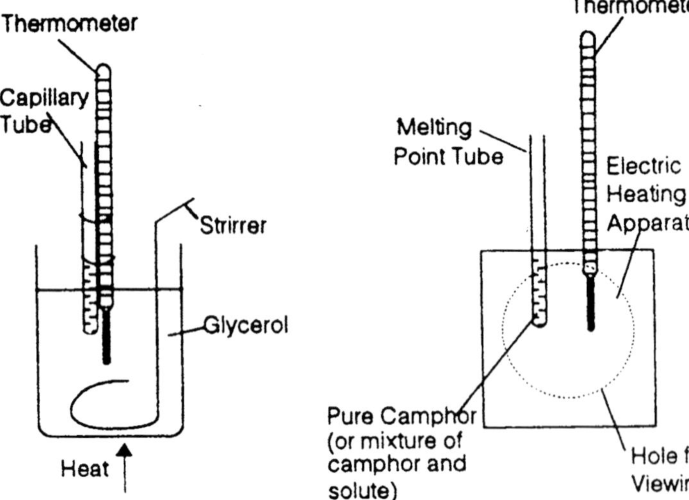

Fig. 3.22 : Determination of depression of melting point by capillary method.

Fig. 3.23 : Determination of depression of melting point electrical apparatus.

The difference of the melting point of pure camphor and the mixture, gives the depression of freezing point. I modern practice, electrical heating apparatus is used for a quick determination of melting points of campho as also the mixture.

The molal depression constant of pure campho is 40°C. But since the laboratory campho may not be very pure, it is necessary to find the depression constant for the particular sample of camphor used by a preliminary experiment with a solute of known molecular weight.

ABNORMAL COLLIGATIVE PROPERTIES OF SOLUTIONS

in the derivation of colligative properties, it was assumed that the molecular form of the solute remains unchanged in solution. Also, the solutions are dilute and behave ideally. In such cases, experimental value of the colligative property is in agreement with the theoretically calculated value.

However, there are certain substances like solutions of salts, acids or bases in water or acetic acid in benzene where the experimental value differs considerably from the calculated value. Such solutions are said to be *abnormal solutions*. The abnormalities observed in such solutions are of two types: (i) association of the solute molecules, and (ii) dissociation of solute molecules.

Association leads to a decease in the number of solute particles and hence the colligative properties will show lower valucs. In case of dissociation, the number of solute particles increases ad consequently, the colligative properties will show abnormally enhanced values.

In order to account for the abnormal behaviour of such solutions, van't Hoff's introduced a factor "i" which is called the *van't Hoff factor* and is defined as the ratio of the *experimental value of a colligative property to the calculated value of that property, i.e.,*

$$i = \frac{\text{Experimental value of the colligative property}}{\text{Calculated value of the property when the solution behaves ideally}}$$

Since the colligative property is proportional to number of solute particles in solution, hence

$$i = \frac{\text{Actual number of particles present in solution}}{\text{Number of particles in solution if it behaves ideally}}$$

or, we may write

$$i = \frac{(\Delta T_b)_{obs}}{(\Delta T_b)_{cal}} = \frac{(\Delta T_f)_{obs}}{(\Delta T_f)_{cal}} = \frac{(\Delta P / P^0)_{obs}}{(\Delta P / P^0)_{cal}} = \frac{\pi_{obs}}{\pi_{cal}} = \frac{M_{cal}}{M_{obs}} \quad ...(1)$$

when M is the molar mass of the solute and ΔT_b, ΔT_f, $\Delta P/P^0$ and π are the boiling point elevation, freezing point depression, relative lowering of vapour pressure and the osmotic pressure of the solution respectively. The subscripts 'obs' and 'cal' refer to the experimental and calculated values of the colligative properties.

(i) *Dissociation of solute* : Consider an electrolyte A_xB_y which partly dissociates in solution yielding x ions of A^{y+} ad y ions of B^{x-} and if α is the degree of dissociation, *i.e.*, the fraction of the total umber of molecules which dissociates and C the initial concentration of the solute, then the dissociation equilibrium in solution can be represented as

	$A_xB_y \rightleftharpoons$	xA^{y+}	$+ yB^{x-}$
Initial concentration	C	0	0
Concentration at equilibrium	$C(1 - \alpha)$	$Cx\alpha$	$Cy\alpha$

The total number of moles at equilibrium

$$= Cx\alpha + Cy\alpha + C(1 - \alpha)$$

$$= C[1 + \alpha + x\alpha + y\alpha]$$

$$= C[1 + \alpha(x + y - 1)]$$

Hence $$i = \frac{C[1 + \alpha(x + y - 1)]}{C}$$

or the degree of dissociation α is given as follows:

$$\alpha = \frac{i - 1}{(x + y - 1)} \quad ...(2)$$

Equation (2) is applicable to any colligative property and provides an important method for calculating the degree of dissociation of a solute. If $\alpha = 1$, *i.e.*, the dissociation is complete, $i = x + y$, the observed colligative property will be x + y times the calculated value. On the other hand, when no dissociation occurs, $\alpha = 0$ and $i = 1$, the calculated and observed values will be equal.

(ii) *Association of solute*: Consider the association of a solute A into its associated from $(A)_n$ according to the reaction.

$$nA = (A)_n$$

where n is the number of molecules of solute which combine to form an associated species. If C is the initial concentration and α the degree of association of the solute, at the equilibrium the number of moles of the undissociated solute is $C(1-\alpha)$ and that of associated form is $\frac{C\alpha}{n}$. The total number of moles in solution is given by

$$C(1-\alpha)+\frac{C\alpha}{n} \quad \text{or} \quad C\left(1-\alpha+\frac{\alpha}{n}\right)$$

Hence the van't Hoff factor,

$$i = \frac{C\left(1-\alpha+\frac{\alpha}{n}\right)}{C} = 1-\alpha+\frac{\alpha}{n} = \left[1+\left(\frac{1}{n}-1\right)\alpha\right]$$

or $$\alpha = \frac{i-1}{\frac{1}{n}-1} \qquad \text{...(3)}$$

If association is complete, *i.e.*, $\alpha = 1$, $i = 1/n$, the observed value of a colligative property is $1/n$ times the calculated value and if $\alpha = 0$, no association occurs in solution, *i.e.*, $i = 1$ and the observed and calculated values will be equal.

COLLIGATIVE PROPERTIES

Those properties of the solutions which depend only upon the total number of molecules of the solute per unit volume and not on its chemical nature are called colligative properties. Four main colligative properties of solutions are as follows:

(i) Lowering of vapour pressure,

(ii) Elevation of boiling point,

(iii) Depression in freezing point, and

(iv) Osmotic pressure.

The colligative properties are widely used for the determination of molecular masses for substances.

Mathematical Expression

From the above definition of colligative properties, it follows that if two solutions are made from different components, they may show identical values of colligative properties which are dependent only one mole fractions in the solution. Thus,

COLLIGATIVE PROPERTY MEASURED ∝ MOLE FRACTION OF THE SOLUTE

Suppose a system of two components A and B (A is solvent and B is the solute) is considered. In this system, w_A is the molecular mass of the solvent whose molecular ass is M_A. Similarly, in this solution, w_B is the molecular mass of the solute whose molecular mass is M_B.

Now number of moles of solvent,

$$n_A = \frac{w_A}{M_A}$$

and number of moles of solute,

$$n_B = \frac{w_B}{M_B}$$

Hence, mole fraction of solvent,

$$x_A = \frac{n_A}{n_A + n_B}$$

and mole fraction of solute,

$$x_B = \frac{n_B}{n_A + n_B}$$

But according to the definition,

$$\text{Colligative property} \propto \frac{n_B}{n_A + n_B}$$

or $$\text{Colligative property} = \gamma \frac{n_B}{n_A + n_B} = \gamma \frac{\frac{w_B}{M_B}}{\frac{w_A}{M_A} + \frac{w_B}{M_A}} \quad ...(1)$$

In the above equation, γ is proportionality constant which depends upon the nature of colligative property.

Equation (1) is very useful because it can be used for calculating the value of any of the involved factors.

ABNORMAL OSMOTIC PRESSURE

When the osmotic pressure of electrolytes is measured, the values observed are much higher than those calculated from the value of V and

T in the equation PV = ST. It is due to the fact that in such compounds the molecules dissociate or associate to the two or more ions and since the osmotic pressure of the solution depends upon the number of particles present in the give volume, the values observed will be higher in case of electrolytes. The abnormal values of osmotic pressure observed in case of electrolytes (*i.e.*, different from those calculated) is known as *abnormal osmotic pressure*.

These abnormal values of osmotic pressure in case of electrolytes are useful in determining the degree of dissociation of the electrolytes.

Plasolysis

The protoplasmic layer lining the cell walls of plant cells or of red blood cells is seipermeable; being permeable to water but is impermeable to the substances dissolved in the cellular fluid. This cellular fluid has an osmotic pressure of its own. Thus when a plant cell is placed a solution of lower osmotic pressure (Hypotonic) than that of the cell fluid, water penetrates into it and is consequently swells up (Fig. 3.24a). But if on the other hand, the plant cell is placed in a solution of greater osmotic pressure (Hypertonic) water diffuse out of the cell fluid resulting in contraction or even partial collapse of the membrane (Fig. 3.24b). The phenomenon is known as *plasmolysis*. This phenomenon has proved to be very useful to the measurement of relative osmotic pressure, De Vries (1884) developed the method. The cells are placed in the solution of different concentrations and the structures of the cells are observed under a microscope. The solution will have the same osmotic pressure (Isotonic) as that of cellular fluid in which plasolysis does not take place.

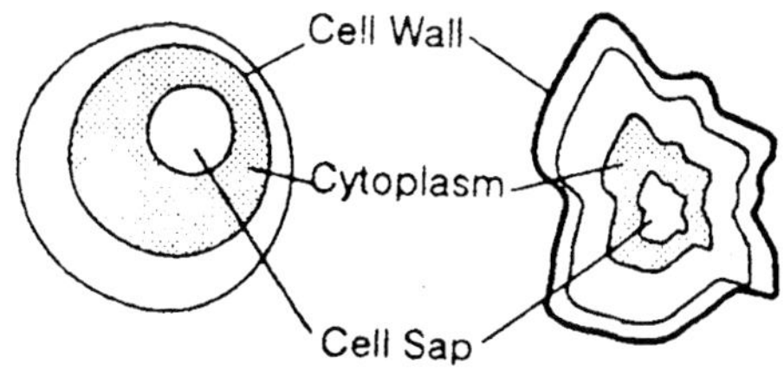

(a) In hypotonic soln. **(b) In hypotonic**

Fig. 3.24

Elevation of Boiling Point

The boiling point of a liquid is the temperature at which its vapour pressure becomes equal to the atmospheric pressure. But the vapour pressure of a solution is always lowered due to the addition of non-volatile solute. Therefore, the solution has to be heated to a higher temperature so that its vapour pressure becomes equal to the atmospheric pressure. Hence, the boiling point of solution having a non-volatile solute is higher than the boiling point of the pure solvent In other words, the boiling point of the solution is said to be elevated. *The difference between the boiling points of solution and pure solvent at a certain constant pressure is known as the elevation of boiling point of the solution.*

In order to understand the relation between elevation of boiling point and lowering of vapour pressure, the vapour pressure curves shown in Fig. 3.25 are considered. In this figure, the vapour pressures of solvent and two solutions I and II have been plotted against temperature. The boiling points of solvent and two solutions are represented by T, T_1 and T_2 respectively.

For dilute solutions, the curves are considered to be parallel straight lines. From the similar triangles CDB and AEC, we get,

$$\frac{AC}{BC} = \frac{EC}{CD}$$

or
$$\frac{p - p_2}{p - p_1} = \frac{T_2 - T}{T_1 - T} \quad \text{or} \quad \frac{\Delta p_2}{\Delta p_1} = \frac{\Delta T_2}{\Delta T_1} \qquad ...(1)$$

In the above expressions, p, p_1 and p_2 denote the vapour pressures of solvent, solution I and solution II.

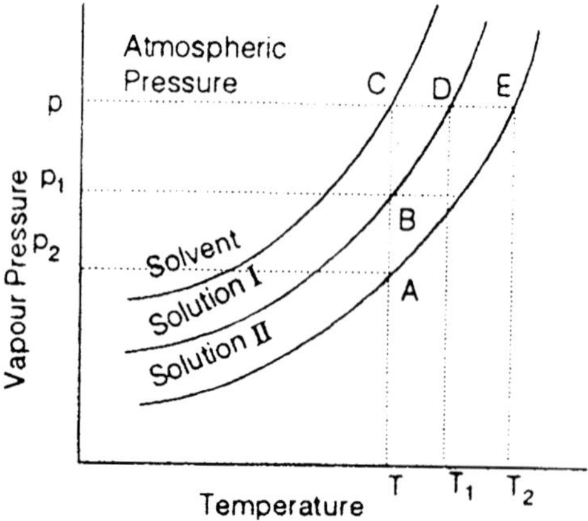

Fig. 3.25 : Elevation of boiling point.

From equation (1), it is clear that

Lowering of vapour pressure $\propto$ Elevation of boiling point

or $\quad \Delta p \propto \Delta T_b$

or $\quad \Delta T_b \propto \Delta p$

But according to Raoult's law, we have

$$\Delta p \propto x_B$$

$$\therefore \quad \Delta T_b \propto x_B \quad \text{or} \quad \Delta T = Kx_B \qquad ...(2)$$

where K is the proportionality constant and x_B is the mole fraction of solute which is defined as follows:

$$x_B = \frac{\frac{w_B}{M_B}}{\frac{w_A}{M_A} + \frac{w_B}{M_B}} \qquad ...(3)$$

where w_A and w_B denote the masses of solvent A and solute B respectively; M_A and M_B are the molecular asses of solute and solvent respectively. If a solution is dilute, $\frac{w_B}{M_B} << \frac{w_A}{M_A}$; then equation (3) becomes as follows:

$$x_B = \frac{\frac{w_B}{M_B}}{\frac{w_A}{M_A}} = \frac{M_A w_B}{M_B w_A} = n_B \frac{M_A}{w_A} \qquad ...(4)$$

From the definition of molality, n_A/w_B represents the molality m of the solution if w_A is taken in kilogram units. Hence equation (4) becomes as

$$x_B = m \cdot M_A \qquad ...(5)$$

On substituting equation (5) in (2), we get

$$\Delta T_b = K \cdot m \cdot M_A = k_b \cdot m \qquad ...(6)$$

where k_b (= K . M_A) is a new constant called molal boiling point elevation constant for the solvent, when *m* = 1 molal, equation (6) becomes as $\Delta T_b = k_b$.

Thus, *the molal boiling point elevation constant for the solvent is numerically equal to the elevation in boiling point which is observed for 1 molal solution.*

From the definition of molality, we have

$$m = \frac{1000\, w_B}{M_B w_A} \qquad ...(7)$$

On substituting equation (7) in (6), we get

$$\Delta T_b = k_b \cdot \frac{1000\, w_B}{M_B w_A}$$

or

$$M_B = \frac{1000\, k_b}{\Delta T_b} \cdot \frac{w_B}{w_A} \qquad ...(8)$$

Equation (8) is of much use because this may be used to find out molecular masses (M_B) of solutes provided the remaining quantities k_b, ΔT_b, w_A and w_B are known.

Units of k_b : The values of k_b are expressed in degrees/molality or as K/m or °C/m.

Molal elevation boiling point constants have characteristic values for different solvents (Table 3.6).

Table 3.6 : Molal Boiling Point Elevation Constants for Some Solvents

S.No.	*Solvent*	*b.p. (K)*	*k_b(K/m)*
(i)	H_2O	373.0	0.52
(ii)	C_2H_5OH	351.5	1.20
(iii)	C_6H_6	353.5	2.53
(iv)	$CHCl_3$	334.4	3.63
(v)	CCl_4	350.0	5.03
(vi)	CS_2	319.4	2.34
(vii)	$C_4H_{10}O$(Ether)	307.8	2.02

SOLVED EXAMPLES

Example 1:

The boiling point of a solution containing 0.20 g of a substance X in 20.00 g of ether is 0.17 K higher than that of pure ether. Calculate the molecular weight of X. Boiling point constant of ether per 1 kg is 2.16 K.

Solution:

Applying the expression

$$m = \frac{100 \times K_b \times w}{\Delta T \times W}$$

In this case, we have

$$\Delta T = 0.17 \text{ K}$$

$$K_b = 2.16$$

$$w = 0.20 \text{ g}$$

$$W = 20.00 \text{ g}$$

Substituting values

$$m = \frac{1000 \times 2.16 \times 0.20}{0.17 \times 20.00}$$

$$m = 127.81.$$

Example 2:

The boiling point of chloroform was raised by 0.325 K when 5.141 $\times$ 10^{-4} kg of anthracene was dissolved in 35 $\times$ 10^{-3} kg of chloroform. Calculate the molar mass of the solute (molal elevation constant for chloroform is 3.9).

Solution:

Here, $\Delta T_b = 0.325$ K, $W = 35 \times 10^{-3}$ kg

$K_b = 3.9$ K kg mol^{-1}, $w = 5.141 \times 10^{-4}$ kg

$m = ?$

We know,

$$\Delta T_b = K_b \frac{w \times 1000}{m \times W}$$

or

$$m = \frac{K_b w \times 1000}{\Delta T_b W}$$

$$m = \frac{(3.9 \text{ K kg mol}^{-1})(5.141 \times 10^{-4} \text{ kg})(1000 \text{ g kg}^{-1})}{(0.325 \text{ K})(35 \times 10^{-3} \text{ kg})}$$

$$= 176.3 \text{ g mol}^{-1} = 0.1763 \text{ kg mol}^{-1}$$

Example 3:

18.2 g of urea is dissolved in 100 g of water at 50°C. The lowering of vapour pressure produced is 5 mm Hg. Calculate the molecular weight of urea. The vapour pressure of water at 50°C is 92 mm Hg.

Solution:

Since the solution is to very dilute, the complete Raoult's Law Equation applied is

$$\frac{p - p_s}{p} = \frac{w/m}{W/M + w/m} \quad ...(1)$$

In this case:

w, the weight of solute (urea) = 18.2 g

W, the weight of solvent (water) = 100 g

m, the mol wt of solute (urea) = ?

M, the mol wt of solvent (water) = 18

$p - p_s$, the lowering of vapour pressure = 5 mm

p, the vapour pressure of solvent (water) = 92 mm

Substituting these values in equation (1)

$$\frac{5}{92} = \frac{18.2/m}{18.2/m + 100/18}$$

Whence m, the molecular weight of urea = 57.05

Example 4:

A current of dry air was passed through a solution of 2.64 g of benzoic acid in 30.0 g of ether ($C_2H_5OIC_2H_5$) ad the through pure ether. The loss in weight of the solution was 0.645 g and of the ether 0.0345 g. What is the molecular weight of benzoic acid?

Solution:

According to the theory of Ostwald-Walker method,

$$\frac{p - p_s}{p} = \frac{W_2}{W_1 + W_2} \quad ...(1)$$

In this case,

w_1, loss of weight of solution = 0.645 g

w_2, loss of weight of solvent = 0.0345 g

Substituring values in equation (1)

$$\frac{p - p_s}{p} = \frac{0.0345}{0.645 + 0.0345} = \frac{0.0345}{0.6795}$$

From Raoult's Law, we have

$$\frac{p - p_s}{p} = \frac{w/m}{w/m + W/M} \qquad ...(2)$$

M, the molecular weight of ether, $(C_2H_5)_2O$ = 48 + 10 + 16 = 74

Substituting values in (2)

$$\frac{0.0345}{0.6795} = \frac{2.64/m}{2.64/m + 30/74}$$

Whence m, the molecular wt of benzoic acid = 122.

Example 5(a):

Air was passed through a solution containing 2×10^{2} kg of a substance in 0.1 kg of water and the through pure water. The loss in mass of the solution was 2.945×10^{3} kg ad that of pure water was 5.6×10^{5} kg. Calculate the molar mass of the substance.

Solution:

Here $(p - p_s) \propto$ Loss in mass of pure water

$p_s \propto$ Loss in mass of solution

Therefore $p - p_s \propto 5.9 \times 10^{-5}$ kg.

$p_s \propto 2.945 \times 10^{-3}$ kg

$p \propto (5.9 \times 10^{-5} + 2.945 \times 10^{-3})$ kg

$\propto 3.004 \times 10^{-3}$ kg

$w = 2 \times 10^{-2}$ kg

$m = 18 \times 10^{-3}$ kg mol^{-1}

$W = 0.1$ kg

$M = ?$

Since $$\frac{p - p_s}{p} = \frac{wM}{Wm}$$

or $$m = \frac{pwM}{(p - p_s)W}$$

$$= \frac{(3.004 \times 10^{-3}\,kg)(2 \times 10^{-2}\,kg)(18 \times 10^{-3}\,kg\,mol^{-1})}{(5.9 \times 10^{-5}\,kg)(0.1\,kg)}$$

$$= 0.183 \text{ kg mol}^{-1}$$

Example 5(b):

In Ostwald-Walker experiment, air was blown through a solution containing a certain amount of solute (M = 0.2785 kg mol⁻¹) in 15 × 10⁻² kg of water and then through pure water. The loss in mass of water was found to be 8.27 × 10⁻⁵ kg while the mass of water absorbed in sulphuric acid tube was 3.317 × 10⁻³ kg. Calculate the amount of solute.

Solution:

$$p \propto \text{Mass of water absorbed by sulphuric acid}$$

$$p - p_s \propto \text{Loss in mass of water}$$

$$p \propto 3.317 \times 10^{-3} \text{ kg}$$

$$p - p_s \propto 8.27 \times 10^{-5} \text{ kg}$$

$$m = 0.2785 \text{ kg mol}^{-1}$$

$$w = ?$$

$$M = 18 \times 10^{-2} \text{ kg}$$

$$W = 15 \times 10^{-2} \text{ kg}$$

We know

$$\frac{p - p_s}{p} = \frac{wM}{mW}$$

or

$$w = \frac{(p - p_s)\, mW}{pM}$$

$$w = \frac{(8.27 \times 10^{-5} \text{ kg})(0.2785 \text{ kg mol}^{-1})(15 \times 10^{-2} \text{ kg})}{(3.317 \times 10^{-3} \text{ kg})(18 \times 10^{-3} \text{ kg mol}^{-1})}$$

$$= 5.7 \times 13^{-2} \text{ kg}$$

Example 5(c):

A sample of camphor used in the Rast method of determining molecular weights had a melting point of 176.5°C. The melting point of solution containing 0.522 g camphor and 0.0386 g of an unknown substance was 158.8°C. Find the molecular weight of the substance. K_f of camphor per k is 37.7.

Solution:

Applying the expression

$$m = \frac{1000 \times K_f \times w}{\Delta T \times W}$$

In present case, we have

$$\Delta T = 176.5 - 158.5 = 17.7$$

$$K_f = 37.7$$

$$w = 0.0386$$

$$W = 0.522$$

Substituting these values

$$m = \frac{1000 \times 37.7 \times 0.0386}{17.7 \times 0.522} = 157.$$

Example 5(d):

1 dm³ of water under a nitrogen pressure of 1 atmosphere dissolves 2 × 10⁻⁵ kg of nitrogen at 293 K. Calculate Henry's law constant.

Solution:

$$p = K_H X_2$$

$$X_2 = \frac{n_2}{n_1 + n_2} = \frac{\dfrac{2 \times 10^{-5}}{28 \times 10^{-3}}}{\dfrac{2 \times 10^{-5}}{28 \times 10^{-3}} + \dfrac{1}{18 \times 10^{-3}}} = 1.29 \times 10^{-5}$$

$$\therefore \quad K_H = \frac{p}{X_2} \quad (\because \quad p = 1 \text{ atm}) = \frac{1}{1.29 \times 10^{-5}}$$

$$\text{atm} = 7.7 \times 10^{6} \text{ atm.}$$

Example 6:

The lowering of freezing point of benzene was 2.33 K when 4.12 × 10⁻⁴ kg of a solute of unknown molar mass was dissolved in 9.13 × 10⁻³ k of benzene. Calculate the molar mass of the solute. Molal depression constant for benzene is 5.1 K kg mol⁻¹.

Solution:

Here,

$\Delta T_f = 2.33$ K, $\quad K_f = 5.1$ K kg mol^{-1}

$m = ?$ $\quad W = 9.31 \times 10^{-3}$ kg

$w = 4.12 \times 10^{-4}$ kg

We know,

$$\Delta T = K_f \frac{w \times 1000}{m \times W}$$

or

$$m = \frac{K_f \times w \times 1000}{W \times \Delta T_e}$$

$$= \frac{(5.1 \text{ K kg mol}^{-1})(4.12 \times 10^{-3} \text{ kg})(1000 \text{ g kg}^{-1})}{(9.31 \times 10^{-3} \text{ kg})(2.33 \text{ K})}$$

$$= 96.87 \text{ g mol}^{-1}$$

$$m = 9.687 \times 10^{-2} \text{ kg mol}^{-2}$$

Example 7:

A brass ..ample composed of 20% zinc and 80% copper by mass metls at 1268 K. Pure copper melts at 1357 K. What is the molal freezing point constant for copper? (Atomic mass of zinc is 65g mol^{-1}).

Solution:

$$\Delta T_f = (1357 - 1268) \text{ K} = 89 \text{ K}, \; W = 80 \times 10^{-3} \text{ kg}$$

$$m = 65 \times 10\text{– }3 \text{ kg mol}^{-1},$$

$$w = 20 \times 10^{-3} \text{ kg}$$

$$= 65 \text{ g mol}^{-1}$$

Since $$\Delta T_f = K_f \frac{w \times 1000}{m \times W}$$

or

$$K_f = \frac{\Delta T_f \times W \times m}{w \times 100}$$

$$= \frac{(89 \text{ K}) (80 \times 10^{-3} \text{ kg})(65 \text{ g mol}^{-1})}{(20 \times 10^{-3} \text{ kg})(1000 \text{ g kg}^{-1})}$$

$$= 23.14 \text{ K kg mol}^{-1}$$

Example 8:

0.440 g of a substance dissolved in 22.2 g of benzene lowered the freezing point of benzene by 0.567°. Calculate the molecular weight of the substance. (K_f = 5.12°C mole^{-1}).

Solution:

We can find the molecular weight by applying the expression

$$m = \frac{100 \times K_f \times w}{\Delta T_f \times W}$$

In this case

$$w = 0.440$$

$$\Delta T = 0.567$$

$$W = 22.2$$

$$K_f = 5.12$$

Substituting the values,

$$m = \frac{1000 \times 5.12 \times 0.440}{0.567 \times 22.2} = 178.9$$

∴ Molecular weight of substance = 178.9.

Example 9(a):

A solution of 0.124 g of a substance, X, in 25.0 l of ethanoic acid (acetic acid) has a freezing point 0.324°C below that of the pure acid 16.6°C. Calculate the molecular weight (relative molecular mass) of X, given that the specific latent heat of fusion of ethanoic acid is 180.75 J g⁻¹.

Solution:

Calculation of Molal depression Constant

We know that

$$K_f = \frac{RT_f}{L_f} \quad ...(1)$$

Here, freezing point of benzene,

$$T_f = 273.2 + 16.6 = 289.9 \text{ K}$$

Specific latent heat of fusion,

$$L_f = 180.75 \text{ J g}^{-1}$$

Substituting in the equation (1)

$$K_f = \frac{8.314 \times (289.9)^2}{180.75} = 3.86°$$

Example 9(b):

A solution of 1.0 × 10⁻² kg of sodium chloride in 1000 g of water freezes at – 0.604°C. The molal depression constant K_f of water is

(1.85 K kg mol⁻¹). Calculate the degree of dissociation of sodium chloride.

Solution:

$$(\Delta T_f)_{cal} = K_f \frac{w \times 1000}{W_m}$$

$$= \frac{(1.85 \text{ deg kg mol}^{-1})(1 \times 10^{-2} \text{ kg})(1000 \text{ g kg}^{-1})}{(1000 \text{ g kg})(58.5 \times 10^{-3} \text{ kg mol}^{-1})}$$

$$= 0.316°C$$

$$(\Delta T_f)_{obs} = 0.0 - (-0.604) = 0.604°C$$

van't hoff factor,

$$i = \frac{(\Delta T_f)_{obs}}{(\Delta T_f)_{cal}} = \frac{0.604}{0.316} = 1.91$$

Sodium chloride dissociates as	$NaCl$	$\rightleftharpoons$ Na^+ +	Cl^-
Number of moles initially	1	0	0
Number of moles after dissociation	$1 - \alpha$	α	α

Total number of moles after dissociation $= 1 - \alpha + \alpha + \alpha = 1 + \alpha$

$$i = \frac{\text{Number of moles after dissociation}}{\text{Number of moles initially present}} = \frac{1+\alpha}{1}$$

Therefore,

$$\frac{1+\alpha}{1} = 1.91$$

or $\alpha = 0.91$ to 91%

The degree of dissociation = 91%.

Example 10:

A solution containing 0.3 × 10⁻³ kg of benzoic acid (M = 122 × 10⁻³ kg mol⁻¹) in 2 × 10⁻² kg of benzene freezes at 0.317°C below the freezing point of the solvent. Calculate :

(i) the degree of association assuming that the acid exists as dimmer in benzene, and

(ii) the apparent molar mass of the acid; K_f for benzene is 5.1.

Solution:

$$(\Delta T_f)_{cal} = K_f \frac{w \times 1000}{mW}$$

$$= \frac{(5.1 \text{ deg kg mol}^{-1})(0.3 \times 10^{-3} \text{ kg})(100 \text{ g kg}^{-1})}{(122 \text{ g mol}^{-1})(2 \times 10^{-2} \text{ kg})}$$

$$= 0.627°C$$

The observed value of $\Delta T_f = 0.317°C$.

Hence van't Hoff factor i is given as

$$i = \frac{(\Delta T_f)_{obs}}{(\Delta T_f)_{cal}} = 0.506$$

From equation (3), α is given by

$$\alpha = \frac{i-1}{\frac{1}{n}-1} = \frac{0.506-1}{\frac{1}{2}-1} = 98.8\%$$

(ii) Since $i = \frac{(M)_{cal}}{(M)_{obs}}$

$$0.506 = \frac{122}{(M)_{obs}}$$

$$(M)_{obs} = \frac{122}{0.506} = 241 \text{ g mol}^{-1}.$$

Example 11:

The vapour pressure of water at 293 K is 17.540 mm Hg and the vapour pressure of a solution of 0.10824 kg. of a nonvolatile solute in 1 kg of water at the same temperature is 17.354 mm Hg. Calculate the molar mass of the solute.

Solution:

Here

$$p = 17.540 \text{ mm Hg}$$

$$= \frac{1.013 \times 10^5 \times 17.54}{760} \text{ Nm}^{-2} = 2.337 \times 10^3 \text{ N m}^{-2}$$

$$p_s = 17.354 \text{ mm} = \frac{1.013 \times 10^5 \times 17.354}{760} \text{ Nm}^{-2}$$

$$= 2.313 \times 10^3 \text{ N m}^{-2}$$

$$w = 0.10824 \text{ kg}$$

$$m = ? \quad W = 1 \text{ kg} \quad M = 18 \times 10^{-3} \text{ kg mol}^{-1}$$

We know

$$\frac{p - p_s}{p} = \frac{wM}{mW}$$

or
$$m = \frac{wM}{W} \times \frac{p}{p - p_s}$$

$$= \frac{(0.10824\ kg)(18 \times 10^{-3}\ kg\ mol^{-1})(2.337 \times 10^3\ N\ n^{-2})}{(1\ kg)(0.024 \times 10^3\ N\ m^{-2})}$$

$$= 0.1837\ kg\ mol^{-1}$$

Example 12:

The vapour pressure of ether (mol wt = 74) is 442 m Hg at 293 K. If 3 g of a compound A are dissolved in 50 g of ether at this temperature, the vapour pressure falls to 426 mm Hg. Calculate the molecular mass of A. Assume that the solution of A in ether is very dilute.

Solution:

Here the approximate form of the Raoult's law Equation will be used.

$$\frac{p - p_s}{p} = \frac{w}{\frac{m}{W/M}} = \frac{wM}{mW} \qquad ...(i)$$

In this case:

w, the weight of solute (A) = 3 g

W, the weight of solvent (ether) = 50 g

m, the mol mass of A = ?

M, the mol wt of solvent (ether) = 74

p, the vapour pressure of solvent (ether) = 442 mm

p_s, the vapour pressure of solution = 426 m

Substituting the values in equation (1),

$$\frac{426 - 442}{426} = \frac{3 \times 74}{m \times 50}$$

whence $m = 123$

Thus the molecular mass of A is 123.

4

PHYSICAL AND CONSTITUTIVE PROPERTIES

CHEMICAL CONSTITUTION AND OPTICAL ACTIVITY

It has been found the optical activity is a constitutive property, *i.e.*, it depends upon the arrangement of atoms with the molecule. The organic compounds having at least one asymmetric carbon atom are found to possess this property.

Asymmetric carbon is that which has all its found velencies satisfied by four different groups or atoms. Compounds contain asymmetric nitrogen or silicon atoms are also found to exhibit this property. Further, it has been found that a substance with optical activity always exists in these forms.

Two of them are rotating the plane of polarized light in opposite directions viz., left and right and the third being optically inactive. Thus if a substance shows optical activity it must have a asymmetric atom in it. For example lactic acid has the formula

```
H   CH3
 \ /
  C
 / \
OH  COOH
```

and is found to be optically active. Asymmetric carbon atom is designated by an asterisk.

According to Le-Bell and Van't Hoff, all the four groups attached to the carbon atom do not lie in the same plane as the carbon atom, but are situated at the four corners of a regular tetrahedron.

So accordingly the arrangements of various groups in space, the lactic acid molecule can be represented in two different ways shown in the Fig. 7 do not have a plane of symmetry.

In other words it is not possible to pass a plane through any of the two tetrahedrons so as to divided them into exactly identical half. Such a carbon atom is called an asymmetric carbon atom.

Optical Isomers as Mirror Image of Each Other

These two models, Fig. 4.1, are not super-impossible, but are related to each other as an object to its mirror image. The exact mechanism by which the molecule rotates the plane of polarized light is not known.

It can, however, be seen in the Fig. 4.1 that in one case the groups are arranged clockwise while in the other anti-clockwise. One of these represents the laevo farmhand the other dextro form.

Recently optical rotator dispersion curves have been used in the study of the stereochemistry of optically active ketones such as cyclohexanone derivatives.

The optical activity of a compound having more than one asymmetric C-atom depends on the arrangement of the groups around each C-atom. Suppose a compound is having two asymmetric C-atoms.

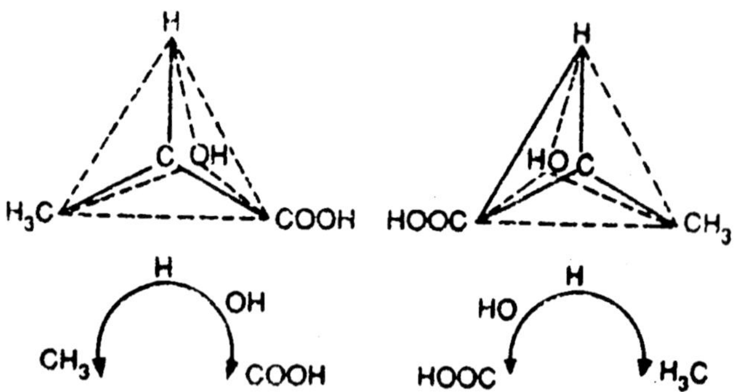

Fig. 4.1 : Mirror image forms of Lactic acid.

If both of them rotate the plane of polarization towards the same direction, the optical activity is enhanced, whereas if one rotates the plane in an opposite direction to the other, then the activity is reduced.

The latter is an example of internal compensation. If the groups around the two C-atoms are identical, the internal compensation results in zero activity and such a form is termed as the *meso-form*.

Thus in tartaric acid ($CH_2HCHOHCHOHCO_2H$) we have the *d, l*, the meso and the racemic forms. Each asymmetric C-atom represents one active centre. This active centre gives rise to two possibilities of optical rotation either towards right or towards left.

Hence a compound having *n*-asymmetric C-atoms will give rise to 2^n such possibilities and hence will have 2^n isomers, *e.g.*, glucose, $C_6H_{12}O_6$, has four asymmetric C-atoms ad hence it must give rise to 16 isomeric hexose sugars.

Principle of Optical Superposition

J.H. Van't Hoff gave the principle of optical superposition which is applicable possible to isomeric substances having several asymmetric carbon atoms.

It may be stated as "*the rotating power of substances possessing several asymmetric carbon atoms refers to the algebraic sum of the contributions of each separate carbon atom which is a definite amount and independent of the configurations of the other atom.*" This can be understood taking the examples of four pentose sugars.

```
      |                         |
HO—C—H + A              HO—C—H + A
      |                         |
HO—C—H + B              HO—C—H + B
      |                         |
HO—C—H + C               H—C—OH—C
      |                         |
      I                         II

      |
HO—C—H + A               H—C—OH—A
      |                         |
 H—C—OH—B               HO—C—H + B
      |                         |
 H—C—OH—C                H—C—OH—C
      |                         |
     III                        IV
```

According to the principle the specific rotation of II should be the sum of the values for the other three isomeric sugars:

Hence $+ A + B - C = (+ A + B + C) + (+ A - B - C)$
$+ (- A + B - C)$

Optical activity is used to confirm the structure but it is not able to disapprove any structure.

OPTICAL ROTATORY DISPERSION

In 1817 Biot reported that the magnitude of optical rotation gets changed with the change of wave length of the light used in the determination. The variation of the optical activity with the frequency of the light is termed as *optical rotatory dispersion.* It can be interpreted in terms of variation of the polarizability of the molecules in light of different frequencies. P. Drude deduced the following equation which gives the wavelength dependence of a great umber of optically active substances.

$$\alpha = \frac{K}{\lambda^2 - \lambda_0^2}$$

where λ_0 and K are characteristics of the substance.

If [α] is plotted against wave length, the following two types of the curves..

(i) A curve showing a smooth increase in rotation (+ or –) with decreasing wave length,

(ii) A curve having peak and trough.

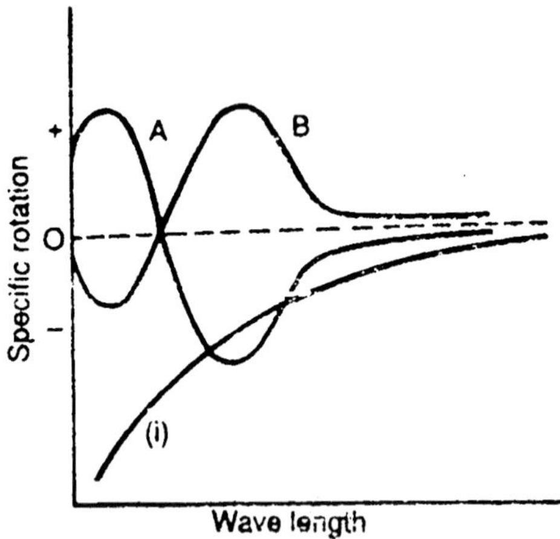

Fig. 4.2 : Optical rotatory dispersion curves.

The curve (i) exhibits peak at a longer wavelength. This is termed as *positive cotton effect* curve. The curve B in which the trough is found at longer wavelength is termed as *negative cotton effect curve.*

Optical rotatory dispersion studies are usually carried out in UV visible range when a functional group of the compound has a weak absorption band. It has been successfully used in ascertain in the structures of complicated optically active compounds.

MOLAR REFRACTION OR REFRACTIVITY AS AN ADDITIVE AND CONSTITUTIVE PROPERTY

It was found by comparing the R_M values for different substances that it is both additive and constitutive property. *i.e.*, it depends upon both the number and arrangement of atoms in the molecule. Thus from a study of molar refractions of a large umber of compounds the constants for different atoms and types of linkages were determined. For example, in a homologous series of aliphatic compounds of difference of CH_2 in composition makes a difference of 4.618 in molecular refractivity. The contribution of other atoms and structures can be calculated like molar volume as follows:

$$\text{RM for } C_7H_{16} = 34.54 \text{ cm}^3 \text{ mol}^{-1}$$

$$\text{RM for } C_6H_{14} = 29.92 \text{ cm}^3 \text{ mol}^{-1}$$

$$\text{Difference}(= CH_2) = 4.62 \text{ cm}^3 \text{ mol}^{-1}$$

$$\text{Thus,} \quad C_6H_{14} = 6CH_2 + 2H$$

$$29.92 = 6 \times 4.62 + 2H$$

$$\therefore R_M \text{ for H atom} = 1.1 \text{ cm}^3/\text{ atom}$$

$$\text{C atom} = 4.62 - 2 \times 1.10$$

$$= 2.42 \text{ cm}^3/\text{g atom}$$

Table 4.1 : Molar refraction contributions of atoms and bonds (Vogel 1948)

Atom or structure	$R_M(cm^3)$	*Atom or Structure*	$R_M(cm^3)$
H	1.028	C—O	4.601
C	2.591	—OH	1.546
Cl	5.844	—COOH	7.226
Br	8.741	—NO_2	6.713
I	13.954	=	1.575
O(>C=O)	2.573	≡	1.977
		6 membered ring	– 0.15
O(R—O—R)	1.764	5 membered ring	– 9.89
O(— OH)	1.518	4 membered ring	0.317
C_3 radical	5.653		
C_2H_5 radical	10.300		

The molar refraction values for some elements and groups based of the refractive indices measured with the D-line of sodium have been included in Table 4.1.

With the help of molar refraction contributions, given in Table 4.7 the molar refractivity of a compound o the basis of its assumed structure is calculated and compared with the value obtained experimentally. This can be understood from the following examples.

1. *Structure of benzene :* Kekule's formula for benzene is:

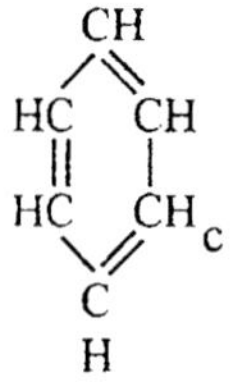

```
       CH
      / \\
    HC   CH
    ||   |
    HC   CH
      \ //   c
       C
       H
```

There are six carbon atoms, 6 hydrogen atoms, 3 double bonds and one six carbon atom ring.

∴ Molar refraction due to 6 C atoms $= 6 \times 2.591 = 15.546$

Molar refraction due to 6 H atoms $= 6 \times 1.028 = 6.168$

Molar refraction due to 3 double bonds $= 3 \times 1.575 = 4.725$

Molar refraction due to one six membered ring $= 1 \times (-0.15) = -0.15$

Total 25.289

The experimental value 25.95 is fairly close to the above calculated value. Hence the Kekule's structure for benzene is correct.

2. *Structure of acetylene dibromide :* The structure of acetylene dibromide is

$$BrCH = CHBr$$

$$2C = 2 \times 2.591 = 5.182$$

$$2H = 2 \times 1.028 = 2.056$$

$$2Br = 2 \times 8.741 = 17.482$$

One double bond $= 1 \times 1.575 = 1.575$

Total $= 26.295$

The observed value is 26.30. Hence the formula of acetylene dibromide is verified. Thus molecular refractivities have been useful in deciding between the alternate structures of the various isomeric compounds.

3. *Structure of acetic acid :* The correct structure of acetic acid can be either (I) or (II).

	$CH_3.\overset{\overset{O}{\parallel}}{C}.OH$ (I)	$CH_3.COOH$ (II)
2C	3 × 2.591 = 5.182	CH3 radical = 5.653
4H	4 × 1.028 = 4.112	— COOH = 7.226
O(C=O)	1 × 2.573 = 2.573	Total = 12.879
— OH	1 × 1.518 = 1.518	
	Total 13.385	

Observed value of R_M = 13.021.

As the calculated value of R_M of structure I has been found to be very close to observed value of R_M, the structure I is the correct structure of acetic acid.

4. *Keto-enol tautomerism :* Molar refraction can give an approximate indication whether one or the other form in keto-enol tautomerism of a compound predominates in its normal state.

The enol form is having double bond and therefore two forms should possess different values of R_M. The calculated molar refractions of the keto and enol forms of acetoacetic ester are 31.57 and 32.62, respectively, hence

$$\underset{\substack{31.57 \\ \text{Keto}}}{CH_3.CO.CH_2.COOC_2H_5} \qquad \underset{\substack{32.62 \\ \text{enol}}}{CH_3.\overset{\overset{OH}{|}}{C}{=}CH.COOC_2.I_5}$$

The enolic form is having conjugated double bond and therefore, an optical exaltation equal to 1.8 is found. The molar refraction of the enolic form should be 34.42. The measured molar refraction of the acetoacetic ester in its normal state is 32. The proportion of enolic form should be given as follows:

$$\frac{32.00 - 31.57}{34.42 - 31.57} \times 100 = 15\%$$

Molecular refraction values such as parachor can be used for elucidation the chemical constitution. Even though the calculated and observed values of molecular refraction closely tally in many cases but anomalous results are also obtained. This is ascribed to the optical exaltation.

OPTICAL EXHALATION

It is observed that when a compound contains ore than on double bond, the molecular refractivity depends not only on the number of double bonds but on their) position also. Thus in case of conjugated system of double bonds (i.e., alternate double bonds there is a marked increase in the value of the observed molecular refractivity than the value calculated from the atomic and the structural constants. This behaviour is known as optical exhaltation.

For example, the observed R_M of isodially,

$$CH_3—CH=CH—CH=CH—CH_3$$

having conjugated double bonds, is 1.76 units higher than the calculated R_M whereas for the isomeric dually, $CH_2=CH—CH_2—CH_2—CH=CH_2$, in which the double linkages are not conjugated, the observed value of R_M is smaller by about 0.12 unit. It has also been found that a carbonyl group, if present along with a double or triple bond, causes optical exaltation. Hence, the experimental value of molar refraction of phorone,

$$(CH_3)_2C=CH—CO—CH=C(CH_3)_2,$$

is 45.39 while the calculated value is 42.85.

$$\text{Optical exaltation} = 45.39 - 42.85 = 2.54$$

If the conjugated double linkages constitute a closed ring as in benzene and cyclo-octatetrene, the optical exaltation is to observed but if the conjugated system is partly within the ring and partly in a side chain as in styree I and acetophenone (II) the positive an only appears *i.e.*, optical exaltation is observed.

$$C_6H_5—CH=CH_2 \quad C_6H_5—\underset{\underset{O}{\|}}{C}.CH_3 \quad —CH_3—C_6H_4—C_3H_7$$

I II III

If there exists a gap in the ring as in α-phellandrene (III), the optical exaltation is present.

REFRACHOR

It is a new physical constant which relates refractive index μ_D^{20} with parachor. It is denoted by the symbol [F] and is expressed mathematically as follows:

$$F = — [P] \log (\mu_D^{20} - 1)$$

Refrachor can be used for elucidating structure but it has not found much application.

VISCOSITY AND CHEMICAL CONSTITUTION

Viscosity has been found to be neither additive nor a constitutive property and therefore it could not be used in deciding between different possible structures of molecules to the same extent as molar volume or parachor could be used. However, it was Dunstan (1909) who discovered an interesting relationship between viscosity and molar volume of non-associated liquids as follows:

$$\frac{d}{M} \times \eta \times 10^6 = 40 \text{ to } 70 \quad ...(1)$$

Table 4.1(a) : Values of $\frac{d}{M} \times \eta \times 10^6$.

Liquid	(d/M) × η × 10^6	Inference
Acetone	43	Unassociated
Toluene	56	Unassociated
Benzene	73	Unassociated
Water	559	Associated
Glycol	2750	More associated
Glycerol	116400	Highly associated

where *d* is the density, *M* the molecular weight and η the coefficient of viscosity of the liquid. This relationship has been employed to know whether a liquid is associated or not. If the value exceeds 70, the liquid exists as associated molecules. Table 4.1(a) shows how the reference can be drawn about the nature of liquids. The values of acetone, toluene and benzene have been 43 56 and 73 respectively, thereby indicating that these liquids are undissociated. On the other hand, the values for water, glycol and glycerol have been 559, 2750 ad 116400 respectively thereby indicating that these liquids are associated and further indicating that glycerol has been much more associated than glycol.

Molecular Viscosity or Molar Viscosity

As M/d represents molecular volume, it means that $(M/d)^{2/3}$ represents the molar surface area. The product of molar surface and viscosity is termed as molar viscosity.

$$\text{Molar viscosity} = \text{molar surface 0215 viscosity}$$
$$= \left(\frac{M}{d}\right)^{2/3} \times \eta$$

It was found by Thorp and Rodge (1894) that molecule viscosity is an additive and constitutive property at the boiling point of liquid. Values for different atoms and linkages have been determined and given in standard charts.

From these the molar viscosity for a compound can be calculated. If the calculated and experimental values come out to be the same, this is taken as a confirmation of the structure of the substance. The values of molar viscosity contributions by different atoms have been given as follows:

Atom	H	C	O (in OH)	O (in — CO)	S
Molar viscosity	80	−98	196	248	155

Rheochor

According to Newton Friend, the product of molar volume and the eighth root of viscosity is constant at least at the boiling point *i.e.,*

$$\frac{M}{d} \times \eta^{1/8} = R$$

where 'R' is a constant called the *Rheochor*. Rheochor, like molar viscosity, is also an additive and constitutive property.

Physical significance of rheochor is that it may be regarded as the molar volume of a liquid at a temperature when its velocity is unity. *Rheochor is not very useful for determining the chemical constitution of a substance.*

The atomic and structural rheochor values (like parachor values) are given in Table 4.2.

It is to be made clear that the rheochor is less useful for determining chemical structures that parachor ad is not used frequently for studying the chemical constitution.

The physical properties may be classified into various categories given below:

Table 4.2 : Atomic and Structural Rheochors

Atom	Rheochor	Linkage	Rheochor
Carbon	12.8	Covalent bod	0.0
Oxygen (in ether)	10.0	Coordinate bond	0.4
(in ketone)	13.2		
Hydrogen (in C—H)	5.5	6-membered ring (hat)	– 5.6
(in C—OH)	10.0	$—CH_2$	23.6
(in HCl)	9.7	$—C_6H_5$	100.7
(in HBr)	12.6	—C(=O)O	36.0
(in HI)	15.0	$—NH_2$	20.6
Chlorine	27.3	>NH	13.6
Bromine	35.8	CN	33.0
Iodine	47.6		
Nitrogen	6.6		

(ii) Constitutive Property

It is the property which depends entirely upon the ode of arrangement of atoms in the molecule, but independent of their number. The optical activity is one such property.

(i) Additive Property

It is the property which depends upon the nature and number of atoms present in a molecule of the compound, such that its magnitude is equal to the sum of the corresponding properties of the constituent atoms. For example, the molecular mass of a substance is equal to the sum of the atomic masses of the constituent atoms.

(iii) Additive and Constitutive Property

It is an additive property which also depends upon the manner in which the atoms are bonded to each other. For example, parachor is an additive as well as constitutive property.

A brief account of more important physical properties alongwith their applications to the problem of elucidating chemical structure has been dealt in this chapter.

MOLECULAR REFRACTION

The refractive index of a fluid varies with temperature and pressure, as these factors alter the number of molecules i, the path of the light. Hence, it cannot be used to compare refractive powers of different fluids in relation to their molecular structures.

To eliminate the effect of these factors, H.A. Lorenz (1880) from the electromagnetic theory of light, and L.V. Lorenz (1880) from the wave theory of light, independently deduced the following theoretical relationship between refractive index and density, which should be constant at all temperatures:

$$R = \frac{\mu^2 - 1}{\mu^2 - 2} \times \frac{1}{d} \qquad ...(1)$$

where μ is the refractive index of a liquid and 'd' its density, R is a constant called the *specific refraction or refractivity*. Multiplying the above equation by , the molecular weight of the liquid on both sides we get,

$$R \times M = \frac{\mu^2 - 1}{\mu^2 - 2} \cdot \frac{M}{d} = R_M \qquad ...(2)$$

The product R × M is denoted by R_M and is called the *molar refraction or molar refractivity*. R_{M1} is characteristic of the liquid and remains constant at the given temperature.

The molar refraction is independent of temperature and pressure, but as is the case with refractive index it varies with the wave-length of the light used. Generally, the D-line of sodium is the light source. If any other source is employed (*e.g.*, the D-line in the hydrogen spectrum) it should be specifically mentioned.

The molar refractivity of a solute, solvent and solution can be determined as follows:

A know weight of the solid is dissolved in a known weight of a suitable solvent. The refractive index and density of the solution are determined in the usual way. If R′ is molar refractivity of the solution, it is given by,

$$R' = \frac{\mu^2 - 1}{\mu^2 - 2}\left(\frac{N_1M_1 + N_2M_2}{d}\right) \qquad ...(3)$$

where μ is the refractive index of the solution N_1, N_2 the mole fractions of the solute and solvent respectively, M_1 and M_2 are their molecular weights and 'd' and density of the solution. The molar refractivity of the solution R', is related to the molar refractivities of the solute and solvent as:

$$R' = N_1R_1 = N_2R_2 \qquad ...(4)$$

where R_1 ad R_2 are the molar refractive is of the solute and solvent respectively ad N_1 and N_2 have the same meaning as before.

The refractive index and density of the solvent are now determined and its molar refractivity R_2 is calculated with the help of equation (2). Substituting this value is equation (4). R_1 the molar refractive of the solutes is calculated.

MOLAR VOLUME OF LIQUIDS

The molar volume (V_m) of a substance may be defined as the volume (generally expressed in cm^3) occupied by one mole of the substance, under specified conditions of temperature and pressure. Mathematically, this can be put as follows:

$$V_m = \frac{\text{Molar mass}}{\text{Density}}$$

The units of molar volume are, those of volume per mole of the substance. It is possible to calculate the molar volume of a liquid from the value of the molar mass and density of the substance.

The density can be measured by using a precalibrated density-bottle, or pyknometer. The density-bottle being convenient at room temperature, while pyknometer can be used for measuring density at various temperatures.

Kopp's Law

It is a well known fact that molar volume is equal to 22.4 litres in the case of all gases at N.T.P. On the basis of this numerous attempts were made to find out if the simple uniformity existed in liquids as well. One of the well known attempt was made by Kopp who measured densities of a large number of liquids at their boiling points which are approximately corresponding temperatures.

Although he could not be able to obtain uniformity of results, yet he established a law called Kopp's law which may be stated as follows:

"The molar volume of a substance is approximately equal to the sum of the atomic masses of its constituent atoms."

Kopp found the following regularities in the molar volumes of liquids:

(*i*) *The isomers belonging to the same homologous series are having nearly equal molar volumes.* An example is that the molar volume of *n*-heptane was 162.8 ml whereas that of *iso* heptane was 162.0 ml. Another example is that the of a volumes of normal and *iso*-butric acids were 108.2 ml and 108.9 ml respectively.

(*ii*) *Any two successive members of the same homologous series of organic compounds were found to differ in their molar volumes by about the same amount.*

For example in the case of aliphatic alcohols, the difference in molar volumes of two successive members (such as methyl alcohol and ethyl alcohol) was 21.4 ml. Further, in the case of aliphatic acids, the difference in the values of two successive members was 22.5 ml.

If similar other series such as paraffins aldehydes, amines, esters, etc., were considered, an average difference of 22.2 ml was found. These observations were found to form the basis of Kopp's law stated above.

Based on the studies of various compounds Kopps compiled a set of atomic volumes. Let Bas (1906) later on demonstrated that the molar volumes exhibited their dependence on the constitutional and structural influences.

The following table records the atomic volumes given by Kopp as well as by Le Bas (1912).

From such data, it becomes possible to ascertain the molar volume of any organic substance and the structure of liquid molecule can be elucidated by comparing the calculated values from practically observed values of molecular volumes.

To demonstrate this let us take the example of ethyl benzoate, $C_2H_5COOC_6H_5$.

Table 4.3 : Volume equivalents of elements

Atom	*Kopp*	*Le Bas*
H	5.5	3.7
C	11.0	14.8
Cl	22.8	22.2
Br	27.8	27.0
S	22.6	—
—O—	7.8	7.4
=O	12.2	12.0
I	37.5	37.0

Le Bas Data

$$9C = 9 \times 14.8 = 133.2$$

$$10H = 10 \times 3.7 = 37.0$$

$$—O— = 1 \times 7.4 = 7.4$$

$$O = 1 \times 12.0 = 12.0$$

(benzene ring) = 1 0215 (– 15) = – 15.0 (no included in table)

174.6 cm^3

Observed molecular volume = 174.6 cm^3.

Hence the structure of ethyl benzoate is $C_2H_5\overset{\overset{O}{\|}}{C}.OC_6.H_5$.

Limitations

However, it was soon found by various workers that molar volume was not pure an additive property. There occurred differences due to constitution as well. For example, atomic volume of oxygen was 12.0 in a carbonyl group ($>C=O$) but 7.8 in a hydroxyl group (— OH). It was also reported that the presence of benzene nucleus reduced the molar volume by 1.50 ml.

In reality it was a mere coincidence with the law that additivity was obtained when liquids were examined at their normal boiling points. But it was soon realised that molecular volume was not purely an additive property. Hence the use of molecular volume in deciding the chemical constitution is limited. Another property, related to molar volume, called *parachor*, has been found to be far more useful for this purpose, as discussed below.

MECLEOD'S RELATIONSHIP—THE PARACHOR

We know that surface tension is due to the inward force o the molecules and hence it is related to the structure of the molecules.

Macleod in 1923 pointed out that

$$\frac{\gamma^{1/4}}{D-d} = C \qquad ...(1)$$

where γ is surface tension of the liquid, 'D' its density and 'd' the density of its vapour at the temperature of experiment and 'C' is a constant. The equation holds good over a wide range of temperature. Multiplying both sides by M,

$$\frac{M\gamma^{14}}{D-d} = MC = [P] \qquad ...(2)$$

where 'M' is the molecular weight of the liquid. The product M × C is called parachor and is represented as [P]. At ordinary temperature far away from the critical temperature 'd' is negligible as compared to D. Then Eq. (2) may be written as

$$\frac{M\gamma^{1/4}}{D} = [P] \qquad ...(3)$$

But $$\frac{M}{D} = \text{molar volume}$$

$$\therefore \quad [P] = \text{molar volume} \times \gamma^{1/4} \qquad ...(4)$$

Thus parachor may be defined as the product of molar volume of a liquid and its surface tension raised to the power 1/4.

If the two liquids have same surface tension under a given set of conditions, their parachors are proportional to their molar volumes.

Suppose, at a particular temperature, $\gamma = 1$. Then, since M/D is molar volume, the equation (3) may be write as follows:

$$[P] = \text{Molar volume}$$

Thus, the parachor may also be defined as *the molar volume of a liquid at a temperature at which its surface tension is unity.*

Parachor has been found to be more useful than molar volume in deciding between different alternative structures of compounds.

Sugden concluded that parachor is largely an additive property. This is supported by the following observations:

1. *The isomeric compounds of the same family* (such as esters, alcohols, etc.) are having almost the same parachor. For instance, there are six esters having the molecular formula $C_6H_{12}O_2$. Their parachors, as included in Table 4.4, are very close to one another.

Table 4.4 : Parachors of Esters of Formula $C_6H_{12}O_2$

Ester	*Parachor*	*Ester*	*Parachor*
Methyl valerate	292.5	iso-Amyl formate	293.6
Ethyl isobutyrate	292.2	iso-Butyl acetate	295.1
Ethyl butyrate	293.6	n-Propyl propionate	295.3

2. *The difference between the parachors of successive numbers of different homologous series is nearly the same,* as show for hydrocarbons in Table. 4.5.

Table 4.5 : Parachors of paraffins

Paraffins *Name*	*Formula*	*Parachor*	*Difference*	*Parachor for one CH_2 group*
Ethane	C_2H_6	110.5		
			40.3	40.4
Propane	C_3H_8	150.8		
			119.3	39.8
Hexane	C_6H_{14}	270.1		
			39.2	39.2
Heptane	C_7H_{16}	309.3		
			35.7	35.7
Octane	C_8H_{18}	345.0		
			79.2	39.6
Decane	$C_{10}H_{12}$	424.2		

From the above table it can be seen that the average difference corresponding to the parachor of the CH_2 group, from a similar study of several other homologous series (such as alcohols, ethers esters, aldehydes, ketones, etc.), has been found to be 39.0.

Atomic Parachors

The values for a given compound are expressed as sum of the numbers and nature of atoms present called *atomic parachors*. Knowing that each CH_2 group has a parachor value of 39, while decane $C_{10}H_{22}$ has a parachor value of 424.2, it follows that

$$\text{since } C_{10}H_{22} = 10(H_2) + 2H$$

$$\therefore \quad 424.2 = 10 \times 39 + 2 \times \text{atomic parachor of hydrogen}$$

$$\text{Atomic parachor of hydrogen} = \frac{424.2 - 390}{2} = 17.1$$

$$\text{Atomic parachor of carbon} = 39.0 - 34.2 = 4.8$$

If the atomic parachors of carbon and hydrogen are known it becomes possible to determine atomic parachors of other elements. For example atomic parachor of oxygen has been obtained from ethers, that of nitrogen from amines and those of chlorine, bromine and iodine from the corresponding halides.

Structural Parachors

It was soon reported that parachor, like molar volume, though large an additive property, has been partly a constitutive property as well. For example, the parachor of ethylene (C_2H_4), which should be = $2 \times 4.8 + 4 \times 17.1 = 78.0$ has been in reality, 99.5. Hence, the double bond should make a contribution of 21.5. Further careful determinations in the case of unsaturated compounds having ethylenic double bond have shown that each ethylenic double bond makes a contribution, on an average of 23.2. Similarly, triple bond has been making a contribution of 46.6.

The values of atomic and structural parachors for different atoms, linkages etc. have bee determined (Table 4.6). The values for some important atoms and structural factors are give below with the help of these the parachor for a give compound is calculated o the basis of an assumed structure.

If this value agrees with the value obtained from experimental determinations of surface tension, the structure is correct.

The values of the atomic and structural parachors computed by Sugden (1924) were revised by Mumford and Phillips (1929). Vogel (1948) revised these values further.

These values are tabulated in Table 4.6.

Table 4.6 : Atomic and Structural Parachors

Atoms, Groups or Linkage	*[P]* Sugden (1924)	Mumford and Phillips (1929)	Vogel (1948)
C	4.8	9.2	8.6
H	17.1	15.4	15.7
O	20.0	20.0	19.8
	12.5	17.5	—
Cl	54.3	55.5	55.2
Br	68.0	69.0	68.8
I	90.0	90.0	90.3
>C=O	—	—	44.4
—OH	—	—	30.2
—COOH	—	—	73.7
$—NO_2$	—	—	73.8
Single bond	0	0	0
Double bond (>C=C<)	23.2	19.0	19.9
Triple bond (—C≡C—)	46.6	38.0	40.6
Rings 3-membered	16.7	12.5	12.3
4-membered	11.6	6.0	10.0
5-membered	8.5	3.0	4.6
6-membered	6.1	0.8	1.4

Calculation of Parachors of Compounds

The parachors of compounds can be calculated with the help of the above table. One example is demonstrated below:

Parachor of Acetone $\left(\begin{matrix} CH_3 \\ CH_3 \end{matrix} \!\!>\!C{=}O\right)$. It may be calculated as illustrated below:

$$3C = 3 \times 4.8 = 14.4$$

$$6H = 6 \times 17.1 = 102.6$$

$$1O = 1 \times 20.0 = 20.0$$

$$1 \text{ double bond} = 1 \times 23.2 = 23.2$$

Parachor of acetone = 160.2 (Observed value = 161.2).

Applications of Parachor in Deciding Structures

1. *Structure of quinone* : For quinone $C_6H_4O_2$, the following two structures have been proposed:

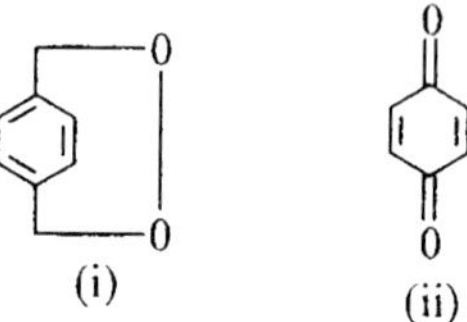

The observed value of parachor for quinone is 236.8, which of the two structure is correct?

(Parachors for H = 17.1, C = 4.8, O = 20.0, double bond = 23.2 and six membered ring = 6.1).

For structures (i) and (ii) we calculate the parachor values separate.

For (i) 6 Carbon atoms = 6 × 4.8 = 28.8

4 Hydrogen atoms = 4 × 17.1= 68.4

2 Oxygen atoms = 2 × 20 = 40

3 double bonds = 3 × 23.2= 69.6

2 six membered rings = 2 × 6.1 = 12.2

Total = 219.0

For (ii) 6 Carbon atoms = 6 × 4.8 = 28.8

4 Hydrogen atoms = 4 × 17.1= 68.4

2 Oxygen atoms = 2 × 20 = 40

4 Double bonds = 4 × 23.2= 92.8

1 six membered ring = 1 × 6.1 = 6.1

Total = 236.1

Since the observed value 236.8 is nearly the same as that calculated value of (*ii*), therefore the true structure of quinone is (ii).

2. *Structure of paraldehyde* : Acetaldehyde forms a liquid polme known as paraldehyde $(C_2H_4O)_2$. The two proposed structures for the polymer are:

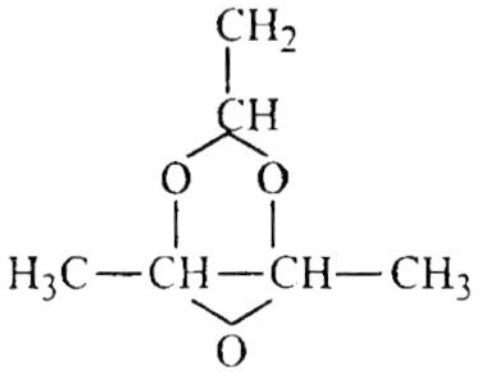

$$\begin{array}{c} CH_2 \\ | \\ CH \\ O \quad O \\ | \quad\; | \\ H_3C-CH-CH-CH_3 \\ O \end{array} \qquad CH_3CH(OH).CH_3CH(OH).CH_2\overset{\overset{O}{\|}}{C}H$$

(A) 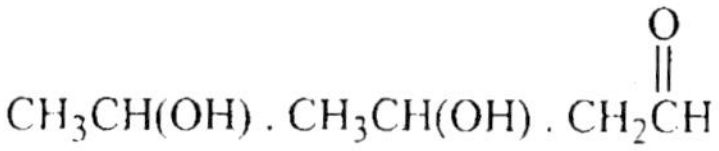 (B)

The value of parachor as calculated from its surface tension is 298.7. Which of the proposed structures is correct? (Parachors of H = 17.1, C = 4.8, O = 20.0, six membered ring = 6.1 double bond = 23.2).

Solution:

We calculate prachors for (A) and (B) separately.

For (A) 6 Carbon atoms = 6 × 4.8 = 28.8

12 Hydrogen atoms = 12 × 17.1 = 205.2

3 Oxygen atoms = 3 × 20.0= 60.0

1 six membered ring = 1 × 6.1 = 6.1

Total = = 300.1

For (B) 6 Carbon atoms = 6 × 4.8 = 28.8

12 Hydrogen atoms = 12 × 17.1 = 205.2

3 Oxygen atoms = 3 × 20.0= 60.0

1 Double bond = 1 × 23.2= 23.2

Total = = 317.2

Since the observed value 298.7 is the same as the calculated value for structure (A), therefore the correct structure of paraldehyde is:

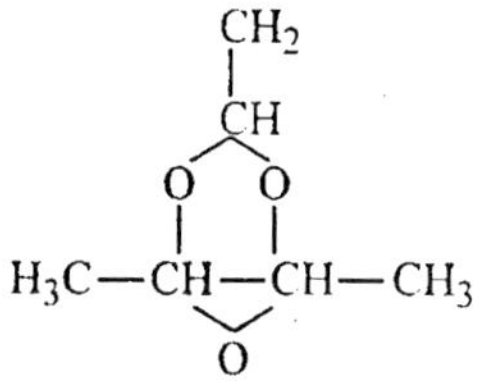

$$\begin{array}{c} CH_2 \\ | \\ CH \\ O \quad O \\ | \quad\; | \\ H_3C-CH-CH-CH_3 \\ O \end{array}$$

(A)

?. *Structure of benzene* : The calculated value of parachor taken fro Kekule fo··nula agrees with observed value which is found to be 206.

4. *Structure of isocanide group* : The parachor value of — NC (isocyanide group) has been calculated to be 65 from the experimental parachor values for methyl, ethyl, phenyl and other isocyanides. The possible structures of — NC group may be given as:

$$\underset{\text{I}}{-N{=}C} \qquad \text{and} \qquad \underset{\text{II}}{-\overset{+}{N}{\equiv}C}$$

Calculated parachor	Calculated parachor
= 12.5 + 4.8 + 23.2	= 12.5 + 4.8 + 46.6 – 1.6
= 40.5	= 62.3

The structure II has been preferred which has also been established by Raman spectra and dipole moment studies.

5. *Odd electro bound I* : The parachor value of odd electro bond has been found to be – 11.6 b Sugden. In the case of SF_6, if all the bonds are considered to be covalent ones then the calculated parachor of the molecule would be 198.2. The experimental value of SF_6 is 144 only. The difference has been explained on the fact that four of the fluorine atoms are attached with odd electron bonds.

   In this way odd electron bonds in various chelated compounds have been proposed.

6. *Deciding the nature of valency* : Parachor provides a valuable tool in deciding the nature of bonds in compounds of nitrogen, sulphur and phosphorus. For instance, the nitro group may be represented by the following three structures:

I	II	III
$-N(=O)_2$	$-N(\rightarrow O)(=O)$	$-N\langle O{-}O$ (3-membered ring)

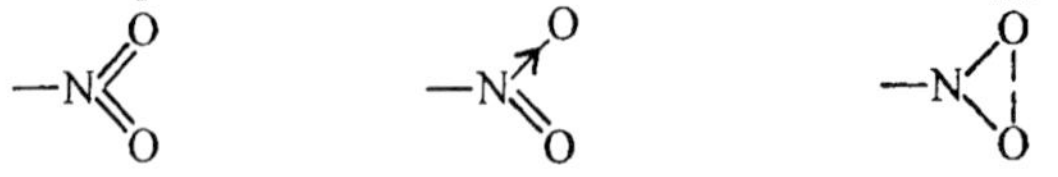

Parachor

I	II	III
= 12.5+2×20 + 2 × 23.2 = 98.9	12.5+2×20+23.2 – 1.6 = 74.1	12.5+2×20+16.7 (for a 3 membered ring) = 69.2

The study of parachors in large number of nitro compounds reveals that the contribution of — NO_2 group is about 73.0. Therefore the structure II is most probable.

7. *Structure of benzil* : Two structures have been proposed for benzil.

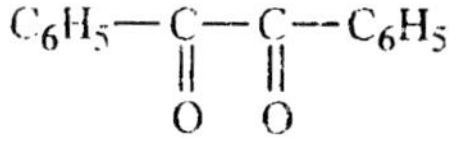

$$C_6H_5-\underset{\underset{O}{\|}}{C}-\underset{\underset{O}{\|}}{C}-C_6H_5 \qquad\qquad C_6H_5-\underset{\underset{O}{|}}{C}-\underset{\underset{O}{|}}{C}-C_6H_5$$

I II

Calculated parachor = 476 Calculated parachor = 464.4

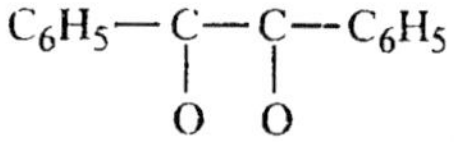

The experimental value of benzil is 480.0. Hence structure I is most probable.

Parachor Anomalies

It must be pointed out that the use of the parachor for the solution of structural problem is not fee from objections. For example:

(i) Parachor measurements indicated that organic oxides, containing the — N_3 group, and aliphatic diazo-compounds have cyclic structure. It appears to be provided by electron diffraction measurements, however, that the groups are actually linear. The erroneous conclusions may perhaps have been due to the failure to take into account the possibility of resonance.

(ii) Serious parachor anomalies exist in several organometallic compounds: in the dialkyl sulphide derivatives of palladium chloride ; having the general formula $(R_2S)_2$ $PcDCl_2$, the parachor equivalent of the palladium atom decreases from 3, when R is methyl, to – 7 when R is amyl.

(iii) Similar to (ii), a steady decrease in the contribution of the metal atom occurs in the mercury mercaptides. Hg $(SR)_2$, and in other series of compounds as the length of the hydrocarbon chain is increased.

In (ii) and (iii), it is probable that as the central atom becomes more completely covered with alkyl groups it becomes less and less able of making its contribution to forces of cohesion and to surface tension. In such circumstances the normal additivity relationships of the parachor might be expected to fail.

REFRACTIVE INDEX

If light is allowed to pass from a rarer medium (*say air*) into a denser medium (*say a liquid*), it is bent or refracted towards the normal. The ratio of the sine of the angle of incidence and that of refraction is constant and characteristic of that liquid (Snell's law). The constant ratio is termed as the refractive index of the liquid ad may be put as follows:

$$\mu = \frac{\sin i}{\sin r}$$

According to the wave theory of light, the ratio of the sines of the angles of incidence and refraction is identical with the ratio of the velocities of light in the two media. Hence, refractive index may be defined as follows:

Thus, $$\mu = \frac{\sin i}{\sin r} = \frac{\text{Velocity of light in air}}{\text{Velocity of light in liquid}}$$

If a ray of light is allowed to pass from a rarer to denser medium, it can be shown from the law of refraction that

$$\frac{\sin i}{\sin r} = \frac{\mu_2}{\mu_1}$$

Here μ_1 is the index of refraction of the rarer and μ_2 the index of refraction of the denser medium. The angle of incidence can never be evidently greater than a 90° and if it is 90° the above equation gets reduced to $\sin r = \frac{\mu_1}{\mu_2}$ or $\sin 90° = 1$.

Measurement of Refraction Index

For the rapid determination of the refractive index of liquids, a number of instruments called refractometers have been constructed. We give below a brief account of the most prominent them which are :

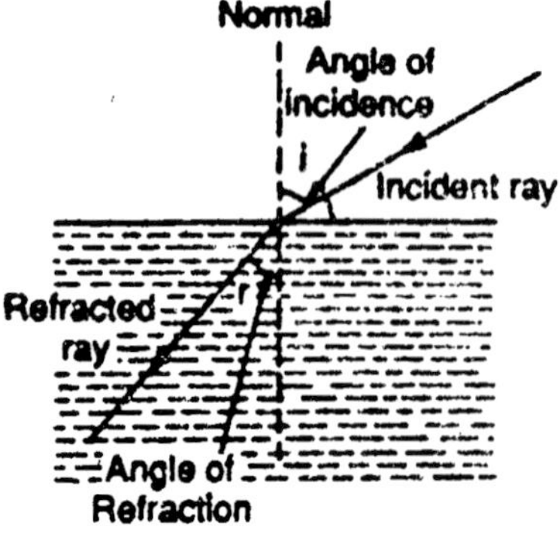

Fig. 4.3 : Refraction of light.

(i) The Pulfrich refractometer, and

(ii) The Abbe refractometer.

1. Pulfrich Refractometer

Pulfrich refractometer is very accurate and simple in principle and is depicted in Fig. 4.3. The essential part of the instrument is a right angled glass prisms with a small glass cell cemented to its top. The liquid to be examined is kept in the cell and a beam of monochromatic light is made to enter the liquid at 'grazin incidence' along the surface between the liquid and the prism. It follows the path of *ABCD* and is observed in a telescope at *D*. If the telescope is moved to make an angle with the horizontal which is less than i, no light could reach it. A very accurate determination can, therefore, be made of the angle i at which a sharp boundary between a dark and light field can be seen through the telescope.

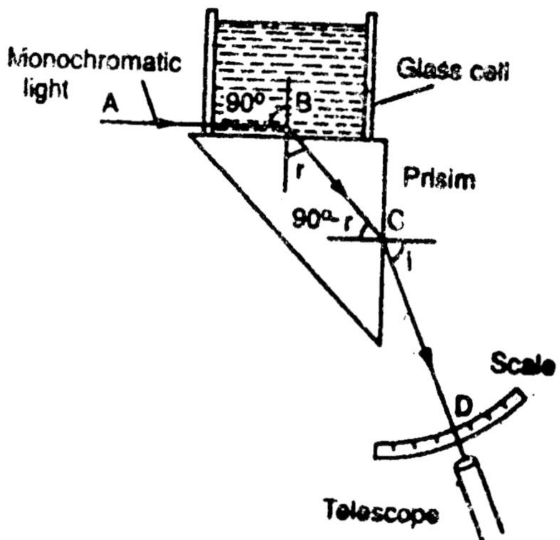

Fig. 4.4 : The optical system of Pulfrich Refractometer.

For a ray of light passing from the liquid into the prism; if r refers to the angle of refraction when the angle of incidence is 90°, we have already stated that

$$\sin r = \frac{\mu_1}{\mu_2} \qquad ...(1)$$

where μ_1 is the refractive index of the liquid and μ_2 is that of the glass prism. It is also clear from the diagram that

$$\frac{\sin i}{\sin (90^\circ - r)} = \mu_2 \qquad ...(2)$$

Bus $\sin (90^\circ - r) = \cos r$, we have

$$\frac{\sin i}{\cos r} = \mu_2$$

or

$$\cos r = \frac{\sin i}{\mu_2} \qquad ...(3)$$

But

$$\sin r = \sqrt{1 - \cos^2 r} \qquad ...(4)$$

On substituting the value of cos r from (4), we obtain

$$\sin r = \sqrt{1 - \frac{\sin^2 i}{\mu_2^2}}$$

and from Eq. (1), $\mu_1 = \mu_2 \sin r$

Hence

$$\mu_1 = \sqrt{\mu_2^2 - \sin^2 i}$$

If the refractive index μ_2 of the glass is known and angle i is measured, μ_1, the refractive index of the liquid, can be calculated. In actual practice, however, it is not necessary to go through the above calculations because the makers of the insrrument supply tables giving refractive indices (μ_1) corresponding to different values of i.

The index of refraction depends upon the wave-length of light employed, the index for red rays being less than that for the violet rays. Measurements of the refractive index referred to D-line of sodium are usually indicated by the symbol μ.

2. Abbe's Refractometer

The principle of this instrument happens to be the same as that used in the Pulfrich refractometer. This instrument is, however less accurate than the Pulfrich refractometer. It is principally designed for the rapid determinations of the refractive index of small quantities of liquids.

(a) *Construction* : A general idea of the construction of this instrument is given in Fig. 4.5.

A and B are two glass prisms. The hypotenuse surface of b is polished while that of A is finely ground. The two prisms are housed in metal casings hinged at H. The two prisms faces can be held i contact with clamp C. A and B can be rotated about a horizontal axis immediately beneath a telescope T. To the metal case carrying the prism, is attached arc arm, R which is able to move along a graduated scale S, the reading on which provides directly the refractive index.

Working

A drop of the liquid is kept upon the surface of prism A. On clamping the two prisms A and B a film of the liquid spreads between them. Light reflected by mirror M is then made to direct towards the prism system. On reaching the ground surface of A it gets scattered into the liquid film. No ray can, however, enter B with a greater angle of refraction than that of the ray corresponding to '*grazing incidence*'. Hence when viewed through a telescope, just as in the case of Pulfrich refractometer the field of view gets divided into bright and dark portions. The edge of the bright portion when coincided with the cross-wire of the telescope provides the refractive index on the scale. If white light is employed, as is the case in practice, a diffused coloured border is seen in the telescope.

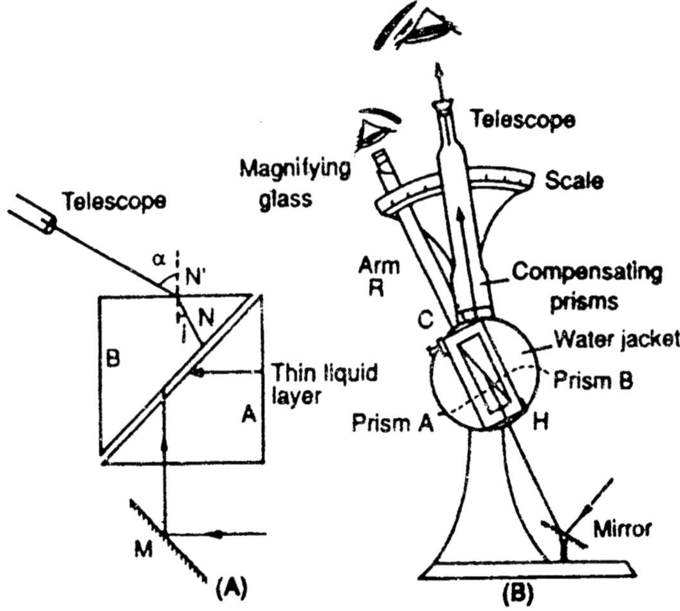

(a) Optical system of Abbe Refractometer shows the course of light ray.

(b) Optical system of Abbe Refractometer

Fig. 4.5

This is made sharp and the colours are removed by the adjustment of two prisms, (not shown in the diagram) attached at the nose of the telescope. As temperature control is of great importance in determining the refractive index of liquids, the prisms A and B are enclosed in a water jacket, J so as to maintain a constant temperature.

OPTICAL ACTIVITY

Plane Polarised Light

A beam of light, proceeding towards this paper and at right angles to the paper, possesses wave components that are vibrating in all possible planes passing through the axis along which the beam is travelling (*axis of propagation*). This is illustrated in Fig. 4.6. Each of the planes of vibration represented in Fig. 4.6 may be considered as the resultant of component waves vibrating in two perpendicular planes, as shown in Fig. 4.7.

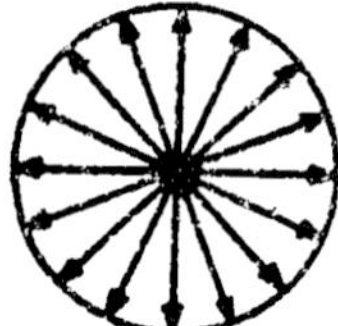

Fig. 4.6 : The circle represents the point of contact of a perpendicular pencil beam of light. The centre of the circle is the axis of propagation of the beam. The double headed arrows represent all possible planes of wave vibration.

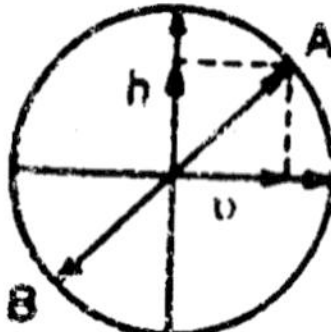

Fig. 4.7 : Illustration of the resolution of planes of vibration AB and CD into horizontal (h) and vertical (v) vector components.

If a beam of light is passed through a properly oriented crystal of the mineral Iceland spar; or calcite (calcium carbonate) the beam is split into two beams and the process is said to be double refraction (Fig. 4.7). The two emerging beams (Fig. 4.8) both have only a single plane of vibration and the plane of vibration in beam *a* is perpendicular to that of beam *b* (Fig. 4.9). In short the crystal is able to separate each wave plane of vibration into horizontal and vertical components b bending one component more that the other.

A beam of light having a single plane of wave vibration is said to be plane polarised as represented by either beam 'a' and 'b' in Fig. 4.9.

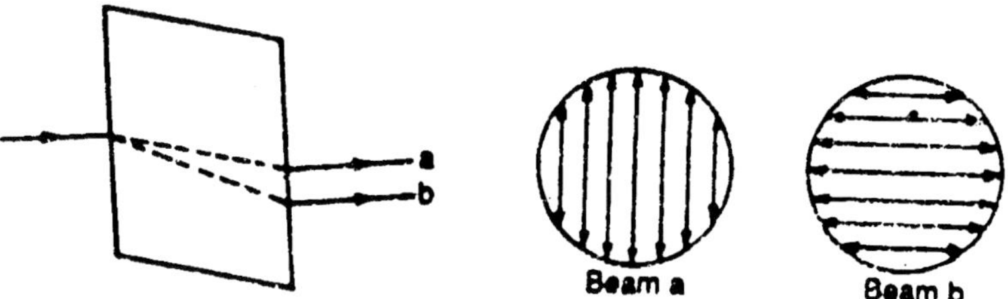

Fig. 4.8 : Illustration of double refraction b a calcium carbonate crystal..

Fig. 4.9 : Planes of wave vibration in beams a and b emerging from crystal.

The generation of a single beam of plane-polarized light may be accomplished b separation of the two beams a and b. A suitable apparatus for this operation was invented in 1828 by William Nicol, a Scotish Physicist known as a '*Nicolprism*'. The apparatus consists of two crystals of Iceland spar cut to certain angles and cemented by canada balsam, as illustrated in Fig. 4.10. A beam of light entering at the left is doubly refracted into beams a and b. Beam 'a' passes through both crystals, emerging plane polarized on the right. Because of the cut of the crystal ad the index of refraction of the canada balsam; beam b is reflected at the crystal juncture and does not enter the second crystal.

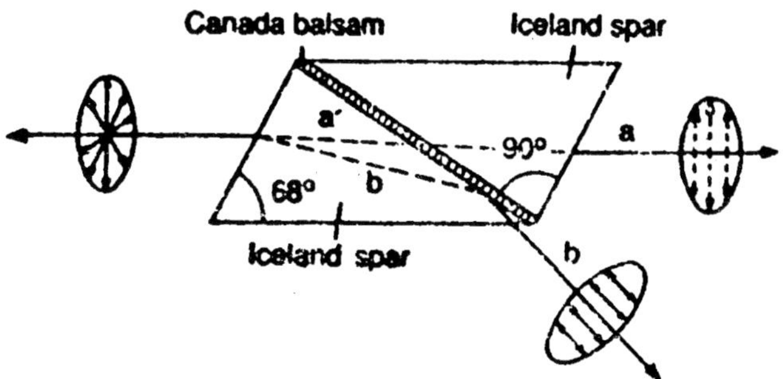

Fig. 4.10 : Production of plane polarised light by a Nicol prism.

Plane polarised light may also be generated by a polaroid, a cooperatively recent invention of an American E. H. Land. Certain crystals said to have the property of *di-chorism*, will absorb light components vibrating in one plane more strongly that those vibrating in the perpendicular plane. Thus a suitable thickness of such a crystal can be used to produce plane-polarised light. Polaroid consists of certain dichroic derivatives of quine the crystals of which are properly oriented and embedded in a transparent plastic.

Nature of Optical Activity

When a plane polarised light passes through certain organic substances it changes its direction of motion. This phenomena of rotation of plane of polarised light b certain substances is called "*optical activity*" and the substance which rotates the plane of polarised light is called "*optical active.*"

Optically active compounds can be divided into two categories: one in which the activity is evident in the solid state only, *i.e.*, due to the crystalline structure of the compounds, and the other in which optical activity is shown by the compounds in the solid, pure liquid, solution or gaseous forms. As the optical activity of the former class has been related to the disappears, *i.e.*, when the substance melts.

This type of optical activity is found with quartz, sodium chlorate etc. Optical activity of the latter class has been related to the molecular structure of the compounds, *i.e.*, this property depends on the arrangement of the atoms in a molecule. As the molecular structure does not get altered b fusion dissolution, or vaporization, therefore, the property gets manifested equally well in these forms.

Dextro and Laevo Rotatory Substances

The rotation of the plane of polarised light ay take place either towards the right or the left.

Rotation towards right : An optically active substance which rotates the plane of the polarised light towards the right is called dextro rotator (d).

Rotation towards left : An optically active substance which rotates the plane of the polarised light towards the left is called *laevo rotator* (l).

The angle of rotation depends upon the following factors:

(i) Nature of the substance

(ii) Thickness of the layer through which the light passes.

(iii) Wave length of the light used.

(iv) Density of the solution.

(v) Temperature of the experiment.

(vi) Nature of the solvent.

Specific Rotation

If 'R' is the observed rotation 'λ' the wave length of light used, 't' the temperature of the solution 'd' is density and 'T' the length of the column of the solution through which light passes, then

$$\frac{R}{l.d} = [\alpha]_{\lambda}^{t} \qquad ...(1)$$

where $[\alpha]_{\lambda}^{t}$ is a constant called the *specific rotation* of the substance is solution for the light of wavelength λ at the temperature 't'.

For practical purposes, sodium vapour lamp is used as the source of light. Then λ is replaced by 'D' the wavelength of 'D' line of sodium. Equation (1) is then written as

$$[\alpha]_{D}^{t} = \frac{R}{ld} \qquad ...(2)$$

when $d = 1$ gm/c.c.

and $l = 1$ decimetre

then $[\alpha]_{D}^{t} = R \qquad ...(3)$

Hence the specific rotation of a substance may be defined *as the angle of rotation produced when the plane polarised light passes through one decimetre length of a solution containing 1 cm per c.c. of the optically active substance.*

Now if the solution contains 'C' gms. of the substance dissolved in 100 c.c. of water then,

$$\alpha = \frac{C}{100} \qquad ...(4)$$

Substituting in equation (2), we get

$$[\alpha]_{D}^{t} = \frac{100 . R}{l . c} \qquad ...(5)$$

The specific rotation is a characteristic of substance.

Molecular Rotation

Optical rotatory power of a compound is sometimes given as a Molecular rotation [M]. This value is by definition the molecular weight m of the substance multiplied by the specific rotation and divided by 100 to reduce the size of the number.

$$[M] = \frac{[m]\alpha}{100}$$

Measurement of Specific Rotation—The Polarimeter

The instrument used for measurement of specific rotation is called a polarimeter, Fig. 4.11. It consists of two nicol prisms A and P. The prism P is called the polariser and the prism A is called the analyser.

Light from source S is allowed to fall on the polariser and it gets plane polarised. If the axis of the analser is parallel to that of P only then light can be viewed through it. But if the axis of A is at right angles to that of P completely dark view is seen. To begin with the axis of A is adjusted at right angles to that of P by moving it on the graduated scale C so that a completely dark view is seen. The solution of known concentration of the optically active substance is placed in the tube in between the two prisms. It rotates the polarised light through a certain angle. To make the field of view dark again the analyser has to be rotated through the same angle. This gives the observed angle of rotation 'R' from which the specific rotation is calculated with the help of equation (5) given above.

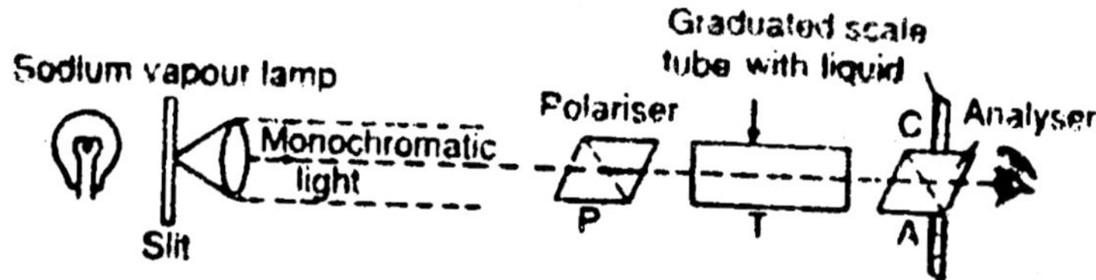

Fig. 4.11

The magnitude of rotation of plane-polarised light by an optically active substance will depend on several factors.

Different wavelengths of light used in the polarimeter will produce different rotations. It is, therefore, necessary to use a known monochromatic (narrow wavelength range) light source. The yellow sodium D-line (5890-5896 Å) is commonly used.

Magnitude of rotation depends upon the number of molecules of optically active substance in the light path ad thus on the concentration of an solution used, and the length of the sample cell.

Other significant variables are the temperature and solvent used (if any) for the optically active substance.

5

CATALYSIS AND KINETICS OF HETEROGENEOUS REACTIONS

CATALYSIS

The word 'catalysis' was first used by Berzelius in 1836 to describe a number of experimental observations which included the discovery by *Thenard* (1813) that ammonia was decomposed by metals and by *Dobereiner* (1825) that manganese dioxide affected the rate of decomposition of potassium chlorate. Berzelius defined the catalysis as :

"It is the phenomenon in which the presence of a foreign substance could accelerate its rate without being used up in that reaction."

He called the foreign substance as catalyst Later on, it was reported that catalyst could also retard the rate of reaction. Thus, the definition of Berzelius was generalised. The new definition of catalyst and catalysis are:

"Catalyst is any substance which can change the speed of the reaction without being used up in that reaction and phenomenon is known as catalysis."

In many reactions, one of the products itself acts as a catalyst. An example of such reaction is the oxidation of oxalic acid by acidified potassium permanganate which may be represented as follows :

$$2KMnO_4 + 3H_2SO_4 + 5\begin{matrix}COOH\\COOH\end{matrix} \rightarrow$$

$$K_2SO_4 + 2MnSO_4 + 8H_2O + 10CO_2$$

The speed of reaction increases as the reaction progresses. This acceleration is due to the presence of Mn^{2+} ions which get formed in the reaction. This type of phenomenon in which one of the products itself acts as a catalyst is known as auto-catalysis.

TYPES OF CATALYSIS

These can be divided into two classes :

(a) Homogeneous Catalysis

In homogeneous catalysis, the catalyst and reactants are in this same phase. Some examples from gaseous and liquid phases are give below :

(i) *Example from Gaseous Phase* : In the lead chamber process for the manufacture of sulphuric acid, nitric oxide gas catalyses the reaction between SO_2 and O_2.

$$2SO_2 + O_2 \xrightarrow{NO} 2SO_3$$

In this example, the reactants (SO_2 and O_2) and the catalyst (NO) are in the gaseous phase.

(ii) *Example from Liquid Phase* : The inversion of cane sugar is catalysed by a mineral acid.

$$\underset{\text{cane sugar}}{C_{12}H_{22}O_{11}} + H_2O \xrightarrow{H+} \underset{\text{glucouse}}{C_6H_{12}O_6} + \underset{\text{fructose}}{C_6H_{12}O_6}$$

Here the catalyst and reactants are in the liquid phase.

The hydrolysis of an ester like methyl acetate gets catalysed by hydrogen ions :

$$CH_3COOCH_3 + H_2O \xrightarrow{H+} CH_3COOH + CH_3OH$$

The conversion of acetone into diacetone alcohol is catalysed by hydroxyl ions.

$$\begin{matrix} CH_3 \\ CH_3 \end{matrix}\!\!>C=O + HCH_2COCH_3 \xrightarrow{OH^-}$$

$$\begin{matrix} CH_3 \\ CH_3 \end{matrix}\!\!>\underset{OH}{C}\;CH_2COCH_3$$

Diacetone alcohol

The decomposition of hydrogen peroxide is catalyzed in the presence of chloride ions.

$$2H_2O_2 \xrightarrow{Cl^-} 2H_2O + O_2$$

(b) Heterogeneous Catalysis

In heterogeneous catalysis, the catalyst is present in a different phase; than that of reactants. Examples are :

(i) *Heterogeneous Catalysis Involving Solid Reactants :* The example for this type is the decomposition of postassium chlorate in the presence of solid MnO_2 which acts as a catalyst.

$$2KClO_3 \xrightarrow{MnO_2} 2KCl + 3O_2$$

Thus, the catalyst (MnO_2) is present as a separate phase from the solid reactant ($KClO_3$).

(ii) *Heterogeneous Catalysis Involving Liquid Reactants :* The decomposition of hydrogen peroxide is catalysed by colloidal solution of gold and platinum.

$$2H_2O_3\ (l) \xrightarrow[\text{Au}]{\text{Pt or}} 2H_2O + O_2$$

Here H_2O_2 is a liquid reactant.

(iii) *Heterogeneous Catalysis Involving Gaseous Reactants :* Combination of SO_2 and O_2 in the presence of finely divided platinum is an example of this type :

$$SO_2(g) + O_2(g) \xrightarrow{Pt(s)} 2SO_3$$

Criteria of Characteristics of Catalyss : A catalysed reaction is found to possess the following characteristics which can also serve as criteria of catalysis.

1. The Catalyst Remain Unchanged in Mass and Chemical Composition

At the end of the reaction, a change in its physical state, colour, etc., may occur, *e.g.*, coarsely grained MnO_2 used in the decomposition of $KClO_3$ becomes finely powdered after the reaction.

2. Small Amount of the Catalyst is Needed

Usually a small quantity of the catalyst can bring about a large amount of chemical transformation. It is because catalyst itself is not consumed during the course of the reaction and is regenerated at the end. For example. 1 gm. of copper in 10^6 litres catalyses the oxidation of $NaHSO_3$ by air. Another example is that a low concentration as one gm atom of colloidal platinum in 10^8 litres can catalyse decomposition of hydrogen peroxide. This is only true in the case of heterogeneous catalysis. However, in case of homogeneous reactions, the rate is proportional to the concentration of the catalyst, *e.g.*, in the inversion of cane sugar, dilute acids act as catalysts and the rate of inversion is proportional to the $[H^+]$ ion concentration.

In many heterogeneous reactions, the rate increases with increase in the area of a catalytic surface. This is able to explain why the efficiency of a solid catalyst gets increased when it is present in a finely divided state or deposited on some active material like asbestos (cf. platinised asbestos).

3. Effect of the Equilibrium of a Reversible Reaction

In case of reversible reactions, the catalyst does not influence the composition of reaction mixture at equilibrium. Thus. it helps to attain the equilibrium quickly. In other words it affects the forward and backward reactions to the same extent and the value of the equilibrium constant remains unchanged.

This was proved by Bodenstein who showed that the use of a catalyst hastened the approach of equilibrium in the decomposition of hydrogen iodide,

$$2HI \rightleftharpoons H_2 + I_2$$

but did not change the concentrations of the reactants or products. For example, the use of platinised asbestos as a catalyst in the combination of sulphur dioxide and oxygen causes an appreciable increase in the rate of reaction but it is not able to increase the yield of sulphur dioxide under give conditions to temperature and pressure.

$$2SO_2 + O_2 \rightleftharpoons 2SO_3$$

4. Inability to Start a Reaction

According to Ostwald, a catalyst cannot start a reaction, but can only decrease its rate. This point since long has been a matter of controversy as there are some reactions in which it appears as if catalyst actually starts the reaction, *e.g.*, perfectly dry H_2 and O_2 do not combine to form water even if they are left in contact for years, but in presence of a little water (catalyst) the reaction proceeds quite rapidly. The reaction in the presence of a catalyst occurs through some alternative path which needs much lower energy of activation. Hence it is speeded up.

5. Specific Nature of a Catalyst

Action of a catalyst is highly specific in nature. That is, a particular substance can act as a catalyst only in a particular reaction and not in all. For example MnO_2 may catalyse the decomposition of $KClO_3$ but not of KCl_4. Highly specific action of a catalyst can be compared to the specific use of a key which can open a particular lock and not every lock (Emil Fischer). Enzymes have also specific catalytic actions. Transition metals such as iron, cobalt, nickel, platinum and palladium are able to catalyse reactions of various types.

6. Nature of the Products is Unaltered by the Presence of the Catalyst

H_2 and N_2 always combine to give NH_3 in the absence or presence of the catalyst. Similarly, SO_2 and O_2 will always combine to form SO_3 whether a catalyst is present or not. But this is not always true. Some exceptions are given below :

(i) CO and H_2 combine to give three different products when three different catalysis are used.

$$CO + 3H_2 \xrightarrow{Ni} CH_4 + H_2O$$

$$CO + H_2 \xrightarrow{Cu} HCHO$$

$$CO + 2H_2 \xrightarrow{ZnO + Cr_2O_3} CH_3OH$$

(ii) Similarly, chlorination of toluene in the presence of a halogen carrier such as iron or iodine and in absence of sunlight, takes place in the benzene ring. But chlorine is substituted in the side chain in the absence of a catalyst but in the presence of sunlight or at higher temperature.

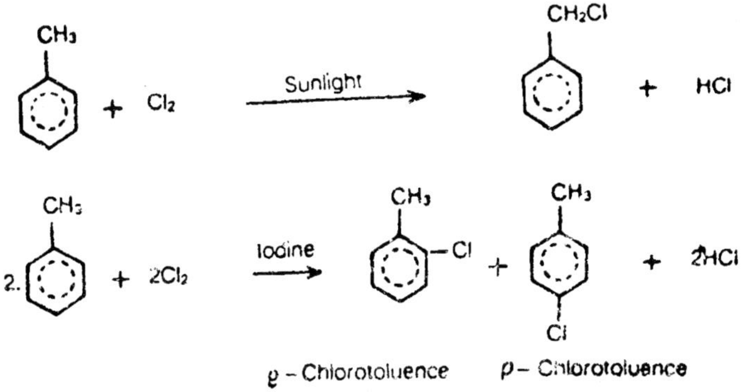

$$C_6H_5CH_3 + Cl_2 \xrightarrow{\text{Sunlight}} C_6H_5CH_2Cl + HCl$$

$$2.\ C_6H_5CH_3 + 2Cl_2 \xrightarrow{\text{Iodine}} o\text{-}ClC_6H_4CH_3 + p\text{-}ClC_6H_4CH_3 + 2HCl$$

o – Chlorotoluence p – Chlorotoluence

g– Chlorotoluence p – Chlorotoluence

Fig. 5.1

7. Optimum Temperature

There is a particular temperature at which the efficiency of a catalyst is most marked. The temperature is known as the optimum temperature. The activity of an enzyme which acts as a catalyst increases exponentially with temperature. If the temperature is raised sufficiently the enzymes are coagulated and lose their activity. It has been reported that activity of enzymes is maximum between 35° to 37° C.

8. Action of Promoters

The addition of small amounts of foreign substances which are not themselves catalytically active, sometimes increases the activity of the catalyst. Such substances are called promoters. In the manufacture of NH_3 by Haber's process, finely divided iron, acts as catalyst, while molybdenum acts as a promoter.

9. A Catalyst is Poisoned by Certain Substances

The activity of a catalyst is inhibited or completely destroyed by the presence of even minute traces of certain substances called catalytic poisons or anticatalysts. For example, in the manufacture of H_2SO_4 by the contact process, a trace of As_2O_3 destroys the catalytic efficiency of spongy platinum. However, vanadium pentoxide catalyst is preferred because it has been found to be less sensitive to poisoning. Similarly, traces of mercury are able to reduce the catalytic of copper for the combination of ethylene and hydrogen to form ethane.

$$\begin{matrix} CH_2 \\ \\ CH_2 \end{matrix} + H_2 \rightarrow \begin{matrix} CH_3 \\ \\ CH_3 \end{matrix}$$

THEORY OF HOMOGENEOUS CATALYSIS

In order for a chemical reaction to occur it is essential that the reacting substances must possess sufficient minimum energy called activation energy. In many cases it is not found to be so.

According to theory of homogeneous catalysis, the function of the catalyst is to bring about reaction between such: molecules which do not possess enough energy to enter into chemical combination by providing and alternative path in which lesser energy of activation is required.

We can thus compare the function of a catalyst to that of tunnel in crossing mountain. In order to cross a mountain at its full height through a tunnel at some lower height, the catalyst provides, thus, an alternative path to the reaction, requiring lower energy of activation. Thus, the catalyst can provide an alternative path, for a reaction to occur at lower activation energy (Fig. 5.2). The various postulates of the theory of homogeneous catalysis are :

(i) The catalyst first forms an intermediate compound with ;the reactant. This reactant with which catalyst combines is often termed as "substrate": when A is the substrate, X is the catalyst, AX is the intermediate compound and k_1 and k_2 are the velocity constants for the forward and backward reactions.

(ii) The intermediate compound then reacts with other reactant molecule (B) to form the product and catalyst.

$$AX + B \xrightarrow{k_3} AB + X$$

This reaction is slow and is the rate determining step. Thus

$$\text{Rate of reaction} = k_3 [AX] [B] \qquad ...(1)$$

where k_3 is the velocity constant.

(iii) The catalyst X which is regenerated in last step may further under go steps (i) and (ii) to form more and more of the products. Thus, the rate of homogeneous catalytic reactions depends upon the concentration of catalyst X. It means that the rate of the reaction will increase if the concentration of catalyst is increased. This can be proved as follows :

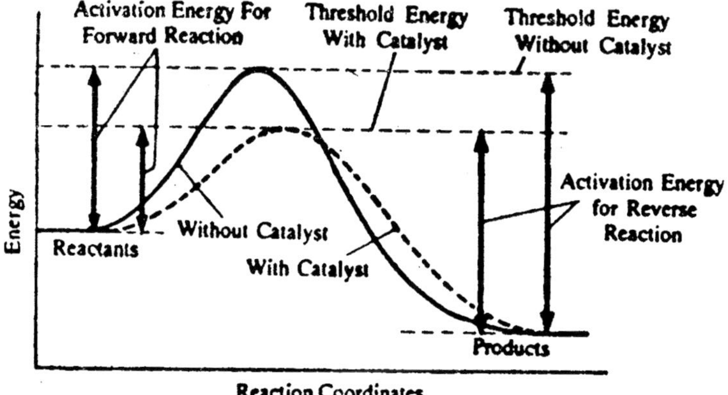

Fig. 5.2

The concentration of intermediate compound [AX], by using postulate of steady state concept, is given by

$$\frac{d[AX]}{dt} = k_1[A][X] - k_2[AX] - k_3[AX][B] = 0$$

or $$k_1 [A] [X] = k_2 [AX] + k_3 [AX] [B]$$

or $$[AX] = \frac{k_1[A][X]}{k_2 + k_3[B]} \qquad ...(2)$$

Substituting this value of [AX] in equation (1), we get

$$\text{Rate of reaction} = \frac{k_1k_3[A][X][B]}{k_2 + k_3[B]} \qquad ...(3)$$

From equation (3), two case may arise :

(i) If $k_2 << k_3$ [B] then Eq. (3) becomes as :

$$\text{Rate of reaction} = \frac{k_1k_3[A][X][B]}{k_3[B]} = k_1[A][X]$$

$$= k1 [A] [X] \qquad ...(4)$$

(ii) If $k_2 << k_3$ [B], then Eq. (3) becomes as

$$\text{Rate of reaction} = \frac{k_1k_3[A][X][B]}{k_2} \qquad ...(5)$$

From equations (4) and (5), it follows that the rate of reaction depends upon the concentration of catalyst although it is neither produced nor consumed in the reaction.

Examples:

1. The reaction between alcohol and sulphuric acid can be explained as follows.

(a) $C_2H_5\ OH + \underset{\text{Catalyst}}{H\ HSO_4} \rightarrow \underset{\text{Intermediate Compound}}{C_2H_5\ HSO_4} + H_2O$

(b) $C_2H_5\ HSO_4 + C_2H_5OH \rightarrow (C_2H_5)_2O + \underset{\text{Catalyst}}{H_2SO_4}$

2. The catalytic action of nitric oxide in the Chamber process for the manufacture of sulphuric acid can be presented in the following manner:

(a) $O_2 + \underset{\text{Catalyst}}{NO} \rightarrow \underset{\text{Intermediate compound}}{2NO_2}$

(b) $2NO_2 + 2SO_2 \rightarrow 2SO_3 + \underset{\text{Catalyst}}{2NO}$

3. The oxidation of HCl by air in presence of $CuCl_2$ can take place by the following mechanism :

$$2CuCl_2 \rightarrow Cu_2Cl_2 + Cl_2$$
$$2Cu_2Cl_2 + O_2 \rightarrow 2Cu_2oCl_2$$
$$2Cu_2oCl_2 + 4HCl \rightarrow 4CuCl_2 + 2H_2O$$

Successes of This Theory

(i) This theory explains the mechanism of homogeneous catalysis.

(ii) This also explains that the rate of a heterogeneous catalytic reaction depends upon the concentration of a catalyst.

(iii) This theory explains the specific actions of catalyst.

Failures of This Theory

(i) This theory does not explain the mechanism of homogeneous catalysis.

(ii) This also fails to explain the action of catalytic poisons and activators.

FUNCTION OF A CATALYST IN TERMS OF GIBB'S FREE ENERGY OF ACTIVATION

It is possible to understand the function of a catalyst by using the transition state theory or reaction rates. In general, a catalyst provides alternate path for the reaction that is having a lower free energy of activation The lowering of free energy is probably attributed to a decrease in energy of activation or a higher frequency factor or both.

From the activated complex theory, it is possible to write

$$k_f = \frac{k_B T}{h} \exp\left(- G_f^{o} / RT\right) \qquad ...(i)$$

where k_f is the rate constant for the forward reaction, k_B is the Boltzmann constant and ΔG_f^{o} is the standard Gibb's free energy of activation.

In the presence of a catalyst, it is possible to write

$$k_f' = \frac{k_B T}{h} \exp\left(- \Delta G_f^{'o} / RT\right) \qquad ...(ii)$$

where (') denotes a catalysed reaction.

From Fig. 5.1, it is evident that the free energy of activation gets lowered for both the forward and backward reactions without altering the overall free energy change of the reaction. This means that a catalyst is able to change the rates of both the forward and backward reaction. But ΔG^{o} does not get changed. Therefore, the equilibrium constant K will not get changed in the presence of the catalyst because ΔG^{o} is related to the equilibrium constant by the relation $-\Delta G^{o} = RT \text{ in } k$. It further reveals that a catalyst helps in attaining the equilibrium position rapidly but does not help in changing the relative proportion of reactants and products at equilibrium.

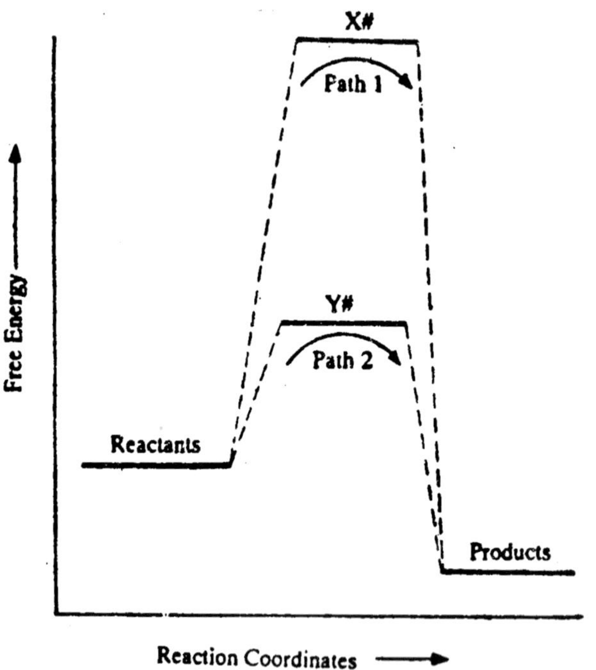

Fig. 5.3 : Lowering of Gibbs free energy of activation of a reaction by a catalyst. Path 1 is without catalyst; path 2 is with catalyst.

Mathematically it is possible to write the rate constants for the forward and backward reactions as follows:

$$k_f = (k_B T/h) \exp(-\Delta G_f'/RT) \qquad ...(iii)$$

$$k_b = (k_BT/h)\ \exp\ (-\Delta G_b'/RT) \qquad ...(iv)$$

On dividing Eq (iii) by Eq. (iv) we get

$$K_{eq} = \frac{k_f}{k_b} = \frac{(k_BT/h)\ \exp\left(-\Delta G_f{}^{'o}/RT\right)}{(k_BT/h)\ \exp\left(-\Delta G_b{}^{'o}/RT\right)}$$

$$= \exp[-(\Delta G_f{}^{'o})/RT - (-\Delta G_b{}^{'0})/RT]$$

$$= \exp(-\Delta G^0/RT)$$

where $\Delta G^o = (\Delta G_f{}^{'o} - \Delta G_b{}^{'0})$

Since ΔG^o has the same value in the presence or absence of a catalyst, K_{eq} remains the same.

THEORY OF HETEROGENEOUS CATALYSIS

The theory of heterogeneous catalysis is based upon the phenomenon of adsorption. The adsorption or contact theory was postulated by Faraday (1833) and later revived by many others. It explains the action of *heterogeneous catalysis*. The action of a heterogeneous catalyst is due to the presence of *free valencies* on its surface. These free valencies offer an opportunity to the reactant molecules to undergo chemical reaction on the surface of the catalyst. The situation may be readily understood by the diagram shown in Fig. 5.4.

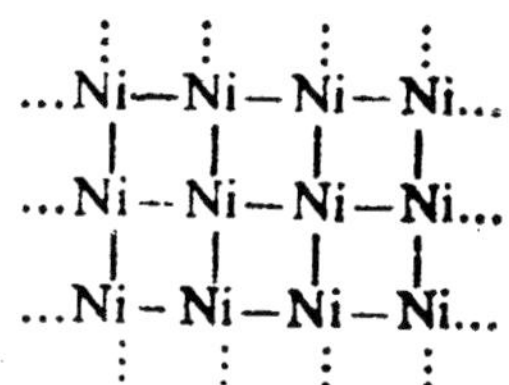

Fig. 5.4 : Free valencies on the surface on nickel.

An atom within the body of a catalyst is joined to the surrounding atoms and hence all its valencies are satisfied : the atom present on the surface of the catalyst possesses a free valency directed outward. According to the adsorption theory, given by Langmuir and Hinshelwood, the mechanism of heterogeneous catalysis involves the followings steps :

(1) *Diffusion* : When the reactants are allowed to enter a reaction vessel containing catalyst, the reactants molecules from gas or liquid phase undergo diffusion on the surface of the catalyst (Fig. 5.5A).

(2) *Adsorption* : The surface of the solid catalyst possesses some isolated active spots (or centres) having residual affinity or free unsatisfied valency forces. Due to these unsatisfied valency forces on the catalyst surface, the molecules of the gaseous reactants get adsorbed to form layers of unimolecular thickness (Fig. 5.5B). Adsorption leads to higher concentrations of the adsorbed reactants on the surface of the catalyst and this, by the law of mass action, should give an enhanced rate of reaction. Best situation is when all the reactants are equally adsorbed. Adsorption being an exothermic process, the heat of adsorption decreases the need of energy of activation.

(3) *Formation of Activated Complex* : Due to the close proximity between adsorbed molecules on the catalyst surface, they undergo interaction to form an activated complex, (Fig. 5.5C). Whenever an activated complex is formed, it is accompanied by an increase in its energy.

(4) *Decomposition of Activated Complex* : As soon as the activated complex is formed, it starts decomposing to give the products and the free surface of the catalyst is regenerated (see Fig. 3D).

(5) *Diffusion of the Products* : The molecules of reaction products diffuse away from the catalyst surface. The heat of adsorption helps in this connection. Now, the fresh molecules may come on the surface of catalyst and react to form the desired products.

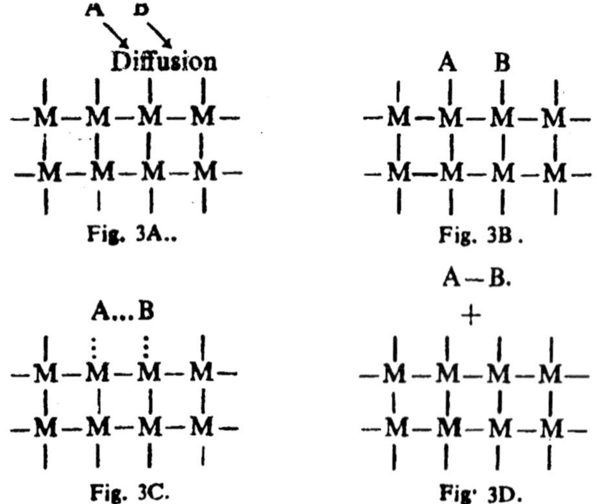

Fig. 5.5

The steps (1), (2) (3), (4), and (5) are consecutive. If any one of these steps is having a much slower rate constant than the others, it will become the rate determining step. Steps (1) and (5) are generally very fast. Further, steps (2) and (4) are usually faster than step 3 though they may sometimes be slower. It is generally accepted that the kinetics of surface reactions can be treated successfully on the basis of the assumptions given below :

1. The rate-determining step refers to the chemical reaction at the surface, *i.e.*, reaction of the adsorbed molecules on the surface, *i.e.*, step 3 given above.
2. Chemisorption plays a significant role in heterogeneous catalysis. In chemisorption chemical bonds get formed between the adsorbate and the surface resulting in a monolayer (Langmuir adsorption).
3. The reaction-rate per unit surface area has been proportional to q, the fraction of the surface covered. The value of q is given by the Langmuir adsorption isotherm.

It is to be remembered that the reason for heterogeneous catalytic activity remains the same as for homogeneous catalysis, *i.e.*, the catalyst increases the rate of the reaction by lowering the activation energy of the rate-determining step. Therefore, although it is not able to disturb the thermodynamically determined equilibrium composition of the reaction system, it tends to increase the rate at which the equilibrium gets attained.

Explanation Offered by Adsorption Theory

This theory explains the following facts :

(i) *Action of Finely Divided Catalyst :* With the increase of disintegration, the free surface area is increased, whereby free valencies or active spots increase which are responsible for the adsorption of reactant molecules. With increase in number of active spots the activity of the catalyst is also enhanced.

(ii) *Action of Promoters :* Promoters themselves get adsorbed on the surface of the catalyst producing discontinuity or unevenness on the surface, thereby increasing the number of active centres. The increase in the number of active centres results in greater adsorption of the reactant molecules on the interface between the promoter and the catalyst where free valencies are crowded.

Increased adsorption means greater concentration, hence higher rate of the reaction.

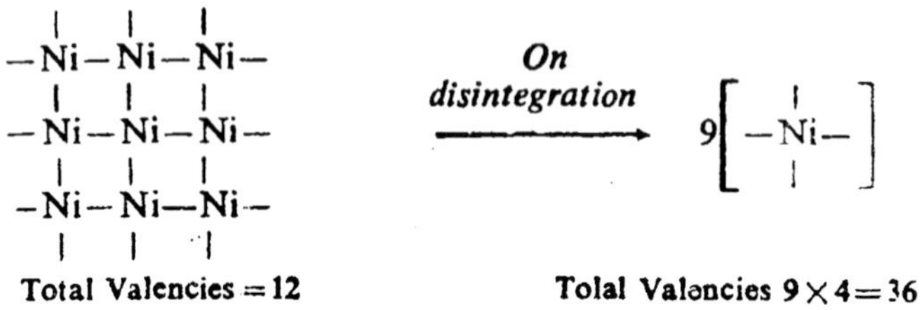

$$\begin{array}{c} | \quad | \quad | \\ -Ni-Ni-Ni- \\ | \quad | \quad | \\ -Ni-Ni-Ni- \\ | \quad | \quad | \\ -Ni-Ni-Ni- \\ | \quad | \quad | \end{array} \xrightarrow{\textit{On disintegration}} 9\left[\begin{array}{c} | \\ -Ni- \\ | \end{array}\right]$$

Total Valencies = 12 **Tolal Valencies 9 × 4 = 36**

Fig. 5.6

(iii) *Action of Poisons :* It is probably due to the preferential adsorption of poisons on the active spots of the catalyst and thus reducing the number of free active spots available for the adsorption of reacting molecules.

(iv) *Specific Action of the Catalyst :* The specific action of the catalyst is due to the fact that the extent of adsorption of the reactant molecule son the catalyst surface and their subsequent conversion into products, depend upon the chemical affinity of the catalyst for the reactant molecules.

QUANTITATIVE TREATMENT OF ADSORPTION (THEORY OF HETEROGENEOUS CATALYSIS)

The quantitative treatment of the theory of heterogeneous catalysis was given by Langmuir. A reaction taking place on a surface is supposed to consist of four consecutive steps.

(i) Diffusion of gases to the surface,

(ii) Adsorption of the gases on the surface,

(iii) Reaction on the surface,

(iv) Desorption and diffusion of product from the surface to the bulk.

Here steps (i) and (iv) are very rapid and normally do not play any role in the overall rate determination process. Also, the equilibrium between adsorption (ii) and (iv) is easily attained and these do not take part in the overall rate determination process. Thus, it is the step (iii) which determines the overall rate and it is the concentration of the molecules on the surface of which the reaction rate would depend.

In the qualitative treatment of heterogeneous catalysis, the Langmuir concept of unimolecular film on the surface is fully accepted.

Irving and Langmuir's concept of unimolecular film on the surface satisfactoriiy explains the observed kinetics. Langmuir postulated that :

1. The gases adsorbed by a solid surface are not able to form a layer more than a single molecule in depth, *i.e.*, adsorbed gas is unimolecular in thickness.
2. There exists a dynamic equilibrium between the adsorbed gas and the gas in the bulk phase, *i.e.*, rate of condensation and rate of adsorption of molecules will be equal.

It is possible to obtain relationship between the fraction of the surface covered and the pressure of the gas at constant temperature mathematically using these ideas. Suppose

θ = fraction of the surface area covered by gas at any instant.

$(1 - \theta)$ = fraction of the bare surface available for adsorption.

P = pressure of the gas.

Now, when gas molecules colloide with unit area of the surface, the rate of condensation of molecules would be expected to be proportional to the pressure, P, and fraction of uncovered surface $(1 - \theta)$. Thus,

$$\text{Rate of adsorption} = k_1 (1 - \theta) P \qquad ...(1)$$

$$\text{Rate of evaporation} = k_2\theta \qquad ...(2)$$

where k1 and k_2 refer to the constants for a given system. At equilibrium, these two rates are equal. Then

$$k_1 (1 - \theta) P = k_2\theta$$

or

$$\theta = \frac{k_1 P}{k_2 + k_1 P} \qquad ...(3)$$

$$= \frac{bP}{1 + bP} \qquad ...(4)$$

where $b = k_1/k_2$ and is termed as the Langmuir adsorption isotherm. Graphical representation of Eq. (3) is shown in Fig. 5.7.

Limiting cases of Eq. (4)

(a) If the gas is slightly adsorbed, *i.e.*, when adsorption is slight either due to very low pressure or due to the low-adsorption capacity of the surface, b is small, and bP may be neglected compared to unity. Hence, Eq. (4) gets reduced

$$\theta = bP$$

i.e., extent of adsorption is directly proportional to the pressure and the reaction will behave as one of the first order.

(b) If a gas is strongly adsorbed, the surface gets covered by a monomolecular thick layer of the gas, *i.e.*, when b or P or both are large, then bP >> 1, and Eq. (4) is transformed into

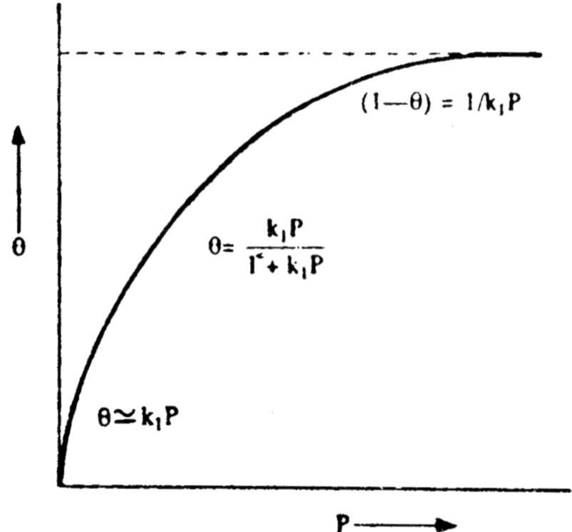

Fig. 5.7 : Langmuir adsorption isotherm.

$$\theta = \frac{bP}{bP} = 1$$

Under these conditions, the reaction rate is constant or independent of pressure and the reaction is considered to be of kinetically zero order.

(c) Another deduction can be made from Eq. (4)

$$1-\theta = 1-\left(\frac{bP}{1+bP}\right)$$

$$= \frac{1}{1+bP}$$

If the adsorption is strong, bP >> 1, then

$$1-\theta = \frac{1}{bP}$$

i.e., the fraction of the surface still available for the adsorption would be inversely proportional to the pressure of the gas.

Kinetics of Heterogeneous Reactions

With the help of the equation derived above, the kinetics of unimolecular and bimolecular reactions can be interpreted.

Unimolecular Surface Reactions

If there is a single reactant, it is first chemisorbed and subsequently, on activation, breaks up into products. If A is the reactant molecule and S the surface atom of the solid, the elementary processes may be depicted as follows :

$$A + S \underset{k_{-1}}{\overset{k_1}{\rightleftharpoons}} AS$$

$$AS \xrightarrow{k_2} \text{Products}$$

where AS refers to the adsorbed molecule.

Suppose, θ be the fraction of the surface covered by A at any instant t and pressure P. According to Langmuir-Hinshelwood the reaction rate should be :

$$\text{Rate} = r = k_2\theta \qquad \text{...(5)}$$

If we assume a steady-state approximation for [AS], we get

$$\frac{d[AS]}{dt} = k_1[A][S] - k_2[AS] - k_2[AS] = 0$$

or
$$[AS] = \frac{k_1[A][S]}{k_{-1} + k_2} \qquad \text{...(6)}$$

Now let concentration of vacant sites, $[S] = C_s(1 - \theta)$
and concentration of occupied sites, $[AS], = C_s$
where C_s refers to the total concentration of the surface sites of the catalyst. On substituting the values of [S] and [AS] in Eq. (6), we get

$$C,\theta = \frac{k_1[A]C_s(1-\theta)}{k_{-1} + k_2}$$

or
$$\theta = \frac{k_1[A]}{k_1[A] + k_{-1} + k_2} \qquad \text{...(7)}$$

and
$$r = \frac{k_1k_2[A]}{k_1[A] + k_{-1} + k_2} \qquad \text{...(8)}$$

On inverting expression (8), we get

$$\frac{1}{r} = \frac{1}{k_2} + \frac{k_{-1} + k_2}{k_2 k_1 [A]} \qquad ...(9)$$

For the gaseous reactions, concentration term [A] can be replaced by partial pressures and Eq. (9) can be modified as :

$$\frac{1}{r} = \frac{1}{k_2} + \frac{k_{-1} + k_2}{k_2 k_1} \cdot \frac{1}{P_A} \qquad ...(10)$$

A plot of $1/r$ against $1/P_A$ would give a straight line having $1/k_2$ as the intercept and $\frac{k_{-1} + k_2}{k_2 k_1}$ as the slope.

Limiting Cases of Eq. (10)

Case I : In the rate expression

$$r = \frac{k_1 k_2 P_A}{k_1 P_A + k_{-1} + k_2}$$

when $k >> (k_1 P_A + k_{-1})$,

$$r = k_1 P_A \qquad ...(11)$$

On integration, Eq. (11) gives :

$$k_1 = \frac{2.303}{t} \log_{10} \left(\frac{P_i}{P} \right)$$

where, P_i refers to the initial pressure of A and P its pressure, at any time t. This equation is of first order with respect to concentration of A.'

Case II : If $k_2 << (k_1 P_A + k_{-1})$, the rate equation (10) becomes as follows:

$$r = \frac{k_1 k_2 P_A}{k_1 P_A + k_{-1}} = \frac{(k_1 / k_{-1}) k_2 P_A}{(k_1 / k_{-1}) P_A + 1} = \frac{k k_2 P_A}{k P_A + 1} \qquad ...(12)$$

where, K refers to adsorption equilibrium constant. Expression (12) which is identical to Langmuir adsorption isotherm can be analysed further, as follows :

(a) At low pressure, *i.e.*, $KP_A << 1$, thus

$$r = K.k_2 P_A \qquad ...(13)$$

and the reaction would be of first order with respect to A.

(b) At high pressure, *i.e.*, $KP_A >> 1$

$$r = k_2 \quad ...(14)$$

and the reaction rate would be independent of pressure and the reaction is of zero order with respect to A.

Eqs. (13) and (14) may be explained by variation of rate of reaction with pressure as shown in Fig. 5.8

Bimolecular Surface Reaction

Now, consider a reaction in which two molecules A and B react on a surface and get adsorbed on neighbouring sites. The process may take place in two ways :

$$A + S \underset{k_{-1}}{\overset{k_1}{\rightleftharpoons}} AS$$

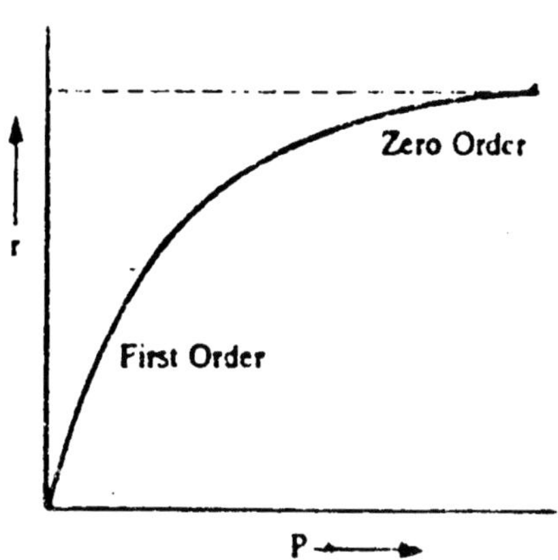

Fig. 5.8 : Variation of rate with pressure.

$$B + S \underset{k_{-2}}{\overset{k_2}{\rightleftharpoons}} BS$$

$$AS + BS \rightarrow \text{Products} + 2S$$

Suppose θ_1 and θ_2 be the fractions of the surface covered by adsorption of A and B, respectively. The fraction of the surface, which is vacant, is $(1 - \theta_1 - \theta_2)$.

The rate of formation of products is given as follows :

$$r = k_3\theta_1\theta_2 \quad ...(15)$$

On applying steady-state approximation to [AS] and [BS], we obtain

$$\frac{d[AS]}{dt} = 0 = k_1[A][S] - k_{-1}[AS] - k_3[AS][BS] \quad ...(16)$$

$$\frac{d[BS]}{dt} = 0 = k_2[B][S] - k_{-2}[BS] - k_3[AS][BS] \quad ...(17)$$

If C_s refers to the total concentration of the surface sites, then we have

$$[AS] = C_s\theta_1$$

$$[BS] = C_s\theta_2$$

$$[S] = C_s(1 - \theta_1 - \theta_2)$$

On inserting [AS], [BS] and [S] in Eqs. (16) and (17), we get

$$k_1[A]C_s(1 - \theta_1 - \theta_2) - k_{-1}C_s\theta_1 - k_3C_s^2\theta_1\theta_2 = 0 \quad ...(18)$$

$$k_2[B]C_s(1 - \theta_1 - \theta_2) - k_{-2}C_s\theta_2 - k_3C_s^2\theta_1\theta_2 = 0 \quad ...(19)$$

These equations are having two unknown variables θ_1 and θ_2 hence, can be solved for θ_1 and θ_2.

If it is assumed that the rate, determining step is the chemical reaction between the adsorbed molecules, then $k_3 \to 0$ and Eqs. (18) and (19) becomes as follows :

$$k_1[A](1 - \theta_1 - \theta_2) = k_{-1}\theta_1$$

$$k_2[B](1 - \theta_1 - \theta_2) = k_{-2}\theta_2$$

$$\theta_1 = \frac{k_1}{k_{-1}}[A](1-\theta_1-\theta_2)$$

$$= k_1[A](1 - \theta_1 - \theta_2) \quad ...(20)$$

and

$$\theta_2 = \frac{k_2}{k_{-2}}[B](1-\theta_1-\theta_2)$$

$$= k_2[B](1 - \theta_1 - \theta_2) \quad ...(21)$$

where

$$k_1 = \frac{k_1}{k_{-1}} \text{ and } k_2 = \frac{k_2}{k_{-2}}$$

On solving for θ_1 and θ_2 we obtain

$$\theta_1 = \frac{k_1[A]}{1+k_1[A]+k_2[B]}$$

and

$$\theta_2 = \frac{k_2[B]}{1+k_1[A]+k_2[B]}$$

On inserting the values of θ_1 and θ_2 in Eq. (15), we obtain

$$r = k_3 = \frac{k_1 k_2 [A][B]}{\{1 + k_1[A] + k_2[B]\}^2} \quad ...(22)$$

When P_A and P_B denote the partial pressures of A and B for the gaseous reaction, Eq. (22) changes to

$$r = k_3 = \frac{k_1 k_2 P_A P_B}{1 + k_1 P_A + k_2 P_B} \quad ...(23)$$

On examining the expression (23), three special cases of important significance may arise.

Case I : If each gas (A and B) gets adsorbed very slightly. In such an even, $K_1 P_A << 1$ and also $K_2 P_B << 1$, so

$$r = k_3' k_1 k_2 P_A P_B \quad ...(24)$$

This implies that the reaction will be of second order and first each with respect to A and B.

Examples of this type include the hydrogenation of ethylene on Cu or reaction between NO and O_2 on glass.

Case II : If one reactant, A, is relatively more strongly adsorbed than B.

Here, $\quad K_1 P_A >> K_2 P_B$

Hence, $\quad r = \dfrac{k_3 k_1 k_2 P_A P_B}{(1 + k_1 P_A)^2}$

i.e., the rate would be of first order with respect to B. But as the partial pressure of A increases, the rate increases to a maximum and then decreases.

Such complicated kinetics has been followed in the reaction between CO_2 and H_2 on platinum.

Case III : When one reactant, A, is very strongly adsorbed. In such cases, we get $K_1 P_A >> K_2 P_B$ and $k_1 P_A >> 1$.

Therefore, the reaction may be put as follows :

$$\frac{k_3 k_2 P_A P_B}{k_1 P_A{}^2} = \frac{k_3 k_2}{k_1} \cdot \frac{P_B}{P_A}$$

Thus, the rate is dependent strongly on the concentration of the strongly absorbed component.

The reaction between CO and O_2 on platinum follows such kinetics.

Retarded Reactions

Surface reactions sometimes become complicated by the adsorption of not only the reactants but also a product of the reaction. In fact, the product may get adsorbed more strongly than the reactant, thus decreasing the effective surface area available for the adsorption of reactant. This results in a retardation of the reaction rate. Suppose there is a reaction

$$A \rightarrow B + C$$

where, A refers to the reactant which gets weakly adsorbed and the product B gets strongly adsorbed. Then the fraction of the surface covered (θ_1) by A can be put as follows :

$$\theta_1 = \frac{K_A P_A}{1 + K_A P_A + K_B P_B}$$

The rate of reaction A will then be proportional to θ_1 and the pressure P_A.

Hence $$r = \frac{k_2 K_A P_A}{1 + K_A P_A + K_B P_B}$$

But when the product B gets very strongly adsorbed, then we have

$$r = \frac{k_2 K_A P_A}{K_B P_B}$$

i.e., rate would be directly proportional to the pressure of the reactant and inversely to the pressure of the product responsible for retardation.

Hinshelwood and Burk found that ammonia decomposes on platinum at 1138°C according to the reaction

$$2NH_3(g) \Leftrightarrow N_2(g) + 3H_2(g)$$

Nitrogen is having no effect on the reaction but the hydrogen strongly adsorbed and retards the reaction rate.

Effect to Temperature on Heterogeneous Reactions

Arrhenius equation, also applicable to heterogeneous reactions, may be given as follows :

$$\frac{d \ln k}{d T} = \frac{E_a}{RT^2}$$

The activation energy (E_a) for a heterogeneous reaction, evaluated from the plot of log k against l/T, is called apparent energy of activation. As the adsorption is temperature dependent, the evaluated E_a would be equal to the algebraic sum of true activation energy (E_t) and the heat of adsorption of reactions (λ_R) and products (λ_P) such that

$$E_a = E_t - \lambda_R + \lambda_P$$

The exact relation is dependent on the nature of kinetics.

Unimolecular Surface Reactions

Case I : If the reactant is very strongly adsorbed (Zero order surface reaction). Here $\theta \rightarrow 1$, and Eq. (5) becomes as follows :

$$\text{rate} = k_2$$

In this case the fraction of surface covered has been independent of the temperature and therefore,

$$E_a = E_t .$$

Case II : If the reactant is slightly adsorbed Under the condition, *i.e.*, $KP_A << 1$

$$\text{Rate} = K.\ k_2\ .\ P_A$$

From Arrhenius equation, we have

$$\frac{d\ \ln(K.k_2)}{d\ T} = \frac{E_a}{RT^2}$$

or
$$\frac{d\ \ln K}{d\ T} + \frac{d\ \ln k_2}{d\ T} = \frac{E_a}{RT^2}$$

But
$$\frac{d\ \ln K}{d\ T} = \frac{\Delta H_{ads}}{RT^2}$$

and
$$\frac{d\ \ln k_2}{d\ T} = \frac{\Delta E_t}{RT^2}$$

Therefore
$$\frac{E_a}{RT^2} = \frac{E_t}{RT^2} + \frac{\Delta E_{ads}}{RT^2}$$

As ΔH_{ads} is generally negative,

$$E_a < E_t$$

i.e., activation energy of this type of reaction gets lowered.

Bimolecular Surface Reactions

Case I : If both reactants are weakly adsorbed. Under the conditions, *i.e.*, $K_1 P_A << 1$ and also $K_2P_B << 1$.

$$\text{Rate} = k_3 K_1 K_2 P_A P_B$$

From Arrhenius equation, we have

$$\frac{d \ln(K_1 K_2 K_3)}{dT} = \frac{E_a}{RT^2}$$

or $$\frac{d \ln K_1}{dT} + \frac{d \ln K_2}{dT} + \frac{d \ln K_3}{dT} = \frac{E_a}{RT^2}$$

or $$\frac{(\Delta H_{ads})_1}{RT^2} + \frac{(\Delta H_{ads})_3}{RT^2} + \frac{E_t}{RT^2} = \frac{E_a}{RT^2}$$

$$E_a = E_t + (\Delta H_{ads})_1 + (\Delta H_{ads})_2$$

or $E_a < E_t$, since ΔH_{ads} is generally negative.

Case II : If one of the reactants gets very strongly adsorbed. If, out of A and B, B is more strongly adsorbed, then we have

$$\text{rate} = \left(k_3 \frac{K_2}{K_1}\right) \frac{P_B}{P_a}$$

From Arrhenius equation, we have

$$\frac{d \ln\left(k_3 \frac{K_2}{K_1}\right)}{dT} = \frac{E_a}{RT^2}$$

or $$\frac{d \ln K_2}{dT} - \frac{d \ln K_1}{dT} + \frac{d \ln K_3}{dT} = \frac{E_a}{RT^2}$$

or $$\frac{(\Delta H_{ads})_2}{RT^2} - \frac{(\Delta H_{ads})_1}{RT^2} + \frac{E_t}{RT^2} = \frac{E_a}{RT^2}$$

or $$E_a = E_t + (\Delta H_{ads})_2 + (\Delta H_{ads})_1$$

It means that the strongly adsorbed product increases the activation energy, thereby inhibiting the overall reactions.

ABSOLUTE RATE THEORY IN HETEROGENEOUS GAS REACTIONS

The absolute rate theory offers a very satisfactory mean to calculate the rates of heterogenous reactions involving the gases. Let us consider a bimolecular reaction between A and B involving a reaction centre, S, *e.g.*, an atom, on the surface. Then

$$A + B + S \Leftrightarrow [A - B - S] \neq \text{Products.} \qquad ...(1)$$

In this type of reactions there exists an equilibrium between, the reactants (A and B) and the activated complex. If C_A, C_B and C_S denote the concentration of A, B and S respectively, the value of equilibrium constant $K \neq$ of the activated state is obtained by applying the law of mass action to Eq. (1).

$$K \neq = \frac{C \neq}{C_A C_B C_S} \quad ...(2)$$

where, C is the concentration of the activated complex. If we consider the partition functions, Eq. (2) becomes as

$$K \neq = \frac{\theta \neq}{\theta_A \theta_B \theta_S} e^{-E/RT} \quad ...(3)$$

where, E denotes the energy of activation for the heterogeneous reacting. On combining Eqs. (2) and (3), we get

$$\frac{C \neq}{C_A C_B C_S} = \frac{\theta \neq}{\theta_A \theta_B \theta_S} e^{-E/RT}$$

or

$$C \neq = \frac{1}{C_A C_B C_S} \frac{\theta \neq}{\theta_A \theta_B \theta_S} e^{-E/RT} \quad ...(4)$$

The rate of the reaction dx/dt for bimolecular reaction is

$$\frac{dx}{dt} = C \neq \frac{kT}{h} \quad ...(5)$$

Substituting Eq (4) in Eq. (5), we get

$$\frac{dx}{dt} = \frac{kT}{h} \cdot \frac{1}{C_A C_B C_S} \frac{\theta \neq}{\theta_A \theta_B \theta_S} e^{-E/RT} \quad ...(6)$$

The rate of the reaction may also be given by

$$dx/dt = k_r C_A C_B \quad ...(7)$$

where, k_r is the specific rate constant. On comparing Eqs. (6) and (7), we get

$$k_r = C_s \frac{kT}{h} \frac{\theta \neq}{\theta_A \theta_B \theta_S} e^{-E/RT} \quad ...(8)$$

The S part of the surface possesses no translational, no rotational but its only vibrational contribution is of the order of unity. It means that the partition function contains only the vibrational factor. Thus $\theta \neq / \theta_S$ may be taken as unity. Hence Eq. (8) becomes as

$$k_r = C_S \frac{kT}{h} \frac{1}{\theta_A \theta_B} e^{-E/RT} \qquad ...(9)$$

The partition functions θ_A and θ_B are determined by the known properties of the reactants. The value of C_S may be evaluated for a sparsely covered surface where it is equal to the number of atoms.

CLASSIFICATION OF CATALYSIS

1. Negative Catalysis or Inhibition

Examples are known in which the presence of a catalyst decreases or retards the rate of the chemical reaction. Such substances are called Negative Catalysts or inhibitors and the phenomenon is called Negative Catalysis or Inhibition. Some examples are :

1. Presence of 1% alcohol retards the oxidation of chloroform into phosgene.

   $$4CHCl_3 + 3O_2 \xrightarrow{C_2H_5OH} 4COCl_2 + 2Cl_2 + 2H_2O$$

2. The decomposition of H_2O_2 is retarded by ;the presence of acetanilide or H_2SO_4 or H_3PO_4.

3. Presence of lead tetra ethyl, nickel carbonyl 1 serves as antiknock material in internal combustion engines.

Explanation : Two possible explanations are available to describe the action of an inhibitor :

(i) Inhibitor deactivates or destroys some other foreign substances present in the reacting system as a positive catalyst, and thus does not involve directly in the reaction.

(ii) In some cases an inhibitor operates by dislocating a step in a multistep reaction. For example, addition of phosphate to a solution of H_2O_2 inhibits its decomposition by combining with existing traces of ferric ions which catalyse the decomposition of H_2O_2.

2. Catalytic Poisons or Anticatalysts

Certain substances when present in the reactants decrease the efficiency of the catalyst. These substances are called catalytic poisons or anticatalysts. Such an effect is observed with a solid catalyst and is found to be of two types :

(a) *Temporary Poisoning :* If the catalyst-regains its activity when the substance responsible for its poisoning is eliminated from the reactants, the poisoning is regarded as temporary. Presence of water vapour or oxygen acts as a temporary poison for iron, the catalyst used in manufacture of ammonia :

(b) *Permanent Poisoning :* If the poisoned catalyst fails to regain its activity even when the catalytic poisons are subsequently removed, the poisoning of the catalyst is said to be permanent. Examples of permanent poisons are given below in the tabular form :

Table 5.1

Name of Poison	*Name of the catalyst*	*Process*
CO	***Iron***	***Haber's process***
AS_2O_3	Platinised asbestos	Contact process
HCN	Colloidal platinum	Decomposition of H_2O_2
Bromine vapour	Nickel	Hydrogenation of oils

Action of the poisons : It is probably due to the preferential absorption of poison on the active spots of the catalyst and thus reducing the number of free active spots available for the absorption of the reacting molecules. For example, the poisoning of platinum catalyst by CO takes place as shown in Fig. 5.9.

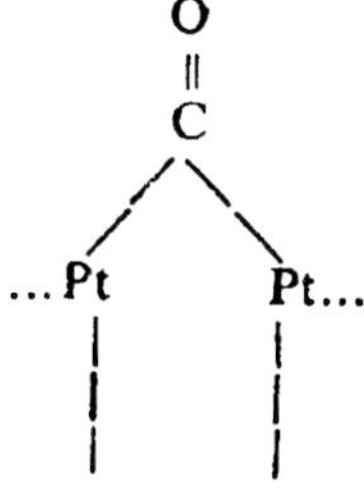

Fig. 5.9

3. Autocatalysis

The process in which one of the products of reaction acts as the catalyst is known as autocatalysis. A few examples of autocatalysis are :

(i) Hydrolysis of an ester is autocatalysed by the acid which is a product of the reaction.

$$RCOOR' + H_2O \Leftrightarrow RCOOH + R'OH$$

(ii) During titration of warm solution of oxalic acid by $KMnO_4$ solutions, the first few drops takes appreciable time before they are decolourised Since the reaction is initially very slow, but after some time the decolourisation goes fairly rapid as the Mn^{+2} ions, formed in the course of reaction, catalyse the reaction.

$$5C_2O_4^{2-} + 2MnO_4^- + 16h^+ \rightarrow 2mN^{2+} + 10CO_2 + 8H_2O$$

(iii) In the action of HNO_3 on copper, NO_2^- ions produced during the reaction act as catalyst.

$$3Cu + 8HNO_3 \rightarrow 3Cu(NO_3)_2 + H_2O + 2NO$$

Nitric oxide formed in the above reaction dissolves in water in the presence of air to provide NO_2^- ions.

Mathematical Expression of Autocatalytic Reactions

Let us deduce this expression by considering the hydrolysis of methyl acetate in which the product acetic acid formed catalyses the reaction.

$$CH_3COOC_2H_5 + H_2O \Leftrightarrow CH_3COOH + C_2H_5OH$$

a	b	Initial
$a - x$	$b + x$	After time t

Suppose, a and b are the initial amount of ester and acetic acid respectively. Suppose, x the extent of reaction, according to the law of mass action, is given by

$$\frac{dx}{dt} - kb(a-x) + kx(a-x) = k(a-x)(b+x)$$

or $$\frac{dx}{(a-x)(b+x)} = k\ dt$$

On separating the variables, we get

$$\frac{1}{a+b}\left[\frac{1}{a-x} + \frac{1}{b+x}\right] dx = k\ dt$$

On integration, we get

$$\frac{1}{a+b}[\ln(b+x) - \ln(a-x)] = kt + C \qquad ...(2)$$

In order to get the value of C, put x = 0 when t = 0, then

$$C = \frac{1}{a+b}\ln\frac{b}{a} \qquad ...(3)$$

On substituting eq. (3) in (2), we get

$$\frac{1}{a+b}\left[\ln(b+x)-\ln(a-x)\right]=kt+\frac{1}{a+b}\ln\frac{b}{a}$$

or $$k=\frac{1}{a+b}\ln\frac{a(b+x)}{b(a-x)} \qquad ...(4)$$

This has been experimentally verified. If the initial catalyst be an acid other than acetic acid, then

$dx/dt = k_1 (a - x) b + k_2 (a - x) x = (k_1 b + k_2 x) (a - x)$

This on integration gives,

$$k_1 b + k_2 a = \frac{1}{t}\ln\frac{a(k_1 b + k_2 x)}{k_1 b(b-x)} \qquad ...(5)$$

Equation (5) is also verified experimentally.

4. Catalytic Promoters or Activators

There is a group of substances which are not catalysts by themselves but when present along with some catalyst greatly enhance their action. They are called catalytic promoters or activators. Some examples of promoters are given below :

Table 5.2

Name of promoters	*Name of the Catalyst*	*Process*
Molybdenum	Iron	Manufacture of NH_3 by Haber's process
Copper	Iron (finely divided)	Bosch process for H_2 from water gas.
HCl or H_2O	$AlCl_3$	Isomerisation of hydrocarbons.

Action of Promoters : It is explained by assuming that a loose compound is formed between the catalyst and the promoter, which possesses an increased absorption capacity than that of pure catalyst only.

5. Enzyme Catalysis

Enzymes are complex organic compounds which are produced by living plants and animals. They disperse in water forming colloidal solutions and are very specific catalysts. As enzymes are having the dimensions in the colloidal range (1000 -- 10000 A°) and their kinetic behaviour is similar to that of heterogeneous process, enzyme catalysis has been referred to as "Microheterogeneous catalysis". Each enzyme can catalyze a specific reaction. For instance, the enzyme diastase produced in the germinated barley seeds is able to convert starch into maltose sugar.

$$\underset{\text{Starch}}{2(C_6H_{10}O_5)_N} + nH_2O \xrightarrow{\text{Diastase}} \underset{\text{Maltose}}{nC_{12}H_{22}O_{11}}$$

Another enzyme known as maltase is able to convert maltose into glucose.

$$\underset{\text{Maltose}}{C_{12}H_{22}O_{11}} + H_2O \xrightarrow{\text{Maltase}} \underset{\text{Glucose}}{2C_6H_{12}O_6}$$

The enzyme known as zymase, produced by living yeast calls, is able to convert glucose into ethyl alcohol.

$$\underset{\text{Glucose}}{C_6H_{12}O_6} \xrightarrow{\text{Zymase}} \underset{\text{Ethyl alcohol}}{2C_2H_5OH} + 2CO_2$$

The enzyme urease present in soyabeans is able to cause quantitative hydrolytic decomposition of urea into ammonia and carbon dioxide.

$$\underset{\text{Urea}}{NH_2CONH_2} + H_2O \xrightarrow{\text{Urease}} 2NH_3 + CO_2$$

Point of differences between enzyme catalysis and general heterogeneous catalysis. The main points are :

(i) *Nature of Catalysis* : Enzymes are non-lying complex nitrogeneous compounds produced by living organisms. They cannot be synthesised by artificial means in the laboratory. On the other hand, the general heterogeneous catalyst may be anything occurring naturally or produced artificially.

(ii) *Enzyme is Consumed During the Reaction* : Enzymes are consumed during the reaction which they catalyse. On the other hand, the general inorganic catalysis remains unchanged chemically during the reaction process.

(iii) *Presence of Certain Inorganic Substances* : Certain inorganic substances such as ammonium salts are needed as food for the enzyme producing. No substances are required for the general type of catalysts.

(iv) *Presence of Co-enzymes* : Co-enzymes are substances which are similar in nature to the enzymes. The presence of coenzyme is essential for the action of the enzyme. In the ordinary heterogeneous catalysis the presence of a promoter is not always essential . A few enzymes, their source and the reactions catalysed by them are shown below :

Table 5.3

Enzymes	*Sources*	*Reaction Catalysed*
Zymase	Yeast	Conversion of glucose into alcohol
Lactic bacilli	Curd	Conversion of milk into curd.
Lipase	Castor oil seed	Conversion of cane-sugar into glycerol.

Characteristics of Enzyme Catalysis

1. All enzymes are proteins and share common properties, They form colloidal solutions and are of high molecular weight.
2. Enzymes are associated with every chemical reaction that occurs in the living system.
3. Enzymes generally accelerate biochemical reactions by reducing the energy requirement (activation energy).
4. Enzymes do not alter the amount or nature of the product.
5. Enzymes do not affect the amount of energy released or absorbed during the reaction.
6. Enzymes retain identity at the end of the reaction, as in the beginning. In other words, they are not destroyed by the reactions they catalyze and so can be used again. However, a given molecule of an enzyme cannot be used indefinitely because it is readily inactivated by heat or action of acid, and so no. Conversely, inorganic catalysis are highly stable and can be used over and over again.
7. Extremely small amounts of enzymes are able to bring about measurable changes.
8. Enzymes catalyze biochemical reactions at significantly lower temperatures. For example, to hydrolyze 5 ml of 1 % starch solution, it is essential to add five drops of concentrated sulphuric acid and boil the mixture for over fifteen minutes. On the other hand, even 100 times diluted saliva containing salivary amylase

would require just 8-10 minutes to hydrolyze the same quantity of starch at only 37°C.

9. Enzymes are specific in their action, *i.e.*, they are capable of acting on a predetermined substrate. An enzyme that can hydrolyze starch is unable to hydrolyze cellulose. For this, another enzyme, cellulose is needed. The degree of specificity, however, varies. Most intracellular enzymes are specific, whereas certain digestive enzymes work on a comparatively wide range of related compounds.
10. Most enzymes can work in either direction, *i.e.*, they are capable of operating reversibly. In other words, one and the same enzyme can catalyze the breakdown as well as the synthesis of the substance. However, in many instances, the reversibility of reaction has not yet been demonstrated.

Factors Governing the Rate of an Enzyme Reaction

1. *Effect of Temperature on Enzyme Catalysis* : Similar to chemical catalysts, the enzyme catalyst is able to decrease the activation energy of a reaction at a given temperature. In reality, the decrease of activation energy by an enzyme catalyst is far greater than that by a non-enzyme catalyst. It is known that the rate of a reaction generally increases with an increase in temperature. However, this condition is highly unfavourable for a living call. Enzymes are, in fact, very sensitive to high temperatures. Due to the proteinous nature of an enzyme, increase in temperature brings about denaturation of the enzyme protein which gives rise to a decrease in effective concentration of the enzyme and hence a decrease in reaction rate. Upto about 45°C, the reaction rates of enzyme-catalysed reactions get increased with temperature. At temperatures greater than 45°C, thermal denaturation of enzyme becomes increasingly significant. At about 55°C, rapid denaturation completely destroys the catalytic function of the enzyme protein. The effect of temperature on the rates of enzyme-catalyzed reactions has been shown in (Fig. 5.10, 5.11).

Effect of pH. Enzymes are sensitive to change in pH (hydrogen ion concentration) in the reaction medium (Fig. 5.11). In fact, every enzyme works best at a specific pH called the optimal pH. Most enzymes display maximum activity at or around neutral pH. Excessive acidity or alkalinity renders them inactive. However, a few digestive enzymes operate either in distinctly acidic or alkaline medium. For instance, the stomach enzyme, pepsin, functions best at a pH of 2.0, where as the pancreatic enzyme, trypsin, has an optimal pH of 8.0.

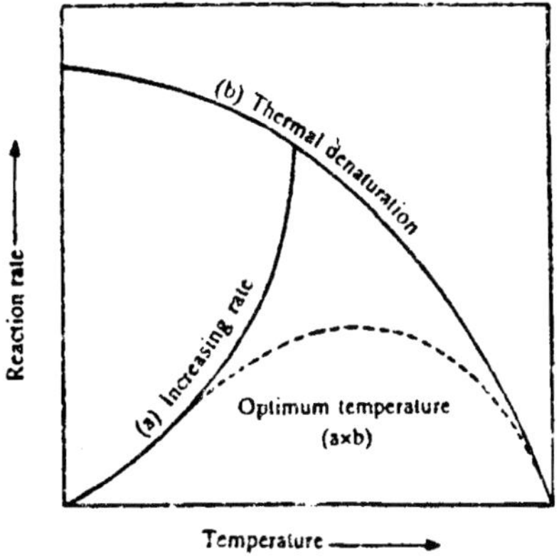

Fig. 5.10 : Temperature-dependence of the rate of an enzyme catalyzed reaction. (a) represents the increase in rate with increase in temperature. (b) represents the decrease in the rate as a function of thermal denaturation of the enzyme; the dashed line curve shows the combination of (a × b) .

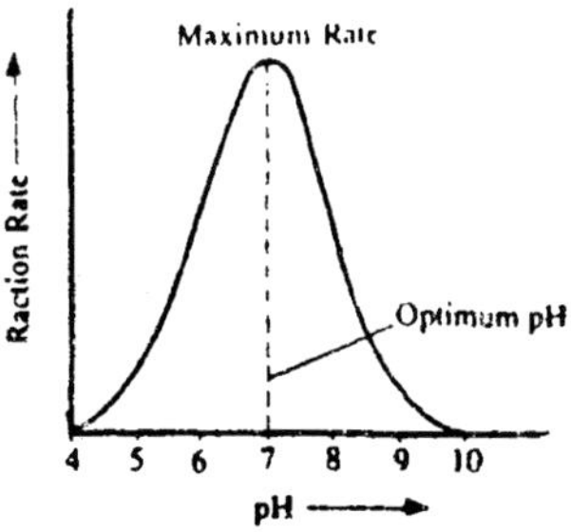

Maximum Rate
Raction Rate
Optimum pH
4 5 6 7 8 9 10
pH

Fig. 5.11 : Effect of pH on the reaction rate of enzymes.

Effect of activator. Many enzymes cannot act on their own and require the help of some substances for their activation and for speeding up the rate of reaction (Fig. 5.12). Such substances are called activators. This activation is due to the effect of certain ions such as Na^+, K^+, Ca^{++}, Mg^{++}, Mn^{++}. You are now with the stomach enzyme pepsin. This is produced in the inactive form as pepsinogen by one type of cells in the gastric glands. Pepsinogen is converted into the active form pepsin by HCl secreted by certain other cells of the glands. Similarly, when pancreatic juice containing the inactive trypsinogen is poured into the duodenum, it comes in contact with another enzyme, enterokinase, secreted by the mucosal layer of the duodenum, which in turn, converts trypsinogen into the active form, trypsin.

Effect of inhibitors. Certain substances called inhibitors slow down the rate of enzymatic reaction (Fig. 5.13). For example, mercury ;and arsenic ions inhibit the activity of a wide range of enzymes. Also, some antibiotics are effective inhibitors for bacterial growth since they hamper their protein synthesis.

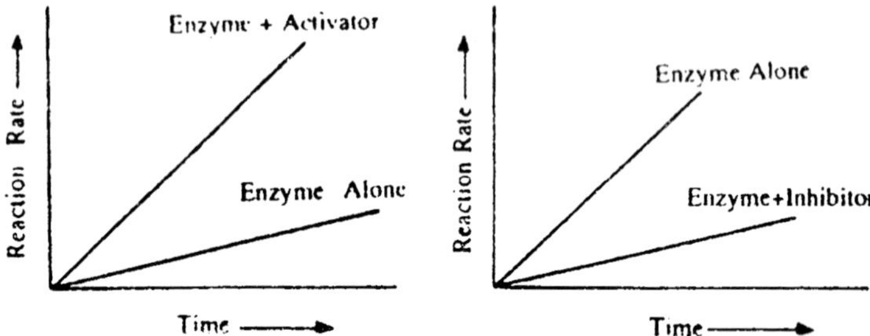

Fig. 5.12 : Effect of activators on the reaction rate of enzyme.

Fig. 5.13 : Effect of inhibitor on the reaction rate of enzymes.

Concentration : The rate of reaction is approximately proportional to the cocentration of enzyme.

Mechanism and Kinetics of Enzyme-Catalyzed Reactions

Biochemists L. Michaelis and M. Menten proposed, in 1913, a mechanism for the kinetics of enzyme-catalyzed reactions which envisages the following steps :

(i) *Step (1) :* The enzyme combines with the reactant (substrate) to form an enzyme substrate complex which remains in equilibrium with the enzyme and substrate.

$$E + S \underset{K_{-1}}{\overset{k_1}{\Leftrightarrow}} ES$$

where, E is the enzyme, S is the substrate, and ES is an enzyme substrate complex.

(ii) *Step (2) :* The enzyme-substrate, complex, ES can decompose to form products with simultaneous regeneration of the enzyme.

$$ES \xrightarrow{k_2} E + P$$

where, P is the product. In the overall reaction $S \rightarrow P$ the enzyme is consumed in the step (1) and regenerated in step (2).

The problem can be tackled using either the equilibrium approximation or the steady-state approximation. Experiment shows, however, that true equilibrium would not be achieved in the fast step because the subsequent slow reaction would be constantly removing the intermediate enzyme-substrate complex. ES. Generally, the enzyme concentration becomes far lass than the substrate concentration, *i.e.*, [E] << [S] so that [ES] << [S]. Hence, the steady-state approximation can be used for the intermediate, ES.

According to the slow rate-determining step, the rate of the reaction is given by

$$r = -\frac{d[S]}{dt} = +\frac{d[P]}{dt} = k_2\,[ES] \qquad ...(1)$$

Using steady state approximation for ES, we have

$$d[ES]/dt = k_1\,[E][S] - k_{-1}\,[ES] - k_2\,[ES] = 0 \qquad ...(2)$$

Now, [E] cannot be experimentally measured. The equilibrium between the free and bound enzyme is given by the enzyme conservation equation, *viz.*,

$$[E]_0 = [E] + [ES] \qquad ...(3)$$

where, $[E]_0$ refers to the total enzyme concentration (which can be measured); [E] refers to the free enzyme concentration and [ES] refers to the bound (or reacted) enzyme concentration. Hence

$$[E] = [E]_0 - [ES] \qquad ...(4)$$

On substituting for [E] in Eq. (2), we get

$$d[ES]/dt = k_1\,\{[E]_0 - [ES]\}[S] - k_{-1}\,[ES] - k_2\,[ES] = 0 \qquad ...(5)$$

Collecting terms and simplifying, we get

$$k_1\,[E]_0\,[S] = \{k_{-1} + k_2 + k_1\,[S]\}\,[ES] \qquad ...(6)$$

$$[ES] = \frac{k_1\,[E]_0\,[S]}{k_{-1} + k_2 + k_1\,[S]} \qquad ...(7)$$

On substituting for [ES] in Eq. (1), we get

$$r = \frac{k_1\,k_2\,[E]_0\,[S]}{k_{-1} + k_2 + k_1\,[S]} \qquad ...(8)$$

On dividing the numerator and the denominator by k_1, we get

$$r = \frac{k_2\,[E]_0\,[S]}{(k_{-1} + k_2)/\,k_1 + [S]} = \frac{k_2\,[E]_0\,[S]}{k_m + [S]} \qquad ...(9)$$

where, the new constant K_m, called the Michaelis constant, is given as follows :

$$k_m = (k_{-1} + k_2)/k_1 \qquad ...(10)$$

It is to be noted that k_m is not an equilibrium constant. Eq. (9) is known as Michaelis-Menten equation.

Further simplifications of Eq (9) can be made. If it is assumed that all the enzyme has reacted with the substrate at high concentrations, the reaction will be going at maximum rate. No free enzyme will remain so that $[E]_0 = [ES]$. Hence, from Eq. (1) we get

$$r_{maximum} \equiv V_{max} = k_2\,[E]_0 \qquad ...(11)$$

where V_{max} refers to the maximum rate, using the notation of enzymology.

The Michaelis-Menten equation can now be written as follows.

$$r = V_{max}\,[S]/(k_m + [S] \qquad ...(12)$$

Two cases may arise :

(a) If $k_m >> [S]$, [S] can be neglected in the denominator of Eq. (12), giving

$$r = V_{max}\,[S]/k_m = k'\,[S]$$

(first-order reaction) ...(13)

(b) If $[S] >> k_m$, K_m can be neglected in the denominator, giving

$$r = V_{max} = \text{constant}$$

(zero-order reaction) ...(14)

These two cases may be shown diagrammatically in Fig. (5)

Again, if, $k_m = [S]$, $r = 1/2\ V_{max}$

Hence, Michaelis constant may be defined as equal to that concentration of S at which the rate of formation of product becomes half the maximum rate obtained at high concentration of S.

The constant k_2 in Eq. (11) is termed as the turnover number of the enzyme. The turnover number may be defined as the number of molecules converted in unit time by one molecule of enzyme. Typical values of k_2 are 100 – 1,000 per second though may be as large as 10^5 to 10^6 per second.

Now one must know the physical reason why the reaction rate of an enzyme-catalyzed reaction gets changed from first-order to zero-order as the substrate concentration gets increased. The answer to that question is that each enzyme molecule is having one or more 'active sites' at which the substrate must be bound in order that the catalytic action may take place. At low substrate concentrations, most of these active sites remain unoccupied at any time. As the substrate concentration gets increased, the number of active sites which get occupied increases and hence the reaction rate also get increased. However, at very high substrate concentrations, virtually all the active sites get occupied at any time so that further increase in substrate concentration will not further increase the formation of enzyme-substrate complex.

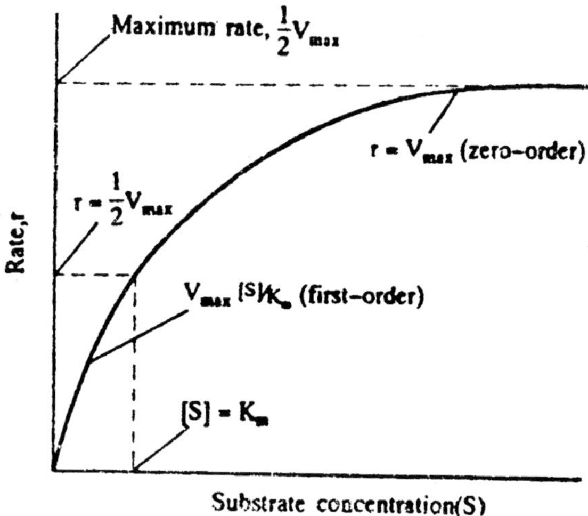

Fig . 5.14 : Kinetics of an enzyme catalysed reaction.

It rather becomes difficult to determine V_{max} (and hence k_m) directly from the plot of r against [S]. However it becomes possible to rearrange Eq. (12) so as to permit some alternative plots for easy determination of V_{max}. Two of the best known methods which make use of the re-arranged equations are described as follows.

1. *The Lineweaver-Burk Method* : This method employs the rearranged equation

$$\frac{1}{r} = \frac{K_m}{[S]\, V_{max}} + \frac{1}{V_{max}} \qquad ...(16)$$

A plot of 1/r against 1/[S] will give a straight line whose intercepts on the x and y-axes are $(-1/k_m)$ and $1/V_{max}$, respectively and whose slope is (k_m/V_{max}).

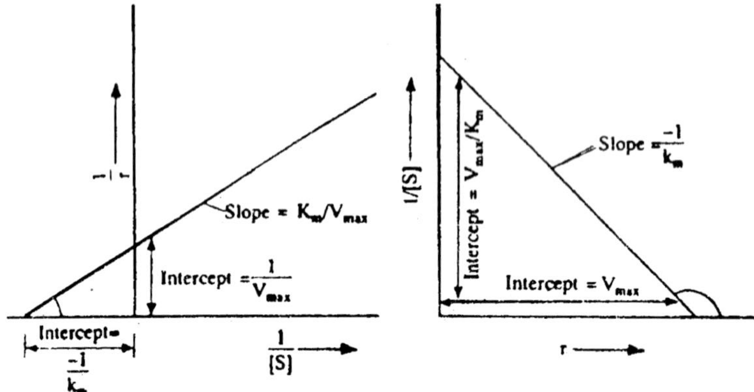

Fig. 5.15 : The Lineweaver-Burk method of plotting enzyme kinetic data.

Fig. 5.16 : Eadie-Hofstee method of plotting enzyme kinetic data.

2. *The Eadie-Hofstee Method :* The method employs the rearranged equation

$$r/[S] = V_{max}/K_m - r/k_m \qquad ...(17)$$

A plot of r/[S] against r would give a straight line with slope equal to $-1/k_m$ and an intercept on the y-axis equal to V_{max}/k_m as shown in Fig. (7). From the graph both k_m and V_{max} can be calculated.

ACID-BASE CATALYSIS

A very considerable number of homogeneous catalytic reactions are known which are catalysed by acids and bases. These reactions are known as acid-base catalysis. When Arrhenius theory of electrolytic dissociation was established, it was shown that the real catalysts are the H^+ and OH^- ions in acid and base catalysis respectively.

Types of Acid base Catalysis. Three main types are :

(a) *Specific Hydrogen Ion Catalysis :* These are the reactions which are catalysed by H^+ ion only. Example is the inversion of cane sugar catalysed by H^+ ions only.

$$C_{12}H_{22}O_{11} + H_2O \xrightarrow{H^+} C_6H_{12}O_6 + C_6H_{12}O_6$$

The rate of this reaction if found to be proportional to the concentration of hydrogen ions present in the solution.

$$\frac{dx}{dt} = k\ C_{H^+} C \text{ cane sugar}$$

(b) *Specific Hydroxyl Ion Catalysis* : These are the reactions which are catalysed by OH^- ions only. Examples of this type are :

(i) The conversion of acetone into diacetone is catalysed by OH ions only.

$$CH_3COCH_3 + CH_3COCH_3 \xrightarrow{OH^-} CH_3COCH_2C(CH_3)_2\ OH$$

(ii) Decomposition of nitroso triacetone-amine is also catalysed by OH^- ions only.

$$CO\left\langle\begin{matrix} CH_2 - CMe_2 \\ CH_2 - CMe_2 \end{matrix}\right\rangle N - NO \xrightarrow{OH^-} N_2\ H_2O + CO\left\langle\begin{matrix} CH = CMe_2 \\ CH = CMe_2 \end{matrix}\right.$$

(Phorone)

(c) *Hydrogen and Hydroxyl Ion Catalysis* : These are the reactions in which both H^+ and OH ions simultaneously act as catalysts. Examples of this type are :

(i) Hrdrolysis of ester is catalysed by H^- as well as by OH^- ions.

$$CH_3\ COOC_2H_5 + H_2O \xrightarrow[OH^-]{H^+ \text{ or}} CH_3\ COOH + C_2H_5OH$$

(ii) Hydrolysis of nitrile is catalysed by H^+ as well as OH ions.

$$RCN + 2H_2O \xrightarrow[OH]{H^+ \text{ or}} RCOONH_4$$

General Acid Base Catalysis : The work of Taylor, Lowry and others showed that the reactions catalysed by H^+ ions seemed to be influenced by substances undissociated acid and even cations of weak bases such as NH_4^+ ions. In short, all the substances which have a tendency to lose a proton can function as catalysts.

Similarly, the reaction catalysed by bases (*i.e.*, H^-) ions are also influenced by undissociated bases or even anions or weak acids such as CH^3COO^- ions. In short, all substances which have a tendency to game a proton can function as catalysts. It is this discovery which has led to a new concept of acid-base catalysis known as general acid base catalysis.

Types : The main types are :

(a) *General Acid Catalysis* : These are the reactions which are catalysed by hydrogen ions, undissociated acids and cations of weak bases. In simple words, general acid catalysis are the reactions which are catalysed by any substance which has a tendency to lose a proton. An example of this type is the iodination of acetone which is catalysed by monochloro-acetic acid and its salt.

$$CH_3COCH_3 + I_2 \rightarrow CH_3COCHI + HI$$

(b) *General Base Catalysis* : These are the reactions which are catalysed by hydroxyl ions, undissociated base and even anions of weak acids only. In others words, these reactions are catalysed by such a substance which has a tendency to gain a proton. Example of this type is the decomposition or nitramide in solution catalysed by hydroxyl ions, acetate ions and H_2O.

$$NH_4NO_2 \rightarrow N_2O + H_2O$$

(c) *General Acid Base Catalysis* : These are the reactions which; are catalysed by hydrogen ions, hydroxyl ions, weak acids, weak bases, cations of weak acids and bases. Mutarotation of glucose is an example of this type.

(A) Mechanism of Acid Base Catalysis

A few examples will be considered to illustrate the mechanism of acid-base catalysis.

(a) *The catalysed transformation of ∝-Glucose in β-Glucose maybe written as*

$$H^+(I) + GH \rightarrow [HGH]^+ \xrightarrow[\text{ment}]{\text{Rearrange}} HG + H^+(II)$$

where, $H^+(I)$ is a proton supplied by acid catalyst, GH is the α- Glucose. HGH^+ is the intermediate complex which is unstable, HG is the β-glucose, and $H^+(II)$ is removed by base catalyst.

(b) *Hydrolysis of Ethyl Acetate catalysed by proton*

This can be represented as

(c) *Decomposition of nitramide catalysed by OH ions*

$$NH_2NO_2 + OH^- \rightarrow H_2O + NHNO_2^- \text{ (unstable)}$$

$$\downarrow$$

$$N_2O + OH^-$$

Kinetics of acid-base catalysis. Acid base catalyzed reactions take place by transfer of proton from an acid to a substrate molecule (S) or from substrate molecule to the base. Hence the reaction between as acid HA and substrate S may be put as follows :

$$S + HA \underset{k_{-1}}{\overset{k_1}{\Leftrightarrow}} SH^+ + A^-$$

$$SH^+ + H_2O \xrightarrow{k_2} \text{product}$$

Immediately, after the start of the reaction, SH^+ will attain steady state concentration.

Hence,

$$k_1[S]\,[HA] = k_{-1}\,[SH^+]\,[A^-] + k^2\,[SH^+]$$

or

$$\left[SH^+\right] = \frac{k_1\,[S][HA]}{k_{-1}\left[A^-\right] + k_2} \qquad ...(1)$$

It is of interest to take into consideration the limiting cases.

Case I : If $k_2 >> k_{-1}\,[A^-]$, then

$$\left[SH^+\right] = \frac{k_1}{k_2}\,[S][HA]$$

Under these conditions the reaction is subject to general acid catalysis. The overall rate of the reaction would be equal to the rate of formation of product, then

$$\text{Reaction Rate} = k_2\,[SH^+]$$

or

$$\text{Reaction Rate} = k_1[S]\,[HA]$$

In other words, it means that the reaction rate is proportional to the concentrations of the substrate and the acid (in molecular form).

Cast II : If, $k_2 << k_{-1}\,[A^-]$, then Eq. (1) becomes

$$\left[SH^+\right] = \frac{k_1[S][HA]}{k_2\left[A^-\right]}.$$

Now consider the dissociation of HA,

$$HA \Leftrightarrow H^+ + A^-$$

which is characterized by

$$k_a = \frac{\left[H^+\right]\left[A^-\right]}{[HA]}$$

The overall rate then is given as follows :

$$\text{Rate} = k_2 \cdot \frac{k_1}{k_{-1}} \frac{[S][HA]}{[A^-]}$$

But
$$\frac{[HA]}{[A^-]} = \frac{[H^+]}{k_a}$$

$\therefore$
$$\text{Rate} = \left(\frac{k_1 k_2}{k_{-1}}\right) \frac{[H^+]}{k_a} [S]$$

or
$$\text{Rate} = k' [H^+] [S]$$

Hence, the reaction rate is proportional to $[H^+]$ even in the presence of HA and A^-. This is a simple case of specific acid catalysis.

Effect of pH on Reaction Rate : We know that the rate constant of a reaction catalysed by H^+ is proportional to $[H^+]$, *i.e.*,

$$k = k_H^+ [H^+] \qquad ...(2)$$

where, k_H^+ is the catalytic coefficient of the hydrogen ions.

On taking logarithms of Eq. (2), we get

$$\log_{10} k = \log_{10} k_H^+ - \text{pH} \qquad ...(3)$$

Hence, a plot of $\log_{10}$ k vs pH is a straight line having slope equal to -1. Also for a reaction catalysed by OH^-

$$k = k_{OH}^- [OH^-] k_{OH}^- \cdot \frac{k_w}{[H^+]}$$

k_{OH}^- is the catalytic coefficient of OH^-

$$\log_{10} k = (\log_{10} k_{OH}^- + \log_{10} k_w) + \text{pH} \qquad ...(4)$$

Hence a plot of log10 k against pH is a straight line having a slope equal to + 1.

For reactions catalysed by both acids and bases *i.e.*, H^+ and OH^- the rate constant, k, is given as follows :

$$k = k_o + k_H^+ [H^+] + k_{OH}^- [OH^-] \qquad ...(5)$$

As Eq. (5) has two terms, they counter each other. Thus, it would be of interest to see its limiting cases. Under low pH conditions the third term is not expected to make much contribution to the overall rate of the reaction and Hence log k vs pH plots must show slope equal to –

1. At high pH value, the second term will not contribute and hence log k vs pH plots should have slope equal to + 1. In fact for such reaction log k vs pH plots show a minima given by,

$$(pH)_{min} = \frac{1}{2}\ [\log k_{H^+} - \log k_{OH^-} + pK_w] \qquad ...(6)$$

The effect of pH on the rate constants for various reaction catalysed by acid and bases are depicted in Fig. 8.

Catalytic Coefficients

Catalytic coefficients are regarded as a measure of the effectiveness of any acid-base catalyst. Actually, the reaction is effected by all the species present in the solution. For a solution having a weak acid HA and its conjugate base, the rate constant is given follows :

$$k = k_o + k_{H^+}[H^+] + k_{OH^-}[OH^-] + k_{HA}[HA] + k_{A^-}[A^-] \qquad ...(7)$$

where, k_0 denotes the rate constant for the uncatalysed reaction and the k_i's denote the catalytic coefficients for the species involved. This is an equation which represents the general acid-base catalysis.

For any reaction in aqueous solution, the catalytic coefficients of H^+ and OH^- are much larger than that for HA and A^-. But in the acid catalysis, the first stage of the reaction involves the transfer of proton from acid to the substrate molecule. Therefore the catalytic coefficient of an acid has to be related to the protonating power and hence the acid. Bronsted showed that this was infect the case. Also the catalytic coefficient of a base goes parallel with the dissociation constant for the base, which is inversely proportional to the ionization constant of the conjuagate acid (K_a).

Acid-base catalysis has been a common feature of organic reactions. In reactions, subject to acid-base catalysis, the first step of a reaction would be the transfer of a proton from acid to the substrate molecule of from substrate molecule to the base. Therefore, it becomes obvious to correlate the effectiveness of a catalyst to the strength of acid or base.

Taylor, in 1914 postulated that there was simple relationship between the acid catalytic constant k_a and dissociation constant of acid k_a *i.e.*,

$$k_a = K_{H^+} + K_a^{1/2} \qquad ...(1)$$

where, K_{H^+} refers to the catalytic coefficient of the hydrogen ion.

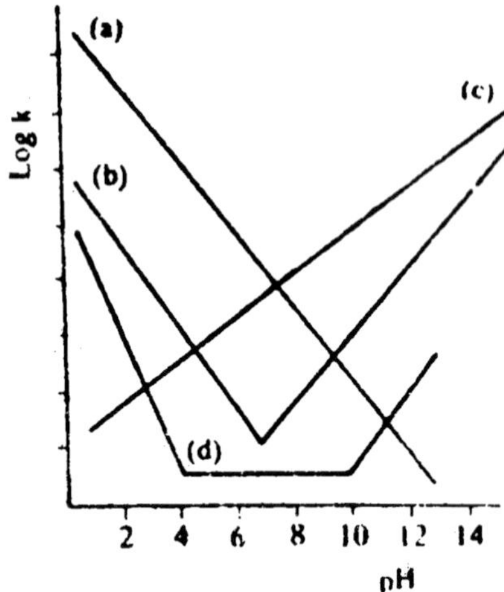

Fig. 5.17 : The effect of pH on the reaction rates for acid-base catalysed reaction. (a) inversion of sugar (b) hydrolysis of esters (c) depolymerization of diacetone alcohol (d) mutarotation of glucose.

Bronsted and Pederson in 1924 gave a more satisfactory relationship between k_a and k_a which is given by following relation :

$$k_a = G_a k_a \propto \qquad ...(2)$$

where, G_a and $\propto$ are constants characteristic of the solvent, the reactions and the temperature. The value of $\propto$ is generally less than unity (between 0.3 to 0.9).

Similarly, for a base catalysis, Bronsted and Pederson gave the equation

$$k_b = G_b k_b^{B} \qquad ...(3)$$

where, k_b refers to the rate constant of base catalysis and k_b the dissociation constant of the base.

The relationship between the catalytic constant of a base (k_b) and the acid constant of conjugate acid is as follows :

For the process

and $$B + H_2O \Leftrightarrow BH^+ + OH^- \qquad ...(4)$$

$$k_b = \frac{[BH^+][OH^-]}{[B]} \qquad ...(5)$$

Let us consider the reaction

$$BH^+ + H_2O \Leftrightarrow B + H_3O^+$$

and $$k_b = \frac{[B][H_3O]^+}{[BH^+]} \quad ...(6)$$

It is also known that

$$H_2O \Leftrightarrow H^+ + OH^-$$

$$k_w = [H]^+ [OH^-] \quad ...(7)$$

From Eqs. (5), (6) and (7), we get

$$k_b \times k_a = k_w$$

or $$k_b = \frac{k_w}{k_a} \quad ...(8)$$

On inserting the value of k_b in Eq. (3), we obtain

$$k_b = G_b'. k_a^{-\beta} \quad ...(9)$$

where $$G_b' = \frac{G_b}{k_w{}^{\beta}}$$

β us again always less than unity.

Eqs. (2), (3) and (9) are known as Bronsted relationships.

If an acid is having p protons bound equally strongly in the acid, and q is the number of positions in the conjugate base to which a proton may be attached, then for acid catalysis the Bronsted equation may be put as follows :

$$\frac{k_a}{p} = G_a\left(\frac{qk_a}{p}\right)^a \quad ...(10)$$

and for the base catalysis :

$$\frac{b}{q} = G_a\left(\frac{p}{qk_a}\right)^{\beta} \quad ...(11)$$

Hammett and Bronsted Equation

Hammett's linear free energy relationship can be applied to the kinetic phenomenon. We will now consider a reaction catalysed by the acid on one homologous series. Hammett's equation with respect to rate constant k_a may be put as follows :

$$\log k_a = \log k_o + \sigma\rho \quad ...(12)$$

and the corresponding equation with respect to the dissociation constant

$$\log K = \log K_0 + \sigma\rho' \quad ...(13)$$

where, ρ and ρ' refer to the reaction characteristic of the nature of reactions and σ is the substituent constant.

Writing Eqs. (12) and (13) as

$$\frac{1}{\rho}\log k_a = \frac{1}{\rho}\log k_0 + \sigma \quad ...(14)$$

$$\frac{1}{\rho'}\log k_a = \frac{1}{\rho'}\log k_0 + \sigma \quad ...(15)$$

On subtraction of Eq. (15) from Eq. (14), we obtain

$$\frac{1}{\rho}\log k_a - \frac{1}{\rho'}\log k_a = \frac{1}{\rho}\log k_0 - \frac{1}{\rho'}\log k_a$$

or
$$\log \frac{k_a}{k_a \rho/\rho'} = \log G$$

$$k_a = G.\ k_a \propto \quad ...(16)$$

where
$$\propto = \rho/\rho'$$

On the basis of this argument the Bronsted and Pederson relationship can be successfully applied to catalysis by a series of homologous acids and bases.

The Acidity Function

Hammett's acidity function is successfully used to measure the relative acidity of media having varied composition and correlate these with the rate constants in various solvents.

It becomes easier to compare the strength of the weak acids and bases by using the values of dissociation constant.

Hammett gave a method for comparing the strength of the strong acids and bases not only in water but also in non-aqueous solvents. Hammett postulated a quantity H_0 which is characteristic of strength of an acid and is based on an indicator acidity scale.

Hammett and Dyrup investigated the behaviour of a series of indicator bases, mostly derivatives of nitroanilines, in sulphuric acid-water mixtures. Hence the indicator base B protonates as follows :

$$B + H^+ \Leftrightarrow BH^+ \quad ...(17)$$

An example of such an acid-base equilibria is as follows :

$$C_6H_5NH_2 + H^+ \Leftrightarrow C_6H_5NH_3^+$$

The equilibrium constant for the reaction represented by Eq. (17) may be given as follows:

$$k = \frac{[BH^+]}{[B][H^+]} \cdot \frac{\gamma BH^+}{\gamma B \gamma H^+} \quad \text{...(18)}$$

where refers to the activity coefficient. Writing expression (18) as

$$\log k - \log \frac{[BH^+]}{[H^+]} = -\log a_H{}^+ \frac{\gamma B}{\gamma BH^+} \quad \text{...(19)}$$

It is possible to determine the values of L.H.S. spectrophotometrically with the aid of a suitable indication base. The quantity on the right hand side of the equation may be defined by a quantity H_o, as

$$H_o = -\log a_H{}^+ \frac{\gamma B}{\gamma BH^+} \quad \text{...(20)}$$

H_o is termed as Hammett's acidity function. For dilute solution, γ_B and $\gamma_H B+$ are equal and $H_o = -\log a_{H+} = pH$ as the activity coefficient change H_o starts to deviate from pH.

The H_o scale can be set up by determining the pK_a of an indicator base spectrophotometrically in dilute aqueous solution.

$$pK_a = pH - \log \frac{[B]}{[BH^+]}$$

It is assumed here that the values of pk_a thus determined will be independent of the solvent and can be used to determine the activity function H_o of more concentrated acidic solutions.

$$pK_a = H_o - \log \frac{[B]}{[BH^+]} \quad \text{...(21)}$$

An indicator having the ratio of $\frac{[B]}{[BH^+]}$ between 0.1 and 10 has been particularly useful.

The acidity function H_o is very convenient for correlating the rates of acid catalysed reaction in the case of processes taking place by a mechanism which includes a stage as in the reaction represented by Eq. (17). For example, the two likely steps in the mechanism of reaction are:

Step 1 : $X + H^+ \Leftrightarrow (XH^+)^{\neq}$ (rapid)

Step 2 : $(XH^+) \neq \rightarrow P$ (slow)

If step 2 is slow and rate determining, then the rate of reaction will be given as follows :

$$v = k^{\neq} [XH^+]^{\neq} \quad ...(22)$$

As the activated complex is in equilibrium with the species XH^+, we have

$$XH^+ \Leftrightarrow [XH^+]^{\neq}$$

and
$$k^{\neq} = \frac{[XH^+]^{\neq}}{[XH^+]} \cdot \frac{\gamma(XH^+)^{\neq}}{\gamma(XH^+)}$$

or
$$[XH^+]^{\neq} = \frac{k^{\neq}[XH^+].\gamma XH^+}{\gamma(XH^+)} \quad ...(23)$$

On substituting $[XH^+]^{\neq}$ in Eq. (22), we have

$$v = k^{\neq}.K^{\neq}[XH^+].\frac{\gamma XH^+}{\gamma(XH^+)^{\neq}} \quad ...(24)$$

The equilibrium constant for the reaction in step 1 may be put as follows:

$$K_a = \frac{[XH^+]\gamma XH^+}{[X]a_{H+}.\gamma x} \quad ...(25)$$

On substituting for $[XH^+]\ \gamma_{XH+}$ in Eq. (24), we obtain

$$v = k^{\neq}.K^{\neq}.K_a \frac{\gamma x}{\gamma(XH^+)^{\neq}} a_{H+}[X] \quad ...(26)$$

The first order rate coefficient may be defined by $\frac{v}{[X]}$.

Then
$$k = k^{\neq} K^{\neq}.K_a.\frac{\gamma x}{\gamma(XH^+)^{\neq}} a_{H+} \quad ...(27)$$

So that,
$$\log k = \log(k^{\neq} K^{\neq} K_a) + \log a_{H+}.\frac{\gamma x}{\gamma(XH^+)^{\neq}} \quad ...(28)$$

or
$$\log k = \log(k^{\neq} K^{\neq} K_a) - H_o \quad ...(29)$$

Thus, it is found that a correlation exists between log k and H_o. The linear relationship between these two quantities can also be established experimentally. A plot of log k against H_0 would give a straight line with a slope of –1.

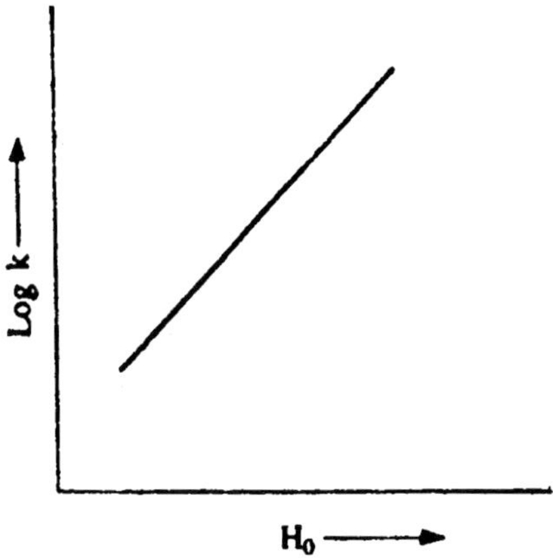

Fig. 5.18 : Plot of log k against H_0 for concentrated acid solutions.